Sisterhood of Jade

WINDS OF CHANGE

BILLI JEAN

WINDS OF CHANGE

Dedication

To Pat—and of course Em.
Thanks for bullying me.

Prologue

The echo of Fiacre's boots was the only sound accompanying him through the dark, deserted corridors of the Citadel of the Dragons. Fiacre held his staff aloft and once again faced the legendary Fountain of Flame. Legends claimed that the sculpture had been created in secret, as a tribute to King Aden, the Golden Dragon. The artisans had crafted the King in his Dragon form, with his wings spread wide — not in aggression but, facing the south as he was, in protection of those who lived in his northern-most land. His wings were said to be so powerful that they could topple the hardest oak forests. Warriors made requests for his breath to coat their shields and armor. One burst of his flame on tinder could keep a home fire lit for centuries. He had been a brave and strong leader, the most noble from a line that had bred honorable warriors since the first of his forefathers had traveled to the north and created a kingdom in that harsh land — a safe island in a stormy sea.

The fountain's waters were said to flow a rosy gold. The mythical firewater had been rumored to cure battle wounds, as well as keep the citizens of this land free of disease. If nothing else, Fiacre knew the water could lighten the spirit and give courage to the hardy folk who had called this northernmost realm their home.

The fountain stood silent now. The flames no longer lit the way for weary travelers returning home. Bitter betrayals had destroyed the once-mighty Dragons, and with them, their people.

Standing here once again, Fiacre faced not only the deserted city, but also the biggest failure of his long life. Emotions he hadn't anticipated made his hands tremble and his heart race. If he were to succeed with all he planned, he had to begin…now. He knew that and yet he hesitated. This path would be painful — not only for him, but also for the ones he strove to free.

"There is no other path." His words echoed on the bitterly cold wind. In his mind he saw the paths that lay before him, the people who must be in place for their goal to be achieved. He bowed his head and opened that force within himself that guided him through the maze of choices. Still he arrived at the point he sought.

"There is no other path," he repeated. He lifted his staff again and circled his hand counterclockwise, murmuring the spell to open the gate hidden in the frozen fountain. There was no other way. The sleepers must be woken. To do that, the cursed must take the field.

As his spell grew in power, the wings of the Dragon swept slowly wider, then just as slowly were drawn inward to create a sheltered alcove. As they folded forward, a light began to glow from within. It grew brighter and brighter until suddenly a crack sounded loud in the stillness and an archway appeared between them.

Fiacre dropped his arms and walked between the king's wings, then on through the gate. He kept up a fast pace, feeling the burning urgency growing in his chest. The line of the king was still strong. Hidden in the depths of their fortress, lives still burned bright within their frozen cocoons. Bright and silently unaware of the passage of time or of the battles being fought for the light, they slept, safely protected by his spells. It was not his spell that would wake them, however, but that of another, from another land. She would come, and when she did, the king would shake off his frozen sleep and once again take up the sword for good.

His mission today had to start the events that would bring about the change. *The smallest of winds can bring about the biggest storms.*

He murmured another spell. This one lit the corridor in a silvery light, revealing cobwebs and centuries of dust on a stone floor. There were no footprints — and with another spell, he ensured that he would leave none either. The air was still and silent. He could detect the faint, steady drum of heartbeats. No other living being walked the frozen corridors.

At the end of the tunnel stood another door, which was solid stone and unmovable, save for the person who held the password. Ancient Dragon runes had been carved in the heavy archway. More were chiseled down both sides — warnings and blessings. Beyond the arch lay the Heart of the Dragon. Three of the king's four children — Edan, Conleth and Keegan — slept within its shelter. The fourth, and youngest, had been lost centuries before. She now resided with him. *Brenyn.* She knew not what she was nor what she had once done—repeatedly through life and rebirth—for the witch calling herself the Black Queen. Soon, Brenyn's memories would have to be restored. He only hoped that when they did return, her Dragon Guard would be there to aid her. He, too, was lost, but there would be a wakening for him as well.

Not by me, though…by the Dream Walker.

Fiacre steadied his grip on his staff and his chaotic thoughts. For magic, he needed a clear, calm mind. Today, it was essential. After several seconds, he calmed himself and opened the flow of power necessary to unlock the spellbound doorway. A whisper of unease rippled up his spine. A touch from outside sent a warning through his flow. There was more to the gate than merely the spell he'd placed centuries before. He followed the touch and found a curse. Someone had embedded it in the stone arch. It hovered over his protective spell like a thin layer of ice on an autumn lake or poison drying on the inside of a wine goblet.

Such spells were dangerous for both the unsuspecting and the person crafting them. The dark magic opened doors that should remain closed. Whoever had spelled his protections had done terrible things.

Fiacre opened his eyes to the other creatures of all the realms. The archway revealed its true self.

Broken chunks of the archway littered the floor. Blood oozed from the stone, resembling sap from a tree, except that it was bright scarlet in color. A fresh flow of it bubbled and slid down the jagged stones in a trickling stream. Evil spells had been chiseled across the bottom left corner of the door and up, diagonally, to the right side of the rounded top. The arch had been broken, and the seal of protection that had been carefully crafted into the ancient stone destroyed. Crumbled stone littered the cobblestones at his feet. Another spell, written in the blood of an innocent had been scrawled along the floor To his right lay a child's bones. One boney hand still lingered in the dried blood of the spell.

Panic tried to freeze him. His breath caught in his throat, yet from within the sacred chamber of the Dragons, he could discern the steady drum of more than one heartbeat.

Careful, lest he touch the spells, he raised his staff and circled his left hand, chanting the counter to the evilness left behind. A shiver of cold air swirled up against him, plastering his robes to his body. The unexpected pressure built and fought him. He strengthened his weaving, calling on the power remaining within the Dragon's citadel without a pause in his chanting. The flow of his magic grew. With a terrible shriek, the curse sudden broke and with it, the cold wind disappeared.

He exhaled and lowered his staff, then raised it in a warding gesture as a crack broke the silence. The remaining structure of the arch crumbled to pieces and the door crashed to the floor. The vibrations echoed through the corridor. No doubt the sound carried up and through the mountains and on through the Twins to the distant keep he now claimed as his own. And if it woke the sleepy witches and drew their awareness to what he'd done?

Then all the sooner we will have done with their evil webs.

A fresh, clean burst of air cooled his skin. The skeleton at his feet turned to ash and blew away on the breeze. He hoped the poor child had been taken to a more peaceful place.

Whoever had left behind such a dark spell and entered had not gotten what they'd wanted. Two frozen bodies lay on the chamber floor. He didn't move. Instead, he let his senses reach out to examine them. A scent of evil lingered over the bodies. Both were women. But more than mere women, they'd been mages. Too bad for them that their magic had led them down the dark path. They had died horribly. His spells and the king's own protections had seen to that. Their hands were frozen into claws that seemed to be trying to dig out their eyes. Dark, frozen blood stained their cheeks. Around their bodies more blood darkened the floor, further evidence of their painful deaths. They would have died slowly and in great agony, a sign that they had fully committed to themselves to the darkness.

May your spirits find peace.

He sent the thought out to them then centered his focus on the cavernous hall. The domed ceiling rose several Dragon heights above his head. When they entered this chamber, they used a passage cut from the mountains and flew below-ground to this, their most sacred sanctuary. A cold breeze blew on Fiacre's cheeks, lifting his hair away from his face and cleansing the room of the lingering stench of evil.

Fiacre had helped build this place, not that the Dragons had needed much help. But it had been with his guidance that they had designed the intricate chips of colorful red, gold and black stones woven in spherical patterns that grew tighter and tighter upon the floor. Beneath the tiles was a hidden chamber built for the Dragon King. Along the walls were gigantic side chambers for his children.

The spells protecting them were intact, but they'd been created to be more powerful than the mages who had used another's suffering to breach the door. Only a Dragon Mage could know the way to waken the Dragons. It had always been so. The family who had sworn their loyalty to the Dragons kept themselves ready to come when called.

Fiacre considered them and found them still strong, yet with only one mage left to help awaken the king from his sleep, much relied on her. If she could not do what was needed when it was needed, many would suffer. He shifted his shoulders and pushed his fears aside. Fears crippled the minds of mages and he knew better than to allow himself such traps.

He considered the dead mages. If they had used their own pain, perhaps they would have made it farther. No one who sacrificed another for gain could pass through to see the King's Heart. But these two had come farther than any others. *Another sign that now is the time to defeat the Black Queen and destroy her evil.*

Fiacre exhaled wearily, feeling the weight of his years more than ever before. The air clouded with his breath. Outside had been bitterly cold, but inside the chamber that was known as the King's Heart, there was a different, deeper cold — a freezing environment that would freeze them from inside to out, if one lingered long enough.

The chill in the air was necessary to ensure the sleep of the Dragons and their Dragon Guards. The ice kept the pain at bay — pain that had kindled the furnace of the Dragons' rage. Losing their lands, their people, their families — everything they had created and nurtured, save each other — had driven the Dragons to near madness. The king's wrath at the loss of his daughter, at the betrayal from within, had burned the castle — save this citadel — to the ground. There had been no need of burials for the massive dead lying in the fields of battle or outside the village huts. In their misery, the Dragons had burned everything. The countryside had been left in heaps of ash after the king had driven the people from their homes. That one act had saved him from the path others had taken—the dark path. The Black Queen sought to drag everyone in this realm down into that evil pit with her.

I placed the Dragons here, away from the pain, from the evil. But evil found them.

Fiacre studied the two dead mages closer. Raven feathers were twisted in the tangled, dirty locks of their long, hair. Both wore fur-lined black capes with more raven feathers woven along the seams. Small bones hung from their necks. Their shrunken gray flesh had tattooed spells along their wrists and up their dirty, bare arms.

He focused on the magic still lingering on their skin. They were known to him, mages of middling power who sought more from the darkest of dark magic. Their sect was the reason he stood here, in a land that had suffered and given everything to ensure the safety of this realm.

Did we fail? Is this the dark I feel building on the horizon? Building beyond our realm? Is she already aware and ready for my every move?

Safety was an illusion. He knew that very well.

Closing his eyes, he leaned on his staff, his head down again, trying to regain a memory from so long ago that it was beyond counting. As a younger man, the way had seemed so clear. Hindsight revealed how one defeat after another had narrowed their choices until finally there had been none left, save one. Hiding the remaining Dragons, sheltering the innocent and burying himself as far away from anyone as he could had seemed like the only way.

No one in this realm now had a memory of that time — save one. Edric, the Silver King, was ensnared in a web of lies he couldn't see through. *Yet.*

Do I see all that there is to see? Can I break the spells binding so many? I must try. We must try.

He opened his eyes and stared into the brighter gaze of the younger him — into a face free of scars, a body healthy and whole, and yet there was agony blazing in there. As if it had just been yesterday, Fiacre was struck with all the pain and sorrow he'd experienced. It felt so fresh that his chest should have been torn open and his heart sliced from its resting place.

With great effort he moved past the agony, past the seemingly bottomless pit of regrets and on to what he needed to do. Beyond his grief, he saw it.

Greer.

Her life force shown bright and pure, like a single thread of gold among a sheaf of dull wool. He pulled that one thread, teasing the life from the memory so he could once again work his magic. Here in the King's Heart, where he'd also buried his own heart, the magic was at its most powerful. If he could create the path, the life he'd tried desperately to save could once again have a chance of living as it was meant to be lived, to walk this realm and accomplish what Greer had been destined to do all the times before. If she were to live again, to fulfill her destiny, his promise to a desperate father would have a chance of being truth instead of bitter hopes that masked the lies. The losses would be…worth the cost.

"Could it ever be worth the cost?" a female voice asked, as loud and clear as if the speaker were standing by his side.

He closed his eyes on the question. He couldn't block the sound of the footsteps echoing toward him.

The scent of roses filled the frozen chamber, making the pain in his chest so unbearable that moisture leaked past his tightly closed eyes. Her hand rested on his shoulder, small and warm, then it was gone — just as she was. *Greer*.

There were other forces in this realm — forces who sought her, called to her, wanting her to come to them and do their bidding. Once she had been the daughter of dear friends, an honorable knight and his beautiful wife. Once she had been all that was pure and good in the new realm of the Dragon, the first seed of joy after more horrors than anyone should be forced to endure. The golden days had not lasted. The storm had risen again and when it hit, had left sorrow in its wake. *Greer*. She had not been killed. Worse, much worse, had happened. She had been taken, stolen from the very ones who loved her most. With her, the king's daughter, Brenyn, had also been taken. They had dared much, the Black Queen and her sisters. They had even taken Brenyn's guard and lover, Oisin.

In this, Fiacre knew they had reached too far, but he had not been able to take advantage of their mistake. Until now, he had not dared come and draw Greer from death.

Greer. She had grown under the evil wings of the Black Queen's spells. She and the other two had become warriors unlike any other before them. Greer's sword had ended the lives of thousands in the service of the darkness. Oisin's had done the same, and as a Dragon, Brenyn's fire had destroyed armies, cities and kingdoms until madness had driven her death. But the Black Queen had uses for them. They were drawn back to her. Oisin after trying to take his life, Brenyn as a child once she lived again and Greer when she'd tottered on the brink of adulthood. Each time they had to fulfill their oaths…save once.

In one of her many rebirths, Greer had been born to a distant king. When she'd grown, she had hidden from the Black Queen's curse. She had lived as a princess…as Gwen. She had died as Gwen, refusing to be Greer, the Battle Hawk of the Black Queen. Her death had haunted Fiacre ever since.

"Was I worth the cost?" Greer's voice asked him.

He opened his eyes and focused on the wisps of memory, the now ghostly, shadowy vision of Greer. His spell had brought her only partially back to this world, but her voice carried as if she were here, in truth, standing before him, though not because he had willed her back as this ghost. He had called her back as herself, not this half-in-death and half-in-life shadow. She had denied his call and resisted him It would seem he needed to convince her to return.

"I made a mistake. I thought you could escape your fate. I thought you were Gwen, and you were—but you were also Greer. You hid, deep within Gwen, but you can't hide forever. You will never be less than the daughter of a warrior…a warrior yourself. It is not birth that makes you. It is *you* who makes you. Choose to live again and I will aid you. I have found a way to break the curse. One chance…only one. You must trust me. I will show you the way."

"And why should I trust you, mage? Did you not desert us? Did you not hide in your cave while the dark grew stronger and stronger?"

He could not deny it and didn't try. "I did. I thought they were gone. With me gone, I believed them unable to rise and grow. I was wrong."

The chamber trembled in response. Greer drew so close that he could feel the spark of her spirit brushing his. Anger filled her eyes. "And what makes you not wrong now?"

He shook his head and smiled. "Nothing."

"Then why would I trust you? I have not been called in…" Her expression filled with pain, then with a snap the anger drew her brow down and her eyes glowed brighter. "I have not walked this realm in ages. The witches who cursed me are no more. I will linger, as you see me now. It's useless to call me."

"No, Greer, the witches are not dead. The Dark Queen and her sisters still weave their webs."

"Then you are a fool. No one can stop them. Look around you. Did they not topple this kingdom?"

He shook his head. "They will call you again. You will be reborn this year, on the Hunter's Moon. They will see you from the moment you leave your mother's womb, and from that moment on, your life will play out again the same as it has every time before—save two."

At his words, Greer's mist form became more solid as more of her seeped through from the spirit realm. Her eyes, the clear, bright gaze he had known, held his with a power all her own. He let her read the truth.

"Two?" She hovered over the mages with a distasteful glance at them, then turned to face him again. She wore a gown. The color might have once been rose. Her long blonde hair wasn't tied up in war braids. It hung down her back to swirl past her hips as she glided restlessly from one side of the chamber to the other.

Surely the pain in his heart would kill him. No one deserved such an existence—not this woman, not anyone. He had sworn an oath to a brave warrior—this woman's father. It burned along his skin, reminding him that he had not been able to keep that promise. *I will not abandon her to this fate.* The lives of too many relied upon him and every single one of them counted. They always had. It was his greatest weakness, and he hoped, his greatest strength. Greer was not broken. Her spirit proved that. Now all he had to do was convince her to trust him — the one person she blamed as much, if not more, than she blamed herself.

"You were born on an autumn morn. I held you in my hands and cut your tie with your mother. You were small and covered in blood and gore, so tiny I feared handling you. I was there. I know. You were not one-ounce evil."

She sniffed after a brief pause and spun away from him. "And? I was after?"

"The next time I looked into your eyes, you were a princess climbing a tree, as free from evil as any I have seen."

Another impatient sniff. "I was never truly a princess."

"You were. Both times."

Over her shoulder, she glanced at him.

"Your mother gave up her right to be a queen to marry your father. If you had not been taken, you would have learned of that soon enough, I imagine. It was one of your father's favorite stories, how he swept your mother right off the throne."

Her form misted to barely there. The pain in her expression didn't need flesh and blood for him to read it. He held himself ready. There would be more pain before this was done.

"Why did you call me here? I have never been to this place." She hovered near the broken door, then over to the mages. He noted she was careful not to draw too near them.

"These are your true people. Your father was a descendant of the Dragons. Because of this, it is here I can call you back to this life. It is here you can come again, not as a babe, but as a warrior," he explained. "You would be ready to fight in this, the last battle, and break the curse."

She lingered closer then moved away with a harsh laugh. "Wasn't the last battle long ago, mage?"

"This one —"

"Will be *the* last?"

"Possibly." He shook his head. "Whether or not it is, if you are there, you will be free of this curse."

She lifted her lip in a sneer that broke his heart. There was so much pain in her, so much anger — justifiable, but dangerous — that he worried again about the path they would take. "Because the Black Queen will kill me."

"No, that will not break the curse and you know it. You will be freed because you will not fight for them, Greer. We will not be alone in this."

She paused in her floating.

"A friend will join our fight — one you knew well."

Her eyes darkened as her frown grew. "I have no friends. I have *never* had friends."

"That is not true. You have many friends."

She surged toward him until her face was inches from his. "I have *no one*. I have never had anyone. Anyone I ever dreamed of was killed long ago, mage. *Every single one.*"

"Not everyone, Greer," he said gently. "Brenyn and Oisin are bound with you."

"And just as trapped." This time the sorrow bled the passion from her voice.

"There is more, another who will join us." He waited for her to lift her head, but she had her side to him, her head bowed. Her hair hung down, hiding her ghostly features. "Jacob survived."

She lifted her head and stared at him with wide, amazed eyes. Her misty form floated back toward the wall. "You would lie to me? You think I don't know that Jacob was killed, even before they brought *down* their darkness?"

Fiacre had to swallow past the pain. Greer had lost much, as had he—friends, kingdoms, lands full of innocent people who had nothing to do with the battle the Black Queen waged, except for living happy lives.

"He has returned to this land. He needs you. The Faye are besieged with darkness. They have him and will continue to torture him. You can free him. You know you can. Together, you and Jacob will defeat this curse. The Silver King will be free of the poison that binds him. The Dragon King will be woken. The Greenway will join us in this battle. Even the Vampires will aid us in defeating the Black Queen. I have seen this."

She shook her head. Her expression had filled with pain and he sensed the chaos tumbling through her.

"I have seen this, Greer. You and Jacob will break more than the curse. Brenyn and Oisin will help bring the Dragons back. Light will again reign."

He watched her expression until she moved away from him, hovering in her mist form against the wall. She said nothing. Her form became dimmer. And yet, for the first time in ages, he held on to hope. His biggest fear in calling her had been that she would simply not come—or if she did come to him, that she would leave before he could convince her. That she was still here had to mean something. It had to mean she wanted to live.

"Trust me." Bowing his head, he drew on the power of his oaths and walked past the mages to the doorway that protected the children of the Dragon. "Let me show you the path. Trust me."

A golden chamber coated in a thin layer of ice lay beyond. The three children of the Dragon stood frozen in the walls. Silent, heads bowed, swords resting tips-down on the floor, hands folded as if in death on the hilts, they waited for the day they could once again waken in this realm. To either side of the Dragons stood a pair of warriors dressed in black and red. Each had sworn to follow their masters into death – and beyond.

The spells holding them kept them safely sleeping until they were again needed, until the lands once more were under a threat.

That time had surely come to avenge the horror the Black Queen had wrought on this land.

He rested his hands on his staff, fighting the sorrow such memories brought. Brenyn had suffered, as had others, but for the Dragon's youngest, the Black Queen had forced her to madness again and again and again. Of the four children of the Golden Dragon, Brenyn was by far the most powerful – and yet she struggled each time she was reborn to master her Dragon's rage. The impact of that anger left Brenyn broken. Fiacre worried that even with his aid, she would spiral into that madness again. His emotions ran high, his fears pushing his sorrow higher. Greer could likely sense his turmoil, perhaps even see it. With magic, it was hard to hide oneself.

"She should not be called," Greer whispered, confirming his suspicions. She knew what he was about.

"She is stronger than you believe. He will give her the rest of the strength she will need."

"With Oisin?" Her tone was icy. "He obeys them" — she faced him — "like I will when they call me. There is no stopping the oaths we swore."

"There is. I need you to be strong. The path will be difficult. If you are strong, you will see the end of this curse. Their curses will end — on you and on them, on all the lands. This I have seen."

Greer hovered closer. There was a light in her eyes that he hoped meant she might be beginning to believe him.

"Once more — for Brenyn, for Oisin, for Jacob...for all of them. Once more, come to this world, and this time, fight for what you truly want."

The fire in her eyes glowed as bright as Dragon fire and she nodded, just once, but it was sufficient. He closed his eyes, whispering a prayer that this time the flame would be enough.

Chapter One

A great wind traveled down from the craggy peaks of the distant Twins, flattening the tall, yellow mountain grasses. The gust carried a billowy cloud of snow with it that tumbled and rolled before dispersing like warm breath on a freezing day. The air stung Greer's face. It also woke visions from the past.

"Steady, Greer."

She blinked. The image of blood splattered on crystal-white snowdrifts didn't release her. An ache in her throat blossomed and her left arm, near her shoulder, tingled as if she'd only just sustained a blow. The injury had happened long ago, in another lifetime. Time didn't matter though. To her, it never did. Today, yesterday, ten years before… The past merely waited for her attention to once again be her present.

"It won't be long now."

Fiacre's voice—serious, yet warm and deep with reassurance—centered her.

The past is over. The present is now.

The meadow lay between her and the pass. Along the way, a stony creekbed snaked toward the orange stone walls of a canyon. At some point in the year, the riverbed had held water — perhaps when the snow had melted and spring arrived here in the high plains. For now, it was a road for anyone passing from the Twin giants to the Forbidden Forest, and beyond.

"Do you sense them?" Greer asked.

Fiacre cocked a scruffy eyebrow. "Yes. Soon…"

Silverfoot sighed loudly, shaking her head hard enough to make the silver on her harness jingle. Greer could understand her impatience. They'd traveled here under cover of the darkness until the moon set each night then on through the day to reach the foothills. Four days of travel, five nights… Brenyn would be all alone and no doubt working far too hard to clean the entire keep. The strain of being away from the keep burned along Greer's muscles. She longed to dismount and end this…before it even started. She wanted to watch Brenyn draw water from the well or make meat pies or sneak scraps to the hounds. Instead, she shifted in her saddle. The mare settled down with another heavy sigh. Greer barely stopped herself from echoing her.

Fiacre chuckled. "The wait is always difficult. Perhaps being less anxious for a fight would be wise, eh?"

Greer wasn't anxious because of the chance of having to battle. Enough blood had been spilled, and yet she didn't see any other way. The Faye had changed. They were dark and filled with rage instead of the calm she had known. As she thought it, she knew that in one of her many lifetimes she'd faced the Faye in battle. *More than once.* "Do you think they will turn away and do as we ask?"

"No. They are filled with hate. Evil has a hold of them…some more than others."

She understood. Evil had a way of winding itself around a person and choking all the goodness out of them. She studied their chosen battlefield once again.

The meadow would be where they engaged. Soon it would be scattered with dead — either them or the Faye, perhaps both. The sheer cliffs of reds and oranges stood quietly and would remain after, a witness to the bloodbath beneath them. Even the heavy mountains standing guard above them were silent — only the wind spoke. It flattened the grass again and took away the quiet with its whistling tune. This time she closed her eyes, shielding them from the biting cold. The wind's lonely song roared around her, filling the space.

The old ones said that when the wind spoke so loudly, the path of one's life is about to change.

Greer considered the thought, puzzled over the odd bit of memory when the cloth of her past had more holes than solid fabric. She preferred the missing pieces. They were better…far better than the memories. The bloody snow was one of those. She'd been warned about the past from Fiacre. Each vision linked to far more dangerous forces. *The Black Queen.* She pushed the thought aside. She would rather not face the implications of the dark witch testing her with visions.

I've returned to do just that — face them, defeat them, break their control and break my oath.

She tensed at her thoughts and had to relax, muscle by muscle. Silverfoot shifted and pranced in confusion until Greer calmed herself. Fiacre waited. He sat silently watching her. She sensed his growing concern.

"There is a spell protecting you, Greer. You are not visible."

She knew that. She also understood that this life was different. This time she had been called by Fiacre, not the witches. She'd decided to answer his call. She'd chosen this time. This time there was only *the* fight. The final battle… *There had once been more than battle and death. There had once been much more…*

The smell of roses suddenly filled the air, bringing a renewed tightness to her throat. A glimpse of castle walls, green with the weight of growing vines covered in a plethora of pink roses flashed through her mind, then the blue, blue, blue of a summer sky so gorgeous that it stole her breath.

She blinked and it was gone. A shiver traced its way down her spine. The memory stunned her, not only with the strength of it, as if she'd just turned to see such beauty, but also with the sharp slice of pain it brought.

Fiacre hadn't moved. He always knew when she battled the visions and he held back so she could sort out her own emotions. This life was proving to be worse — or perhaps better — than the others. She hadn't been born as a child who grew up unaware until suddenly she experienced an urge for something — or someone. *The Black Queen's call.* This time, she'd been brought here as she was now — an adult already prepared to fight. And she would fight — for her freedom, not for some mad witches who wanted to crush the world under their boots.

Fiacre had warned her that the visions and memories would be harder to control. If they were going to win her freedom — and that of her friends — there was no time for her to discover who she was, who she had been or who she couldn't be. *I'm Greer, a warrior. I'll fight their control and break it if I can…or die trying. Nothing more, nothing less.*

The thought brought pain. She swallowed and tipped her head skyward to examine the horizon. The pale blue was barely visible behind the heavy blanket of gray clouds. It might snow again instead of the flurries that currently disappeared and reappeared. They were so high up that the snow might stick. Down below, where the warmth and safety of the keep had surrounded her, spring had already arrived. Up here, Father Winter still held reign.

She gazed out across the land, knowing this was not the first time she'd seen the glory of this place — the tall peaks of the mountains, the long, sloping foothills covered with ash and pine, oak and mighty elm that met and were fenced off by the ridges of the canyons in front of her. The bored sighs of her mount, the shaking jingle of her gear and the solid presence of the mage next to her were also familiar...and yet, not so poignant, not so filled with bitter pain. There was only the coming battle, the attempt to change a path that might never be altered.

"I did not know you before," Greer said.

Fiacre hid his surprise well, but not well enough. "No. We did not meet before."

"You found me."

"I searched and found you, the same as I found Brenyn."

"She was small, wasn't she? A child." It was important, suddenly vital that she knew this.

Pain flickered across Fiacre's old face. The lines traveling down from the sides of his mouth deepened. "Yes. I found Brenyn first. You know that. She was a child."

"Yes. You saved her and that was when you learned how to find me."

"I knew of your suffering, Greer. I'd been searching for you since...since last you were here. Do you remember that time? Is that what troubles you?"

"Yes. No. I remember...everything, if I choose."

"Such things are dangerous."

"I know." She focused on the Twins. "I know not to bring those thoughts to life."

"Good. This is good, Greer. You must listen to me. The potion—"

"Will only work for so long."

He walked his gelding closer and took her arm, meeting her eyes with a pained expression on his aged face. There were scars among the wrinkled folds. She often wondered how he had gotten them, but she'd never asked. Such things would make no difference. "This is the way, Greer. This is the way to end this curse."

"It was an oath, not a curse."

"It is both. It can be broken. You have suffered enough. Believe me. If you don't believe anything else, believe this."

Believe. It had been so long since she had thought of anything. Blackness had been her only companion— and the soft sleep that came with it. Belief was sharp and it was painful, and worse, it brought with it the memories—and regrets—that she had tried so very hard to erase. *Roses bloom in the spring. The petals last the summer and when they fall at last, their scent mingles with the cold air of autumn leaves.*

A wolf's howl carried to them. She snapped her attention from her past and to the present. The wolf sounded achingly alone. At first, she thought it was part of the sudden flow of her own thoughts.

Fiacre's mount, Storm Cloud, pranced. The ringing of the reins sounded overly loud. Silverfoot shifted under her. Greer put pressure on her legs and the mare stilled. Fiacre circled Storm Cloud once, scanning the trees along their left, across the dry creek bed.

Another lonesome howl echoed behind them. The wolf — or wolves — had drawn closer.

She pulled her sword free of the scabbard. The weight, length and balance of the blade fit her perfectly. It had been crafted during ages past. Fiacre had gifted it to her in a chamber far from this place under the watchful frozen gaze of an ancient king. A ray of sun broke from the heavy-bottomed clouds, shimmering on the sharp edge of the blade's length like a lover's caress. Along both sides of the steel, runes scrolled down until they joined at the hilt and formed a looping knot. There had once been another blade, similar but far different. The runes on that blade choked her with oaths she'd not wanted to swear, to women she dared not disobey.

"Beware, Greer. Your focus is here...now."

She glanced over at Fiacre, seeing the sternness in the deeper lines on his face. His eyes were bluer than the sky and more like the biting cold of a frozen lake than the warmth of a sunny day. Power filled them. She soaked it in. She wanted everything to disappear forever so she didn't have to be here, again, in this realm that had taken so much from her.

Fiacre turned his mount in a circle, scanning the forest on their left with an intensity that drew her out of her self-pity. Something was there...in the deep shadow of the forest.

From between the trunks of two tall pines a wolf emerged. It held its head alert, staring at them with the singlemindedness of a hunter. Seconds went by with its gaze locked on them, then it lifted its head and howled again. Then, surprising her, it trotted toward them. As it grew nearer, the air around it shimmered until the light coming from it was too bright, so she shielded her eyes. When she could see again, a man walked where the wolf had been.

"Easy... Alrick is here to aid us," Fiacre warned.

She allowed the nervous mare to prance in a tight circle but didn't take her gaze off the warrior. He wore mail, much like hers, with a sword at his hip. His brown hair blew away from his stern features. She thought his hair overgrown, as if he normally wouldn't have grown it to such a length. When his gaze met hers, it seemed as wild to her as the wolf's. A shaft of sunlight shimmered down on him and his eyes flashed amber then back to dark brown.

He halted a few feet away. "Fiacre."

"Alrick." Fiacre bowed in his saddle. "You are well met. We have need of your skill."

The words surprised her. The warrior stood at ease, his body relaxed, as if he and Fiacre were old companions.

"You are after Jacob," he said.

Jacob. The name tried to bring strong visions from the past. She refused them. A bead of sweat trickled down her spine. The breeze had quieted for the moment. The air was still chilly enough that she shouldn't be so warm.

"Yes. Will you aid us?" Fiacre asked.

The question distracted her from the sweat building on her skin.

Alrick didn't answer. Instead, he studied the canyon. After a long pause, he sighed heavily and crossed his arms, facing them again. His eyes were tired, the whites bloodshot, perhaps with exhaustion. He was thin, either from time on a trail or naturally. She couldn't say which. Even still, she didn't doubt his strength. He might look like a man who'd not slept in days, but the Lykae could fight. She didn't doubt his strength one bit. He would be an asset in any battle.

"I've been tracking Jacob for days, ever since I caught his scent," Alrick explained. "They've been traveling through the canyon from a gate in one of the border towns. I would have struck before now, if not for your missive."

Missive. She knew Fiacre had communication with others, but the thought that he had reached out to this man, obviously on a trail, surprised her. Fiacre's sight was strong if he could locate this man on his hunt.

Fiacre stilled his horse before he said, "Then you will allow him to accompany us?"

"He's better off with you," Alrick replied.

"As would you be. You are still searching?"

She frowned, unsure about their conversation. Alrick's eyes narrowed and he stared off past them, into the depths of the forest. His expression reminded her of someone with no hope of finding what they sought.

"Aye."

Fiacre drew his horse closer to Alrick. "I know what you truly seek beyond Jacob. You look for your mate. She is not lost to you. Do not give up hope."

Alrick narrowed his eyes. It didn't hide the rise of intensity in them. He struck Greer as a desperate man. There was strength in him. She recalled the ways of the wolf. They were fierce fighters, and once on a trail, they never gave up. They also mated for life. And if their mates perished, they would soon follow.

The Lykae were little more than slaves. They were the guardians of the Vampire. There had always been rumors of Lykae independent of their masters. She sensed Alrick wasn't one of these. He was…other. It was in his eyes—or perhaps, she thought, in his bearing. *Not of this realm. Of another.* A memory of a great hall, dark with shadows save for a large fire in a central hearth, came to her. She stood, silent and watchful in the shadows while around her people celebrated. The Black Queen lounged on her throne, feet from her, and bragged of journeying to a far-off realm where she had laid the seeds that would bloom when she needed them.

A blast of icy cold wind caused her to blink rapidly and the memory disappeared. The surety that this man was from another realm remained.

"I'll aid you this day, then continue the search."

"We will need you before this is over, Alrick. The battle for all the realms will happen here. When it does, we will need strength on our side if we hope to win."

"You've seen this?" Alrick demanded.

"Yes. Soon the sides will be drawn. We must be prepared."

Silence followed. Greer waited. They did not need her counsel. The wind cooled her. At the same time, the memories tugged, and without something to do, she felt them growing stronger. The massive hall called to her. There were memories there that she knew she wouldn't want to recall.

"Sides... I'm not sure we're ready to join sides, mage. Our realm has enough to manage without traveling here to aid this one."

His insolence startled her enough to bring her back to the here and now. Fiacre only smiled.

"Is anyone ever ready? And still, your companions must come or else your realm will fall, as well as this one. The Heart Realm is the center. If it does..." Fiacre lifted a shaggy eyebrow. "You know this. Why debate with me?"

"I'm not debating." Alrick laughed. It was a surprisingly warm sound. "There is no hope for my people to journey here. The gate to my home realm is closed." Alrick scratched his jaw and squinted at Fiacre. "The gate Aubrey fell through is gone," he said, sounding as if he wished to clarify what he spoke of. Gates were protected by the Silkies. She recalled this from before and knew that such gates were not easy to destroy.

Fiacre raised his eyebrows.

"Not gone, then?" Alrick muttered.

"No. Once a gate has been created, closing it requires more than mere spells. Your mages were able to put up a barrier, but the gate is not destroyed. The Silkies protect the other means of travel. Even they are hard-pressed to keep the ways closed. It is not within my power to do so." He shook his head. "No, the ending is drawing nearer. Jacob is at the center."

Was it her imagination or did Fiacre's glance stray to her then off again? *Jacob.* She had once known a man named Jacob. The thought brought with it such pain that she clenched her jaw. The scent of roses filled the breeze. She knew it wasn't real. Not now. It couldn't be, and yet, there it was, sweetening the bitter cold air.

"He, with your aid, will change the Vampire Kingdom. It's essential that this occurs, just as it's essential that your friends arrive here…soon."

"I have no control over that. The Vampire Kingdom does not parley with the Lykae, mage."

"They will listen to him." Fiacre pointed to the still-empty meadow and the cliffs beyond. "And the Lykae will follow you. The winds of change are here. Perhaps for now you would do better to stop and see what these changes bring."

Alrick's frown was firmly in place, more so now than before. "And the girl?" he asked, as if Greer couldn't speak for herself.

"I am Greer." The mare danced, as if sensing her building unease. Greer steadied her without taking her gaze from Alrick's.

"Greer," Alrick repeated.

His gaze weighed her worth and she resisted the desire to sit straighter in her saddle.

"Tell me, Greer. What is your part in this?" he asked.

Before she could respond, Fiacre moved and blocked Alrick from her view — and her from his, she noted.

"She is here to defend me and to help gain Jacob from the Faye. Do not tell me that the king of the Lykae judges women less fit for battle than men."

"Not if I want to keep all my body parts intact." Alrick laughed. "You and a single warrior against the Faye that are coming through this canyon?"

Fiacre's gelding pranced closer to her mare, revealing Alrick again. Her face felt warm. She met his gaze and refused to be baited by him.

"Greer is enough to reach Jacob, free him and bring him to us. With your aid and my magic, we will hold this day," Fiacre said.

"I see. Why do I sense more?" Alrick tipped his head slightly. "*Greer* means watchful, doesn't it?"

She shook her head, unsure what he meant.

"Vigilant, perhaps. It's an old name in my realm. Perhaps here it has other meanings," Alrick said.

"Greer is my name, nothing more," she offered. Another, more powerful name bestowed on her by evil had meaning. It was a name she hoped to never hear spoken again.

"Mm-m." Alrick turned his sharp gaze to Fiacre. "I will do what I can." As if his agreement had announced their coming, she heard the clank of metal, the thud of hooves and the creak of wagons.

Silverfoot pranced. Fiacre stared off into the canyon. "They have arrived."

Alrick gestured to the forests he'd come from. "I'll take them on from the flanks. Are you going through the middle to Jacob?"

"Yes." She released her knotted reins, letting them fall on her mare's neck as she pulled on her shield. It was a welcome weight.

"Jacob must be freed, no matter the cost." Fiacre met her eyes with a solemnness in his that stressed how important this one man was to him.

Her heart felt as though it missed beats, then raced to catch up. *Jacob is a common name.*

"And the Faye?" Greer asked.

"They cannot continue through these lands." There was sorrow in Fiacre's tone, but a firmness she understood.

"The less of them the better," Alrick muttered.

"They are not all responsible for the current—" Fiacre began.

"We can debate later, mage. Now we need to prepare ourselves."

From the curved banks of the stream, a company of warriors appeared as if out of the thin air. It was a trick of the land, she knew. Still, for a moment, it seemed as if the rocks and dirt simply gave birth to the warriors.

One blink and the illusion was broken. They were real...glaringly real. The orange cliffs outlined the silver and black gear they wore. The colors fueled an anger that grew in her heart. Silver and black should *never* be worn by these warriors. The colors were forbidden. Gold and blue, the colors of warmth and sunshine, were the truth—not the silvery dark corruption of the Black Queen.

"Steady. We knew they would come. This is what we wait for. This is who we must stop," Fiacre said.

Greer acknowledged him with a distracted nod. Fiacre was a mage, not a warrior. A warrior didn't glance away from the enemy. She could sense Alrick preparing, tightening his armor, checking his gear and moving to her left.

"Be ready. We must be fast. Do not let them kill the prisoners," Fiacre warned.

"There's no chance of that," Alrick said gruffly.

The next second, she could feel the tingle of magic. Fiacre waved his staff in a circle. Blue light flowed behind his path, opening a gate to a world cast in shadows. Six warriors appeared—not living men, but ghosts of the men they'd once been. Fiacre had explained their role to her. They owed Fiacre their lives and had given their word that even after death, they would come to his call. She'd often sparred with them, and the bite of their blades was real enough. The leader, a tall warrior with an evil scar running diagonally from the corner of his mouth to up along his cheek, lifted his sword in greeting.

"What in the—?"

"Easy, Alrick. They are with me. Do not let their form fool you. They are here to battle, the same as you."

They could not stay for long periods of time, but with their aid, cutting through the enemy would be far easier—if Alrick calmed down. His dark eyes flashed amber and he shifted his feet as if he wasn't sure whether to attack or stand. With a glance at her, as if to confirm what he saw, he stayed steady. "Right. Let's do this."

The Silver King's warriors would be no match for her, Alrick and the six undead.

A cry went out from the Faye. They had been spotted.

Within the blink of an eye, the Faye formed a line in front of the three wagons. Another contingent marched from the rear to stand behind the first. Two riders walked their horses forward. They were confident, sure of their numbers, and didn't realize that the weight of their elvish pride would drag them down to death.

She could feel the power in her body, poised, ready to strike. *I am Greer. I am here to aid Fiacre.*

But another name whispered through her mind, one she couldn't deny.

Hawk. I was once their hawk, swooping down on armies and destroying them for the Black Queen and her two minions, The Three. The memories tried to take over, but Greer pushed back, refusing to let them. Still, an image of her bloody sword surfaced. *I will never be theirs again. Never again will I be their Hawk.*

The remembered name sent a ripple down her back, but nothing—not this place, the cold, the Faye, even Alrick and Fiacre—could stop the fierce rush of battle-readiness coursing through her as the Faye positioned themselves to fight.

Chapter Two

Oisin knew consciousness visited him rarely.

Pain. Cold. Ice. These were his constant companions. Nothing else existed. His body was a distant part of him, packed tightly in ice that should have killed him long ago. But throughout the years, these three variables remained. Nothing else — no sound, no sight, no escape. Nothing, just the painfully cold ice.

No, there is fire. A flame. My *Flame. Hair the color of the summer sun on the fields of wheat. Eyes the color of the deepest forest ponds reflecting the warm light of tree and sky on its silky surface. And her lips, softer than the petals of a rose, forming the words that would hold me to her forever.*

Out of nowhere, a slow warmth heated him, dispersing the chill until, with a suddenness that would have made him bellow in pain if he could, it vanished. His body trembled, experiencing heat for the first time in ages. The awakening was agony.

Dread knotted his stomach. Oisin knew what warmth meant. A new kind of pain would begin again. He clung to the vision of Flame — her eyes filled with love, staring into his, her hands, soft and cool on his face as she lifted her face to kiss him. The image melted away on the river of pain. He couldn't hold in the agony. A cry built in his throat. Only his clenched teeth kept it in.

Sounds intruded on his agony. He shut them out and tried to reclaim the vision of Flame. More sound intruded. And with those sounds he understood. *They come for me.* Panic took the place of the pain. It was a panic so deep, so horribly consuming, that if not for the bonds of ice, he would have clawed at his face to tear out his own eyes — anything so he could be of no use to them. The ice held him. If not for it, he would have driven a knife into his own heart to stop what was to come.

Flame. She will suffer again. They will destroy her mind. I will lose her again. A rush of images flashed by, too fast for him to gain anything from them save the love he felt for his Flame. It was so deep that it was a part of him. A glimpse of sun-kissed hair and pale, creamy skin and grey-green eyes filled with pain held his, then were gone. The images changed, slowed and he saw her, truly saw her. She wore a gown and had her hair tied back as she knelt by a well, drawing water from it. Something made her look up, and a dog came bounding into the image, wiggling and playfully seeking her attention. She gave it, petting the dog while talking happily to it. The image blinked away, but not before he knew. *Brenyn. She lives as Brenyn, not Flame. She lives free of them. I must reach her. I must protect her.*

With a suddenness that vibrated deep in his body, the ice encasing him broke. Each column toppled with an enormous crash. Even free of his prison, he couldn't move, could barely breathe, as sensations attacked from all sides while he tried to comprehend how he'd been able to see Brenyn. The vision hadn't come from the Black Queen. He knew her wretched touch. This had been…different—clean, pure, true.

He blinked and blinked. The vision had left him and so had his ability to process the sudden change to his existence. All around was white—ice and packed snow, walls, floors, a ceiling far overhead…all in white with a glimpse of blue sky far down a tunnel of whiter white.

His first breath was so treacherous that it clawed at his air passages. He choked and coughed without successfully gaining any of the urgently needed air. Another desperate gasp was just as difficult until a voice spoke.

"Silence," a woman demanded.

Ice once again seized his throat, freezing his breath. *That voice. That terrible, dreadful voice.* In that instant he was aware. In a flash, his life, all the different versions of it, flew past his inner eye, and in the center, a new, more melodious voice spoke to him in his mind. *"She lives again. You are needed. You must find her. You must protect her."*

"Poison, our weapon, our deadly warrior… You are ours to yield, ours to waken. Waken now and once more do my bidding," the witch commanded.

Poison. Sword. They call me these things. Poison. Sword. Weapons made to kill. I am a living sword and with me stands my Flame…No! I am Oisin. My Brenyn…where is she?

"This time you will be more," the voice in his head promised.

He held himself still, sure that the witches had no clue that there was another voice speaking to him, weakening their spell and giving him hope. *"Who are you?"*

"Shh… In time you will understand. Until then, stay strong."

"Waken, Poison. Do my bidding and once again repay your debt," one of the women ordered.

No. Not a…not a…weapon. I am a man. I am…

A face hovered just out of focus, then another, both cutting deeper than the freezing ice attacking him. *Brenyn and Greer. The Flame and the Hawk. They live!*

He could still sense the witches below him on the snowy ground. They were shouting their spells, using words they'd used hundreds of times before, but this time, they were weaker. Still there, but weaker.

The different voice in his head said, *"You must not let them know. You must be partially bound to them or else they will kill you."*

He wanted to argue, to fight such an idea, but the spells were binding him slowly, bit by bit. A cry built in his throat. It came out as a strangled groan. Fisting his hands, every muscle in his body drew taut. He threw his head back and fought the witches' bonds. *I am not a weapon. My name is* not *Poison. My name…is…*

"By the raven's blood, I command you." Warm droplets splattered his face, burning like embers from a great hearth. "By the power of The Three, awaken and pay your debt." This time, the voices spoke in unison, the tone horrific and filled with dark power. The Black Queen was using her two sisters to bind him once again. The horror of that knowledge settled deep, piercing him to the core.

"Do our bidding once again," they sang in unison.

More droplets sizzled against his skin. More binding spells tied his will down and imprisoned his mind. "You are ours to command, Poison. Awaken, Poison, and once more do as we wish!"

Death. Poison.

He opened his eyes. Before him stood the three, their eyes blackened, their souls far darker. The witch's brow was smeared with red to indicate her pact with forces dark and dangerous. Her sisters wore the pendants in the shape of an eye on their chests that were crafted out of bone, a symbol of power that they'd traced with fresh blood. More bones adorned their headdresses and even more were visible in their wild hair. Feathers twisted with mud and blood were twined within their manes and hung from their wrists and shoulders. Their capes were lined with the silver fur of the winter wolf, and all along the collar were woven feathers from a thousand ravens. Blood stained the white snow at their feet. More dripped from their fingertips.

He stared at them. Deep down his hatred blossomed. He pushed it down. He could not be affected by their horrifying visages. They were no more important to him than the snow at their feet or the whisper of wind against his face.

"Poison. Come… come to me." The black-haired queen beckoned to him with a hand more claw than human limb.

Poison stepped down from the dais. The ice that had held him for so long crunched overloud in the silence of the chamber. His steps were steady and strong, controlled by the curse that bound him.

And yet… With this waking something else lingered, allowing him to retain a small slice of his own consciousness. Someone else remained with him. *A Dream Walker?*

Is that the voice of hope I heard?

It was fleeting, and as much as he wished it were big enough to free him now so he could kill the witches, he knew the voice spoke with wisdom. He would have to bide his time and wait until he could break away and seek out Brenyn.

If the witches sensed a weakening, they would kill him. He let his gaze wander over them, careful to keep his face impassive.

Eager, maniacal expressions filled the three witches' faces. They obviously rejoiced in their power and could not see that their security was built on a flaw, a crack in their hold on him. For if he could think beyond their commands, he could feel — and if he could feel... *Then the Dragons may yet survive.*

If they did not realize it. If they did sense it, they would grow furious. It was always the trapped animals that fought the hardest.

He firmed his grasp on his waking mind. He would have to wait, watch and work at widening the crack in their control to a gap, to a door and ultimately to a way out of the curse that bound him.

At the queen's feet, Poison knelt on one knee in homage. "What is your will, my queen?"

"Death, Poison. Always death." She caressed her blood-stained fingers over his jaw, tipping his head up so that he was forced to stare into the madness of her eyes. "And, of course, a bit more." Her touch made his skin crawl. He endured it. Nothing they did produced the desired results. It never had. He would never lie with them. His heart and body belonged to another.

In a fury at his body's lack of response to her stroking, the Black Queen screamed curses at him and scratched his chest with her sharp nails

"Easy, sister. He is of more use than to warm our bed. There are many others to choose from for that privilege."

The Black Queen hovered over him, still enraged. He would wait to test their strength — and if the crack remained... *I will be free. We will be free at last.*

He buried the vengeful thoughts as deep as he could. *Time.* In time he would destroy them. Before that, he would be free.

We will be free at last, Brenyn. They will never force you to kill again.

Chapter Three

Jacob was dreaming. He knew he was. Still, he couldn't stop himself from reaching out for the curtain that separated him from seeing who lay beyond the sheer fabric. He reached and reached. The curtain moved as if by a breeze. It didn't lift. He couldn't reach it. No matter how hard he tried, his fingers were never close enough to grab hold.

It was essential that he rip it free from the curtain rod. He wasn't in a room — not one he'd stood in for centuries, at least. Long ago, in another world, he'd once raced down corridors of stone and hidden in rooms like this one when he'd played with other children. With *her*.

Wooden shutters would have been closed in the winter, a fire would have been lit in the hearth and the woven tapestries on the walls would have depicted scenes from the hunt. Furs would have covered the cold, stone floors. Goose down would have filled some mattresses, while others would have been filled with straw or sometimes wool left over from the clippings of the sheep.

Those days had been long ago.

In another lifetime.

He was no longer Jacob, the stray brought up by the cooks and befriended by the youngest of the four princesses. He was no longer the brave warrior heading off to win himself a reputation worthy of a princess.

That life had been taken from him.

He knew this.

The scent of roses filled the air.

He was Jacob — Vampire, killer and monster to the people of his old realm — and his new one. Jacob, who lost his life when he tried to save a witch. Jacob, who fought and fought and fought on the sands. Faye watched…cheered. He killed and killed. Friend? Foe? It didn't matter. They had died, and when they had, he'd drunk from them if he could, anything to avoid the poisoned blood the Faye fed him. Only he wasn't on the sands. He wasn't fighting. He wasn't killing.

It's a dream. I'm dreaming.

The scent of roses filled the air.

Roses he knew.

How? Where are they coming from?

The breeze didn't hit him. He sweated. He burned. Drops of perspiration stung his eyes, trickled down his back. No coolness eased his suffering. He opened his mouth to shout, sure that his vocal cords worked, yet no sound emerged.

The scent was there. Roses, but not just any roses — not the poignant, heavy fragrance of the high beauties… It was the light, sweet scent of the small, wild roses that grew on the castle walls. They had always struck him as being even more beautiful for their wildness, as was the beauty of the woman behind the curtain. He knew it, knew her. The curve of her neck, the long lines of her back, the gentle sweep of her hip, the small, perfect shape of her hands... She knew him. She knew him like no one else ever would.

Her name was there...on his tongue. He could say it. He wanted to shout it. What was it? His head felt full, heavy with fear, and a desperation suddenly filled him. His heart—that traitorous organ that obeyed him because he wouldn't let go of his humanity—felt squeezed by a fist.

A buzz filled his head. Not his head...the air. *Wasps? Bees?*

Shouts. Battle cries. The sound of dying. He knew it well enough to know that it belonged nowhere near her. She would never be touched by such ugliness. No battle would reach her, leaving behind scars no amount of time could erase. Nothing like that would harm her. No one would ever dare.

Was that true? Did he know? Had she suffered? Had she been touched by the pain brought on by struggle and loss?

She moved, shifted as if she were going to walk away, yet faced him instead. He held his breath and waited for her to lift the curtain.

She came closer. The outline of her heart-shaped face took the rest of his breath hostage. Delicate cheekbones and jawline, the aching sweetness of her cheek, skin so soft he had to be careful when he touched her, all became clearer...c loser. She had to come closer. He had to read her eyes, see the horror there when she saw him, recognized the monster facing her.

She stopped suddenly. Did she know? Sense the change in him? The coldness that was always there, holding him hostage?

Time went by and nothing changed until, with a suddenness that shocked him, she turned her head. The long flow of her golden hair brushed the curtain. He watched the fabric rise like a wave then slowly fall as her hair eased away. The scent of roses overpowered him. He reached out again. He couldn't touch it. The curtain still lay beyond his reach. He knew it was too late. She was leaving, running from him.

He shouted. He knew he did. His throat ached with the force of his yell, yet no sound emerged.

He fought to reach her, had to reach her. Had to make her see he wasn't a monster. He'd tried not to kill them. On the sands, he'd struggled, refused the blood, refused to raise his sword and taken blow after blow. Nothing he did then, or now, mattered. He couldn't move. Couldn't fight the need to fight. Couldn't fight her, couldn't forget her, couldn't have her, couldn't…

Cold surrounded him. Cold that crept up from his toes, holding him in place so tightly that he couldn't move. It reached his chest, freezing his heart, then slid upward, even as he fought to free himself.

Before it covered his face, he found the power to shout.

One word left his lips and echoed around him, even after the ice froze him. She didn't turn. Even after the curtain flapped in the breeze and lifted enough to give him a glimpse of her rose-colored gown and long, flowing golden hair, she didn't face him, didn't gaze up at him with tears and sorrowful hope filling her eyes. No, she was leaving him. But that wasn't right either. He'd left her, hadn't he? She wouldn't have left him. He'd been the one to leave.

Then why do I feel she's coming closer? Why do I smell roses? If I'm frozen, wouldn't the roses be long gone?

Chapter Four

At the very rear of the army, a canopy of deepest black caught Greer's eye. There were several wagons with warriors confined behind bars. The cages were tall, with sturdy bars up the sides and over the top. Nothing protected the men and women inside from the harsh weather. They'd be drenched in rain and freezing in the cold bitterness of winter. Now they were lined with warriors standing, gazing out at them. She couldn't see their faces. She felt certain they were eager for release.

One carriage stood out from the others. It was enclosed with heavy black drapes. The cloth fluttered wildly in the wind, perhaps wanting freedom as much as the men and women in the cages.

The warriors were used for sport. Games, Fiacre had said. She felt a sudden kinship with them, a deep sensation of painful awareness. Since waking from death, emotions came at her as sharply and suddenly as attacks in the dark. Greer drew in a deep breath, trying to deal with the sudden empathy for the captives.

She focused on the army of Faye soldiers with their bright armor and shining banners. A surge of anger rushed her at the sight of them. She clenched her hand on the reins and worked on not tensing her entire body. Her mare shifted, either sensing her confusing emotions or feeling the tension she couldn't control.

"Greer," Fiacre called. His voice seemed far off. In her mind she saw the Faye attacking, killing men, women and children without thought. "Greer."

"Yes." She blinked back the rage, the pain and the horror. *Did you not do much worse?*

"Do you see the black wagon?" Fiacre asked.

"Yes." The wagon was the only one curtained and guarded so heavily. The other wagons were open cages with two soldiers on horses and one on the seat, driving the horses forward.

"Good." Fiacre drew closer. "It is the warrior within the black wagon who we need. Free the others if you can." Fiacre leaned over and caught her arm. His grip was firm, strong. Relief settled over her like the warmth she felt when she slept under her furs. During those times, when the fire burned low on the hearth, she felt whole. The emotions receded as she focused on his face. "He's rising. I can feel him fighting their magic. Be careful."

"Always."

Fiacre released her.

"Aye, he might not recognize friend from foe." Alrick adjusted his armor. "He cannot be exposed to the light of day. Ensure that you cover him and that he is not further harmed." He glanced up at the clouds.

"He might survive in this. He's strong. Be cautious. He might be suffering from the poison they feed him."

There was no need to ask what poison Alrick spoke of. It was clear that whatever it was would muddle the hidden warrior's mind.

"Why do you block our way?" The Faye warrior had ridden up to within a hundred feet of them. He rode a stallion of purest black. His helm would have reflected the sun like a star if the overhead clouds were not blocking it. Still, she knew him as a commander.

"You have people who do not belong to you," Fiacre responded. "Release them and return to your forests."

"None of these prisoners are your people."

"Neither are they yours. Release them and we will let you leave this place."

The Faye commander laughed harshly and motioned to them, then to two men behind him. "Bring them along. They will make a nice addition."

Fiacre didn't respond. Instead, he gave her a slight nod. It was all the signal they needed.

Alrick started running toward the Faye without a glance at her.

She steadied her grip on her sword, lowered her visor with her sword hand, and her mare burst into a gallop. The visor limited her vision. It also concentrated it. The Faye stood between her and what she needed. A slight lean in her saddle and her horse leaped forward even faster. She passed Alrick. He was already past the first wave of Faye and engaged with the second line of warriors.

Fiacre sent out a spell. To her it looked like sunshine flooding a dark room. The Faye scattered, some crouching on the windswept grass with their hands over their ears as if to block a horrible sound. Others attempted to control their suddenly wild horses. Those who were able to withstand the onslaught and stay on their feet were suddenly engaged in battle with the warriors made of mist.

Through the chaos, she raced to the wagon.

A group of warriors broke free from their company and tried to stop her. The sun reflected on their silver visors and hid their beautiful features. She could still identify them as the enemy.

Fierce rage filled her. She broke upon the ranks with a savageness that left dead warriors in her wake. More tried to intercept her, screaming battle curses as they attempted to block her from her goal. Each stroke of her sword silenced those cries and left death behind.

Circling her mount, she spied two of the warriors falling to the grass, never to sing their songs to their forests again—if they even remembered how. More took their place as if they knew what she sought and, having broken from Fiacre's spell, were determined to stop her. She charged through. Her sword drank their blood until her arm and shoulder burned with the strain. She shifted left, right, back, forward, twisting and turning in the saddle to stay astride as she fought her way ahead. Slowly she gained ground, but at the cost of lives that had once shown bright and pure for hundreds, perhaps thousands of ages.

Above the sounds of battle, she heard shouts, not of challenge but of desperation. *The prisoners.* She circled her mare, spying what caused them alarm. Fallen torches must have lit the dry winter grass, for the area blazed. Smoke and the heavy scent of burned flesh filled that side of the battlefield.

As if from far off, she heard a shout from Fiacre. The wind grew to hurricane force. The fire spread toward the Faye and away from the wagons. The Faye fell back. A path broke to the wagons.

She put her cheek against Silverfoot's sweat-stained neck. "Now, Silverfoot... Run!"

The smell of horse and leather was strong, but not powerful enough to rid the air of the stench of blood and death. She tightened her legs, and the mare leaped over fallen soldiers, immediately dodging two who tried to stop her with wicked-looking pikes. Greer kept her seat by sheer luck.

Shouts rose above the cries of her enemies — the prisoners in their carriage. Greer spared them a glance. They had broken free. Two Faye lay dead at the side. The Faye were now separated — ones fighting Alrick and the six warriors and the ones racing to the wagons to secure the prisoners. Fiacre shouted and another bright light blasted the field. Where it touched the silver-and-black warriors, they fell to their knees, pulling their helms off so they could cover their ears.

A spear whistled by Greer's ear, bringing her attention back to her target...the downed carriage. An arrow thudded against her helm. She jerked the mare around and sought the bowman, only to have a barb smack into her left breast. Luckily, it hadn't penetrated the hardened leather. The pain was enough to bring her focus to the warrior readying another arrow.

A woman.

As Greer registered this, the archer let another arrow fly.

Greer shoved it aside with her sword and charged. As she rode, she swung her shield out and down, catching the woman by surprise and throwing her onto her back. Her bow swung outward in an arc. Greer sliced it in half but left the woman alive and scrambling backward like a crab.

Greer sought her bearings as she slowed Silverfoot. Out of the confusion, another warrior ran to face her. Dressed in richly detailed black-and-silver armor, with his heavy broadsword held high and ready, he raced at her as if she were the only opponent on the field. Worse, he blocked her access to the carriages.

She ducked low again, patting the mare to reassure her, then leaned forward, ready to battle whoever she needed. The field narrowed. Her vision became focused on him. All else fell away. He was injured. His left side dragged a fraction. There was blood on his silver armor, where his shoulder met his neck, more than enough to slow him. It didn't matter. She took it all in and processed it, even as she charged.

At the last moment, the warrior shifted, taking a stance with his sword held at the horizontal that would cut her horse out from under her. Such a move would cripple a horse for life, if not outright kill it.

Anger burned the fatigue from her arms and strengthened her resolve. The sounds of battle stilled. Burned flesh now filled the freezing smoke-filled air, making her want to sneeze. The tingle was there. It was a minor detail on the periphery of her concentration. The warrior opposite her was everything.

The warrior crouched lower, sword at the ready. She veered to his right at the last possible second. At the same time, she kicked her feet from the stirrups and spun in her saddle to jump down. The move landed her in a roll directly behind him. Before he could compensate, she shoved her blade through his lower back and out through his chest.

Time returned to normal.

He gurgled out an inarticulate sound that might have been a word.

"Horses are not your equal. You should never attempt to take the life of one," Greer told the dying man.

His hoarse grunt could have been agreement. She didn't pause long enough to find out.

She released him. Her sword slid from his body with a wet sigh. She bent and wiped it on his black cape, glancing around her as she did, then she whistled for Silverfoot. Alrick was off to her right, fiercely battling three warriors. As she watched, he dispatched one with a strike to the neck then swung his sword diagonally and took out another. Facing off with the third, he gave a wild cry and bashed his head into the man's then, gripping his armor, threw him off.

Alrick was fine.

The mist warriors were taking care of the rest, and while the battle continued, she took off on foot, the mare following obediently behind.

The carriage she sought was down on its side mere feet from her.

The other prisoners were fighting the few Faye that had rallied to try to force them back into their shackles. She ignored a shout and sprinted the last few feet, then shoved one section of the heavy black cloth aside.

Inside the protection of the wagon, a warrior glared at her. Dark spots seemed to wink to life in her vision. Her legs went weak. She grabbed the side of the carriage for support as the world spun her too fast. She couldn't catch her breath. A flash of something, the scent of roses and the face of a boy with smiling brown eyes burst through her consciousness then was gone.

The prisoner remained. The contours of his face, even twisted in pain and rage, were still familiar to her. Darkest brown eyes and a furrowed forehead arrowed down black eyebrows she knew would kick up if she said something amusing…

This is… This is…

A shout from behind startled her. She spun. A man dropped two meters from her. A ghost warrior caught her eye before drifting away. *I need to free this man and take him to Fiacre. That is what I need to do. Nothing else matters. No memories. Not now.*

She turned back and landed flat on her back. Her breath exploded from her in a ragged gasp. Before she could recover, a hand, as cold as her knife blade in winter, caught her by the neck and dragged her upward.

The emotions she'd not had time to control roared at her with such speed she couldn't process them. They were a violent storm destroying everything in their path.

Jacob. This is my Jacob.

No barrier stood between the sorrow, the joy, the love, the betrayal and the desertion, nothing but her refusal to remember. She'd been born once, twice…multiple times. She'd been found, used to inflict horrific damage on people and killed again and again, only to be reborn. Only once out of all those circles of pain and death had she lived, truly opened her heart and mind to her existence. This man stood at the center of that life. The moments — that life she'd experienced — had been locked away, hidden so that she'd never be tempted to try again. Now those memories and the emotions that belonged to them demanded release.

She couldn't focus on breaking free *and* burying a life she never should have had.

"What trick is this?" His strength astounded her. Eyes bloodshot and wild with passion met hers. Like a strike of lightning that revealed the nighttime landscape, everything but his face disappeared.

"You think to trick me with Gwen? I will do nothing for you!"

The hand at her throat tightened, cutting off all air. The sound of *that* name, of a woman she'd tried desperately to be then just as desperately to forget, wounded her deeper than any injury she had ever suffered in battle.

Desperate to escape, she fought him. Hits to his forearm did nothing. She tried kicking him but he didn't even blink. With a suddenness that again startled her, he released her and staggered backward, appearing stunned. There was fresh blood on his chest, more on his upper thigh.

She tried to breath and ended up coughing and gasping for breath. She thought she heard him say, "The roses were real."

It made no sense, but at the same time, it did. The scent filled the air. It always had. The Rose Kingdom was named for the pink roses that climbed the stone walls of the castle. That was long ago and couldn't be real. She refused to accept such things. It was winter in the mountains. Nothing bloomed now. The past was the past. It couldn't be changed. It couldn't be re-lived. Edward and Elspeth, the loving king and queen who had raised her, were long gone, along with the thousands of citizens who called the Rose Kingdom their home. *They died —*

She shut down the memory and focused on Jacob. He stood bent over, his hands on his knees. There would never be another Gwen. She could never allow another Gwen.

"It's not a trick." With a hand at her throat, she straightened. "I'm not Gwen. Gwen is dead." Her voice had roughened from his hold or from the fist her emotions had on it—she couldn't tell. The words were like lies on her tongue. They had to be the truth. She would not re-open the painful wounds of a past that had destroyed her. She tried desperately to replace the cocoon she'd lived in since waking—the emotionless, dreamless cocoon that kept the memories at bay.

Jacob was bent over as if she'd strangled him. At her words, he stared at her. His wounded expression, so confused and filled with pain, sliced through her heart.

She tried again. "She's gone. I'm Greer. Fiacre sent me to free you—" She got no further. Jacob grabbed her again, this time with a grip on her upper arm.

"You're lying." His forehead creased with the force of the emotions filling his eyes. There was desperation and something else, something she couldn't allow. Hope.

"No. I'm telling the truth. She died long ago." She swallowed at the look of anguish deepening the lines on his forehead. It was for the best. She needed the cocoon, the barrier between herself and the world. She needed Fiacre. He could replace the cold, frozen feeling. "We must go. We—"

"What Faye trick is this?" His grip tightened until she was surprised that her bones didn't crack. "Answer me!"

"It's not a Faye trick—"

He dragged her closer, so close that she could see the red in his eyes as well as her own reflection in his dark irises.

"You—"

"Look around you!" she demanded. "Don't you see them dying?" She shoved at his chest, gripping his tunic when he didn't move. "I wasn't sent here *by* the Faye. I killed them to try to reach you—to free you!"

His gaze broke from hers for only a second. In that time, she knew that with a twist of his head, he'd categorized every inch of the field. And he wasn't worried…or letting her go. She shoved at him again, desperate now. He was cold, like marble that wouldn't move, no matter how hard she pushed. By his pain-filled expression, he didn't even realize she wanted him to let go. His skin against her palm was so cold… Jacob had been like a hearth—toasty warm.

He's not the same and neither am I. She knew that wasn't entirely correct. The warmth of the man she had once known might be gone, true. She knew it didn't matter. This was still Jacob. *Still Jacob. But I am not Gwen. I never was Gwen. That way lies destruction.*

Lies. She could feel her heart filling with urges she couldn't allow. That look in his eyes, that pain… She knew how to soothe it, how to touch him, speak to him, hold him. *No! The Three will find me, and when they do, they will destroy him and everyone else. Truth. His life may have changed, but he lives. They will take that, or worse, twist it to their will.*

Despairing, she stopped trying to break his physical hold. "I have lived many lifetimes. I always return as you see me now." She touched the center of her chest with her free hand and pulled at his grip on the other. This time, he seemed to realize that his grip hurt—or else her words were getting through. He dropped his hand then stood there, the painful expression still etching lines on his face. Meeting his eyes hurt. He was damaged. Perhaps blood cravings had altered him – or the poison Alrick had spoken of, or perhaps because he was no longer mortal. *No longer Jacob, and I'm no longer Gwen.* "We are both no longer the same."

As if her words had lit a spark, he glowered at her. "You *are* Gwen. Do you think I can't tell? Look at me!" He gestured to his chest. "I'm a Vampire. I can tell with one scent that it's you!"

The rage in him eclipsed even the wildness in his eyes.

She understood what he meant. "You're right…and wrong. It was always me…Greer. Gwen was but one short lifetime of the many I've lived and it ended in tragedy. I tried to be something other than I am." She battled her own anger now. "I can never be anything but what you see now. This. A warrior. Do you see a princess? Do you?"

He dropped his gaze to see more than her face, but not for long. His eyes fixed on her temple, where she could feel the blood from a blow, which reminded her that her helm had tumbled free when he'd knocked her onto her back. She reached up and wiped at it with her wrist. She hadn't registered the hit. Now she could feel the warm blood dripping down her brow. Her hands were nicked and sliced. Her body was encased in sweat. No princess would ever sweat, let alone lift a blade in battle.

The memories suddenly broke free, enraging her rather than drawing her downward into sorrow. She stormed closer to Jacob and shouted, "Look around you! We're in the middle of freeing you. All *this* is because of you. We have no time for talking! No time for any of this! We need to leave! *Now!*"

Instead of backing down, he narrowed his eyes and glowered at her. "We have time. All I have is time!" Suddenly he had a grip on her again, this time dragging her back to the carriage as easily as if she were no more than a child. His strength, even clearly injured, stunned her. In the shadow of the carriage, he stopped. The clouds lifted from the sun, spilling bright light in patches on the field.

Does he know when the sun will shine?

"Explain this. And I warn you that I have no patience for lies."

"Explain? I just did. I'm *not* Gwen." She broke his hold. "She died. Died long ago!"

Stubbornness etched lines on his face that she knew so well. He wasn't going to budge. Even the meager sunlight didn't deter him.

For some reason a bubble of space still existed around them. If only the fight would reach them, then she could avoid this. *Fiacre will make me go with him. I will have to help him.* The pain of that made her eyes sting. The past was there. She had merely to reach out and all of it, all the feelings, the experiences, the…love she'd felt for this man would be there. *Not again. Never again.* She met his eyes, buried the past and strove for the chilly existence before she'd opened the curtains and met his eyes. *This time I will be nothing more than a warrior.*

"Long ago I made a choice, one that I have paid for repeatedly. I have been reborn over a dozen times, and each time I am called to fulfill my duty. This time is different. This time, Fiacre called me. This time I have a chance to break the curse. Fiacre needs you. He believes you can aid us in ending this." She gestured to the Faye and the battle taking place mere feet from them. Jacob's gaze didn't waver from hers. The painful lines etched on his face eased. "Alrick is here." He narrowed his eyes at the name. She rushed on. "Soon, others you know will arrive. That is what is important. Ending this," she hissed the last, feeling the weight of his gaze like a brand on her skin, "not who I once was, one time out of a dozen lifetimes. That life didn't matter. *You* didn't matter." She threw the last at him, determined to make it the truth. It sounded false, even to her own ears.

Jacob didn't answer. He didn't blink. He didn't move. He stood towering over her, his beloved face bruised and bloody, his shoulders broad and strong, and yet, she couldn't imagine leaning against them and letting him ease her burden. *Gwen is dead. The woman he loved is dead. I killed her. He will die as well if he believes otherwise.*

"You're a reincarnate."

She shook her head. Stubborn. "No." This, she wouldn't allow. "I am Greer. Long ago, I was born not far from here. Since then I have been reborn, each time with a different name, but it is me, always *me*." *Except once.*

"Then you *are* Gwen—or you were." With a thunderous expression, he demanded, "Why are you denying it?"

"Because it makes no difference. Gwen is *dead!*" She drew a breath and tried to ignore the butterflies flipping and dancing in her stomach. "Long dead. Her life was nothing."

His eyebrows dipped down so low over his eyes that the skin between them furrowed. It was a forbidding look. She had no fear of the sudden anger, though — not from Jacob. She never would.

"We have to hurry. Fiacre is —" she began.

"I won't hear more of this —"

"Good! Stop talking. I am *not* Gwen. I am Greer, and we need to go!" She flung her hand out to point at the bloody battlefield.

He didn't take his gaze off her. "Exactly."

For some reason that one word caused her a rush of panic. She saw him flex, knew something was wrong and attempted to step back. Too late his hand landed on her arm in the vise-like grip from before. She tried to pull away. Suddenly she knew she had been seconds too late.

The world disappeared. Blackness suffocated her. Nothing, not Jacob, not the cries of the dead, not the cold breeze from the mountains existed. Then, as if she'd broken free from a deep dive beneath the Emerald Sea, the world resurfaced. Only it wasn't the battlefield, and she wasn't standing under the shadow of the Twins.

"What have you done?"

"Sleep."

The one word circled and circled in her head, dragging her downward. She clung to her anger and kept it like a light in the building darkness.

Chapter Five

Brenyn sat up in bed, her heart pounding. *The warrior. He's close. He's...* Indistinct images hovered, still there if she could only close her eyes and fall back asleep. The idea filled her with a mixture of fear and anticipation. Which was stronger she couldn't say. *If he's more than a dream, I should be afraid. I should go tell someone right now.* She didn't move. Fiacre and Greer were still gone. She was the only one in the keep. Suddenly that knowledge sent a shiver down her back and made her heart leap. It was far too easy to imagine someone else being there, walking down the corridors, coming closer and closer. She closed her eyes and steadied her breathing. There was no sound save those she made. No one walked down the corridor. No one reached for the handle of her door. Nothing changed in her room. She listened until her ears hurt.

Sighing, she lay back down and stared up at the moonlit ceiling. *On the morrow, I will let the dogs sleep in* here. *At least with them, I will be forewarned. If there is someone…which is silly. There is no one. I'm alone.*

The images slowly began to fade out of reach. *A dream. Another dream, nothing more.*

Sweating even though her hearth barely warmed the room, she tried to force her brain to accept the reality that her small room was empty. No one stood over her, no one watched her during the day as she went around doing her chores, no one hovered close by in case anyone dared harm her.

Silence filled the room. Even the fire didn't pop and crackle. She almost got up, just to add wood so that some sounds kept her company. Instead, she rolled onto her side so she could stare at the embers and reassure herself that the room was deserted.

In her dreams, her warrior didn't speak. Yet, in them, somehow the silence wasn't as empty. When he came to her, she knew what he was thinking — or not really thinking — but what he would have said if he did speak. His presence always filled in the silent loneliness. Sometimes when she woke, she felt a pang of sadness for his loss.

She flipped over onto her back. The glow of the moon coming through the closed shutters meant it was still deep night. If there was a man, a big, handsome warrior who visited her, the midnight hour seemed appropriate. The middle of the night, the time when day fought with night, had always frightened her. He would have kept her warm, curling her close to his bigger, warmer body so she could sleep, knowing she was truly safe.

Silly. No man waits for me. No one yearns to hold me. I simply miss Greer and Fiacre.

The small blue vial of potion beside her bed would help her sleep. It would also relieve the dreams. She'd once gone four nights without it. The dreams had been frightening — but clearer than ever before. Sometimes she wished she had never left them. Sometimes those moments were better than waking. Sometimes… *I wish I could stay asleep.*

Brenyn sighed and pulled the covers up to her chin as she turned to her side. A trail of hot tears slid over the bridge of her nose. She wiped them away. They were useless. Tonight, all her worries were terrifyingly real. Deep inside, where she hid her biggest doubts from Fiacre, she believed what she dreamed was a past she couldn't recall when awake. Memories. *What if I have dreams of memories — like Greer?*

Greer had memories. She had arrived one night, naked and freezing, in Fiacre's tower, whole and alive after coming to them from beyond the veil. Her dreams were filled with memories of her past lives. Even her waking hours could be suddenly filled with memories. She took a potion. It seemed to make Greer cold and absent in ways that concerned Brenyn.

She feared even more that part of Greer had remained behind, that part of her was still beyond the veil — walking the world of shadows. Brenyn had spoken to Fiacre about it and the mage had claimed that Greer would return slowly and only when she was ready to face her pasts. *Pasts.* Greer had lived several times. Fiacre had called her back to try to break her curse.

Alone, with the days filled with useless tasks, Brenyn had begun to worry that she, too, had once lived before. Why else was she here? Why else had Fiacre, a great mage, found her and brought her to such a place? How did one child out of so many homeless, starving souls gain his attention? She wasn't special. The only thing special about her was Fiacre.

She stared at the glass bottle. Fiacre didn't drink such potions. Yet, since her first day with him, she'd always taken it. Only once in childhood had she disobeyed Fiacre. She could still remember him finding the full vial. He never grew impatient with her, never scolded, never raised his voice. She could remember the feel of his hand on her arm, the look of intensity in his eyes and even the light, shimmering icy blue from his gaze as he questioned her without speaking.

He'd been scared. Frightened. She could see that now. As a small child, she'd been too scared that he'd throw her out to see it was his fear that had made him so upset that day.

It wasn't until she'd grown that she'd intentionally not taken the potion. After the four nights, she'd noticed that her dreams had been much more vivid. She'd dreamed of Greer and the warrior. It made sense to dream of Greer in battles. She *was* a warrior. And the warrior with wild, sun-streaked hair fit too. He made her heart ache, though, as if he meant more to her than anything else in the world. It was silly, insane and dangerous. After the four days, her fifth dream had sent her back to the potion. She'd dreamed of him again. He hadn't been in a battlefield. He'd been in a bedroom. He'd hovered above her, his expression filled with warmth and...something else. She'd woken breathless, her heart racing and her body covered in sweat. She ached, longing for something she didn't understand.

The potion stopped the dreams. Now she worried it stopped other things too.

Sighing, she closed her eyes then opened them when she couldn't keep them closed. Everything had changed once Greer and Fiacre had left the keep. The lonely, empty halls had never bothered her before, but now, knowing she was the only person there made her heart ache. She missed explaining to Greer that she needed more to look forward to than simply preparing for war. Greer needed to prepare for life. She missed explaining to Greer how she would find a farmer to marry, not a muscled warrior who had biceps bigger around than her thigh. *A warrior is strong. He could be a protector when the battle reaches us. What if Fiacre doesn't need me any longer? What if he forgets me? What if he doesn't return? What if he returns and no longer needs me?*

Anyone could cook and clean. Many could do so much better than a girl who forgot to start the bread early enough for them to have it with their first meal. The village women, for example, could. They could clean the entire keep in less than a week, while for her it took days and days and days to simply tidy one room.

I can't fight. I can't call the ghost warriors. I can't see the line of protection around the keep. I can't help with the battle. When the battle begins, I will be forgotten. The worst of her fears were that she was already forgotten. *I will be forgotten, and if I die in the upcoming battle, no one will remember the smaller-than-average girl who used to clean a keep for the great Fiacre. Not even Fiacre.*

"No, that will never happen. Fiacre saved me from the streets. He brought me here. He will care for me." A few deep breaths and she focused on the potion. It would ease her sleep. It would also remove the warrior. "I want a farmer for a husband, not a warrior. I want a calm, kind man, with a small bit of land and laughter in his eyes." *The warrior has eyes that glow with laughter.*

She reached for the bottle. "No. His eyes were amused…at me." The potion hit her tongue. It was bitter and laced with something tingly. It would help. "I have to stay here. I have to stay and wait for Fiacre."

The potion warmed as it went down. She curled her knees up higher to her chest, burrowed under her bedding and closed her eyes.

Chapter Six

Jacob caught Gwen—or Greer—in his arms. His stomach protested. It didn't matter. He'd hold her this way until his last breath. He cradled her close to his chest and breathed in the scent of her. Tears—*goddamn tears*—blurred his vision. There was no one near, not a living thing for miles upon miles. He controlled himself and wiped away the damn wetness. He'd brought her to the only place he knew well enough. It was the start of his journey in this realm that he had once called his home. That fact hadn't hit him until he'd passed the gate with the others and the scents and *feeling* of being back where he'd started had hit him. Then it was too late to do anything about it...if he could have. He'd come here to save a woman—a mage named Aubrey. He'd ended up taking a full quiver of arrows to the chest. It was a better location than the battlefield or the prison where the Faye had held him.

The ruins were deserted. As far as he could tell, no living creature called this place home. Nothing, at least, within a hundred miles. Unfortunately, that also meant that there was nothing else here either. A stone ruin, half reclaimed by the forest, was the only shelter that existed. Two towers stood with gaping holes where the stones had fallen to reveal the dark interior. It would do.

He settled Gwen on the grass. Blonde hair, shaven at the sides and twisted in braids down the middle, spilled free onto the wet grass. She'd always worn her hair long and free-flowing down her back. Not once had she worn war braids. Never had he seen a mark on her... And yet, this woman—*Greer* had fresh wounds and, under those, the sign of older scars.

It doesn't matter. This is Gwen.

Memories of her resurfaced as if he'd just opened a door to his past. All the years he'd held those images locked away, he'd known that if he dwelled on the past, he'd never be able to survive. Now all those memories had broken free in their rush to remind him of every single second he'd spent with this woman. They were rich with details he'd never consciously noted—the way the sun had shimmered on her hair that day at the beach, the day she'd dived deeper than any of the bigger kids and fetched a speckled stone. She'd been so happy. She'd smiled for days. But on that afternoon, she'd spun toward him and her hair had fanned out like the golden wings of a hawk. The bright happiness in her eyes had sparkled brighter than the sun. Her laughter? Gods, her laughter. That time she'd snuck into the armory and oiled one of the guard's equipment so that when he tried to grip his weapons they'd slide right from his grasp. Climbing trees. Climbing walls. Trees. Towers. Always going higher, until she'd reached the very top of the mountains that sheltered their home. Nothing had stopped her.

Except death.

He clenched his fist near her cheek then drew in a lungful of air and searched her face. He saw the differences, the marks Gwen had never possessed. They were small scars—just white lines that outlined the story of a warrior, not a princess—but they were there. They'd been put there through experiences that Gwen had never had. Wars. Battles. Fighting. Gwen had been a princess from a family that held with traditional values. One of those values was that princesses did not go to battle. They did not carry a sword, nor did they show aggression.

Or climb trees.

An image of her that last day—beautiful and sad—surfaced. Roses had bloomed all around them, and a few petals had landed in her hair. He'd picked them out gently, so he didn't have to face the tears in her eyes. She'd not let them fall. Gwen had never given in to tears easily. Her eyes had shimmered like jewels, though. He'd never given her jewels. As a poor orphan, he'd had nothing, so he'd left her to seek glory so at least he would have that to give her.

She'd worn a rose velvet gown. The perfect princess. Even her hands had been soft and held perfectly at her waist while she waited, quietly and regally, for him to leave her behind.

She hadn't always been a princess. As a child, she'd been wild—so wild that he'd worried for their safety. As they'd grown, she'd become less the wild child and more the...princess. Or, if he were honest, the caged hawk—beautiful, but with no possibility of being what it should be...wild.

He'd watched and said nothing as the girl he'd known all his life had slowly been smothered and replaced by the princess. She'd only revealed once how unhappy she was, and he'd soothed her by explaining that a princess couldn't run around without slippers — or in trousers and a tunic, or...all the idiot things that had driven her into the role of princess and further away from a common warrior.

But this? This woman was a warrior...and she hadn't been alone.

Fiacre. A legend. The mage was aiding her. *Why?*

Alrick had been there, too.

There was much he didn't know, but there was also an equal amount he did understand. The mage had fought the Faye. He'd had Gwen aiding him, and with them had been Alrick. That meant that whatever events had passed since his captivity, his realm was still linked to this one. And even with the poison still muddling his thoughts, he knew he didn't want Gwen within a hundred miles of the Faye — or Alrick and Fiacre. Alrick would use her. Fiacre would do the same. *Why? And why free me?* He had an idea that when she woke, she'd tell him.

Behind him he felt the tremble of magic. He drew a knife from her hip and spun. No one, not even Fiacre, would take her from him. Alrick, he would not try, but the mage...

"Jacob. Hold up, man!" Alrick shouted. Beside him the mage stood, filled with power and brighter than the forest around him. He held up a hand and wore an expression likely meant to pacify Jacob. It infuriated him.

"Don't come a step closer." His fangs had dropped, causing him to slur the 's' on 'step'. He shut his mouth and gripped his knife in the ready position.

"Jacob. You have questions."

"Aye, you must listen, eh? Just listen." Alrick held his hands up higher, as if that would help Jacob chill.

It did. The king of the Lykae didn't often try to placate people. Jacob straightened with a wince as his stomach injuries burned at the pull. "I don't need answers. How do we return home?" If he could get her home then he could work out why she'd insisted she wasn't Gwen and why she thought that life wasn't the most important of all her lives.

Alrick glanced behind Jacob at Gwen then met his eyes. "We don't. Home is coming here. Listen to the mage. The girl is—"

"She's with me!" His fangs sliced his lip. Power filled his muscles, making him tense, ready for attack.

"Yes, apparently she is." Alrick spoke in such a dry tone that Jacob shook the aggression off and tossed his head.

"You're pissing me off."

Alrick grimaced. "I can see that. Maybe you should listen to Fiacre, eh, and hold off on the instincts?"

Jacob pinned the mage with his gaze. "This is Gwen. No matter what name she uses now, this is Gwen."

Fiacre raised a hand, palm out as if to calm him. "I know what you want, what you see, Jacob. There is more. There is always more," he added.

"You don't know shit about—"

"Jacob, I get it. Truly, man," Alrick said. "I get it. If you want this to have a happy-ever-after, you need to listen to the mage. That woman is yours. We get that. You still can't take her. You can't protect her."

"Why can't I? She would be safe with me!" *If I can leave this realm, she'll be safe.*

"No. She isn't. She won't be. She's got to be free, man. Listen to the mage, Jacob. Would I allow anyone to deny you what is yours without a reason?"

Jacob wanted to refuse it all, to throw the logic aside and take Gwen away.

He drew in a pine-scented breath instead. He held it, understood he didn't need to breathe, understood why he'd always hung on to his humanity — *for her* — and still couldn't stop himself from letting the breathing continue.

He exhaled heavily and studied the facts. He was a Vampire. His body demanded blood. His wounds demanded sleep. The man facing him, Alrick, was owed a debt. Above all else, Jacob trusted him. Jacob had vague memories of facing Alrick on the sand, of wanting to kill him. Fortunately, he'd not succeeded.

He understood all this in less time than it took him to draw in another breath. An unnecessary breath, he reminded himself.

Meeting Alrick's eyes, he nodded hesitantly.

Alrick sighed and sheathed his sword. To Fiacre he said, "You've got a few minutes to explain, mage. I'd make them count."

Fiacre rested his hands on his staff. He had a short beard and wispy white hair. His blue eyes were keen and sharp, though, reminding Jacob of a cerulean sea the morning after a storm. Strength radiated from him. He banked it, but it shone brightly.

"I know what you sense. You sense this woman is yours. As a mortal, you knew her. As a Vampire, you recognize what you denied so long ago."

"I never denied —"

"Don't lie to me!" The shout was so unexpected that Jacob snapped his mouth closed. "You left her, did you not? To seek fame. Instead, your life was taken from you."

The battle, the darkness, the panic and painful bite, then the change hit him all over again. It had been agonizing. He'd begged to die during the worst of it. He could still recall their laughter, the scent of metallic blood on the leaves, the taste of it on his tongue as he brought down his first and only kill, his captain. The painful memory was as fresh now as it was when he'd opened his eyes and stared into the empty gaze of his friend. It all came crashing back — the horror, the pain, the loss and more. How he'd left Gwen, knowing she'd wanted to beg him to stay but hadn't because she'd known he wouldn't. They'd been a close as any two people could be. Short of sharing their bodies, they'd shared everything. The fact that they'd never consummated their love had only made it all the deeper. He'd known he'd hurt her — and badly — by leaving. He'd done it anyway because he'd thought he knew what was right for them.

"Are you reading my mind, old man?" *Worse, making me remember?*

Fiacre shook his head. A sadness had replaced the anger from moments before. "No, Jacob. I have no need. I know the story, you see. I know why you left and what occurred when you did."

"I sought to be worthy of her," he whispered. Truth, but not the whole truth.

Fiacre's expressive old face frowned so that his wrinkles were deep grooves. "She was never yours. She owes an oath to The Three."

Jacob tensed all over again. He sought Alrick's gaze and saw the serious acceptance there. Alrick knew this. *The Three.* The Dark Queen and her minions. The Black

Queen to some, and her two sisters, the lieutenants or captains or much worse, the enforcers of her will. They were said to draw the very blood from the land and leave it dry, to topple kingdoms and conquer lands without lifting a finger. They used their power, quietly, secretly, behind the scenes — but sometimes, they rose up and took power. When they did, all bowed before them — or suffered gruesome deaths.

But this is all rumor. Stories to keep children in bed, nothing more. Gwen couldn't have owed them a thing. She could never have even talked to them, let alone made a pact with them.

But she claims not to be Gwen — or not to be her now, because that Gwen never mattered.

His head ached as if someone had driven a spike into it rather than into his chest. If he had the potion the guards had given him, the pain would go away.

The Three were legendary evil. He had a faint sense that there was more to that, something he should recall. The pain in his head made thinking difficult. He'd thought nothing could be worse than the drugs the Faye had used to poison the blood they served him, but now he knew that there was something far more painful — wanting those drugs and not having them. *I'm a damn drug addict.*

"They will call her to them, if they can," Fiacre warned. "I keep them at bay…for now. If you take her from me, if you go without my protection on her, you might as well take her to them and let them have her."

Jacob stared from the old man's lined face to Alrick's scruffy one. The king of the Lykae needed a shave and a haircut. What they were saying made no sense, either because he didn't want it to or the drugs were messing with him…or? *It's crazy.* But Gwen's scent still held him in place. She was here. Therefore, so were the two men facing him with their insane stories. *And if they're here, does that mean that the Black Queen wants Gwen?*

"This shit sounds insane, Alrick."

"Of course. Our lives *are* insane, Jacob. How many battles have we lived through? How many lives have we ended? How long have we walked alone, always wishing we could find more? And where do we find it? Here?" Alrick threw his arms up then anchored his fists on his hips. "Think, Jacob. Can it really be a coincidence?"

Jacob's head throbbed at him, demanding the Faye drugs or sleep. He stiffened his shoulders, tightening his abs in the process, and winced at the damage there. "You found your mate?"

Alrick stared at him with a frown better served to an enemy. Jacob didn't budge. Fiacre didn't speak. That was a rare thing, Jacob assumed. Alrick's expression didn't waver, until finally he snorted and looked out over the forest. "I sense her," Alrick finally admitted.

And can't find her? "How is that possible?"

Alrick sighed and met his eyes again. "Magic, I assume."

Fiacre raised his bushy eyebrows as if to say, 'probably'. Alrick continued after the mage simply stayed silent. "She's here. That I know. Just knowing is enough...for now." Another heavy sigh. "It'll have to be the same for you. I'm guessing that Greer told you she's not this woman you knew. And instead of listening to that, you shifted her here. Nice choice."

"I thought the gate would still be here," he said, sounding defensive.

"You cannot take Greer away from this realm, Jacob." Fiacre shook his head. "I know you wish to protect her. She can protect herself. The princess you knew is no longer there. If you loved the girl, Gwen, then it was Greer you loved, unless it was merely the princess you wanted."

Jacob had the mage in his grip before he knew he was going to move. Alrick grabbed his forearm, but Fiacre met his gaze calmly.

"I loved Gwen. I loved her, and this woman, whoever she calls herself, still has that love."

"I doubt that." The feminine voice behind them was laced with amusement, but most of it was cold, hard fact. The chill of a blade against the back of his neck didn't surprise him as much as Alrick's grin. Alrick dropped his grip and shook his head.

She'd poised her knife exactly where, if thrust, he'd lose all sensation of his body. He'd recover, sure, but first, he'd fall on his face. He eased his grip on Fiacre.

"Step back. Raise your hands. Keep them where I can see them."

"You sound like a cop." He stepped back, though, with his hands up.

Fiacre grimaced. Alrick simply folded his arms, indicating that in no way was he prepared to help. Hopefully, it wouldn't be needed.

"Never" — she leaned closer and the blade burned where she sliced him. The warmth of her body caused a great deal more pain — "do that to me again. *Never*."

"Got it."

Her body heat receded, and she walked around him, her knife still in her hand. Her eyes were filled with vengeance. Gwen had never looked at him with such rage. He'd never given her a reason to, either. She stopped by Fiacre, assessed the old man's neck, then gave Alrick a flat stare before facing him.

"How did you know I'd bring her here?" he asked, more curious than anything else. His anger had evaporated.

"I knew you would never take her anywhere near the Faye. This was the only option." At Fiacre's words, she lowered the knife, but she kept it in her grip. "Jacob, we need to know that you understand what we face."

His head ached as if it'd been cleaved with a butcher knife. Through the pain, he could still follow their insane plan. He might not remember it — the drug had done a job on his memory — but he could follow simple logic, even if it wasn't very possible. "Understand? It sounds like incredible odds with no chance we're going to win."

"That's about it." Alrick laughed. "I knew you'd get it."

"Does this mean you agree?" Fiacre grimaced, which brought all his thousands of wrinkles together to form deeper lines. No doubt the mage had much to worry over. Gwen simply stood, ready for anything, her blue eyes on him with more animosity than he felt necessary.

The drugs the Faye had fed him sent the world spinning and his aching head pounding. He wanted to leave this place, to sleep then wake with Gwen there. From the look of his new companions, he'd get one thing.

Gwen — or Greer — by his side or near his side. And to have her there? He'd have to go along with this mad scheme. *Another battle.*

He sighed. "I'm in." He'd do his part, but he'd have to ensure that when the dust settled, they survived. Until then, he'd have to stay close and, if he had to, convince the woman staring daggers at him of exactly who she was.

Chapter Seven

Evie's office usually soothed the senses. She'd designed it herself. The walls were soundproof. The furniture was comfortable and elegant. Her desk had been crafted by the best Faye woodworkers and her chair was of the highest quality that money — her money — could buy.

"It's all for nothing," she said.

The man sitting facing her across the glossy surface of her desk didn't respond. It wasn't to him she spoke, and by the look in his crystal blue gaze, he knew it.

Even her chandelier had been commissioned from the best artists. It shimmered and shown with brilliance. It was a muted, understated sophistication she had grown more and more fond of.

Now it will all be lost.

She tapped an elegantly polished nail against the small parchment he had delivered.

"They await your reply."

"Yes, they do, but I have none to give." She didn't stand. Her legs probably wouldn't support her. The man across from her didn't turn violent. He nodded, just once. That was all it seemed to take for her heart to race and her stomach to feel as though he were wringing her guts with his big hands.

It was too late to take it back. It was too late for a lot of things. The decision had been made and had been the moment she'd lifted a finger to aid someone she should never have touched.

Do I regret it? Is that what this is? No, she decided. *This isn't regret. It's an ending. That's all.*

She would close her club. There would be no more *Evie's* here or on any of the other realms.

"I will give them your answer in two days. You have until then."

Surprised, she studied his face, trying to read what he meant. She would have had better luck making sense of the Mona Lisa's smile. His face was glacier-like, his eyes sharp. Cold intelligence filled the depths. She'd heard him correctly. He was giving her time.

That could only mean one thing.

She'd underestimated him. She'd seen what he wanted her to see. The broad shoulders, the bulk of him, the sheer *size* of him—a weightlifter with the height and build—and, of course, the scars of battle on his face to reinforce the image. She saw a rugged sprinkling of what would become a beard if he didn't shave soon, his long hair tied back from a strong face and of course, confidence. He oozed confidence.

He looked like any other big, powerful man.

At first, even second glance.

Blazing under that exterior was intelligence, the kind that comes with patiently waiting, watching and, only when the move was secure, taking it. And this move, this chance he was giving her, must mean that she had something he wanted. *Please let him be smart enough to know I won't deliver anything or anyone that will upset the balance.* She almost laughed. *Isn't this why we're sitting here?*

She smiled at the irony and nodded politely. "Thank you, I w—"

"Do not thank me," he said, clipped, to the point and with a pause she was loath to break. Thankfully, he did. "In repayment, tell me who this is." He took out a piece of parchment from his shirt pocket. Instead of handing it over, he rubbed a corner as he stared at whoever was drawn on the page.

She waited, not about to rush him. If he gave her two days… *We might survive. Will he? Who is he?*

His casual shirt, an elegant black button-down paired with charcoal trousers and matching suit jacket, didn't help her in the least. He could be anyone, except he wasn't. He was much more. The muscles, the silent stare, the sureness in his gaze… He wasn't of this realm. He had long brown hair that was bleached halfway down from the sun and tied back from his face. He had dark sideburns and a lowered brow, as if what he was concentrating on needed his complete attention…her.

Silkie? Can he be a Silkie? He has the sun-darkened flesh, the bleached hair, the muscle…

He studied her as closely as she studied him. It sent a chill down her spine. There was no emotion in his gaze, no reflection of his thoughts, other than he was thinking, considering, weighing her worth—or not *her* worth. He was not evaluating Evie the woman, but Evie, the all-realm mistress of pleasure. Her heart skipped several beats. *He knows. He knows I'm bound by much more.*

She couldn't resist peering at his forearm, her fear growing in leaps and bounds at what lay there. It was on his left arm, inside—displayed for her, she knew—three circles traced with red runes. The reality of that forbidden mark, the knowledge that across from her sat not just a messenger, but an evil that no one had lived beyond meeting, chilled the heat his attention had created. Suddenly there wasn't enough oxygen in the room. The centuries of life disappeared and the moment became longer than any other in existence.

It took all her willpower to lift her gaze from his arm to his face—and even more to meet his eyes again. There was no change in his impassive expression, no sign that he knew she now understood who he was, other than a slight lift to one eyebrow.

Once upon a time he'd possessed another name. Throughout the centuries, the only one who had remained was *Poison.*

The Three will make their play. After all this time, they will call in their debts. Have they waited and orchestrated this from afar to only now reveal themselves and flaunt their triumph?

Can he betray them? Is that even possible?

Slowly he placed the parchment face-up on the desk.

A sketch of a girl. Evie glanced up to see him watching her with an intensity that made her swallow the instinctual protest she would have spoken. Matchmaking had been her talent at one time. Even now she felt the stirring of her awareness waking.

"May I?" She indicated the paper.

His eyes didn't narrow, they twitched. He also stayed leaning forward, as if in the process of jumping up — or over the desk to snap her neck. It would be easy for him to reach her and even easier for a man his size to kill her. She was unprotected here, in her most secure location. Why would she put safeguards around an already-ultra-secure room?

She swallowed past a dry throat and lifted the paper closer. Everything she had built, everything she'd endured, rested on what she could do for this warrior.

The girl on the parchment was finely drawn. Every detail was filled in, from the tips of her fingers to the top of her head. Evie guessed the man across from her was the artist. He watched her now, waiting as if ready to take the sketch back at any moment. It was precious to him, just as the girl was. "I might be able to find her name…"

"I want to know where she is."

"Where…?" She refocused on the drawing. The girl was dressed as a peasant from another time or realm. Evie studied the room. He'd sketched out a high, narrow window displaying the view of two mountains. The room she didn't know, but what lay outside of the window she knew. *The Twins.*

"Did you draw this?" She glanced up long enough to see his nod. She had to buy time, had to see if what he wanted from the girl was truth. "And this room? Did you see this? A vision of this?" Surely, he hadn't been there.

"I saw this room and her."

"I cannot tell you who she is, only that I know where she is," Evie offered.

"Where?"

It wasn't a question as much as it was a demand. One they both knew she had to obey, and yet this was far beyond her and even, she guessed, him.

The Three bound him. That meant that they might be guiding him in this as well. It made no sense. *Why give two days?* The Three would never show mercy. It wasn't their way. Poison, by The Three, also never gave chances. He'd never left anyone alive. Or had he? People spoke of his deeds. How did they learn of them if he hadn't left *someone* alive?

Evie felt a headache coming on. More than that, she felt the girl's energy, a fire that had yet to bloom. Linked to that, to her, was this warrior, and through that link was the shattered remains of…*ice*. Ice lay in broken shards around him, and in his arms…this girl.

It wasn't from his strength the ice had been broken. It had been from the girl. *So, he does break the bonds – or will with the girl's help. Or did in the past… The two of them will become one. He will trade one binding for another, yet one he will wear willingly – if he finds her. If he protects her and if she steps in and fights for him.*

Or has she already done this? The kaleidoscope of images suggested that the two of them had lived and loved many times before. A tingling of memory teased her until, with a start, she had it. The Hawk, the Flame and…the Sword—or, as he was sometimes called, Poison. Greer, Brenyn and Oisin—the Dragon and the Dragon Guards. They had disappeared when the Black Queen and her two lieutenants had risen to power. *The Three.* And they had taken three warriors and bound them with curses. When The Three had made their bid for power, they had released their warriors—Hawk, Flame and *the man facing me.*

And he was free. Free of them and searching for his Flame… *Is the Black Queen's power diminishing, then? Does this mean the time of the prophecy is now?*

Oisin. His freedom had to mean something. It wasn't much, but it was enough. Even the slimmest of cracks could break a dam.

"I won't ask again," he said.

Evie opened her eyes. Her vision — of him and the girl — was superimposed on top of him sitting across from her. For a moment, the phantasmagoria of color made her nauseated She blinked until he again sat alone across from her. His dangerous eyes were intense with demand.

"These are the Twin Peaks, and from this angle, she is north of the Dark Forest, but —" She paused, unsure how to continue. She wanted time, *needed* time. If *he* sought this girl, it was one thing. *If the Three want her…* "I will not reveal more unless you assure me this is for you and not" — she dared to point to his tattoo — "anyone else."

He lifted that eyebrow again, higher this time. *Disbelief,* she thought, *or perhaps respect.* She imagined for a moment that he might smile.

"Me. Only me."

Evie took the time to assess his dangerous, icy stare and felt the shift in the upcoming storm. He'd found a way to chisel away at their binding. Could it be enough to free an entire realm from the Black Queen's control?

"You must go to the Heartland." And she must go speak with a certain witch. The end, she feared, had come. "Fiacre protects her. She lives with him in the Rose Court."

His expression slowly eased into something far less threatening. It still wasn't easy to meet his eyes. She had the feeling that what she'd said had brought him relief. He did smile then, and his fearsome demeanor fell away to reveal merely a man—a dangerous warrior still—but a man all the same. "Surely the gods jest."

"If they do, it escapes me how."

He stood without another word. A winter blast of snow-filled air settled against her heated face, then he was gone.

She stood as two of her men entered. No doubt they'd been blocked from her room by whatever magic the warrior possessed.

Before they could ask questions, she warned, "Be ready. We travel today."

Simon, who'd been with her the longest, asked, "Where?"

"First, to go see a witch, then…" Her gaze landed on the bookshelf across from her—the one that held, among other things, the ability to see into the future. "We'll have to see."

Neither man said a word. Their concerned gazes spoke loud enough.

Chapter Eight

Brenyn waited at the gates of the keep with a torch in hand. She could sense Fiacre coming closer, like the sun rising. A shiver whispered down her back. It wasn't from the cold. She'd bundled up today without having to glance out of her window to see the heavy clouds and fierce breeze. The woolen stockings and heavy layers under her gown kept her warm enough. Even in the chill of early evening, she wasn't cold. No, the shiver came from something else — or someone else.

When Fiacre arrives, I must tell him of the warrior...the dreams.

Even as she thought it, she shivered again. Fiacre had sent an owl ahead to say they would arrive tonight. She wanted them to return. At the same time, she dreaded it. The nights had been long. The potion wasn't working. When she woke, the images vanished like smoke on the wind. During the day, while preparing the rooms or making a meal, images of a tall, handsome warrior would sneak in on her.

Hopefully, that could end now that her friends were returning. She raised on tiptoe and peered into the dark, saw nothing and eased back down. Restlessness made her want to pace. She was too tired, her mind too full of worries, to stand there any longer. *They'll be here and everything will be better.*

But was that true? Being alone had its advantages. She could talk to the warrior with no one around. Or *practice* talking to him. There was never a response, not during the day. When she first began to fall asleep, whispered responses came to her before the dreams swept her away.

Once Fiacre and Greer returned with their guests, she couldn't go around explaining to a man that wasn't there why she couldn't leave with him. And leaving with him was what he wanted. She knew that like she knew that tomorrow she'd have more work to do than the day before and the day before that one.

She'd prepared two rooms today, expecting the new residents to want a space of their own. Only, at midday, another owl had arrived. This one with word that only one room need be cleaned.

Does Fiacre think I can unmake a room?

She anchored her torch into the rusty hoop on the gate and reminded herself that she was tired, and Fiacre was always thoughtful and kind. He'd sent an owl ahead to explain there would be one less, not to change what she did during the day. All the rooms needed to be cleaned anyway. He'd told her that some time ago, even before Greer. She tried to imagine the cold, barren castle filled with people but couldn't. The main hall had always been cold and empty, the corridors dim and silent.

The sound of horses echoed through the gloaming. Squinting into the dark beyond the circle of her torch light, she spotted Fiacre's white hair. Then, beside him, the outline of Greer's slim, straight form on her gray mare. A mist swirled around Greer, and another image of Greer caught her by surprise—Greer, her armor blood-drenched, her shield broken and hanging uselessly from her arm, her face bruised and slashed from her eyebrow to temple.

Horrified, Brenyn stumbled backward, her hand up to ward off such a vision.

"Brenyn, it is glad we are to see you." Fiacre's gravelly voice, the warm tone solid and firm, broke the vision as suddenly as someone shutting a door on the winter wind.

She attempted a smile. It came out odd because her face felt odd, as if she were still out of doors in that cold winter storm. Trying to shake the after-image, she concentrated on Fiacre. He stared at her with a worried frown

"Brenyn, you are well?" Fiacre moved his horse closer.

She nodded, hurriedly realizing she was holding them back from the warmth of the keep. "Yes, yes, of course. It's good to have you back." She dared a glance at Greer and was relieved to see that Greer looked tired, not drenched in blood. "Greer, the mare still hasn't foaled."

Greer smiled. It eased the icy chill from her eyes. "I'll check on her. She should drop soon." Greer dismounted, holding her right shoulder oddly. Sweat and dried blood stained her shirt collar. Her armor showed signs of wear, not wet, fresh blood.

"Brenyn..." Fiacre dismounted. She hurried to his side and took his reins. Fiacre clasped her shoulder. "Are you well?"

"Yes. Yes, I'm well."

He seemed about to ask more, but his gelding welcomed her with a tired sigh, nudging her for a sympathetic pet on his forehead. "You missed me, yes?" she whispered to him, rubbing his soft nose.

"He is tired, as are we all." Fiacre smiled and squeezed her shoulder. "It's good you are well. This is Jacob." He motioned to the man still astride his horse. His eyes were almost closed, as if he were in pain. "He will need rest to help with his recovery—and perhaps something for his head."

"Of course... I brought a few of your potions to the room I cleaned for him." She glanced at Jacob again, noting his brown eyes and dark, downward-slashed eyebrows. His black hair hung partially in his eyes and down in a disarray to his shoulders. It was his eyes that caught and held her attention. There was pain in the depths. "Jacob, you are most welcome."

Jacob's gaze skimmed hers then moved on quickly. Wincing, he raised his hand to his head and squeezed his forehead. At the same time, he swayed dangerously on his horse. Fiacre surprised her by reaching Jacob's side before her and helping Jacob down. She exchanged a worried glance with Greer. She didn't think Fiacre could support such a tall warrior and rushed over. Fiacre wrapped an arm around his waist and draped Jacob's arm over his shoulder.

Greer moved to Jacob's left just as Jacob collapsed against Fiacre. Together they supported him as his head fell forward and his legs gave out. Greer grimaced but took more of his weight.

Brenyn clasped her hands together, unsure what to do to help. "What should I do? Do you wish to leave him here?"

Fiacre chuckled. "No, I'd rather you leave the horses. They're tired. They'll make their way to their stalls. We have to get Jacob indoors," he said, sounding strained.

She worried he'd harm himself.

"Go," he added, more in a grunt than a word.

"I have his room ready." She half-ran next to them. "It's on the second floor."

"Good."

"I will go ahead and fetch your things." She ran ahead and opened the small door within the massive keep's gates. The smaller door was still large enough for two men to walk abreast. She hoped it would be wide enough for the three of them. Fiacre turned sideways and Greer did the same. They passed through with only a few muttered words from Fiacre. She closed it and quickly ran after them.

"Go on and make sure his fire is lit," Fiacre ordered.

She hurried on ahead. After a few feet, she paused. She felt oddly exposed, as if the eye of evil had settled on them, aware now that they had lost a warrior.

He's freed himself and they know. They know. They always know.

The words fed her fear, but not because she understood them. She didn't. They weren't hers. She stopped at the second-floor landing and scanned the meadow in front of the forest. In the shadows of the trees, she thought she saw the outline of a person—a woman. She wasn't certain how she knew, but whoever stood there wasn't alone. A tall, broad-shouldered warrior stepped out of the shadow of the woods and stood beside her. The moon suddenly broke from the clouds. She thought she spotted a blond beard on the warrior, and the flash of pale skin from under the woman's hood, then the moon disappeared behind a cloud and the figures were gone…if they were ever there.

Be ready. When he arrives, you know your time has grown short.

The words still lingered in her mind when Fiacre arrived with Jacob and Greer. They were so busy getting Jacob into the bed, his boots off and his wounds cleaned, that Brenyn kept the words and her worries to herself.

* * * *

"Your majesty, Thane has arrived."

The Silver King lifted his gaze from his goblet's deep, rich burgundy depths. The oblivion he could find in the cup was only fleeting, after all. Lilith, his trusted advisor, was absent, away again on the business of his realm, and with her gone, the whispers were louder. The present came into focus, if muddled, and was still too close for him to bear.

"Your majesty, did you hear me? Thane has arrived."

At one time, the man standing two steps beneath him had been like a brother to him. They had fought together, drunk together, learned the ways of women together. Now he was a ghost, an imprint from a past canvas filling him with pain. Together with pain came anger. His vision blurred dull red, and through it he gazed at the world.

A thought surfaced. *Lilith will return soon.* When she did, he could once again retreat to the darker recesses of his innermost chamber.

"Is that so? And where is he?"

His brother's second son stepped from behind one of the dozens of columns supporting the high ceiling of the palace's throne room. His armor was crusted in dirt and the rust of dried blood. Dark circles bruised his eyes. There was no black cloak blowing from his shoulders and flapping in the breeze as he walked closer, no shine to his long hair and no beauty to his swollen, damaged face.

"Uncle." He bowed and it lacked the grace usually shown by one of the royal family.

Edric considered him. As if a breeze blew the clouds from his mind, he saw his nephew clearer than he'd seen anyone in a long while. A deep shudder traveled through him, shaking the very foundation he'd built a kingdom upon. *How can this be my nephew? How can any one of my people suffer such a defeat?*

"Leave us." A flick of his wrist and the room emptied as silently as the wind blowing through the willow's heavy branches outside the hall. "Speak, nephew. What has brought you to me in such a condition?"

Another bow of his nephew's head was followed by a stare filled with dismay. "We were attacked."

Rage engulfed him, completely controlled him to the point that his hands shook with the force of the emotion. *How long has it been since I felt so deeply?* For a moment the question ran circles in his mind, growing wilder and wilder. With it, the rage lifted and a wisp of something else grew clearer...another emotion. It was shock followed by outrage. Both feelings battled until he forced himself to speak again. "No one would dare such a thing."

His nephew bowed his head again. "We lost our caravan of fighters and all their arena guards in the Twin Pass two days ago."

He stared at his nephew, speechless. *Fighters? What fighters?* Caravans he knew. They brought supplies from the Greenway. A memory of Lilith saying that his people needed to be entertained rose in his mind. She'd said that the seasonal celebrations were not enough, that the joy in the forest was not enough. And he had said... He had said... *I let Lilith deal with them.* She had given them what they'd wanted. He had understood. Give *her* what she wanted, and under her ministrations, his sorrow would fade. *At what cost?* He had cared not. Nothing else mattered save the next dose of oblivion.

This bordered on blasphemy. No Faye should suffer wounds such as his nephew wore, and yet here he stood, perhaps scarred for the rest of eternity. His anguished expression was filled with the horrors he'd endured and the losses he'd suffered.

"The mage, Auld Fiacre, lives. It was he and his magic that defeated us."

Edric tilted his head, unsure he'd heard correctly. Fiacre had always been a friend of the wood.

"And there was a woman, a warrior unlike any I have seen in many an age. She rode into the battle and left death behind her. She was unstoppable. And yet she sustained wounds. If the mage protected her, he didn't do so completely."

A woman warrior unlike any other. And she rides with Fiacre. "She was wounded. You are certain?"

"Yes, my brother got several touches on her."

"And he is?" Edric glanced around the empty hall, expecting Dillion to appear. When no one approached, for no one stood in the hall, he allowed his gaze to access Thane. Sorrow filled the depths of his nephew's crystal eyes.

"Dillion fell on the field of battle. He is dead, your majesty."

"Dead?" It was incomprehensible. A royal son, dead before he had walked this realm to its fullest, before he had been loved and been betrayed. Edric closed his eyes, overwhelmed with a bitter sadness so great that he sought the wine and drank greedily from the laced sweetness in his cup. The sorrow receded and he focused once again on his nephew.

"She is one of the immortal families?"

"I did not see her close enough to sense this, Uncle. I was kept back by warriors crafted from mist."

Auld Fiacre. Why now? Why after such time? Does he sense it too? The build-up to the end? The long-awaited climax to a story drenched red with the blood of our countless battles...?

Edric bowed his head and considered the small, plain circle of silver on the first finger of his right hand. The band reflected the light as beautifully today as it had on the day it had been bequeathed to him. Had the time come to move at long last? Was his journey finally to end? The pain to finally be over?

The mage had weaknesses. Everyone did, even the Silver King. The thought made him want to laugh. *Yes, I did have – at one time. No longer.*

"Go to your rest," he said to his nephew. "Go and be with your family and share in the loss of your brother. Rest. Soon we will have our revenge, and when we do, I will need you by my side."

The younger Faye clearly saw this as a privilege. Edric knew better. It was a curse, not a blessing. *Those who love and abide by me, die because of me. Isn't that what you said, mage? Because I couldn't see the truth. I see it now. You've schemed and you've waited, like a spider, ready to strike.* He fisted his hand around the delicate cup and felt the metal dent under his fingers.

"Thank you, Uncle." Bowing again, a bit more gracefully, his nephew walked from the hall, a barely visible limp in his stride.

You have wounded us. I wonder if you will like the results. He lifted the distorted goblet and threw it against the nearest column, spilling what was left of the oblivion he wanted on the tiles of his hall. The red stain spread far wider than he would have imagined.

Chapter Nine

The corridors of the castle were a jumble of confusion. Torches were a rarity and only existed along one wing. The black depths of the other hallways were hidden in shadows that Jacob had trouble piercing.

A Vampire could see in the dark, not that his sight helped now. His system hadn't recovered from the poisoned blood. A constant buzz, as if somewhere close by a million bees had built a home, vibrated through his ears. His sense of the moon's rise and fall didn't exist. Not once in his long life had he failed to know the exact rising and setting of both the sun and moon. Those celestial giants always brought some comfort. At the very least they'd shared his lonely existence. Now, not only could he not locate the moon, but he couldn't see by its light. The paths seemed to be cloaked in tar. Walking down the hall, he felt as if the sticky darkness clung to him, restricting his passage.

Of course, he knew that was the drug the Faye had fed him, not the empty corridors. After several nights, he had hoped to be free of their vile potion. But it seemed the Faye had done a number on his mind. Everything made either perfect sense or no sense at all, like the sensation that he walking through tar when such a thing was impossible.

Up ahead of him, a narrow window provided a slice of moonlight. His footsteps were the only sound. No one else walked the deserted keep that Fiacre had taken him to, and yet the sensation of suddenly being watched made him pause in the silver light of the moon. To his direct left, down two floors, slept the girl Brenyn. She brought him meals and timidly asked about his health. A few of the nights when he prowled the confines of the keep, she walked the outer corridors, either sleepwalking or as restless as he was for fresh air. Tonight, she slept in her room, safely tucked away behind the thick walls.

To his left and far, far higher, in a tower with rickety, unsafe stairs, Fiacre either pondered the ways of the universe or else slept at his massive worktable. It was hard to say by his heartbeat. Awake or sleeping, it beat a steady, strong rhythm. At this hour, Jacob assumed the old man slept, but knowing mages the way he did, Fiacre could as easily be watching Jacob prowl the keep.

Below Fiacre and near Brenyn was the one room he avoided. *Her* room. She slept. During the day when he tried to sleep, she pushed herself to exhaustion. She started her day before the sun rose and ended it when the sun dipped down to rest. He was aware of her every movement. Sleep for him was brief, and even then, it wasn't the healing third sleep that he needed to rid himself of the Faye's poison. He tried to block her out, but to him, Greer was like a drug, much more addictive than the Faye's swill. Every day, instead of resting properly, he traced her movements. She rode each day, far out from the keep — too far, in his opinion. She practiced swords either by herself or with magical beings, because even though he could hear the strike of sword-on-sword, he sensed no living warrior sparring with her. Brenyn could have been the person, yet he knew she didn't enter the practice arenas.

He sensed that Greer slept deeply now. Her heartbeat soothed him and at the same time made him restless.

There was no one else there. Horses, chickens, cows, a few goats and field mice — that was it, other than the three mortals he shared the enormous keep with. If Fiacre had been serious about bringing in an army, there was certainly enough room.

For now, he was concerned with one thing — recovering his mind and body. He still felt weak. He was aware enough to feel embarrassed by the goblets of blood Brenyn brought him — not that the girl ever made a mention of them...or even of his being a Vampire. His spine stiffened at the implications that he couldn't hunt for his own blood.

He jumped to the window casement, a once-easy move made difficult by his weakness. The view outside sent ripples of awareness down his arms. He'd slipped on a pair of leather trousers that had been left folded neatly for him in the wardrobe, along with boots that fit like a glove and a simple shirt. The shirt was homespun linen and the boots the kind that used to be made by men and women who knew how to craft such things to last through mud, water and years of wear and tear. Memories of the last time he'd worn such clothes were so clear that they could have been only yesterday, if he didn't know for a fact that centuries had passed. *In a world far from this one. Why does this feel familiar? Why does this view hurt worse than the damned Faye arrows in my chest?*

The moonlight revealed rolling meadows. Beyond them stood the shadows of a forest. Beyond the trees rose mountains. *The Twins.* He knew this view, knew the mountains. knew these walls.

It was almost too much to consider, but it had to be. He had to know the truth. There were gaps in his memory since his capture, but nothing had damaged his memory of a life he'd once lived — only his refusal to think about it.

With a muttered curse he launched himself skyward, shifting to the form of an eagle so he could feel the wind on his face as his powerful wings rode the flows of air. He hadn't always been a Vampire, but since his change, he'd learned how to survive and be the strongest he could be.

Below him, the land grew sharper. He savored the feel of the wind and the power of his wings as he circled the wood until he spotted what he sought. He dove and flowed to man-form again to sink his fangs into an elk buck. The hot, wild blood surged through him, filling him with strength. He released the stag before he'd taken too much for the creature to survive. It lifted its head and bellowed as staggered off, crashing through the woods. Its call roused the forest.

Another elk broke out from the trees, head down, ready to knock him off his feet. The buck's hooves pounded the ground like thunder. Jacob surged upward and landed on the elk easily. The hot tang of its blood rushed through Jacob's body, waking him more and purging the poison still clinging to his mind.

He jumped clear of the animal and landed on his feet, feeling more like himself than he had in far too long.

The forest quieted as he centered himself. In the distance he thought he heard the caw and cry of ravens, the blood scavengers of battlefields. If it were ravens, they didn't come into view.

To the north, he sensed a village and the farmers who lived on the outskirts. Farther down a river, another bigger village existed, and beyond that another — all of them along the river that brought its waters out to the sea. In the mountains, he sensed no life other than the animals that always called the wild home. It was through the mountains, though, that the Faye lived in the woods they loved. And it was through the Twins that he'd been freed. Alrick had been there but had left him to chase after his mate. Even though Jacob had been hurting and suffering from the Faye drug, he knew Alrick would return.

Jacob took a deep breath, feeling no discomfort from his wounds. His mind was clear and his body strong with no pain when he tightened his muscles.

He concentrated back toward the keep and sensed the two women and Fiacre, along with the dogs, horses and other domestic animals. Along the forest, he felt the presence of wolves. None of them possessed the Lykae mind. Far, far to the south, he sensed Vampires. They were yet unaware of him. And back toward the north, beyond the mountains, he could sense the Faye. They were oddly different, as if they were of two peoples instead of one. He faced the shore. Nothing beneath the water registered. He wasn't sure if he would have known what lay under the dark seas.

I know this land. I've always known this land. It was true. This was the Rose Kingdom, the birthplace of his past-self and the birthplace of his present Vampire-self. He started walking, pushing aside branches until he found a dim reminder of a path under the heavy branches of ancient oaks. The trees were huge in both height and girth. And if one looked closely, disregarding the new-growth forest at their feet, they could see how the trees formed a straight line with a path leading underneath their mighty branches.

He turned in a circle and studied the landscape then the outline of the path. He started walking again. After what felt like hours, he came to what he'd dreaded finding.

An archway.

It was crumbled. Gray chunks of mortar and fallen stones sprinkled the overgrown forest floor. The arch still stood where once anyone who wished entrance to the Rose Kingdom would see the glory of the land through the beauty of the arch's delicately balanced artistry. Rose vines strangled it now. The carvings along the columns were hidden and those that were revealed were discolored and mute with weathering. He touched a visible word. *Welcome.* The rest of the greeting had disappeared with time. No roses bloomed on the vines. It was too far in the season for them to survive.

"It was always a welcoming sight."

Jacob didn't face Fiacre. He did drop his hand from the arch, though, and cross his arms. "How did this happen?"

Fiacre sighed heavily. "Time did this. Time and the evil we must destroy."

"Where were you when they were attacked? When they were killed?"

"I was…elsewhere."

He faced the mage and studied his ancient care-worn face. There was sorrow there and pain, along with no small amount of regret.

Jacob had known King Edward and Queen Elspeth. Of course, he'd been no more than a common boy, but he'd known them. They had not been like any of the kings and queens he'd met later in his life. They'd been a happy couple with several children. A common boy was welcomed in friendship by their youngest daughter, Gwen. She'd met him beside a city well, and after helping her draw up water, she'd invited him to see her secret treasures under an ancient elm deep in the palace gardens. From that day on they'd been inseparable. Until, of course, he'd left her and she'd died.

But the royal family had been kind to one lost boy and given him more than he could have dreamed – a place among them, and with it, the love of their daughter. Gwen *had* loved him. At one time all he'd ever wanted was to prove himself worthy of that love. But he'd failed and she'd died, and by the look of the arch, her entire family had also perished.

Fiacre knew. He'd come to the court. Jacob could remember the occasion, and even running into the mage – literally – once. Fiacre had steadied him and, looking deep into his eyes, the mage had smiled at Jacob's stuttering apology. He'd been a mage, a magic user of such renown that Gwen had questioned Jacob endlessly on what exactly Fiacre had said and what he thought of the mage. Fiacre had merely squeezed Jacob's shoulder and murmured, "Take care, young master."

That had been all he'd said.

Gwen and Jacob had debated for days whether he'd meant more than merely not running into adults. Gwen had been convinced that Fiacre was sending Jacob a secret message.

Jacob stared over at the man who'd either shrunk with age, or else Jacob had merely grown to a height that made Fiacre appear small and old. There was power in the mage's eyes and flowing through him. Jacob could scent the magical thunder of him on the air. Even so, Fiacre seemed fragile in appearance.

"Why couldn't you save them?" His question came out sounding more like an accusation than he'd intended. "Even if you were far away, I can't believe you didn't feel...something."

Other than shaking his head sadly, Fiacre didn't appear offended. "By the time I did '*feel something*', it was too late. Not even King Edward's entire army was enough to stop the fall of his kingdom. The Black Queen wanted her pawn. What she gained was far worse — the destruction of a kingdom that had stood for all that was good in this realm."

"What do you mean, 'pawn'?" Jacob wanted to call the words back the moment he said them. He knew. *Gwen.*

"Greer. She has always belonged to the Black Queen — or, since first she was born into this world." Fiacre leaned on his staff. "You need to remember one thing, Jacob. We can win. This time I have called them back. It wasn't the witch who tossed her net and pulled Greer and Brenyn back to this realm. It was I who brought them here."

"To what end? To theirs? This plan is too thin. It's a house of cards. One strong shake and the whole thing falls down."

"Perhaps. But perhaps too many people are prepared to ensure that none of these plans fail. The Three have made enemies. They stretch themselves too thin. Think, Jacob. Think. Delilah is known to you. She ruled the Scarlet Coven in your realm. You knew her as evil and yet your companion Emerald broke free from her control."

Jacob stiffened. Emerald and Warren were dear to him. If Emerald had broken free from her coven's control, they could be happy. As soon as he thought it, he grimaced, knowing the couple too well. They'd be in the thick of this scheme. Circerran no doubt had Emerald aiding her, and if so, Warren was with her. "You play with people's lives, mage. Gwen, mine, others... What if it all fails?"

"If it all fails then it will be no different for us than if we do nothing. The Three, if they win, will either win because we do nothing or they will win because we try to beat them and fail. But" — Fiacre raised a gnarled finger — "if we try to beat them and do, then we have rid this realm and the seven realms of their evil."

"That's a lot of ifs." It was also true. Jacob studied the flows of air, scenting Gwen immediately. Her heartbeat was steady in the rhythm of sleep. She would stand by Fiacre to death. He knew it like he knew the sun would rise in five hours and twenty-two minutes. Her life hung in the balance, and if what she'd said was true, it was the first time in her existence that she had a chance to break free of the Black Queen.

"I've waited centuries for this chance, Jacob." Fiacre spoke his name as if they were old acquaintances. "I will not allow it to pass us by. You may very well doubt it every step of the way, but you will take the steps I need."

It wasn't a question. And behind his words lived a threat, one that only a mage with the loyalty of Jacob's heart could level. If Jacob didn't commit himself, Gwen would be forever gone.

Jacob met the old man's gaze. "I will do what I can."

"That, you may find, is more than even you understand. But for now, it will do." Fiacre smiled and, with his staff in hand, headed back toward the keep.

Jacob sighed and walked after the old man. Mages spoke in riddles. It had always been so, but if Fiacre could free Gwen from her torment, then Jacob would do all he could to aid him. And if once she was free and still insisted that her life with him had meant nothing, then Jacob would have to help her see her mistake. It was logic, and if he'd gained one thing from his life as a Vampire, it was the ability to see logic—and help others to see it as well.

Chapter Ten

The warmth of Aubrey's hearth kept her small cottage comfortable, even in the deepest of the winter. It also provided her with a place to heat her tea. Nothing was better than a cup of tea when the weather outside was damp and cold.

In a comfortable chair by the hearth, the only annoyance in her home slept sitting with his head rested on his fist, his big feet up on a stool. Greyson.

She was tempted to wake him. He'd been a thorn in her side for days, possibly weeks. Still, he'd cut wood, stacked it neatly by the front door, brought more of it in than needed, and milked her cow, gathered eggs and fixed the squeaky door. Of course, he'd done it all without complaint. One could argue that he needed his rest and deserved her gratitude.

She could argue quite the contrary. It went against the grain to say nothing, but that was exactly what she did. No doubt the silence didn't fool him. Greyson was many things. A fool, he was not.

And the truth was, she wouldn't wake him because she needed a rest from him. If she woke him, the first thing he'd do would be to check on her, as if two months weren't enough for her to recover. As if him doing all the chores she cherished weren't enough of a reminder that she still couldn't care for herself. .

She refused to acknowledge the discomfort of walking to the kettle to pour the water over her tea. Her feet would heal. With wounds such as she'd endured, the release of pain happened slowly. There would be no more sitting or lying abed, though. That had been made clear to everyone, Greyson included.

He slept soundly for a man who did so sitting. He never snored, even when he did lie down in bed. Better, he barely spoke. When he did, she had to admit she was loath to hear him. Always he had something sound and reasonable to say, except for the fact that it was in complete opposition to what she wanted, typically getting things done — cleaning, washing, getting out of bed.

At least she'd won a few battles. She now had free rein of her home. If her feet didn't ache so badly, she was certain she'd be enjoying it much more.

A knock at the door got Greyson out of his chair and a gun in his hand within a blink of her eyes.

"Greyson, really?" she murmured. *Does he think me unable to protect my home?* Clearly, he did. Since her capture, everyone seemed to feel she had lost her abilities and her common sense.

He gave her a look she'd grown to know meant he'd heard her and he wasn't about to budge.

"Enter," she called out. "Evie has come to call," she added to Greyson as she pulled her favorite clover honey down from the shelf by the hearth. She'd

111

gathered the honey herself. The memory was a sharp reminder of how much her life had changed, a reminder she shouldn't have needed.

The door opened and Evie, lacking the makeup and exotic clothing she wore in her club, entered with two very large men directly behind her. They both ducked under the mantle, then stood scanning the room, Greyson, his gun, then her.

Aubrey ignored them. They were here to protect Evie. And since Aubrey meant her no harm, they would behave.

"Evie, just in time for tea."

Evie removed her black down jacket and folded it over the back of one of the ladderback chairs circling Aubrey's table. "Thank you, Aubrey. It's good to see you up and well." Evie paused after pulling out a chair and cocked an elegant eyebrow at Greyson. "Greyson, I believe you won't be needing the gun. We come as friends."

Greyson holstered his weapon and still managed to look dangerous. He stayed standing with his arms crossed as he stared at the two men. No doubt all three men understood that no violence would occur on this night. And yet, they all stood ready in case it did.

"Come. Sit. *Sit.* I won't have anyone standing while we have tea." Aubrey motioned to the cups at Greyson's right. He cast her a glance that she chose not to acknowledge, then reluctantly brought the cups to the table.

"Thank you. There's honey and milk if you wish." She was relieved when Greyson sat. Then she realized he'd positioned himself facing the other two men and too far from the table to enjoy tea with them. It wasn't polite. At least he wasn't demanding to know what they wanted. She let it go.

"I hope you found my home easily enough." She'd opened her protections to allow Evie access as soon as she'd sensed her. The spells had realigned as soon as Evie had passed through. Hindsight suggested that she'd have been better off waking Greyson and discussing this with him. To do so would have suggested he had a say in what she did, and that, more than anything else, had stopped her—notwithstanding his tiredness.

Evie lifted a hand and brushed her hair back from her forehead. "We did. Thank you."

Aubrey poured the tea and indicated the scones she'd baked just that morn. "Help yourselves, please." She passed first Evie, then both men, a cup of tea, then handed one to Greyson. He accepted it and gave her a steady stare that seemed to say much more than his words ever did. He was concerned. He wanted to know why she'd not told him about company. And more, he wanted to discuss with her how she shouldn't keep things from him.

Since her capture, he'd been more vocal than ever before on her hiding things that could endanger her life. Before the capture he'd never said a word, so logically anything he said now was more. The only thing he hadn't spoken of was what she most wanted to hear—why he cared, why he was here, and more…what he felt for her, and even more importantly, what he was going to do about it.

"Thank you, this is wonderful. Chamomile?"

"Yes, with a bit of ginger. It keeps the body well and the mind strong."

"Mm-m, it's very good." Evie set her cup down and curled her hands around it. Her two men ate their scones in silence, their eyes watchful but relaxed. Greyson simply waited and watched.

Aubrey sipped her tea and let the warmth ease her.

Changes whispered on the wind. She could feel the way the land waited, hushed and anxious, for the shift in the never-ending power struggle between dark and light. Evie wasn't entirely a surprise visitor. Evie had many roles. One of them was ancient and all but forgotten by those who now lived.

Aubrey remembered and knew that if Evie were here, they had reached the eye of the storm. *Will I be strong enough to do what needs to be done?* Her capture had been...difficult. Worse than the torture had been the doubts, but never had she doubted her abilities, not even when her parents had buried her deep underneath her family home and faced death to keep her safe. Not even when she'd first woken to a world so changed that she had sought solitude to simply survive. Now she sought solitude out of fear — not fear of being recaptured or killed, but of failing, of not having enough strength to aid those she had grown to love.

"You know why I've come." Evie met and held her gaze. Aubrey could read the answer there, if she wished, but she ducked her head, breaking eye contact to gather her thoughts.

The tea settled heavily on Aubrey's stomach. She was glad she'd not taken a scone. "Ah, I would no' claim to that." She sipped her tea, cursing her accent and how much it revealed of her state of mind. Greyson no doubt heard it and understood how shaken she felt. Evie, well... Evie knew all, didn't she? There was nothing she could do to keep her fear from the seer, but still she tried. "I know you have certain abilities. If you've come to me, you must have reason."

Evie lifted her tea and took another sip. There was a slight tremble to the cup as she lifted it, sipped, then set it down. "I think most people don't realize what you are—or what you were."

Aubrey shifted. She had not anticipated the conversation to turn to her.

"They know only that Circerran found you buried beneath the remains of an ancient keep. They have no idea why you were there, nor the importance of where you were."

A chill shivered over Aubrey's spine, traveling down so fast that she almost shuddered. "And what does that have to do with this visit?"

"Everything." Evie laughed. It sounded strained. "And nothing at all."

"I see." Aubrey understood. Evie was blind for the first time in ages. If she used her sight, if she once again chose a side, the Black Queen would paint a target on her back—if she hadn't already. Relief settled Aubrey's nerves to a manageable level. At least her heart seemed to regain its normal, steady beat. If Evie could not see, there was a chance she would not know much more about Aubrey than mere whispered rumors.

"Do you?" Evie leaned forward, the intensity of her gaze blazing from her eyes. "I was there when your family's home was brought down to ruin and rumble. I was there when the Black Queen tried to eliminate the Dragons. I was there when the mighty Fiacre was brought to his knees. I was there when we lost all that was good in the seven realms." The sight didn't shimmer in Evie's eyes, but knowledge burned bright.

"I was there when your family protected the remaining Dragons with their lives—when they locked you away to keep you sane and save you for a time when you would be needed."

Aubrey didn't dare glance away from Evie's intense gaze. She could sense Greyson's questions building and the next words Evie would speak forming behind her lips. The flows of magic had slowed, and the air had paused as the world seemed to hold its breath. Aubrey felt the flows cling to her, trying to drag her down into that dark, endless hole of blackness—to escape and return with such power that nothing could stop her. It was madness. But it was the madness the Faye had tried to turn her toward. The torturers had tried to bring her to the pit, and through their words and whips, force her to willingly take that step down a path that would end the pain. A nudge in one direction or the other would have pushed her into that pit. But she'd survived because of one thing—an oath her family had given centuries before to a king they'd died to protect.

That oath, and nothing else, had saved Aubrey from turning. She was weak, too weak to have endured their methods. The only weapon to fight them was that oath. But it was secret, so secret that what Evie spoke of was forbidden knowledge. No one outside of her family should have known of their oaths to the Dragon King.

Evie sat back, crossed her arms and changed the course of Aubrey's life with her next words.

"It is time to wake the Dragon."

The words washed over Aubrey and, instead of her panic increasing, something deep inside her awoke. Warmth, the clean, wonderful warmth of home and security, slowly calmed and comforted her. *The time is here.*

Greyson sat forward. There were protests on his lips. She could clearly see them forming without even reading his mind. She stopped him with a hand on his arm. The contact with his skin reminded her that once upon a time she'd wished for a normal life, a man to love her and a home to call her own. That wish had died on a forest floor. She closed her thoughts on the memory. She had freely given her oath to the Dragon King. She was still bound by that promise. It triumphed over all else…even love.

But Evie was breaking rules. Aubrey opened her own sight, and through the swirls of magic that made up her home, she saw Evie clearly. The seer had made a choice as well and now stood to fall from the knife's edge. *Why?* Aubrey sensed fear in Evie, but no conflict, no decision that was forced on her or one she would gain from. But it wasn't her duty to come to Aubrey with such announcements. *Is it? Who reins in the seers?*

"Explain yourself, Evie. Is it not the duty of the seers to see, not to interfere?"

Evie's expression tightened. "It is. Yet, when the balance is destroyed, then we must act to restore it." She set her cup down firmly. "The balance has long been askew. Long before I allowed Ajax to use my gate from world-to-world, too," she muttered. Leaning forward, she said, "Since I allowed passage, and since they have begun to move their pawns, I was left with no choice but to become involved."

The passion in her tone worried Aubrey. Evie had more power than merely seeing into the future. Her 'clubs' were there to actively monitor the balance. Her sight was without measure. Her divinations had been passed down from generation to generation. It had been ages since her people had taken part in the balancing of good and evil. Legends spoke of such events — truly horrific battles that had ended in pain and misery.

Aubrey opened her eyes to the magic that made up the world beyond the walls of her home. There was an uneasy flow of colors, as if they sought to find something and couldn't. Some blended, which was expected, but others that should have flowed easily against each other seemed to have no contact. The browns, greens, blues, yellows and reds were muted in places and darker than normal in others. It looked like a piece of rumpled fabric left out too long in the sun. Where the sun had touched the folds, the fabric had faded. And where the sun hadn't been able to bleach the color from it, the colors were dark.

Aubrey's unease grew. "There is great disquiet in the balance. I have seen this since awakening in this realm."

"I see the same." She leaned forward. "This is our chance to regain the balance. That is why I've come and why you must fulfill your oaths."

Amazed, Aubrey asked, "You've seen this?" King Aden stood, frozen in his grief. His lands were no more. His kingdom was held in a spell that none could break. The last battle would be won if and only if he and his Dragons took to the field. The Black Queen had stopped all chances of such a thing occurring.

"Think, Aubrey. Why is the evil here becoming so...predictable? Why have we re-opened the gates between the realms? Sloppy. It's all sloppy" — she pointed a finger at Aubrey — "and you know it. Your capture was planned. Think, Aubrey. Why? Why take you and not kill you?" Evie sat back in her chair and sighed impatiently. "My sight will tell you what you already know. It is time to act. The Heartland is where the balance can be restored. I believe the Black Queen has began to lose her grip on power."

Hope bloomed in Aubrey's chest. If such a thing were true, much could be done to force her to weaken even more. Already her evil sister, Delilah, had lost much in this realm. Emerald had broken the ties that bound her to the Scarlet Coven and, in doing so, had broken Delilah's control over in this realm, possibly others. Was Karina also weakening?

A chill shivered down her back. They had not shown themselves during her torture, but if they had been controlling the Faye, then...

She focused back on Evie. "And you know this without using your sight?" At Evie's faint nod, Aubrey asked, "How?"

"Poison." Evie's gaze was intense. "He has broken free from their curse."

Aubrey almost let her cup of tea fall from her grip. She tightened her hand on it and realized she'd stood only when her feet throbbed a warning at her. Greyson also stood. He frowned deeply from her to Evie. "Who is Poison?"

She barely heard him. If the queen had lost her most valuable players, was it true? Was the time for her to act upon them? "This is true? They've lost their grip on them?" Her heart was beating as if she'd run a race.

"I believe so. He came to me."

"Why?"

"He sought his Flame."

Aubrey sank down in her chair and, without realizing it, took Greyson's hand. "This... That means... How?"

"I don't know how!" Evie smacked the table and stood. "If I use the stone, they will know! Already they know I used the gate to aid you and yours. But if he's broken free, that might mean..." Evie sat heavily. "It might mean he won't report back to them. It might mean—"

"You're protected, and if you aren't, you wish for protection." Aubrey understood Evie's visit. If Evie used her stone and the queen had power over her, she would be forced to see for her. If she didn't use the stone, she would be safe. Coming here had been for two things—to warn and to seek shelter. "Does Fiacre know?"

"I assume so. My spies tell me that he has found Jacob."

Greyson leaned forward. "And the Vampire is well?"

"He will be, if he's not," Evie snapped. "That's beside the point. My spies also discovered that Fiacre rode with a woman warrior, and a wolf joined him. They broke the Faye line and freed the captive warriors, one being Jacob."

"Your spies seem to know a great deal." Greyson sounded accusing, as if Evie had withheld information.

Aubrey softened his words with, "This is good news. Would the wolf be Alrick? And the woman... Could you be saying Fiacre has...Greer?"

"I believe he has both—and soon all three. The Hawk, the Flame and soon, the Sword. He is destined to be by their side. It must be so. In the last battle—the battle to align the balance—all of them *must* be on the field. In order to defeat the Black Queen and her lieutenants, we all must be prepared, yes?"

Aubrey wondered. There were ancient texts, prophecies that suggested other, far more dire results were needed to end the queen's rule. The three legendary warriors were pivotal, but in order to break their cycle of birth and rebirth in the service of the Black Queen, a sacrifice that no battle could provide would be needed. *One of them will have to willingly give their life.*

"Slow down. Who is this Sword?" Greyson had heard, it seemed, enough. "Hawk? Flame?"

Evie gave him a steady look, but Greyson could do much more to aid them if he had all the facts.

Aubrey considered how best to explain, then spoke, "The three we discuss were cursed at a time when the Dragons fell. Poison is the name the Black Queen gave him. But he is also called Sword. He is always the protector of Flame. The three of them ride into battle and leave nothing but destruction behind."

"And if they've broken free, this is good news for us? Explain." Greyson's voice dipped lower when he was frustrated. For a man who liked things a certain way, dealing with her and all the other folk that made up this realm must be difficult.

Feeling a bit sorry for putting him through so much, Aubrey tried to explain. "Evie is speaking of a battle that can put an end to darkness, meaning the evil we're trying to stem here in the Heartland and in the other realms. It is no coincidence that there is more and more evil arising. The Changelings, the dark covens, the increase in discontent among the wolves, the Vampires turning to darkness, the demons in the Faye Realm... All of it can be traced back to its beginning. The Black Queen is a witch with ties to such evil that to meet her eyes can draw a person down into the depths of madness. She has not simply sold her soul to darkness. She has sacrificed *other* souls to ensure her power.

"She is by far the most dangerous adversary. She and her sisters, or lieutenants, have long followed the deeper, darker magic, but for all their terrible power, they are pawns, much as we are for the light." She paused. Greyson listened, and no doubt understood her very well. Her accent had nearly disappeared over the past few months in his company and now that she knew what lay ahead, her nerves had steadied.

"Sword, Hawk and Flame are rumored to be descendants of the Dragons. Some legends say only the one is a Dragon and the other two her guards. And still other legends claim only the Hawk, a woman called Greer, is descended from the Dragon warriors. Some of these legends are true. I believe they are, at least. I believe that the Black Queen forced them to take oaths that make them do her will. And her will was to bend every nation to her rule. She used the three warriors to lead her legions and, under their direction, they destroyed entire kingdoms. They have done so because of the spells that bind them." She gathered her thoughts, recalling easily the different prophecies, and most importantly the one she considered vital if the time had arrived for them to overthrow the queen. It would not merely be in battle that the cursed warriors would break her dominion. It would be from a sacrifice. Otherwise, they would have found their freedom long ago—not that it helped her figure out how to explain it to Greyson.

"You're telling me that three warriors were pivotal to winning battles?"

Evie snorted. "They aren't merely warriors. I nearly peed myself when Poison arrived." She picked up her tea again and shook her head before sipping. "They are... How do you say it? Powerful?"

"Unstoppable," Aubrey added.

Evie pointed a finger at Greyson again. "And if he has broken the curse, then it might be possible that the other two have as well, which would mean they would be fighting with us, not against us."

Greyson's frown deepened. He was obviously attempting to synthesize it down to what he could handle. "Why now?"

"If his beloved is once again taken, he will willingly follow."

He gave Evie a steady look. It was obvious that was not what he'd asked. "And his beloved is one of these two women."

"Yes. Brenyn, youngest daughter of the Dragon King Aden."

Aubrey sucked in a breath. "You know this as fact?" *If this rumor is truth, then what else is truth? Can I ask Evie?*

"Yes." The one word seemed to suggest that there would be more information forthcoming.

"And Greer. She is the daughter of the King's Dragon?" Aubrey asked. She knew the stories, that the most honored of all warriors stood to the left of the king. Legends spoke of him finding true love and leaving his king for her. He, along with his family, were then destroyed by evil. It was a warning to all warriors seeking more from life than service, perhaps, but maybe there was truth at the core.

"Yes."

Then it must be her who makes the sacrifice...or Brenyn — the child kidnapped from the king, the beginning of his sorrow and rage. Or Oisin, the warrior who lived for his love? Will he sacrifice himself? She felt a headache coming on. They had all suffered, all sacrificed themselves in different ways. How could they not have? Lifetime after lifetime, they had been forced to live and kill for evil.

"What you're saying is these warriors have some sort of protection that makes them unstoppable? And they work for this group of witches?" Greyson asked.

Her mind whirling with possibilities, Aubrey glanced at him then at Evie. The seer raised her eyebrows, leaving the answer for Aubrey to tackle. She debated and finally explained, "I believe they can be stopped, but always before, when they fell in battle, the Black Queen went into hiding. Much like a spider, she stays out of sight but continues to create her webs. Her two sisters do the same. Delilah, for example, came here and headed the Scarlet Coven, creating such evil within them that they may be forever cursed."

"Delilah was the witch at the gate when you were captured? The one who wanted Emerald?"

"Yes." Aubrey had only the stories Circerran had told her of the encounter near the gate to go on, but she knew that Emerald had broken away from Delilah. And hadn't Circerran said that Delilah had been expelled from this realm back to the Heartland?

"And if we kill these witches, then they will lose their power here and in this other realm?"

"Yes," Aubrey said, then added, "and no." Before Greyson could demand an explanation, she went on. "There are prophecies. One says that there will come a time when the sword will be cleansed of poison. This is Oisin freeing himself of the queen. When this happens, a prophecy warns that the Dragon King will take to the field with his three lost children. It is then that the free nations must go into battle. If they do, then the free nations will end the dark queen's power." She kept to herself the sacrifice that must be made but felt like she'd done a pretty good job of condensing thousand-year-old texts into a manageable size. When she glanced at Evie, she thought that Evie's eyes flickered with more intensity, but the seer stayed silent. Clearly, she knew there was a great deal more. Greyson, on the other hand, did not stay silent.

"And this Poison you call Sword or Oisin... He is what sparked this belief that now is the time for this epic battle?" Greyson was intelligent—almost to a fault. She knew he had heard her slip with 'prophecies' not 'prophecy' and would later question her on it, no doubt when no one was around.

"Yes." Evie raised her tea and sipped it.

Greyson glanced at her with a look that said he didn't believe such a simple answer fit the kind of action Evie was calling for.

Aubrey agreed but kept that to herself. "Yes. I can feel the world waiting."

"We must act, then, yes?" Evie sat straighter.

"Hold on." Greyson held up a hand. "How did this Poison, Sword, whatever—"

"His true name is Oisin," Aubrey offered. "The women are Brenyn and Greer."

Greyson had a way of saying she was being silly without saying a word. He did it now, and she lifted her chin.

"They would prefer those names, I believe," she added.

"Mm-m." Greyson settled his arms on the table. "How did he break free from these witches?"

Evie shrugged. "A Dream Walker."

Aubrey blinked, squinted at Evie then shook her head. "A Dream Walker? There has not been a Dream Walker in centuries." *Longer, possibly.* "What makes you believe one could break him of the queen's spell?"

For the first time, Evie looked uneasy. "I might have spoken to one."

Aubrey paused with her cup in hand. "You...spoke." She shook her head and set her cup down. "Evie, you spoke with a Dream Walker?"

"Why is that odd? What is a Dream Walker?" Greyson demanded.

Instead of answering, Aubrey stared at Evie, surprised when the seer shifted in her seat and looked uncomfortable. An odd ripple echoed through Aubrey's lines of protection, as if a wind had blown them aside.

"Evie?" Aubrey whispered, feeling a chill settle on her skin.

Evie glanced at her companions. Neither man spoke. At her slight wave, one stood, went to the door and opened it. A woman in a cloak with a hood hanging down to shadow her features stood just outside.

Greyson got to his feet again. She was thankful that he hadn't taken out his weapon. She stood and suffered his worried glance. She checked her lines of protection. They were still in place. The slight push on them must have been the woman standing at her door. Such a thing was...should be...impossible. She glanced over at Greyson and gave him a slight shake of her head. He lifted his eyebrows. No doubt adding a new line of protection around her home—possibly armed guards—was in her future.

"Well," Evie murmured and gave Aubrey an apologetic smile. "I thought she could explain far easier than I could."

The woman didn't move to enter, but at Evie's words, she pushed back her hood to reveal close-cut blonde hair that accentuated the delicate features of a Faye princess—only this was no princess. Aubrey opened her sight for the third time. The bright golden aura of the woman shone from her like someone had gathered a million fireflies in their cupped hands.

"Dragon Mage," she murmured, bowing her head. "It is an honor to meet you at long last."

The heat leeched from Aubrey's face. Next to her she was suddenly aware of Greyson. He shifted his feet. Fearing he'd drawn his gun, or worse, she glanced at him. He gave her another look loaded with words he didn't need to say. She felt as if everything in her life had suddenly sped up and found an ache building in her throat for all the chances she'd let go by without saying a word to this man about how much he meant to her. With effort she swallowed and faced the Dream Walker. Seconds had passed, but her path had suddenly become unchangeable, as if someone had carved it out of stone.

"Dream Walker, you are welcome to enter my home. May the light shine on you," Aubrey murmured, bowing her head in respect.

"And guide you as you find your path," the woman responded. She lifted her head and smiled, revealing an impish air to an otherwise-solemn expression. "We have much to do and not much time. The Dragon has slumbered long enough. If we have read the signs correctly, 'tis time to wake him."

Aubrey felt her stomach tighten painfully. *The Dragon King.*

The Dream Walker sighed as she took Greyson's favorite chair by the hearth. "I will have to see to setting the Silver King straight, first. He has been tricked far too deeply for far too long. It will take time, but a few days' journey will be well worth it. You agree it must be done?"

"Danu save us," Aubrey whispered. "The Silver King? You will…break the spells on him?"

"It seems that waking those who sleep is as important as freeing those who are bound."

The flows of magic were shifting, realigning and forming around the Dream Walker. She used the flows to travel, for the Dream Walker wasn't truly in this room, in this time or even in this realm. Somewhere her body slumbered while her mind journeyed wherever there was need. Aubrey had known one other such as the woman facing her now. She, too, had come in time of need…and had forever changed Aubrey's life. In all her interactions with that Dream Walker, Aubrey had never seen such vibrance. If her power was this great, what did that mean for the events that would surely follow? *It means that not only my life will change, but many others as well.*

"What must we do?" Aubrey asked.

"We?" The Dream Walker's smile dimmed. "You, Dragon Mage, must journey to the Heartland and wake the Dragons." The Dream Walker focused on Greyson and her smile returned. Aubrey took one look at his face and knew why. Greyson was going to be a problem. His brow was lowered, the skin above the bridge of his nose grooved with the force of his worry.

"And I suppose you will go with her?"

Greyson practically growled his response. "Damn right."

Aubrey and Evie exchanged a look of horror at his disrespect, but the Dream Walker merely laughed. "Good answer. Very, *very* good answer."

Greyson seemed content, but Aubrey felt a sharp spike of fear pierce her heart. The coming battle wouldn't be easy. There were sacrifices that must be made. *What will stop him from becoming one?*

Chapter Eleven

The wind blew the leaves Brenyn had just swept into a neat pile by the door back into the hall. She considered giving up. It was tempting. In the end, she banished the leaves out of the door and down the steps with more forceful sweeps of the broom. Sweat blossomed on her brow and ran down her temples. She wiped it off with a sleeve and kept at the leaves, determined to rid the courtyard of them. With so few living trees in the castle commons, she couldn't fathom where the leaves even came from. The forest, perhaps, or the many gardens lining the halls? Wherever they came from to litter the corridors, she wanted them gone. Magic would be a fine gift. No doubt Fiacre could shrug a shoulder and vanish the pesky things forever.

She paused and leaned on the broom. The work wasn't necessary. With Fiacre in his tower and Greer off hunting for a stag—more for the blood than the meat—Brenyn had time. Jacob slept—or if he didn't, he said very little when she entered his rooms.

There is enough going on in my dreams, I suppose.

The thought filled her with guilt. She should have spoken to Fiacre by now about the woman she'd seen in the woods. The last week had been busy, too busy to bother him. Excuses, she knew.

Indistinct images hovered, still there if she closed her eyes. She no longer needed sleep to see these visions. They waited, even when she was awake, to deepen her knowledge that her life would soon change. The idea filled her with a mixture of anticipation and fear. Which was stronger, she couldn't say, because sorrow colored everything else. At different times of the day she would suddenly feel her throat tighten and her eyes sting. Tears rose up inside her like the tide, swallowing the slim shoreline beneath the keep's walls.

Even now, just pausing in her work, tears blurred her vision. They burned hot and disappeared against her skin. Her temperature had grown unpredictable. At night she no longer dared light a fire in her room. She was certain Fiacre would want to know, but she wasn't sick. She was simply hot all the time…or deathly cold. It was as if her body temperature was no longer hers to manage. And it was essential that she remain in control. *Control. Remain calm. Always remain calm.* She knew the litany, understood that Fiacre had made it the most important thing in her life — as important as her nightly potion. But Fiacre was busy. Everyone was busy and she couldn't help but wonder if they, too, didn't have secrets that they'd rather not reveal, like hers — that soon enough, she might *not* have control. Immediately her mind switched from producing tears to cold dread.

The questions that tumbled through her were chaotic. *Will he find me in time? Does Fiacre know? Does he want him to find me? What if he isn't free? What if the woman is wrong?*

The image of walking through the snow, barefoot and naked, came to her again. The soles of her feet hurt from the cold. Where she stepped, the snow melted. She'd glanced back and seen that she'd left a trail of steaming footprints in her wake. The sensations were so clear. She rubbed one booted foot on top of the other and closed her eyes, unwilling to believe such visions but unable to stop them.

The images had free rein. They blossomed and grew in detail, taking her breath away with how real the freezing winter landscape felt. Her nose tingled when she drew in a sharp breath. Her fingers throbbed and her toes echoed the sensation.

There was only one reason she could think of for such things to feel so real. It was or had once been real.

She knew it and believed it, because she had to. She had to trust that what she dreamed, what she saw, was truth. And if it was, then *he* was real, too. She needed him to be real because the thought of him being merely a dream made the tears, barely held in check, threaten to fall.

Brenyn reviewed what she was sure of. Greer knew what she dreamed was true. She fought the past because she couldn't accept it, and Jacob was part of that pain. He'd hurt Greer — somehow. Greer had lived before. Jacob must have been in one of those lifetimes. And if that were true and Greer's dreams were memories that haunted her…

Then my dreams mean this is not my first life, either.

What if her dream warrior had also hurt her? The fear and panic increased, and the heat simmering in her body rose.

"Remain calm. You must remain calm."

With a cry she dropped the broom on the cobblestones and scanned the courtyard for the source of the voice she'd heard so clearly. It was not a woman's voice, either. It was a man's deep voice…*his* voice.

"Show yourself." Fear had her heart racing and worse, her temperature rising. Sweat blossomed on her forehead. As soon as it formed, it burned away.

"I am not there, yet. Calm. Breathe. You must remain calm."

"How can you speak to me like this? Where are you? I don't want you here. I don't want you to speak to me!" Her body trembled so hard that her arms and legs shook.

A sense of unease crept over her — not her own, from him. *"You don't mean that."*

Tears filled her eyes and blurred the light gray of the cloudy sky beyond the castle walls. She blinked her gaze back into focus. She'd cleaned this courtyard since all those years ago when she'd first come with Fiacre to the keep. These walls were her home. If that were true, why did other walls call to her, white walls with the softness of beautiful carvings etched on their surfaces? She focused on the safety of the here-and-now. These walls… The roses that grew on them… They slept their winter sleep. For now, they were brown, dried vines choking the wall, but in the spring they would blossom and fill the courtyard with their perfume.

But there were other flowers — small blue and purple blossoms that grew out of the melted snow. There were other courtyards and other palaces. And there was always, in every one of those places, this man. *Oisin.* The name floated to her and created such a wash of tenderness and warmth that new tears flowed from her eyes. But her temperature began to lower and her heart rate slowed as panic began to be replaced by something else. It was a sense of rightness, she realized.

"I don't mean it. I'm afraid," she whispered. "I don't understand what I know and what I don't know, what I see and what I dream. I...can't see the difference any longer."

Relief settled over her from him. It felt as though he had brought her close to his chest and held her tight. She didn't understand it but let the comfort ease the residue of fear that still nagged at her.

"Never fear me. I will never harm you."

She brushed at her tears with her fingertips. "I don't fear you. You...are necessary. I see that now. I feel incomplete. Alone."

"Wait for me. I come to you, but I cannot reach easily. I must take the roads men use to remain hidden."

He didn't say why he hid. She felt the cold rush of goosebumps and skirted the full knowledge of what he hid from.

"You are strong. Remain calm. I will reach you soon."

"I will," she promised, unable to keep the distress from her tone. It was the truth. Even before the woman's voice in her mind, she'd known this day would come, that *he* would come...for *her*. Always for her, because without him, there was no her, and without her, there was no him. They were two parts to a whole.

"Don't fear me. I will protect you."

"No one can protect me." It was the truth. And now, she knew, that it had always been so. Not even Greer... Not even this warrior, the one the witches had named Poison... *That is not his name. It is Oisin.* "But I do not fear you."

Suddenly she saw a clear image of his dark eyes and heavy brow, the smile she knew was only for her and she felt the gentle touch of his hand on hers. His love made life bearable and, at the same time, unbearable.

"You shouldn't come here. I shouldn't be here. I will only harm them." The thought of saddling up the gelding, leaving this place and never returning to these lands was an urge she almost couldn't resist. She took a step toward the stable.

Fear, something she would have sworn her warrior didn't know, surged through to her from whatever link he had forged between them. *"You've only just woken. You cannot leave now. I come. Greer is awake. Soon we will be together again. This time we will be free."*

"We will never be free. They will come for you. They will put you back in the ice, so I will come for you and when I do, they will have us both…as they plan."

"They will try. I am free now, little one. Someone aided me. And you? Always you have saved me."

She covered her mouth with both hands to hold in her cry. "The last of the Dragon Guard were killed long ago." She could see their bodies, broken and silent on the hillside. But even that wasn't true. Greer and Oisin were the last. Her honor guards…to their deaths. Always to their deaths.

"So much doubt… I will be there. Wait for me. Tomorrow eve or the next morn. Do not doubt so much, little one. Believe. Believe in me, if nothing else. As often as you have saved me, I have saved you."

The heat dissipated and her tears fell. She sat on the steps, unaware of even walking to them. Head bowed, she let the tears fall. A longing for warm arms, for the steady beat of a heart under her cheek, filled her. "Hurry then. I wish to leave this place."

"I will. You know what we have to do."

"Yes. I know." *Fight. Again.*

His presence disappeared, but not completely this time. It wasn't as strong, more of a sensation of him, but it comforted her to know that he lingered.

The horses neighed in their stalls, wanting to be fed, and far above in Fiacre's tower, a light came on as the mage lit the candles in his study. Greer was no doubt worrying over Jacob. While Jacob was...either wandering the keep or pacing his rooms.

For now, they all waited. For now, she would continue to help them the only way she knew — by cleaning, cooking and tending to them all. One day — very soon, she guessed — they would need her to do much more than serve them foods she made with her own hands.

They'll need me to help gain our freedom. Is such a thing possible? Truly possible? For the first time since waking from a dream of a warrior with startling bright eyes, she wasn't confused. The memories would come. She would have to let them and hope that when they did return, she was strong enough and brave enough to face them.

"Very well, but until then, I have a mare to see to and perhaps a life to bring into this world." With images of a baby colt in her mind, not a tall, broad-shouldered warrior, she picked up her broom and headed to feed the horses.

Life will change. It will be a change with a chance of freedom, perhaps even freedom from bonds we don't see.

* * * *

Greer woke to a feeling of unease. By all rights, she should have been sleeping. She'd tried her best to wear herself out during the day. But she threw the furs off and stood, ignoring the cold stone floor as she walked to her balcony. She opened the double-shuttered doors and stood drawing in deep breaths.

The wind was fierce, blowing the waves up until they crashed like white foam at the base of the cliffs far beneath the castle walls. Each time, she swore she could feel the salty spray. It was the rain, she knew. She wished suddenly to dive down into the salty water and leave the pain behind.

She didn't move. She couldn't. Such an end was cowardly. She closed her eyes, imagining it anyway. The soft caress of water surrounding her and easing the pain that was tearing her apart, erasing the image of Jacob's tormented expression.

He hadn't spoken to her since they'd brought him there. He'd not accused her with his eyes. He'd not spoken in a voice ravaged with emotion. He'd wandered the keep at night and held his silence during the day. Fiacre blamed the drugs. His wounds were part of it and so was the lack of blood. But she knew better. He would not be defeated so easily. Jacob had always planned, strategized and worked a problem until he came up with a solution.

Except there was no solution for them. She had been brought back to fight—possibly to the death—again. She wasn't like Brenyn and Oisin. She couldn't watch Jacob suffer and die—or have him watch her do the same. She shut her eyes to the visions of Oisin driving a sword into his own heart, only to have the Black Queen stop him from completely dying. Each time he'd fought them harder and harder, but nothing had ever ended his capture and spelled sleep in the ice.

And now? Brenyn was here before me. I was brought back as I am. Where is Oisin, then? Does he still linger in the ice, waiting for Brenyn to wake him?

She drew in a deep breath of icy sea air and opened her eyes to dispel such thoughts. There were no answers unless she asked the questions, and she hesitated to ask too much of Fiacre. The truth wasn't always kind. Jacob thought he knew a truth — that she was Gwen deep down, the princess he'd known — but the truth was that she had merely hidden from a fate she couldn't alter…until now.

Fiacre needed her and he needed Jacob. Without having to ask, she'd gone out, taken down a good-sized doe and brought back enough blood for Jacob. Brenyn had wrinkled her nose then accepted the bucket of blood. Brenyn had even said she'd left him a cup and that when she'd returned to his rooms, it'd been gone. So, he was aware and trying to recover. He simply didn't seek any of them out. Even Brenyn barely got a word from him.

Greer knew that if she entered his rooms, there would be more arguing, or worse, memories from the past she couldn't keep denying that they shared.

And tonight, the past lingered closer than ever. She'd struggled to keep it at bay since the battle. Once she'd opened the curtains on that carriage and seen his beloved face twisted in rage, it was as if the mist that had protected her from feeling, from living, from being here again, had been stripped away.

His presence left her with nowhere to go, no way to avoid the pain, no way to fight it. It sliced her with every breath she took. Even on the salty breeze, the scent of roses tormented her — the small pink kind that loved to climb castle walls, a reminder of all she had lost, all that she had let be destroyed and all that she had naively wanted.

She closed her eyes and held on to the stone balcony as tightly as she could. The weathered stone was cold and wet. The rough surface scraped her fingers. Even that small discomfort could not hold back the memories and guilt trying to overtake her.

Gwen. Gwen is who he sees when he looks at me. Does he know it was me looking at him through Gwen's eyes? It was always me — and yet, not… I hid, and because of me, all he loved was destroyed. And now, I once again pay the price — and so will everyone who is near me. Gwen is all I ever thought I wanted. In the end, she wasn't enough — not for him and not for me — a princess, bound by ties too tight for breath, let alone freedom to be myself. And that is who he sees…Gwen.

Tears should have been a thing of the past. Feelings should have been of no consequence. There was the upcoming battle, and there should be nothing more. But with him here, with seeing him again, all the hopes she'd once had — silly, stupid dreams — surfaced and wouldn't be ignored.

A bird — possibly a seagull — cried high above the incoming storm, and for a moment, its darkened wings flashed through the clouds. It dove and became clearer. It wasn't a seagull, but a hawk.

Golden wings with a darker head. Sharp talons, sharper beak, a killer. *I was the Hawk and Brenyn was the Flame. Does Oisin, her Sword, travel to us, even now, to protect her?*

At her thoughts, the memories would not be held back. She couldn't bear to think on Brenyn and Oisin or

Jacob, so she dove deeper, to the beginning — to her, to Greer, the child who had once been.

Down a narrow cart path, a girl skipped, her long sun-kissed brown hair tied back into two braids that bounced behind her as she went. She wore a gray gown covered with a plain linen outer tunic, but someone had lovingly stitched pink roses along the hem and collar. The lush green expanse of hydrangea with their heavy blue flowers lined the forest path, sharing their beauty with the small, pink tea roses that trailed up the cherry and apple trees. The fields were ripe with corn and smaller plots with potatoes and sunflowers. It was the forest that they entered, and the path wound through a tunnel of living greenery to help keep the heavy rains off weary travelers.

The girl wasn't weary, nor was she aware of anything other than the smell of flowers on the day, the sun shining through the clouds and a happiness so great that it burst from her in bits of song. She was small, no more than ten or fewer winters. She went along the well-worn earthen path as if she'd been down this lane thousands of times before.

"Kelli! Wait for me."

A laugh was all the response Greer received until, with a spin, the child smiled at her before taking off again.

Greer's view skipped upward, away from the child, and she tipped her head back to see the blue of the cloudless sky. The trees above her were so dense that she could only spot patches of azure through the woven protection.

From ahead, Kelli cried out in a startled gasp.

Greer's vision turned back to her sister. Her heart seemed to stop and she froze. If Greer could have screamed, she would have.

Kelli had stopped in the path, her body half-turned to Greer. Her small face was frozen in pain, her child's hands wrapped around the shaft of an arrow planted like a slender sapling in the center of her narrow chest.

Fear tasted like metal in Greer's mouth as she ran. Her heart had started back up and now beat so wildly that she felt lightheaded. No matter how hard she ran, she got no closer.

"Kelli!" Greer stumbled to a stop as her sister knelt in slow motion. Kelli's eyes filled with tears and her small brow furrowed in confusion. Then, without a word, she crumpled onto her side, one arm outstretched toward Greer.

As if her fall had been a signal, a rush of bitter cold raced through the trees, turning them white with frost. A whirlwind brought with it leaves the color of blood. They circled over the child then covered all of her from view, save one small blood-stained hand.

The cry of birds directly over her head dragged Greer's gaze upward from the fallen girl. She ducked as two ravens winged downward so close that she felt their passage. Crying, they circled amid the storm cloud of leaves. In their beaks they held springs of strawberry blossoms. The white petals seemed too delicate and pretty to be laid upon the blood-red leaves covering her sister's body.

She blinked, feeling dizzy, and stumbled on the trail, now in search of the archer. She could see no one. The trees were empty, the trail deserted and even as she kept walking, she still could get no closer to her sister.

"Who are you? Show yourself, you cowards! Why did you do this? Why?" Her scream echoed through the land. The forest seemed ill-at-ease, as if it held its breath, waiting for something far worse to arrive.

Suddenly, from behind where the child lay, two women appeared. They were dressed in long, heavy black cloaks that barely fluttered with the force of the wind. Their image brought a freezing terror. They stood motionless near the fallen body of the child, their staffs held in their hands, the ravens landing on their shoulders as the leaves blew and danced around them. Their wild black hair was greased back with white mud that also adorned their cheeks in sweeping slashes. Dark pigment blackened their eyes, as if they wore masks. Even from a distance, she could see that their gazes were pinned on her.

"Cowards? Such words from one who has so much to lose."

Greer trembled so badly that she felt as if her legs would give out, and like the child, she would crumble to the ground. She couldn't, and held herself strong. She tried to speak. Her lips were sealed shut.

The witches smirked at her as if they knew she wanted to curse them and was unable. In the next instant, they threw their heads back and cawed like the ravens, revealing sharpened white teeth and blackened tongues.

Greer's head fill with agony at the sound, as if they'd driven blazing hot spikes deep into her skull. She cried out and gripped both sides of her head, pressing on her temple for fear of her head exploding.

As quickly as it began, the sound and the pain vanished.

Another bird winged down from the middle of the storm of leaves. As soon as its claws touched the earth, a woman dressed in heavy furs, with her long auburn hair tangled among the pelts, walked from between the swirling leaves. Her hands were tattooed with scrolls of red and black down to her fingertips. More tattoos colored a mask around her eyes like the other women. They outlined her eyes in red and reached up and into her hairline.

Raven feathers were twisted in the intricate knots of her hair, creating a crown that was anchored into a heavily jeweled headdress of black leather. More leather encased her body. It was tooled with swirls sprinkled throughout with thousands of glittering pieces of metal and stones.

Greer tried to close her eyes, to block the sight of her. Instead, she was held, as if by an invisible hand.

The witch opened her mouth and flies poured forth in a viciously buzzing swarm. They raced toward the ancient forest, and Greer thought the trees swayed in horror from the ravenous hunger of the cloud.

As suddenly as the swarm began, it vanished. The wind stopped. The silence after the onslaught was deafening.

Time seemed to stand still. The three stared at Greer, unspeaking. The intensity in their gazes drew her. In a flash, she knew. Kelli would live again. Her parents would not be taken, tortured, as she watched. Her village would remain, her brother would grow to a be a man, and her parents would have another child…

This moment would stop. More, it would forever be undone. Kelli would rise, and once again skip down the forest paths.

From the trail, behind the three, a man appeared. He raced to them, shoving branches aside as he sped along a path trying to hold him back.

With a suddenness that took her breath, she knew he would die if she did not…

Agree.

As suddenly as she had become Greer, the young, ignorant village girl, she drew in a breath and was again Greer the warrior who had been called to this realm.

The memories were slow to release her. She did not force them away. Instead, she accepted the past, accepted that this memory, more than any of the others, was essential. She knew the events that were about to play out and knew the finality of them — the horrors she would endure because of a past so distant that it was beyond counting bore on the events that would take place all too soon.

The crowned witch had held out her hand and she had taken it. She'd had no choice. The two black ones, with their barbed bows and notched arrows aimed at her father, had taken away any choices, save one. But it had been her free will that had caused so much pain. He had still sped toward them, his broadsword drawn, his face filled with purpose, and yet it had not been the witch's death that had darkened that day. It had been Greer's, because above all else she had loved her father — her family — and nothing was too high a price to pay to ensure their safety. At least, that was what she'd thought back then.

The witch had beckoned to her with black-stained fingers. Greer had gained her feet. And the young girl she had been had known the path she must take. To save her father's life — and through him, her mother and even her sister, lying so still on the grass — she had to take that hand.

She had closed the distance between them. The storm cloud of leaves had erupted once again and cut her off from everything else — her father's distant shout, her mother's scream, even the view of her beloved Kelli.

She had taken a breath filled with the scent of wet leaves and rich blood and grasped the witch's hand.

As their palms had met, the witch had tightened her grip. The very center of Greer's palm had burned with an icy viciousness. The forest, her fallen sister, her mother, her father, everything except the painful grip of the witch holding her hand had disappeared, to be replaced by even greater anguish.

The memories finally released her and the world she walked now resurfaced. Sea-scented air chilled her. She gasped in a breath, choked on it and tried again, gaining her balance bit by bit. The icy blast of the rain still wet her face and had, in fact, drenched her clothing, but she clung to the discomfort to help dispel the pain and sorrow of that long-ago choice.

She had sealed her fate on that day. Even now, the circled knot of three ravens on her palm tingled.

They were drawing closer. She could sense it. *Is this the real reason for Jacob being here? To weaken me with memories?*

They should have known better. Pain was part of her life. Each time she had come back to this realm, pain had always been there. She'd lost everyone she dared love. The witch had lied about that. From the beginning, she had deceived her, but Greer had learned. She hadn't simply survived each time—until the odds were too great and she'd die— she'd learned. The queen was insane. Only death could cure her madness.

Fiacre can end her…with my help. She fisted her hands and tried to keep from striking out as frustration and hurt strangled her. *Calm. Stay calm. Jacob is here. He is here for a reason and not merely to aid in this battle. Brenyn is here. And Oisin? Will he come here as well?* The image of Brenyn's warrior wasn't clear to her. It was as if he stood frozen behind a sheet of ice. For some reason, she felt certain he'd broken free. She wouldn't search for him, knowing that such a thing would call attention, especially after a memory had surfaced. She simply had a sense that Brenyn's warrior wasn't trapped in the ice any longer.

She stepped away from the balcony. The ocean held no answers. The memories would continue until she had faced what she feared most. And this time, it wasn't the witch queen.

Jacob. He sees Gwen when he looks into my eyes. What if he always will?

Chapter Twelve

Edric surveyed the ranks of his warriors as he rode through them. It wasn't until he had passed several perfectly straight lines of bowmen that they realized their king rode among them. A cry began then, and the shout grew until the air vibrated with it.

He turned his steed to face their shining ranks and the metallic sound of them coming to attention echoed afterward in the silence.

Over twenty thousand strong faced him, their helms bright, their shields held proudly. His people blazed under the sun. In the past, their enemies had run from the sight of them. Ballads had been written of their marches. Legends spoke of the valor of the Faye, and yet...the past was a misty blur filled with pain and betrayal.

He sighed. The heaviness of memories weighed him down. The past was golden, sliced sharper for all its beauty. The gold and blue were forever banished from his realm, replaced with the silver, a brighter, more pure light that complemented the black of his heart.

"The southern troops are situated at the border?"

"Yes, your majesty."

"And the Vampires?" He glanced to his captain in time to see the distasteful lift of his lip. "They have set up their part?"

"Yes. The last word we had from them was that they have scouts scoring the countryside for him."

The Silver King snorted. Vampires could never be trusted. Their weakness was too great. Lilith had not returned, though, so he was left to rule his people once again. He bit back the question he asked daily—where she was—because each day he got the same answers. And he could admit that each day his need for her diminished. The pain of the past was a distant storm, no doubt ready to break him. For now, he had other things on his mind, such as killing a mage who had dared take the lives of his people.

"Send out our scouts. I want word from their lips when the warrior is secured. He must be brought to me, not to their bloodthirsty queen. Understood?" If the mage wanted this man so badly, he'd come out of his keep, so Edric felt it equally necessary to capture him.

"Completely, your majesty."

"And what else do they report?"

"There is a woman with him." Drustan stilled his mount, then continued, "We learned of her through other sources."

"Other sources?"

"The Greenway spies."

The Greenway wished peace. Such sentimentality was foolish. It could also be useful. "And? Who is this woman?"

"I have no idea. The spy brought this." Drustan handed over roll of leather.

Edric unrolled it and froze. Upon the pale surface of the leather, a hawk in flight stared at him. "Why wasn't I informed immediately?"

"I only now received the report."

"Who is this spy? Where is he?"

"She, your majesty. She is there." His captain pointed to a figure standing in the shadow of an archway on his left. At first glance he thought Drustan had been mistaken. The slim figure could have been a boy. Then he took in the close-cut blonde hair above a face far too beautiful to be any boy. So were the curves under her armor.

He squinted over at her, uncertain why she needed further study. Odder still, he was unable to stop himself from cataloguing her every nuance. She wore a long-sleeved blue tunic under a cloak of dusty gray. When she tossed the cloak aside, he saw no insignia. Someone had taken time to add a flattering embroidery along the insides. A silver wolf cape rested over her shoulders. Both the cloak and the fur could have come from any of the ragtag people who littered the countryside outside his kingdom.

She could be northern, perhaps, or just as easily from the high mountains of the south. Still, her clothes were well made, which intrigued him. She also wore boiled and tooled leather that would have served a prince. Her hand rested on the pommel of a long sword she wore with the practiced ease of a fighter. The leather wrist guards were well kept and as well-made as the rest of her clothing. The wrist guards had nicks and slices, and so did the chest armor. Her weapons weren't merely for show, then. Even more intrigued, he contemplated the chances of this messenger, with this message, arriving at this moment.

Fate was a fickle female, wont to caste her dice whenever she wished. This was beyond even her usual.

"She looks more like a warrior-princess than a spy."

"She is a warrior, surely." Drustan grimaced. "I am doubtful she is of noble birth."

"Doubts are for the weak. Facts are what I need." For some reason, Drustan's distaste offended him. At his tone, apparently ever keen to his moods, Drustan simply bowed his head in acknowledgment.

"How long has she been working for us?"

"She is new. The last time we received word from any of our informers, we were told there would be a new messenger. She arrived with the correct wrist tattoo and her message."

"Tattoo?"

"The spies are in a guild. They all wear the blue tunics and have the inside of their wrists inked with an eye."

Edric shifted in his saddle. After so long, to be this close to finishing this, to be done, either in a final death or to finally destroy the remains of a kingdom that had joined with the witches to mortally wound him, should be all he concentrated on, and yet… "She is new."

"Yes, your majesty." Drustan shifted his gaze to the girl then back to Edric. "Do you recognize her?"

Sighing, Edric turned to survey the pinks and golds of dawn above the Winter Gate. It was going to be a glorious day. The cool breeze from the north would ease them as they rode. The sun would warm them as well. His troops waited, still unmoving, while he considered what to do with this new toss of the dice. "She's not of our race. What do I know of such beings?

One looks very much like the next. Bring her over to me. And get her a horse. I want her to ride by my side."

Drustan bowed and did as he had been instructed. Edric knew he had shocked his captain. His people didn't reveal emotions as readily as others, it was true. After a lifetime, outward signs were not necessary. Still, Drustan obeyed, surprised or not. No question. No hesitation.

When was the last time I spoke with Drustan? Edric frowned, unsure when he had exchanged more than a few words with anyone. The haze of the pain and the burn of the past agony lingered, clouded all else. Ruling a people as docile as his took none of his time and no effort, not when he'd had Lilith. Yet he no longer had Lilith. She had abandoned him, and when asked, his people would not meet his eyes nor answer him. All they would say was that Lilith hadn't returned.

Why is that a good thing?

He was once again taking up the mantle he'd worn far longer than some scrap of a girl spy who had walked this realm. *Then why does she draw my attention?*

He turned his head to study her. Drustan spoke with her. For some reason, it appeared she didn't respond with the same kind of obedience his people had mastered. She glanced across the sea of warriors at him once, then focused on Drustan. By her hand gestures, he guessed she was arguing stridently with his decision. Several of his warriors openly stared. A few of the lines showed signs of crumbling.

His captain appeared resolute. Surprising Edric, the girl seemed as equally determined.

Edric dismounted. The shifting in the lines ceased. He handed his reins over to a waiting groom and walked through the flawless ranks.

"And *I* said, I delivered. I want to be paid. Then, if his *majesty* wishes company on his march, he will have to suffer yours. Mine is too costly."

"I'm certain I can manage the fee." Edric expected shock, perhaps embarrassment at being caught talking as if he were…a pampered aristocrat. *Have I become spoiled? Perhaps.*

She sighed heavily, crossed her arms and, her face set in a cool expression, regarded him as if he'd taken the tarts from the banquet feast of the High Moon Celebration and claimed he'd not, while the crumbs dusted his lips.

"There is more I wish to learn from you," he added when she didn't speak. "I can pay, of course."

Her eyes were outlined with a soft charcoal—not black, merely a slight darkening to make her thick lashes appear even thicker. Even more fascinated up close to her, he tried to find a flaw to her beauty. She wasn't Faye, after all. Only Faye women were flawless. Yet the more he sought a mistake in her creation, the more he realized that there were none. Her face, with its smooth lines and high cheekbones, slim, elegant, small nose and delicately arched eyebrows, was a work any artisan would have paid handsomely to recreate.

She lifted one eyebrow at him impatiently. "I am *not* one of your servants—"

"I do not possess servants."

That got a twist of her lips and a sigh, as if he were being difficult.

Drustan tensed, not doubt ready to throw the woman out of the forest for such disrespect.

Edric shook his head ever so slightly.

His captain stepped back, giving them space. She was gorgeous enough and delicate enough to make him wonder if she couldn't be a pixie. *And cheeky enough.*

"I want to be paid."

"Fetch her gold," he murmured absently to Drustan. His captain, one of the most highly trained of his men, saluted smartly and headed off to fetch the girl's gold, like a servant he'd claimed he didn't have. *I may not have servants, but people do fetch me anything I wish.*

"So, where are we off to with such a big army? If it's to the Vampires, you can count me in. I'd like to see them handed their fangs."

He had the urge to change directions completely, head off to take Celenia's head and place it at this woman's feet. The Queen of the Vampires wasn't his enemy, not any longer. She'd aided him when he'd been betrayed. Sadly, he considered lying. The little spy had a gaze that made him wonder if she wouldn't be able to hear the truth. "Sadly, no. I go on a journey through the Twins."

"And that just happens to be where I'm going. Imagine that."

Another laugh escaped him. "I have not planned this" — he indicated the army in case she'd missed it — "to follow a single woman."

Her expression thoughtful, she turned to accept her money when Drustan returned. "Thank you. You know, you might want to ditch the war gear. You'd make a fine manservant."

The captain of his most elite guard grimaced. From behind him, a palace stableman handed over the reins of his snowy-white stallion. A dappled gray trailed after and was given to the girl. Tall, well-muscled with a dainty head and soft eyes, the gray was by far the prettier of the two horses.

"Yours, I presume?" he asked the woman.

"Of course."

Drustan lifted a single eyebrow at her arrogant answer.

"Was this another payment? She's a fine horse."

"She is a fine horse, but she is not a payment."

"Ah, I see." The ranks began to shift again as the sun rose higher. Edric considered for a moment more why this girl interested him, then let the thought go. "We must ride. Before we do, I should know your name."

With a sharp glance up from tying her saddle bags closed, she said, "Loralei."

He frowned, certain he'd not heard her correctly. "Laura Lee?"

"No. Loralei Alexia."

A Siren. For whom else names their child, 'she whose singing lures men to their destruction'? Is it her voice that's so enchanting then? He glanced at Drustan. By the disapproval on his face, Edric guessed her voice didn't sound as charming to his captain. She posed a dilemma if she were, in fact, a Siren. There was one Siren with the Silkies, a woman with a voice that could freeze the land in her cold sorrow. Another one had been forgotten in the mountains. No other of their race had survived.

Or did they?

It was all so long ago. He reached up and pinched the bridge of his nose.

"Headache?"

"Yes," he answered, dropping his hand. She watched him now, as if waiting for something. Him to move, he supposed. "Are you prepared to leave, then?"

153

"With you?"

"It would seem so."

He didn't understand the anxiousness in which he waited for her reply — or his relief when she nodded. Both worried him. Once she took her reins and launched herself up onto her mount, his worry eased.

Sighing, she positioned her satchel, gathered her reins, surveyed his people then him and seemed not in the slightest impressed. "Shall we go? The sooner were leave, the faster we are done."

"I'm afraid no matter how soon we leave, it will not speed up the length of the coming battle. Best to enjoy the ride."

At her steady stare, he walked to his own mount, his mind on what to do with the woman he'd invited along to war, more than on the upcoming war.

If he kept them at a steady pace, would he be able to see more of her? Each night they camped he could spend in her company. Surely if she were a Siren, he would know. *And if she is a siren? Does it matter that I once made it my life's mission to destroy them all so that no other man would fall under their spell?*

As soon as they passed under the Winter Gate, the girl joined him. Without any kind of respectful greeting, she asked, "Why are you going to war again? I wasn't clear on that bit."

Chapter Thirteen

Jacob waited until Greer went back into her room before he settled himself on her balcony. Something had happened to her. For a time there, while he'd watched, her gaze had gone chillingly blank. Her arms had collapsed limply to her sides and she'd slowly knelt on the freezing balcony and stayed that way, as she stared into nothing. *No, not nothing.* At something so painful that her hands and shoulders shook with the force of her tears.

He'd seen pain before. He'd lived for over seven centuries. Pain was part of that life. Her gaze — *Gwen's* gaze — had been pinned on something so painful that it brought her to her knees and tore him up inside to watch.

He waited until he could hear her steady breaths indicating sleep before he entered her room. Hers held little in the way of comfort. There was a bed, with the bedcurtains partially closed, and a small table next to it with an unlit candle, a cold hearth, a round table with two chairs. and a bear-skin rug on the floor. There was also a tall cabinet for her clothing and a plain wooden chest with her sword and sword belt resting on top. Nothing more. No paintings. No tapestries on the walls to keep off the chill.

It looked like a room someone stayed in, not lived in.

Her wet clothes were laid out neatly on one of the chairs in front of the hearth. He'd dried his with a thought. *What am I doing in here? Torturing myself. Fiacre spoke the truth. She spoke the truth. This woman is much more than the girl I knew. But…she's still Gwen.*

He walked to the bed on legs that seemed to have a mind of their own. As he drew closer, he tried to steel himself for the sight of her, and still it nearly drove him to his knees.

Gwen. There was no doubt in his mind. This was Gwen. This woman, lying on her side, was Gwen. The curve of her hip, the dip of her slender waist, the lean line filled in with soft hills was Gwen. *But she's more, isn't she?*

He swallowed painfully and crouched next to her bed. Her fists were curled under her smooth cheek. People had tendencies, tics, that, no matter what they did, they were rarely conscious of and, even when they were, couldn't stop. He knew he ducked his head when he couldn't face whatever challenge presented itself — and ground his teeth. Both had been pointed out to him often enough by over-observant companions.

Gwen had fisted her hands — when she walked, when she sat and when she slept. Her hands had always been either loosely clenched or tightly fisted. She had to work at holding her hands at her waist, loosely clasped like a good princess.

She'd once confided in him that she clenched her fists to keep her fear inside.

He'd never understood what a princess had to fear. *What does a warrior woman have to fear?*

The cold, uncaring woman who'd held a knife to his throat wasn't the woman sleeping on the bed. This was a delicate, beautiful creature. A sleeping beauty.

Pink lips slightly parted, she grimaced and murmured in her sleep. The furs slid down to reveal the delicate angle of her shoulder and the slender length of her leg. Gwen was golden, always had been—golden haired, golden skinned. Unlike the pale beauties of her time, she had a natural *alive* coloring. She always had. Her time in the sun had merely turned her into a shimmering beauty.

He bowed his head, clenched his jaw, breathed her in and knew that no matter what was said, no matter what anyone told him, this was the woman he had loved. *How is this possible?* He fisted his hands and a broken laugh escaped. *I ask this when I've been confronted with the impossible time and time again? Bryson found Isobel after centuries of her being buried alive.*

His gaze locked on Gwen's face again as if she drew him like magic. *Are you in there, Gwen? Spelled into this warrior woman? Changed from the princess I knew to this fierce fighter? Or were you always the warrior, gazing out from Gwen's beautiful eyes?*

Fiacre's words rumbled in his memory, too clear, too *true* to be denied.

Gwen would never lie to me, never indirectly or directly do something so painful to me.

He searched her sleeping face. There was no peace to her rest. She shifted again and mumbled words he couldn't understand. The murmured whispers sounded distressed. Her mouth tightened and her smooth forehead furrowed. With a suddenness that had him reaching backward to catch himself on the wooden floor, she twisted in her bed to lie on her back. Stunned, all he could do was hold himself there, arm behind him, leaning back as he stared at the beauty she'd unknowingly revealed.

The mounds of her breasts were incredibly soft-looking, peaked with twin pink nipples and the lightest of pink areolae. Her ribs appeared small under them, her slender stomach flat and toned. Yet all of her was shaped with such femininity that he couldn't drag his eyes away. Never in all his existence had he seen such beauty. He squinted at her, unable to soak in all she'd unwittingly exposed. He leaned forward and barely stopped himself from brushing his hand down her smooth skin. Instead, he gritted his teeth until his molars ached and pulled the furs all the way up to her delicate collarbone.

There was a red scar on her right shoulder, the size and length suggesting a knife wound, and a bruise on her upper arm. Suddenly, she threw her left arm up, nearly touching him. The scent of roses was clearer now. Stronger. He traced the pad of his forefinger over her brow. The tension there eased. She sighed and turned to her side, toward him, fists nuzzled under her cheek once more.

Stunned, he simply stared. How many times had he seen Gwen sleep? Always like this, as if seeking comfort. The thought made him frown. Gwen had been well loved. Everyone had adored her, but…she'd been alone—always alone—except when she'd been with him. He couldn't resist touching her soft skin again, just a light graze of his hand up her shoulder. The feel of her drew his body tight, pulling his muscles bowstring-taunt. His mouth filled with moisture as need rushed him.

In torment, he gazed at her. *How is this possible? Gwen is dead. I lost her long ago.* The thought brought another dose of agony and more confusion. *If she died, then who is this?* His thoughts circled. He didn't know what to think. His body had no doubts. His arousal pulsed, sending demands he knew there were no chance of meeting. He shut his eyes, not strong enough to keep his hands off her with her so close.

A kiss. That was all I ever took from Gwen. No, I didn't take it. A rough laugh escaped his control. *She took it from me. Gave it to me.* The memory sliced what was left of his heart to shreds—bitter and sweet at the same time.

He opened his eyes, dispelling the pain, searching her sleeping face, half-hoping she would wake and find him here.

This is not Gwen. The thought battled the vision before him.

A breeze, wet with the scent of the sea, cooled him. He pulled the fur up again to cover her shoulder. *If this is not Gwen, who is Greer? Why does Greer look like Gwen? Smell like her. Fill me with regrets?* Fiacre spoke the truth. Gwen was Greer…or Greer had been Gwen.

He dipped his head, his mind in confusion, but his awareness of the truth was growing stronger as he stood. As soon as he did, he froze. A knife blade rested—no, not rested—*pressed* to his throat. *Again.*

She left the blade in place and walked around his side to face him. He was aware of her nakedness at a level that made it hard to think of anything else. With all his willpower, he kept his gaze fixed on the gray eyes of a now-very-awake woman but shifted his feet to keep a few inches from her. She hissed at him and the knife sliced a line along his throat.

"You seem determined to slice my throat."

Her gaze smoldering, she didn't drop the knife. "What are you doing in here?"

"I thought that was obvious." He jerked his chin toward her exposed body. She made no indication that her nudity bothered her. Why should it? She was perfection—strong, lean, yet rounded in so many perfect ways. "Your master thinks I will save the world."

She quirked a brow. There was no sign of humor in her eyes. Anger burned there instead. "And you thought you'd start in my room?"

Hardly. There were many things he wanted to do with this woman, but none of them would be fighting her, even with a knife at his throat. "You'll have to slice deeper to make an impact."

"I know how to kill a Vampire."

Anger spiking, he shoved it down and tried for calm. "Do you? Well, go on. I've died before."

"Don't tempt me." There was something in her eyes now, something desperate she was trying to hide.

He leaned into the knife and took hold of her wrist, forcing the it tighter. "If you hold a knife to a Vampire, use it!"

She tugged her arm, her expression turning panicked. "Release me!"

He held on just a bit longer, either to torture himself or to show her he was in control. He wasn't sure. As soon as he released her, she pointed at the door with her knife. "Get out."

"I want to, I do, but before I do, I think we should talk." He turned his back, like a gentleman and because her body was imprinted on his brain anyway, and said, "Perhaps you should dress."

She made no move, merely stood there, apparently fuming at his back.

After a long, drawn-out silence, he shrugged. "If you'd rather stay as you are, I will not complain."

Movement behind him, the lightest of thuds as she jumped down from her bed, then the sounds of her dressing. He waited, willing his arousal down. It eased reluctantly. The scent of her was going to be a problem. There was only one way to minimize it. He stopped breathing. There were a few uncomfortable minutes to endure as his mind began to panic, no matter how much he repeated to himself that he didn't need to breathe. By the time she was dressed, though, he had himself in line…mostly.

"What do you want?"

"I think we'll start with answers to my questions, before we move into wants, eh?" He faced her and regretted it.

Dressed in a simple blouse and trousers, she looked bold and breathless. *No woman should ever be this beautiful.* He could detect the darker shadows against the linen of her shirt. The tight points of her nipples were surely meant to torment him. He refused to glance away from her face again. To do so would surely lead him into something that he would regret.

"Who are you?" His voice sounded like he'd swallowed sawdust.

"I am Greer."

He rolled his shoulders impatiently. "And? I know this. I heard you the first time. *What* are you?"

"We discussed this already...on a battlefield. You dragged me off. Remember that?"

He refused to let her sidetrack him. "I was drugged. My mind was not clear. I remember some of it. Alrick."

She nodded at his questioning glance.

"Fiacre being...a mage. Confusing plans for a battle." Not much, really. "Explain again, why you look, sound and smell like Gwen and are trying to convince me you aren't."

She squinted at him as if to see whether he was kidding her. With a disgusted roll of her eyes, she sat in one of the two chairs. He chose to stay where he was, far enough that her impact was lessened. "I am not Gwen. This is who I am." She gestured to the room — or else the keep, perhaps the realm. "I'm a warrior. Fiacre believes we will be able to stop the battle that is building."

"What do *you* think?" Her calm frustrated him. He wanted her to be upset, distraught, filled with torment — like him. Or else on fire with the passion he could barely suppress.

"I think that Fiacre is a mage. He has visions of what will be. If he believes we can do this, we must try."

"So, we — the two of us — will somehow stop all the evil in the world — not only in this cursed realm, but also in other realms as well? Maybe all of them, is that it?"

She broke eye contact and peered past him, at the curtains blowing inward from the sea breeze. She was so beautiful that his throat ached and so removed it felt as if she were on another plane. When he thought she would not reply, she met his gaze again.

Expression pensive, she said, "I only know that Fiacre is strong. He has been able to bring me here — as you see me now, not as a babe reborn to this world. Now he has brought you here. Soon, others — people from your realm, as well as this one — will arrive. The pieces are falling into place. How can I not believe him, or at least try to do what he wishes of me, if there is a possibility of success? If I fail, then I will fail trying. This, I think, is all we can do. Try. Believe in him and try."

She sounded like Gwen, the lines of logic all fitting exactly as they should to build a truth she could believe in. He opened his mouth to reply. Instead, he asked what he truly wanted to know. "Are you...related to the woman I knew?"

She met his eyes and shook her head.

"Gwen was not your...grandmother?"

"No."

He ground his teeth at the truth in her tone. Fiacre had not lied. This meant he had to think but couldn't leave her, not yet.

"You look like her. Smell like her," he said. "You sleep like her. You smile like her." He punctuated each sentence with a stab of his finger. "You even sit like her!"

Eyes wide and in an incredulous tone, she asked, "Do people sit differently?"

"Yes!"

She slowly stood, eyes on his as she drew her sword from the scabbard next to her. Holding it perfectly balanced in her hand, she twisted her wrist and circled the blade in a lazy arc.

"Does this look like Gwen?" She flicked her wrist again and held the blade with her left hand as easily, as perfectly as she had with her right, pointing the tip at his throat again. There did seem to be a method to her desire to slice it. "Was she strong enough to wield a sword for hours and fight? Was she brave enough to charge into a field of Faye to save the life of one ungrateful man? Could she have killed to break you free?" Breathless and beautiful, she faced him, her weapon an easy extension of herself. "Tell me," she commanded, her gaze as sharp as her sword. "Could *Gwen* have done these things?"

"A Vampire. You forget that I'm a Vampire, not a man." He turned from her and, to prove it, punched the hearthstones. A crack appeared. Dust billowed down at his feet. Head bent, he tensed his muscles and with a silent snarl fought the urge to leave her behind, along with the truth that he couldn't bear to say aloud.

No. Gwen would never have been strong enough. That wasn't the truth either. Gwen had been strong. Gwen had held it in, hidden it from everyone, even him.

"I didn't forget." Her touch on his arm burned. "You're still a man, Jacob. Vampire or not, you haven't changed."

He turned his head to find her close enough to scent the soap she'd used to wash. Her eyes had always fascinated him. Now her hair, so different from before, caught and held his attention. It was still as golden as summer sunshine. It glimmered on the sides where she'd shaved it closer. The braids must have taken time to bind. The effect made his hands itch to touch the massive mane of twists and ropes that flowed down her back.

"I haven't changed. If you truly look, you will see I am still the same." She whispered the last so softly that even with his Vampire hearing, he barely heard her. Her hand trembled, so unlike the steady grip of her sword. As if she'd hit him in the head he understood, saw more in that moment than he had before. Saw her, for the first time. *It was always her, staring out at me. Hoping I'd see her, and each time...I let her down. She's Gwen. She's more than Gwen.*

He swallowed painfully and sat on the stones of the hearth to clutch at his head to stop the confusion. "You're tearing my guts out, woman. I don't want to hurt you. I don't want to hurt. I can't be a stranger to you. I'll call you Greer, or Gwen or whatever you want. It makes no difference to me, as long as I can know you, see you, be here with you and have you acknowledge that you know me. I don't care how many times you've lived or how many battles you fought or warriors you've killed. Do you think my hands are free of blood?" He lifted them as if he could still see the deaths on his fingers and palms. It wasn't difficult to imagine the stains from his sins. He met her eyes and knew she would always be the only woman he'd ever loved. She deserved the truth.

"I killed when they changed me. I killed Ewan, my captain. *My friend,*" he whispered, unable to stop the words. He was horrified by the confession, all the same. All the centuries since that wild night seemed to evaporate and he was once again covered in his friend's blood, full of his friend's life. He'd vomited until only bile had spewed from his lips, then crawled under a stony outcrop and curled into a ball of misery. He'd stayed there, until finally he'd gotten up and gone in search of his friend's body. Ewan had lain where he must have dropped him, in a fall of leaves, at the bottom of a hill under an ancient oak. Black beetles and other insects had scurried from his corpse when Jacob had lifted him from the ground. He'd ignored them and carried his friend to the border of the Rose Kingdom.

He'd dug him a grave with his bare hands. It hadn't been hard. His strength, even starved, was greater than any mortal's. "I took his life and, like a coward, buried him in the ground without a marker."

Suddenly, she knelt at his feet and took his hands in hers. Her eyes were like diamonds in the moonlight. "Jacob, you can't blame—"

He shook his head and swallowed so he could continue. "I can blame it on the blood need, on the frenzy, but I *killed* him. No one will ever convince me otherwise." He stared into her eyes and saw the anguish there. If what she said was true—and how could it not be?—then she shared his pain. The Black Queen would have forced her to kill and keep on killing each time she lived. She had fought and killed to free him from the Faye. Was that blood on her hands or his? If what Fiacre had said were to be believed, the Faye were also under a spell.

"I won't try to convince you," she whispered. There was acceptance there, but also an opening for more of his confession.

"I gave him a burial. I didn't let the animals"—he choked on a laugh—"other than me, tear him apart. It was important to bury him. I killed him. It was my fault he never returned."

She shook her head. Either at his words or at the tears shimmering in her eyes, he didn't know.

He clasped her hands between his and held on.

"I love you," he managed. His mouth didn't seem to be working properly. The words came out sounding slurred. "Whether you still love me or not, I need to hear. I don't care if you're not Gwen, or if you are. I see you. I see *you*. I always did, always have. I was just too cowardly before to accept it."

She surprised him by pulling her hands free and stroking his face with her fingertips. "There has never been anyone but you in my heart." Then, catching him again by surprise, she leaned closer and, meeting his eyes, closed the distance between them and offered him her lips. He wrapped his arms around her and pulled her closer to his chest. Even though he knew his heart didn't beat to keep him alive, it beat now, for her. Her flavor filled him—fresh, clean, warm and slightly tinted with the sweet wine she must have had with her meal. It didn't matter. He was addicted. The first sweep of his tongue along hers caused him to deepen the kiss for more. He didn't have time to worry over pushing her too fast, too far. She tugged at his hair and pressed his mouth to hers, seeking more as if she were as starved for him, as he was for her. He had her on his lap before he knew he'd lifted her from the floor. She tasted of life, of love, of times long forgotten, but most of all, she tasted of warm, hot woman—of *his* woman.

He broke free to stare at her flushed face and brilliant eyes. "You are the only one I have ever loved."

She touched his lips with her fingers. "There are reasons why we should not take this further, Jacob." His gaze sought hers, but she avoided his eyes. "We will face impossible odds. If we do survive, it will be more than a miracle," she whispered.

"Then there is no time to waste, eh?" His humor sounded flat, but to his surprise, she caught his eyes and slowly smiled, revealing the familiar dimples he'd missed all these years. His heart felt painfully full.

"That might be true," she admitted, causing him to hold her tighter as she traced her finger along his jaw down to chest. She sighed softly and met his eyes again. "I still want us to go slowly."

Was there fear in her voice? He frowned and caught her hand, pressing it to his lips so he could kiss her palm. "We will take all the time we're given. I've waited centuries. A few more days won't matter."

"Days, eh? What if it's months?" Her dimple resurfaced, then she closed the distance between them and kissed him again, softly this time, exploring and tentatively seeking his response.

He wrapped his arms around her, and she reached hers around his neck and plastered her chest to his. Her warmth bled into him. The fullness of her breasts amazed him. The flavor of her lips nearly broke him, but he kissed her with every ounce of love he'd ever felt for her. Gwen, Greer... It didn't matter. The name didn't matter. Only she mattered.

Far too quickly, she pulled away and, with eyes wide but filled with happiness, she stroked his face with her fingertips, making his heart feel like bursting—among other parts of him. If she was startled or worried over his obvious arousal, she didn't show it. She leaned closer and kissed him lightly, feather-light kisses that turned longer and longer, until she let him take over again and love her.

Months? He would give her years, a lifetime. She was all that mattered.

Chapter Fourteen

"There is a change in the air, sister."

Meredith lifted her head from the book she pored over. Her long black hair hung in unwashed tangles over her shoulders and down her back. Karina watched her wave her hand over the enormous book. "There is. We've waited long for this."

"You should have seen it coming, Delilah," Karina added to her younger sister.

Delilah wore the black guise of their oaths. The black paint glistened in the light from the hearth where she tinkered with some herbs. She'd lost her place among the Faye. They had no time for the Silver King's poison cup and corrupt court now, not that she'd been able to recover the loss of his troops. Some of the Faye had begun to question her influence on their king.

"The wind appears fickle, sister. It blows for us. Wait and see." Meredith, their queen, could read much more than the winds. In this, Karina found herself doubting her for the first time in her existence. Their prize warrior walked free, his companions either alive and hiding or still unborn. The former seemed unlikely. Why would Meredith waken him if not to bring the other two to him? Always before, the Dragon's daughter had woken him after years of misery.

Karina wondered if Meredith had realized her power was slipping After centuries, the time had risen again, and yet she had done nothing. Delilah had done worse than nothing. She'd failed.

And was there punishment?

Not even a good strapping.

Delilah's failure to bring Emerald to them should have — at the least — been met with blood and pain. The Scarlet Coven was lost, a memory of the greatest coven to have ever existed. And was there retribution? Were the Jade Coven bitches groveling in the dirt like the dogs they were?

No. They'd fought and, worse, won the battle she and her sisters had orchestrated to bring them all to their knees. The potion had been successful. It had not only changed the magic folk but it had also shifted the dull mortals. If given correctly, both were reduced to nothing more than their servants. Animals, really. Animals with gifts Karina had bred into the potion. They had an opportunity to harness the most powerful immortals and put leashes on their throats. There would be no more need for deception and lies, for working in the shadows.

Such power they could have, and what did her sisters do to earn it? To keep it alive?

Nothing.

For far too long, Meredith had simply watched as they lost their foothold on this and other realms. Her prize pet, the Silver King, had addled her mind — or else corrupting his people and turning him into little more than a lap dog had been her only true desire.

Karina rolled the idea over and over in her mind. Meredith had been slighted by Edric. That was true. Karina had been there when the Faye had denied Meredith's advances and chosen another over her. Was that all that drove her queen, the woman, the sister, who she'd given her loyalty to centuries before? A man? The mere destruction, the total devastation of one man and his kingdom couldn't be all Meredith wanted.

Karina dreamed of millions bowing to her, heads to the ground as she walked by.

She had no tolerance for failure or small-minded goals.

The loss of the Faye who Delilah had taken with her to secure Emerald's capture, let alone the energy spent crafting a trap, should have gotten Delilah crawling on her stomach and begging for mercy from Meredith's temper.

Instead? Meredith had taken Delilah with them to waken their prize. *Poison.* And the two of them had celebrated by fornicating with men. Both had been drunk on witch's brew and filled with the sexual instincts of a bitch in heat.

And where was Poison now? Meredith could no longer sense him — hadn't been able to for some time, possibly from first waking him.

Karina slit the raven she held down on the table from throat to stern. She imagined doing the same to Torque's witch, while he watched. While his bonded lay already gutted on the floor in front of him, she'd have him strapped and sliced for her pleasure. There was no doubt in her mind that Torque and his immortal club of fools had something to do with their loss of

Poison. Who else would dare interfere in what had been theirs for centuries?

The raven cawed loudly then dropped its head onto the wooden surface as its life left it. She squeezed its body and collected the blood in her bowl. "We will lose this battle if we do not test the wizard's strength."

Meredith lifted her head again from her study. The madness in her dark eyes hadn't changed over the centuries. It had deepened to possess her completely. Her soul she'd given to the spells they worshiped. Her inner self, that child who had scavenged and scurried out of the way of the powerful, and who had survived and flourished, gaining strength and respect as she grew, stared back at Karina. The sizzle of power rippled through the room, then settled back on her sister's shoulders. "The wizard Fiacre?"

The name made Delilah pause in her fiddling. She tilted her head, spilling her icy blonde hair down so it touched the hearth stones. The guise was one of Delilah's favorites, outside of her true form. To Karina, Delilah looked like a Faye whore more than a mage of such power that she had once ruled a coven by herself. Of course, she'd done so at the orders of their sister and queen, Meredith.

Many had trembled at the mere rumor of their approach. The Black Queen and her two lieutenants… They were known as 'The Three'. Folk trembled at the mere mention of them. They wore many names, in many languages, among many people. Always they worked to gain their power over the masses. As long as people feared them, names were like guises. They could change as they needed them. Karina had been a witch among the high mountains of the Siren's lands and a Seer among the ancient tribes of men far to the south of Greenway. Her sisters had done the same, each place and each guise crafted to keep the darkness growing through their lies and deceptions. For centuries they'd worked in the shadows, until finally they'd succeeded in piercing the Silver King's heart, and, with him under their thumb, they had set out to destroy the Dragons. From there it had been easy to keep the lands in fear and control the people with them.

Karina longed for more. It was time to step into the light. In the New Realm, they had begun to do just that. The changelings, the deceptions among the Wolf Clan, the lies told to the Vampires to aid them in breaking from their fool king... All of it would be for naught if they lost the Heartland.

Already the Sirens were returning. The Silkies had sent envoys to the New Realm. The Sea Folk would soon rise and join them. The Wolves were grumbling, and more and more of the Vampires were listening to them. Even the Greenway were said to have found hope. If the Dragons woke, the destruction of all they'd built would be complete this time. She could feel it. The wind had indeed changed. If she could not get Meredith to see it, then she would have to force events that would make her queen even less...stable. Reigns changed, after all. Karina couldn't have devised a better opportunity to step up into the position of the power suited to her.

"Do you think he has gained power that I would not be aware of, sister?" Meredith asked in a silky voice that warned Karina to step softly.

She buried her ambitions and sealed the pathways in her mind. "I think he is crafty and should be collared and caged."

"Such bloodthirstiness, Karina." Meredith *tsked* and smiled, revealing the black-stained teeth of their calling. Without their guises, they were hideous. Delilah rarely allowed hers to slip. Even when she rested, she kept her body young and supple. It spoke of weakness.

Meredith let her guise fall whenever she wished, as if the spells were nothing more than clothing that she no longer chose to wear. Karina also slipped in and out of hers with ease, her favorite being a small calico cat and her next, the body of a young, strong warrior woman that she now wore.

"It goes with the image, I suppose," she muttered, just loud enough for Meredith to hear.

As expected, Meredith laughed heartily. Their queen like rough humor, the raunchier the better. From the hearth, Delilah watched her closely. Delilah was no fool, even if she'd failed foolishly.

"Shall we spy on the old man?" Meredith asked. "He is often lax in his guard. Shall we pay him a visit to show him his lines are weak and worthless? I find myself bored of these texts. Shall we have some fun with the mighty Fiacre?"

Delilah brushed off her hands and rose to her feet.

Karina didn't wipe her hands free of the blood. She loved the feel of something's life on her hands — or their last bit of life.

"We can test the garden. Do you think he knows the evil that was done there? In his precious Rose Kingdom?" Meredith's singsong voice was sprinkled with madness and with the cunning and sharpness that had drawn Karina to her so many centuries before. She needed to take care that Meredith never suspected the power she sought.

"I doubt he knows much of anything, my queen." Karina smiled and drew her power from the death around them. The circle of children's bones on her neck sizzled along her skin, reassuring her that there was always power within her grasp.

"Let us play, my queen." Delilah's eyes glowed bright. "It has been far too long."

"It has, hasn't it, sisters?" Meredith cackled again, but the sound filled Karina with hope. The queen had begun to unravel, and the more power she used, the more the madness spread.

Chapter Fifteen

Greer allowed herself to feel Jacob's strength. His body was tight with muscles she wanted to touch and taste. Every dream she'd never allowed herself begged her to take as much as she could from this night, this moment, this time in his arms.

She wanted him until she ached with the unfamiliar feeling, but they hadn't moved toward sharing themselves yet. She was content to feel him, with his arms curled around her while they lay in her bed, watching as the night eased away beyond her open shutters. Being in his arms was like nothing she'd ever experienced before. While Brenyn had Oisin, she'd chosen to live alone. She'd feared growing close and losing someone, but it had always been more than that. After this man, no one would do. She had spoken the truth. Her heart belonged to him.

Jacob's passionate words still burned in her ears, still sliced a painful line deep in her heart. For such a strong man to be reduced to this had broken past her resistance. How could she deny what they both wanted? But could they have it? Could they survive it? *Can I survive if I lose him?* That thought held her back. He'd respected her wishes, even when she had felt how great his desire was for her. She might not have bedded a man but knew the ways of such things. Jacob was a big man—in all ways. But he was a gentle one as well. She had no fear of him or of sharing her body with him. She already shared her heart, but such an intimate, physical experience would take its toll.

"I want you, Jacob. It isn't that," she assured him, touching his jaw with her fingers to assure her that he was still there, even though his body lay tight to hers. She could feel the evidence of his erection, a long, thick bar of hotness pressed to her hip. He didn't try to hide it, but he didn't press her to do anything about it. For her part, she could feel her own heat, a soft, lovely slickness to her body that she'd never experienced before. Just the press of his thigh, tight to her womanhood, gave her pleasure.

"I know. There's no need to explain. I understand."

She kissed his jaw and snuggled closer.

He bent his head to capture a kiss when she tipped her head upward. His stomach tightened under her hand as she stroked it. After releasing her lips, he met her eyes.

"We will have years ahead, eh? My only fear is that I'm too cowardly to let you out of my sight." He stroked her braids—his eyes on her hair, then on her face, her eyes, then back to her hair again.

Such words made her throat feel tight and tears burn her eyes. She dipped her head, kissing his throat to get herself under control, then lifted to meet his gaze. She wanted to imprint every sensation, every glimpse of him, for a time when she might not have him.

"You were many things, but never a coward." She laughed, but it came out choked with the tears she struggled to keep from falling. "Only when it came to cliff jumping with me."

He grimaced and brushed his palm against the hair she'd shaved short from her temple so that her helm would sit tight to the sides of her head, then surprised her by tumbling her to her back and resting against her. That tantalizing erection of his felt branded to her. He moved his hand to her waist, making her body sizzle to life. "I was. I saw how fearless you were, and I worried you'd be harmed. I was relieved when you stopped your adventures."

It was her turn to wince. There was more between them than her hiding that she'd been more than Gwen. The past didn't hurt as much as it had before, though. Perhaps talking about it helped. Their adventures had usually been her doing what she wanted, whether diving from the clifftops or climbing the highest trees to see the baby eagles. A princess didn't do such things. She'd tried so hard to be a princess.

"I know." She sighed. "I tried to hide, just as you tried to be something you didn't need to be — a warrior, with all the dreams only the young believe are possible."

"Valor." His brow wrinkled at her nod. "What are you saying? That I shouldn't have tried to be worthy of you?"

She shifted her head to stare at him better. "Do you think killing people makes you worthy?"

He winced again then surprised her by smiling. "It makes no sense now, centuries later. Back then I was young. I was in love with a princess. It was the only way to win you."

She stiffened. "I wasn't a prize."

"No." He turned serious. "I was a foolish young man. Can you forgive me?"

There was pain there, in that memory. He'd walked away from her. He'd left her, even knowing she'd been unhappy with more than him leaving for the border. At his words, the pain eased and slowly faded.

"You hurt me." She met his eyes and held them. He tightened his grip on her hip. "I had you—then I didn't."

He didn't back away from the accusation in her tone. His eyes were the same, filled with intelligence and such love that it was without end.

"Then the attacks happened. I wasn't there…here." He gestured to the room.

She had never been in this wing of the castle. This room had most likely belonged to a servant or a warrior. The royal family rooms were off limits. She couldn't go there for fear of being drowned in memories. Her father, her mother, her rowdy brothers… All of them were gone now, just like Kelli and… She saw an image of her da, that last day, just before she'd taken the Black Queen's oath, and it threatened to fill her with sorrow. She wouldn't let it. Not now, not when she had Jacob back.

"The kingdom is different. Until I walked under the Rose Gate, I didn't believe it possible. The changes are difficult to accept, but with time it comes," he noted.

Relieved that he didn't want to discuss the fall of the Rose Kingdom, she found she was eager to speak.

"The centuries have been harsh to the land. The seas have caused most of the damage. The beach we knew is no more. There is a path down the cliff, though, but nothing like what we used. There is no more sand on the beach. There are smooth stones, though. The rivers have changed, too. Where we once rode through the wood, along the small stream" — she glanced at him to see him still watching her with interest — "there is a river so wide it's hard to see the distant shore. The two villages grew on its banks. Those places were never here before," she said, thinking of the small cottagers they'd known. There had been a child who would see them riding by and run out, smiling and trailing along with them. They'd often stopped for water and entertained the children with stories of the king. "The cottagers are gone and the fishermen's families moved away — or perhaps moved inland to take up a new craft."

"You know a lot about the area."

"I patrol often. Fiacre wanted me to ensure the villagers were safe. I also fetch supplies."

"Is that safe? If the Black Queen is after you, shouldn't you stay here hidden, not off collecting potatoes?"

"We grow our own potatoes." She smiled when he grunted. He trailed his hand over her stomach, then on to her side and up almost to the swells of her breasts. It was hard to concentrate on what they were discussing. "It's safe. Fiacre keeps me hidden. Besides, Brenyn loves to go to the village markets. She always hums for days afterward while she cooks."

Jacob shoved his hair off his forehead The gesture was familiar enough to make her heart do odd things. His shirt was unlaced, so she could see the strong muscles of his neck and throat. She hadn't seen him without a shirt since they had been children.

"Is she...the housekeeper?"

Greer laughed, caught off guard by the question and the way he asked. He bent his head and kissed her, stopping her laughter instantly as heat suffused them. His mouth was hard to release. She ached for more but held back, enjoying the hot taste of him. He pulled away only to stun her with kisses along her jaw, then neck, before he swept kisses along her collar bone and back up to a spot behind her ear. Her body grew so restless that she stroked her hands up his back, under his shirt, and felt his solid smooth muscles.

He chuckled and lifted his flushed face. "I'm trying to behave, here. Talk to me. Why is my question funny?"

She blinked, trying to ease the arousal from clouding her thinking. *Brenyn.* He'd asked about Brenyn.

"She's like me, a reborn. This time Fiacre found her and brought her here. She always fights the memories." She paused and considered what to say. Jacob took her hand in his and brought it to his warm lips. She forgot about everything but him. She wanted him to touch her, to keep on kissing her, but she also simply wanted him. Here. Always.

"Why would that mage bring you back then here?" Jacob winced. "You died here."

That mage. No one would doubt his mistrust of magic. No doubt he had reasons, but with Fiacre, there was no reason not to trust in him and many reasons to believe. "Fiacre called me back, Jacob. He convinced me to return. I must believe he sees a path that will lead us out of this. I've died here, it's true," she said and held up a hand to stop his immediate grumbling. "I've died in the snow, the rain, the mountains and deserts, in fields of flowers, in fields of mud, under fallen horses—"

"Right. Got it." He turned to his back and placed his arm behind his head. "I haven't died. Only once have I gotten close. It's not as easy to kill a Vampire."

"Good."

He turned his head to gaze at her. She lifted on an elbow to stare down at him. The sight of him swelled her heart. He was so handsome. He always had been. The girls of the keep had sought his eye often enough. She'd often worried about them, until she'd realized that no matter how many times they tried to gain his attention, his gaze always sought hers. Now, in her bed, with words said between them that both warmed her heart and terrified her, he made her feel jittery, fearful, unsure and happy all bundled together. The fear tried to eclipse everything else, but she didn't allow it. Fiacre had to believe they could survive. She clung to that with all her might.

"You need to be strong. *We* need to be strong." She took his hand. It was rough with callouses along his long fingers and broad palm. It was reassuring to feel the potential strength. "They will come soon. I can feel it. They are powerful and devious. Cunning. The bond I gave will hold. We must find a way to defeat them before that happens." Panic felt as if it were cutting off her air. Her heartbeat pulsed wild and heavy. *If Fiacre is wrong…*

"We won't let that happen." Jacob pulled her closer, so she was now half on top of him. Where they touched, he seemed to warm. A shiver tingled along her skin. It was easy to imagine all of him touching all of her. Faced with Jacob, the love she had always felt for him since first meeting the young boy filled her to overflowing. She wanted to take in the texture of his hair, to touch his jaw and know what the bristle felt like against her body, to know all his weight pressing her down... "We're strong. Trust in me the way you trust the mage."

She blinked to refocus her mind. His brow was arrowed downward, his eyes dark with worry. How could he worry over such a thing? "I trust you."

"Fiacre must have a plan he believes will work," Jacob said in a soothing tone as he stroked his hand down her back and up to her shoulders. "We don't let them know you're...here. 'Aware', whatever, 'awake'. *Here*, whatever the plan is."

She worried her lip, seeing all the flaws in Fiacre's plan. Jacob must have as well, because his frown had deepened. "No plan is sure," she warned.

He laughed and shook them both with his merriment. "No. No plan ever is. This one sounds insane."

"It's not. Fiacre knows what he does." She rested her arms on Jacob's broad chest. "He convinced me." She tapped his nose to make him blink. "If we try his plan, he believes it will end the curse, and more than merely that—"

He captured her hand and kissed her fingers. "Free the Silver King, break the Lykae free and stop all the evil in the seven realms."

He meant it as a joke, but she cupped her hand against his face. "It might. Who is to say that evil is stronger than good? I didn't choose to be a warrior of death. They did. There must be a way to stop them. I can't believe that in all the realms evil like this is stronger than good."

He placed his hand over hers, keeping it on his face, but didn't respond, which was just as well. She needed to make him understand what they were fighting and what would happen if they failed. And if the queen got hold of her, she wasn't going to kill for them again...not this time. There had to be a way for her to resist them. Suddenly time seemed too short. Each second, each breath she drew, each moment with him, was a gift. If they found her, they would call her, and she would come. And when she did, she would disappear and the warrior who obeyed their demands would remain. If Fiacre could stop that, he would have said. He would have reassured her that he had a way to stop them — and he hadn't.

"Jacob, you have to watch me closely. If they manage to take me, or worse, control me from a distance even, you need to watch for any kind of change—"

"Slow down. Take a breath. Easy," he murmured.

"I know what you think. You think nothing bad will happen. But you and I know that is not true. Something bad could very well happen. If they find me, if they control me and I can't say anything, I will kill you...all of you. You can't let that happen."

His expression was thoughtful as he pulled her hand back down to his lips. "I'll simply tie you up and throw you in a cell. It worked for me. A few drugs and" —he kissed her fingertips, then continued —"once we kill the witch, we'll let you out."

She realized that the warm glow in her chest had grown to fill her. "Are you making a joke?"

His grin was slow. It filled his eyes, eliminating the pain. He tipped her to her back again with a swift move. The size of his arousal against her hip hadn't dimmed. Neither had the heat of her own. "It's an idea."

Not letting him know she wanted to smile, she shook her head and reminded him of the danger. "It's a terrible idea. I... I'm strong, stronger when they control me. I won't be alone either."

He surprised her by brushing a kiss along her jaw, then lower and lower, nearing the swells of her breasts. She held her breath. "Do you mind? I can't help myself."

She couldn't help the laugh that escaped. It spilled free as if there had never been a time when she didn't laugh.

"What?" He scanned her face.

Instead of answering, she pulled his head to hers and kissed him. At the same time, she turned on her side to curl as tight to him as she could — except where she caressed her hand down to explore the contours of his hard erection.

He groaned heavily and turned her to her back. She almost protested, but he suddenly had his mouth on her nipple. A burst of pleasure soared up her spine and made her moan. She almost didn't catch his hand sliding over her stomach to cup her possessively.

She moaned louder, a sound that she had no control over and had never made before, but she couldn't stop it — not with the heat of him all around her and his hand bearing down on her so perfectly. He pressed his fingers to a spot and she arched her hips, seeking more. Under her palm, his erection hardened even further.

"I have to taste you." He shoved her blouse upward and his mouth was suddenly on her bare chest, leaving hot, wet trails of pleasure behind as she tugged at his belt. He groaned and, with a frantic look at her that seemed to reassure him, he brushed her hand with his knuckles as he released his breeches. Suddenly, she had his arousal in her hand. It was so velvety smooth, yet so hard and hot that she lost herself in the feel of him.

"Easy... Don't be afraid," he whispered, slipping his warm hand along her stomach.

"Never. Don't stop. Oh, Jacob, don't stop."

"Just this, just this. We'll wait for more," he said in a voice deep and rough with passion. The thought made her lightheaded and at the same time grounded.

At that moment she didn't care about anything as long as the need for him, for this, was satisfied.

She took his mouth in a passionate kiss, and with his hand over hers, began to stroke him. He groaned into her throat and, after a few long passes under his guidance, he released her hand. As soon as she did, he tore her breeches open and began stroking her skin so that the tight need that had been building suddenly rushed her with such desire she could barely think, let alone explore the curves of his muscles. He slipped a finger inside her and rotated his palm. The result was so sudden and so wonderful that she gasped for breath and broke their kiss. Pleasure tumbled through her, spinning her up and away. In the grip of ecstasy, she heard him groan and his thick penis jerked in her hand. He clasped his hand over hers and, within a few tighter strokes, warmth spilled out from him in time with low moans.

Her own excitement grew and another burst of pleasure caught her in its grip. She panted through it and when she could think again, Jacob was there, gently kissing her cheeks and neck. She didn't want to let him go ever again. Their lips met and his kiss broke a barrier inside her that she never wanted there again. When he broke the kiss to place warm caresses of his lips on her face, she sighed and ran her fingers through his hair. She still held him in her other hand, but his flesh did not possess the steely hardness from before he had succumbed to pleasure.

He pulled up and rested on one elbow. His eyes were warm with passion and his face still hectic with color.

She soaked it in, him, the sensations still tingling through her, and most of all, him being there, with her. *If I never have a lifetime of this, then I will still always have this moment.*

"Don't," he whispered and brushed a kiss to her cheek.

"Don't?" But she knew. Jacob had always been able to read her. She felt a chill settle along her skin, as if he were already gone.

He brushed his knuckles over her cheek, then pulled her close so he could press kisses over her collarbones. The caresses were so light that they tickled. They both laughed when she tried to find spots that used to make him squirm. He practically leaped from the bed when she found one, then he tackled her backward, making her laugh so hard that it was as if her muscles had turned to water.

"Careful, you. I know your weaknesses, too." He attempted a serious face, but his grin broke through and spoiled it.

Content, she watched him pull off his shirt and use it to clean her hand. He had no inhibitions about being half-naked, not that he should have. His now much smaller manhood lay in a bed of dark curls, but with swift motions, he cleaned himself then tossed the shirt to the floor. With the same economy, he laced his trousers then pulled her closer so they were both on their sides, facing each other, arms and legs intertwined. "Don't think this is the only time we have," he warned. "I plan on wooing you properly."

"I thought you'd done that already." She touched his hair, brushing it back from his forehead, and let the memories of doing the same rise to the surface. He'd always been so intent on doing whatever he'd been doing that he'd not given a thought to his hair. She loved it, though, how dark it was and how silky soft. It'd curled when he'd let it grow. He had never cared about it. It had only occurred to him when it was in his way. Once he'd let it grow so long that he'd been able to pull it back into a knot. She'd been sad when he'd shown up with it cut short again. To wear under his helm, he'd explained.

He lifted an eyebrow and considered her. "I tried, but I knew I needed more, even if you didn't believe it. No." He kissed her stomach then pulled her blouse down. "I mean to take our time. I want you ready."

With that he settled back down on his side and sighed.

She thought she had been ready, obviously so, if she had climaxed so quickly, but kept her thoughts to herself. If he had more wooing to do and it ended in more pleasure, she would not discourage him. *Perhaps not tonight, though.* She yawned and got a smile from him when she did so. The moon had set, and the first blush of dawn filtered through her open shutters.

"Will you sleep now?"

"No. I need little sleep," he said after a moment of simply lying beside her. The look on his face made her face feel warm.

"I have to go on patrol soon," she said.

"Really?" He ran a hand through his hair and gave her a grin. "I'll go with you."

"But…" She glanced out the window at the blush on the horizon.

He stiffened. With a suddenly serious expression, he said, "I can stay awake in the day. I'm ancient, remember?"

"On the battlefield… You knew then, when the clouds came in."

Abruptly, he sat and rubbed his hands over his face. There were scars on his body, long slices done by a sword or knife. Sighing, he dropped his hands. "Let's go then, shall we?"

The abrupt change in his behavior sent a stab of cold down her spine. Reaching out, she touched his arm. "What's wrong?"

He rose from the bed and her mind went a little blank at the sight of his bare back. All those muscles, all the lines and all the…skin—naked skin of a man she wanted back in bed with her.

"I'm wondering about a few things. That's all. Let's go on this patrol."

She got up and tried not to feel hurt by his sudden coldness. She found her boots, put them on, then comforted herself in gearing up. If he regretted the passion they'd shared, she would be better off. They would be better off. She knew this, and yet she glanced over at him and wanted to have him pull her close again.

As soon as she gathered her sword and sword belt, he said, "Ready?"

Instead of responding, she simply nodded. *If this is all we have, I will be content with it. I will carry it with me for as long as I have.*

* * * *

Jacob shifted in his saddle. A coldness had settled between him and Greer. She rode next to him but she didn't speak, and when he tried to break the silence, her responses were one or two words at the most.

He knew why.

He'd held her in his arms and forgotten the changes that made having her, truly having her as his, impossible. *Am I that person who wishes for something then isn't satisfied when I get it?*

The cloudy day made it possible for him to ride with her. If there'd been an attack and the sun had shone down on the field, he'd have been unable to aid her. Or he would have done all he could and died trying. He was ancient, but the sun would forever be between them.

I'm a Vampire, and no matter what she is – Gwen or Greer – she's still beyond my reach.

A gust of wind blew hard and cold from the north. The scent of snow built on the air. At the least something would soon be upon them. By the look of the storm clouds staying low and heavy from the north, he bet on rain, maybe even snow

They'd been out on horseback for well over an hour. He sensed no one near, and other than the villages far up the river, there was no sign of much more than a squirrel or a few fleeting birds in the ancient trees. To their south and west, he sensed a pack of wolves, but not the kind he hoped for. Not Lykae. "Where did Alrick go? I remember him giving me attitude."

She glanced over and some of the chill left her features. "He went in search of his mate. He will be here soon. Fiacre made it clear that we will need him if we hope to convince the wolves to join us."

"Alrick's found his mate." He struggled with the idea. "I'm not sure what to think of that. He's been alone for...ages."

They navigated up a ravine. Greer rode like a warrior — light, easy in the saddle, with complete control of her gray mare. Why wouldn't she? She'd always been good with horses.

"Perhaps that's why he didn't continue with us to the keep," she said when they reached the top.

"Perhaps." He dropped his gaze to her right palm, where he could just see the white lines of a brand. He moved his gelding closer and touched her hand. She glanced sharply at him. *Does the contact feel as good to her? Or is the chill of my skin shocking?* "They gave you this?"

She pulled her hand away and fisted it. "Yes."

He considered what else to say. She'd not asked who he meant, but then, she knew. She knew a great deal that he wanted to know. "What does it mean?"

He thought she wouldn't answer, but kept his peace, waiting in case she simply needed time. They'd known each other inside and out and still he'd misjudged her once before. He'd been fooled into thinking she wanted to be a princess, but the truth was that she'd never sought such confinement. She'd only ever wanted him — a simple man. That was the problem. He wasn't a simple man.

After several minutes of riding, they reached an open meadow cut through by a branch of the river that would eventually become a smaller stream. They walked their horses across the shallow water and up the grassy turf on the far side. Greer stopped and allowed her mare to drink. He did the same.

She didn't glance over at him, but said, "It binds me to…her. It is part of the oath."

"Hmm-m." He knew of such bindings. A burn like that was magical. What would happen if it were removed? Would she be free of their control? Fiacre would know. He watched the way her jaw flexed. She held herself in check, keeping the pain that simmered at bay.

"What is Fiacre's real game?"

"Game?" She frowned over at him. He'd surprised her with the change in topics. *Does she think I want her to relive the events that brought her such pain?*

"He wants me to bring the Vampires to our side, correct?"

"Yes."

He laughed. "That simple, eh? This means we need to travel there. I won't leave you behind."

The comment brought another frown, but she glanced away, studying the terrain instead of him. Her profile was beautiful. Even under the cloudy skies her hair shimmered golden. He could remember the feel of it under his palm and fisted his hand to keep from reaching out to her.

"And what will you be, my traveling snack?" he asked.

She grimaced but didn't turn back to him. "The Vampires are slowly becoming surrounded. Their lands are dying. Their source of blood is dwindling. They must travel farther and farther for what they need. The wolves help, but even they become restless."

"How do you know this?" he asked

"Fiacre has spies everywhere," she replied.

Jacob lifted his eyebrows. 'Everywhere' was a bit much.

"He has sought the best time for this, Jacob. He woke me." She swallowed and turned to face the other side of the brook again. Even dressed in the hardened leather and dark colors, her skin glowed beautifully. No one would ever think of her as anything other than a woman, even in her gear. The delicate lines of her neck drew his eyes. His fangs tingled, but not from thirst. While kissing her he'd not once thought of blood. But he did want to sink his teeth into her and taste her as elementally as he could. "He found you," she said, breaking through his lustful thoughts, "and located Brenyn. He has spies within the Vampires."

"Brenyn. She has a part in this — and here I thought she simply brings me my meals." He meant it as a joke but didn't get a smile from Greer. She grimaced. He knew Brenyn was more. There was something about the slim, quiet woman who spoke to him. It was almost as if he'd known her before — or not known her but sensed more to her than what simply appeared, perhaps even more than she knew.

"Brenyn is much more than a girl that 'brings you your meals'. She is…" She hesitated then finally faced him. There was something in her gaze that made his senses alert. Pain, he realized.

It's not enough that I doubt her wanting me. I have hurt her, too.

"She has always been with me. Every time I awaken, Brenyn is there, along with another. We have many names and none of them good. We bring fear and leave behind slaughter." He tightened his hand on his reins at the unshed tears in her eyes. "Most know us as the Hawk, the Flame and the Sword."

He moved his horse closer and took her hand. It was cold. Her fist remained tight until he took it and kissed it. "Forgive me. I didn't mean to cause you pain. I'm a fool."

She laughed, but it was a broken one.

"Don't. You don't need to talk about this —"

"I don't?" She laughed again. "Do you think that makes me any less than what I am? I am the Hawk. Brenyn is the Flame. Her bonded is the Sword. You know these names. You know what I've done. You know what we've all done. We're monsters."

Jacob winced. *How have I been so wrong?* "Those are names from legends meant to keep children in their beds." Jacob intertwined their fingers. "As are the stories of Vampires."

She exhaled and one tear slipped from her control. "We are much the same, are we not?"

"We are nothing alike. I've not suffered like you. I —"

"You have. We both have. Is that why you close me off?" she demanded. "Don't you regret sharing a path we can't continue down? I'll be called. I'll be forced to serve her or I'll die on a battlefield. Who would choose that?"

"What are you talking about?" He tried to grab her hand again but she avoided him. "You're not going to die and you're sure as hell not going back to her!"

"You can't say that. I understand, Jacob." She shook her head, either at him or the tears trying to break free. "It's for the best. We both have —" A shrill cry interrupted her and from the trees birds broke from the trees, winging off to leave.

He sensed something on his left — warriors. "Hold. There are a dozen coming toward us."

"I sense them." She didn't draw her sword or buckle on her shield. Calmly, she got herself under control, far easier than he did, and focused on the forest.

"Who are they?"

As he asked, the first of them broke from the trees. He circled his mount to keep them in sight, but none drew their weapons. They wore rough leathers but were clean enough, with traces of blue swirls on their bare forearms and cheeks. One, the blond-headed leader, had blue smeared on his forehead and a talisman of intertwined knots of blue stone around his neck. His broadsword was enormous, and he wore a bow crossway over his chest. A full quiver of long arrows attached to his saddle.

"My lady," he shouted, raising his hand and halting his men. They spread out, relaxing in a loose band, some getting water while others simply stared from him to Greer.

"Arne, what news do you have?" Greer called.

The warrior, Arne, motioned to Jacob. "Who is your Vampire friend?"

The men grinned as if he'd made a joke. One spat without taking his eyes off Jacob. There was no love of Vampires here, but neither was there any real animosity. He didn't have a quiver of arrows in his chest, after all.

"The name's Jacob. And you are?"

"Jacob." Arne sounded the word out, like he was practicing, but didn't give his name. Instead he tilted his head and examined Jacob as if he were sizing him up for a suit. "You are the warrior Alrick spoke of. He sends his regards and a warning. The Faye are on the march."

Greer frowned from Arne to the horizon, where the tallest of the three towers could just be seen through the trees. The storm clouds over the keep had turned dark blue, almost black. There would be a storm, either snow or rain, but it had yet to be decided. He bet on either, and soon. Nothing was worse than a battle in a muddy rainstorm.

"Is this good news or bad?" he asked.

"It's not good," Arne said. He shrugged. "There is a rider with them. Not Faye. She wears the clothing of the Greenway spies, but…"

"But?" Greer asked, frowning deeper now.

Arne squinted at the storm before finally offering, "We have some doubts over her truly being one."

Jacob could have used more substance. If someone wanted to talk, they should say something.

Greer didn't seem to mind. She simply asked the essential question, "When will they be here?"

"A week, possibly less, possibly longer."

Jacob ground his teeth. If this was an example of the spies Fiacre had in his pocket, Jacob worried for the whole mission.

"That storm is growing. It comes all the way through the Twins — snow in the pass and rain down below. It will make traveling difficult." Arne shifted in his saddle and winced.

Maybe he has saddle sores. Jacob tried to rein in his impatience. Did the man have anything to report?

"Edric may ride behind it, but if he keeps on, he'll be in the Dark Wood within the week."

A week to the Dark Wood. That was only a few days' ride for an army. That meant they had less than two weeks, possibly even only a week to prepare for a possible confrontation with the entire Faye nation.

"What news do you have of the Silkies?" Greer asked. She seemed calm. Her color was even, her eyes bright, and there was no hint of worry in her body language or tone.

"None. All is silent from them. Only the Siren and her Spartan send word that reinforcements will arrive. In time, you want to know? I'm not certain."

"Where is Alrick?" Jacob asked when the man walked over and bent to fill his waterskin.

Arne shrugged. "He was headed for the Faye. It seems he thinks his mate is with them."

"His mate is a Faye?" Jacob asked.

Arne laughed. "No. He thinks the woman that rides with them is his."

"A Greenway spy?" Jacob couldn't imagine. Alrick was a man with a high opinion of himself. Rightly so, perhaps, but a spy...? How would Alrick handle having someone like that as his? Jacob supposed he'd be so overjoyed to find her that he wouldn't care if she was a belly dancer for the Playboy Bunny Mansion. Maybe. Hopefully. Alrick was tough, but he could admit mistakes, and he'd stayed here, looking for her. That had to be a good sign. Jacob would have to hope for the best. Alrick deserved happiness.

"We doubt she's a spy." Arne motioned to a man with red hair and only a few blue swirls at his temples.

"She wears the gear, but she borrowed the clothing from the spy guild. They wouldn't say who she was, only that she was given whatever she wanted by their master."

Jacob wondered. If she wasn't a spy, she must be a witch. *Alrick and a witch.* That might actually be worse. Alrick was notorious for not trusting magic. Could a bond trump such a deep-seated belief? Love could, but was the bond wolves felt as strong? Derrick loved Samantha, but Derrick had never had the hatred of witches — and Vampires, for that matter — that Alrick possessed.

"Fiacre will know. We should return to the keep. Will you stay with us?" Greer asked.

Jacob tried to stay focused.

"No. Fiacre will need news of the Lykae. Without Alrick, we will go to see what can be done. Look for us within the week. We would very much like one of Brenyn's meals."

"I will tell her." Greer turned her mare and started off.

"One more thing," Jacob said. "Do you know a witch named Aubrey?"

The men were in the act of leaving. At his question, they froze. All attention turned to him. It was clear they did, and even clearer that he'd asked something important to them. Instead of Arne speaking, a man who'd held back under the shadows of the trees walked toward him. Behind Jacob, Greer had stopped. The man walking toward him could have been Aubrey's twin — same clear gray eyes that flashed blue, same dark hair, and while he had a strong jawline and chin, the angles of the face were too close for them not to be at the very least related.

"Aubrey Mac Cinaed."

"I believe so. We've never exchanged surnames, but she's a smallish witch with long dark hair. And when she uses her magic, there are tattoos like the ones you wear revealed in her flesh." No one spoke, but there was a lot going on in the group. "She was captured and taken to this land. Since freed, but she...comes from here, eh?"

A sudden slash of lightning followed close by thunder that was so loud his ears rang caused his horse to rear. He battled it back, turning it this way and that to stop it from racing off. By the time he had it settled down, Fiacre stood with the men and Greer watched him with a look of concern.

"Fiacre will talk with them. We should go," she said, turning her mount to the keep, and entered the wood.

Jacob gave the men and Fiacre his attention, but they were deep in conversation. Whatever they discussed, he wasn't welcome. The dark-haired warrior glanced at him then focused back on Fiacre. It didn't matter if Aubrey had come from this land, not really. He followed Greer, catching up to her quickly.

"Why did you ask them about Aubrey?"

He shrugged. "It seemed important at the time. There are a lot of loose ends being drawn together."

"What do you mean, loose ends?"

"You and me. Aubrey and her capture. Alrick and his mate. Fiacre and this upcoming battle. It seems like a lot. Brenyn..." Regardless of what Greer had told him, he considered the girl who brought him his meals. She didn't seem to fit in this story. A battlefield was no place for her. "Brenyn... She's such an...innocent. Why do you fear her remembering?"

Greer blinked a few times, clearly not following his jump from topic to topic. "I'm not certain what I fear. I only know that she will soon recover her memories. I struggled this time, not wanting to feel them." She faced him fully for the first time since he'd held her in his arms. "She is never easy with our rebirths. She will need Oisin. He aids her in ways she needs."

She broke away from Jacob's gaze and studied her hands.

"She seems a very innocent soul," he finally said. "There are legends, even in my new lands, of the names you spoke of, but what do they force you to do?"

"Kill. Kill until the lands are drenched in blood, until every kingdom is under their rule, until Brenyn bursts into flames, Oisin drives a sword into his own heart and I fall under a sea of swords."

He tipped her head up with a finger under her chin. Their eyes met and he saw the fear she held at bay. It pierced his heart.

"That is what we are fighting to avoid, Jacob. If we can't stop them, I will destroy everyone you have ever called a companion. Their power flows through me and I am unstoppable. Believe me when I say that the legends you have heard are true. The three of us led legions of warriors, and under our guidance, nations fell." She stopped for a breath then continued before he could speak. "I can sense them coming closer. I can feel it. We don't have much time before they notice that I have not only been born but have been brought back as I am now. I'm amazed they haven't noticed that my birth has not occurred. Fiacre might be to blame for that."

"What do you mean?"

She lifted a shoulder. "Brenyn is here. Oisin has broken free from them. I would have been born years ago. They must know."

"But they haven't sought you out?"

"I only know he has hidden me before…"

"Ah, yes. Well, he needs to continue doing so." He didn't want to ask he what she thought of him, but suddenly, after her revealing so much, he had to.

She spoke before he could ask what she thought of him being a Vampire. "I have forgotten what it's like to talk at such length. If we are to be successful with this campaign, especially with the Vampires, I will have to try harder to be around other people."

"Ah, yes. The Vampires." He felt the urge to expose it all, to reveal the weakness she wasn't seeing—the flaw in their renewed love.

"What?" She studied him with a slight frown marring her smooth skin. "What is it?"

"Why are you so easy with me being…a Vampire?" The words came out forced, as if he'd had to drag them from his very lungs. Now she would realize what he meant, what he was and what they could never have.

She met his gaze and suddenly started laughing. It burst from her so hard that she seemed to need to support herself with a hand on his chest. Her mare stood still, no doubt as stunned as he felt.

"Is it that funny?" he asked.

"No, no." She said it but couldn't stop her laughter. "Jacob, I'm sorry…sorry."

"Sorry for laughing? Don't be." If this is what she thought of his question, of him—

She suddenly sobered and took his face in her hands, shocking him with her closeness. "Of all the things to worry over, why worry over being strong enough to survive? To be strong enough to fight beside me. For me"—she moved her hand to his chest—"your heart beats."

He couldn't lie to her, couldn't make her believe he was anything other than what he was—the real monster. "I make it beat. I did from the start."

"I don't care. I only care that maybe, just maybe, we have a chance to live, that I have a chance to know what it's like to be loved."

"A chance?" He took her hands and lifted them to his lips, kissing her fingertips. His vision of her blurred but he refused to allow himself to blink for fear of losing her. She was warm to his touch, her face no longer cold but filled with worry — that he didn't love her. "I love you. I love you so completely that I want to shift you from this place and hide you away like a princess in a tower." He covered her hand with his. "But you have to realize that I am a Vampire now — a strong one, true, but with the limits that my new life has burdened me with. If the battle is in full daylight —"

"Then we will make it cloudy. Jacob" — she drew her horse even closer until their legs were pressed knee to knee — "is that why you shut me out?"

"I didn't... I..." How could he explain?

Her gaze remained intense and in it he saw love, love and a knowledge that humbled him. She knew what they risked, loving each other, and she still wanted him. "I love you, Jacob. I want you for mine. Now. Tonight," she whispered. "For as long as we have. I don't care if you are a Vampire or a soulless zombie. You're mine. If you —"

He kissed her until they were both breathless.

"I want you to be mine, for now, for always." It was an oath he meant to keep.

Chapter Sixteen

Brenyn startled awake. At first, nothing penetrated the pitch darkness, not even the embers from her hearth. Then Morning, the pregnant mare, nudged her. She'd fallen asleep in the stables. Morning stood with her head down, still enormously pregnant.

A soft snort was the only acknowledgment Brenyn got for being there.

Whatever sound had wakened Brenyn was gone now. She stretched and her neck protested. After a night sleeping upright, it made sense. One spot hurt more than the rest until she massaged it lightly. As if jealous, the mare nudged her almost off balance. Brenyn laughed and barely caught herself from falling over. She gave the mare a fond rub on her velvety nose.

"You poor thing. Soon you will not be so tired — or maybe you will. A small babe to take care of might make you wish you hadn't gotten loose and let that stallion near you."

The mare snorted.

Outside it was very dark. Brenyn tried to gauge how long she'd slept. There was no moonlight tonight. No starlight. The stable was dark as pitch. She guessed it was far into the night.

"Well, it must be late if I'm this stiff." She rose to her feet and brushed the hay and barn dust from her gown.

A sense of unease lingered, nagging at her like a hangnail. Greer's behavior worried her. Her friend had been distressed since returning with Fiacre and Jacob. The signs were small, but there. She guessed it had to do with Jacob, and worse, Fiacre. The sense that Fiacre wanted more from Greer than she could give filled Brenyn with dread. Greer had been called to aid them. She knew that until they'd left to find Jacob, that fact had remained distant, as if there were a storm brewing on the horizon.

Now Brenyn sensed the storm coming closer—or worse, that it had arrived and hovered over them.

Attempting not to think about it, she concentrated instead on seeing better. Slowly, her eyes adjusted to the dark enough for her to make out shapes. She didn't leave the stable, though. Instead, she listened to the night sounds that were so familiar to her.

The dream had come to her again.

Just like the others before, it had felt real. She shivered a little, reminded of the cold, icy wind in her dream. She'd been naked, barefoot, walking through snow that burned her feet because it was so cold. None of that had mattered. She'd known she had to keep walking. There was a man trapped in ice. He had needed her. He was a warrior. He needed her fire. She'd known that soon the cold would disappear under the beautiful heat of flames.

204

She gripped her head with both hands to stop the scattered images. Such things were dreams, nothing more. The sense of urgency remained. *He's trapped.* As quickly as the thought surfaced, another followed like an echo. *Not any longer... He's free.*

It was true. She tried to sense him but felt no connection. *Did I sweep the courtyard yesterday or is that the dream and this real?*

More anxious now, she turned her attention to the mare and stroked her nose, trying to block the panic that was building. The poor thing was enormous. Her sides were swollen and her stomach hung, tight as a drum. Her time had to be soon. With a nudge, the mare let her pass, so she could open and close the stall door. There was much to do. She shouldn't have slept. The keep would be dark. It was her job to light the torches along the passages they used. Since she was the only one to walk the corridors, she didn't worry too much.

Greer would be in her chambers. Jacob would be in his. Fiacre would be in his tower. She should go up to him now and explain everything — the dreams, the woman in the woods, everything. *He will know what is dream and what is not.* She felt better for the decision. Butterflies whirled in her stomach, but they weren't unpleasant. They gave her strength. *He is my strength.*

The thought didn't cause her to panic again. It soothed her enough to leave the mare and barn behind. Minutes later she slowed, suddenly realizing that instead of taking the small hall to the tower courtyard then the steps up to Fiacre's tower as she had done hundreds of times before, she'd walked to the small garden, deep within the unused sections she'd yet to clean properly.

A shiver rushed her skin. She'd been here before...many times.

It was an unspoken agreement between her and Fiacre that she should never venture into the oldest sections of the palace. And yet, it was next to the statues of warriors long since gone from this world that she sometimes found herself when she wandered the keep.

For some reason, when she was here, sitting on the edge of the silent, broken fountain, that she could think. The long-dead trees and weeds overflowing flowerbeds surrounded by broken statues didn't interrupt her thoughts with questions. They didn't create more questions from their answers than she'd had before she'd asked her own questions. No, the garden stood silent, but it was a listening silence that seemed to help her settle her fears whenever she stepped within the faded walls.

Tonight, she needed to think — not about the dream or the mysterious woman in the woods or about her warrior promising to come to her then disappearing from her consciousness.

None of these things were as important as Greer.

And what Jacob's arrival meant to her friend.

There was no mistaking the pain in Greer's eyes. Greer hid from her feelings. Fiacre explained that the way he'd woken her made Greer distanced from the world. The emotions and memories would take time. Brenyn feared seeing that Jacob had stripped Greer of those protections and made her face whatever it was she feared.

Why fear? Jacob will not hurt her. There is no evil in him. She knows him from her past. Does that mean she fears what she feels for him the way I first feared my warrior?

Then there were her other worries for Greer—of Greer hurt, of Greer covered in blood, of Greer battling for her life on a muddy field.

Brenyn squeezed her hands together as a glimpse of Greer, her battle gear drenched in blood, her fair hair covered in sweat and gore and her face black with soot and smudges of blood and dirt, rose from the depths of her mind. Greer shouted. Brenyn could see her mouth moving and her neck straining, and yet no sound reached her. Instead, everything else became crystal clear. The scent of smoke, of mud and horses, of leather and steel—and under it all, the stench of death hung on the air and made her gag.

The image changed. Greer stood on a hill littered with fallen warriors. The wind blew her hair back like the wild wings of a hawk. She shouted again and raised her sword, poised to strike whatever she faced. Blood covered her shield. A huge dent caved in the middle crossways. Brenyn could still see the standard in the center.

The Three Ravens.

Brenyn shivered. It felt as though ice filled her veins.

In the vision, Brenyn turned and faced the colors of the fallen. *Green and Bronze. The Greenway.* Then she turned again and faced a man with wild brown hair tied back from his strong face. There was a slashed scar through one heavy eyebrow. He cocked that eyebrow upward at her as he said something she couldn't hear.

Horror filled her at the wounds he'd suffered and she stepped back. A wash of blood covered half of his handsome face from a deep, long head wound at his hairline. A black-and-blue bruise marred his cheek and his broken shield hung from his left arm. He dropped it and stepped closer to grab her by her upper arms.

Brenyn met his gaze again. His bright eyes glowed with strength. His expression changed to concern. He seemed to shake her. Sweat beaded and fell down the sides of his face. She wanted to feel his warmth, but she couldn't.

The ice had arrived. It had trapped her. It was too immense. The pain too great.

He suffered. Greer suffered. The warriors all around her suffered. She had made them suffer. Without her, no one would fight. There would be no more battles, no more dead, no more… Brenyn felt it deep in her core.

Brenyn tipped her head upward to break his beloved gaze. Ravens filled the sky. They blocked the sun. Then he was there, his eyes fierce and…and…

The vision released her so suddenly that Brenyn stumbled to her feet, tried to catch a statue to help her keep upright, sliced her hand down the rough surface then slipped to the ground. Her knees cracked painfully on the paving stones. The double hurt brought tears to her eyes. She reached up to wipe at them and realized her cheeks were already wet.

The Hawk's ready to strike. And with her, the Sword rode alongside his Flame. Forever they would return until they had fulfilled their oaths, until everything good was destroyed and darkness ruled the land. Unless a sacrifice was made of love and —

The ice vanished. Heat filled her, rising so high that she opened her mouth to scream. At first no sound emerged, then it shrieked from her as if her pain could be dispelled by the wail.

* * * *

A scream echoed through the keep and tried to pull Jacob from the depths of kissing Greer.

He resisted. The reality of her lips on his, eager and demanding, was better than any dream. Greer's body was tight to his, allowing him to caress every curve of her. A real, honest warmth rose from inside his core to suffuse his body from head to toe. He felt alive. Even his *hair* felt alive.

Nothing compared to this woman. She touched him, sculpting her hands to his muscles, his face, his shoulders and into his hair. She pressed herself tight to his erection, riding it through their clothes with such passion that he was near to bursting — again.

He held on by a thread. She needed to want it, to need this, to be ready for what he wanted to show her.

Her kiss grew demanding, seemingly wanting the same things he wanted, hopefully enough to make her ready for him. He ached in places that had gone unchecked for… He couldn't remember. He tightened his hold on her luscious ass and guided her hips to a heavier glide over his cock. It felt so good that he had to arch his hips and groan as his seed rose to near explosion. He prayed that she was just as hot, just as ready.

He could feel her heat through their clothing, the scent of her arousal tainting the air, and he knew she had come once already. Another climax was rising in her. If she hit it, he'd tear their clothes off and show her such passion that she'd never want to leave his bed.

Another scream, this one saturated with pain, rushed through the keep. His ability to ignore it, to resist reality for one more minute while he lost himself to loving this woman, vanished as he located, then recognized, the sound.

Brenyn?

He broke away from Greer's lips and held her in place, panting when he knew air wasn't necessary, so he could listen for another scream, but Greer stole his ability to think. Her eyes were sleepy, the passion there as high as his. She frowned, pulled his head to her and pushed down on his tortured erection.

Another scream echoed up from the keep. Suddenly the door to her room slammed open and struck the stone wall with the force of a wind so strong that it brought with it fallen leaves. Greer startled away from him. He swung her behind him while he used his Vampire skill to call his sword to hand. Nothing entered the room or jumped out of the corridor to attack. Instead, Greer shoved past him, jumped down from the bed and grabbed her sword from the hearth as she ran from the room.

It took him a second of shock to put the pieces together. His body still demanded hers, still beat at him like an eager drum. He shook his head and forced his brain to work the problem—a scream, an odd wind, leaves that belonged outside, inside. Greer gone…

"Greer! Slow down!" He took off after her, aware that she ran barefoot ahead of him and he'd have to call her boots later because she wasn't going to stop to put them on now. "What is it?" He knew. *Brenyn.* The scream had faded. Still, he could hear the echo of it. "What's with the wind and damn leaves inside?"

She glanced at him as she ran. "They've found us."

"What?" Jacob stumbled on the stairs. The enormous keep possessed a vast network of stairways. They were slippery as shit. Greer didn't slow. He slipped halfway down, caught himself on the railing then went down the rest of the stairs two at a time and still didn't beat her. He clothed himself in a new shirt and jerkin, then demanded, "*Who* found us?"

From above, boots hitting the floor were pounding closer. Fiacre could run for an old man.

"The Black Queen." Greer ran through the main hall. Her bare feet didn't appear to slow her down. He sped up to keep up with her. "It has to be her. Brenyn is...fragile. They would strike at her first."

"Greer!" Fiacre's bellow resounded off the walls. "Greer!"

"We're down here!" Greer stopped so suddenly that Jacob had to catch her so he wouldn't knock her off her feet when he barreled right into her. She steadied him with a hand on his chest. "Are you feeling well?"

Offended, he stiffened. "I'm fine. You stopped too suddenly."

"Greer?" Fiacre's call was closer.

"We're here!" Greer shouted loud enough to be heard on a battlefield. "We're in the —"

Fiacre appeared at the top of the stairs. He saw them at once. With his staff in his hand, he took the stairs at an alarming rate for his age. "Hurry. She's in the old garden."

Greer turned and headed down the right-hand corridor from the main entryway. The other corridors were open halls with tall, narrow windows that rose a hundred feet or more from the floor. Paintings depicting epic battles decorated the arched ceilings and, even after all this time, were still visible. He knew this hall, but the arched wooden door wasn't familiar. It led into an open-air corridor with carved buttresses and delicately sculpted columns. Trees lined the way, their greenery in most cases overgrown and yellowed, spilling out and on top of the low walls in between the beautiful arches.

Greer ran, either unaware of the debris on the tiled floor or immune to the sharp sticks, blowing leaves and dirt. He ran after her, hearing Fiacre right behind him. He slowed to pace himself with the old man. "What's going on?"

"Our lines are being tested. They may have reached her, but they can't touch her."

"Who's testing us? The Black Queen?"

Fiacre gave him a studying glance and muttered the answer as if Jacob had dragged it from him, rather than asked a question. "Yes."

He couldn't help himself from shouting, "What? I thought you were hiding Greer and Brenyn from them!"

A storm of old leaves struck, attacking from the crumbling garden in a whirlwind of sharp edges and blinding dirt. Jacob raised his arm to keep most of it from his eyes. A leaf sliced his cheek and another cut his hand. He whipped his arm around, but that did nothing.

The wizard shoved his staff at the whirlwind and shouted one word. The wind died. The leaves fell to the floor and silence descended on them.

"I am. My protections are still on them. This is different." Fiacre gave him a wrinkled frown as he lifted his staff and banished another whirlwind of leaves.

Jacob caste the heap of lifeless leaves a glance as he ran by. They remained grounded, but would they stay down?

Fiacre and Greer slowed to a halt. Jacob stopped at the edge of what once might have been a beautiful garden. Greer moved to stand under the entrance but went no farther. Her face was fixed in an expression of concern. He followed her gaze and understood why. Brenyn lay on the ground beside an old fountain. She was on her side, her face turned to them. Blood glistened fresh and bright on her chin. Fiacre motioned Greer back when she tried to go to her.

"Don't." Fiacre sounded gruff, never a good sign when dealing with mages. "Let me see if I can wake her."

"It's the memories, isn't it?" Greer asked, trailing the old man into the garden.

Jacob followed, feeling a chill settle over his skin. Unspoken was Greer's fear that it was much more than the memories. *How can memories hurt someone?* As he walked deeper into the garden, the chill on his skin magnified. It could have been Fiacre. Jacob didn't believe it was, though. The garden had its own magic.

Fiacre settled next to Brenyn. Slowly, as if fearing to harm her, he lifted her upper body off the cold stones and into his arms. Her lashes fluttered then stilled on her too-pale cheeks.

Jacob studied the garden, the open walkways on each side, the lack of roof above them, then the drab bushes and lifeless trees. He'd never been in this garden before. He and Gwen had been all over the keep as children, but this garden wasn't known to him. The door, he didn't remember, either. But the hall... The paintings on the ceiling... He recalled those.

This place spoke of spells or worse. Something created tension in his muscles. *A threat.* There were a variety of ways to attack. The garden didn't feel safe, and not just because of the openness. *Something deeper. Older.*

"Is there a spell on this place?" he asked.

Without lifting his head, Fiacre said, "There is an ancient darkness in this part of the palace. It has been deserted for many centuries. I fear this is a combination of that evil and the Black Queen or her lieutenants prying."

"Then why is it not barricaded? Why let her come here?" Jacob would have destroyed it or blocked the passageway. "A spell? Anything to keep her out."

"To use magic against magic only increases the power of it. It would have drawn her here even more than if I'd simply asked that she not come here."

Jacob shook his head at such logic. "Forbidding a place also makes it impossible to keep from trying to sneak a look."

Fiacre glanced at him. His blue eyes shimmered with light...power. "True. It only magnifies with magic. She ventures here from time to time. Until now, those times were harmless. She is remembering. The lines have been tested. This was a memory that brought Brenyn great pain." Fiacre glanced over at Greer then back at Jacob. "An old memory filled with pain would be one way they might try to break my spells."

"I see." Jacob muttered the words but didn't really get what the old man was saying. He thought Fiacre might mean that the girl had remembered something terrible about her life—Greer's life, too. From what Greer had explained, that could be one of many horrible memories. Battles were not pretty. They were not heroic. They were muddy, bloody, insane fights to the death with more pain and gruesome ways to kill a man—or woman— than Mel Gibson could portray in any movie. Even *Gladiator* or the Spartan battle movie,

300, that the Spartans enjoyed mocking, wasn't close to the real horrors found on a battlefield.

For him, the worst wasn't when his life had been in danger of ending every second. It had been after — when he had barely been able to move, when his arms had felt made of lead, when his wounds had pounded for attention. It had been then, when he was too filthy with death and too tired to care, when he'd had to walk, sometimes crawl through the mud, blood and dead bodies for hours simply to be free of it all. And even then, the stench of war had clung to him and his hair, body, armor, the very air he breathed, the food he tried to eat. Nothing was worse, in his opinion, than those hours, days, weeks after a massive campaign.

Brenyn had lived through lifetimes of those battles. And with her, she'd had to endure friends living and dying beside her. Before her. After her. She'd died. That reality hurt him in ways he hadn't had time to process. He didn't know the woman well, but what he did know was that no one deserved such a fate.

He'd lived alone. He'd distanced himself from everyone. Only recently had a few of his companions broken past his defenses and become important. *And look where that brought me. Here.* With a woman he thought he'd lost. *How do I protect her — a legend in herself — from a legendary evil known in all seven of the realms. Can I?* He shifted his shoulders. He would. She was everything. He'd made an oath.

He'd been in more battles than he cared to remember. He'd always put a distance between himself and his companions. Now, watching Greer, seeing the anguish on her face, he realized that he was more of a coward than he'd ever understood. She lived, not only when she'd been Gwen, but when she'd been reborn, each time as Greer, the warrior. She loved Brenyn, and he could only imagine how she suffered to see her friend—a friend who appeared in all her lives—enduring pain and hardship. She'd said Brenyn was fragile. Watching Greer now, imagining her living through Brenyn and this warrior Oisin's deaths, over and over and over, had also made her fragile. Greer was both fragile *and* strong.

He'd no longer be alone. He'd also no longer be protected by his solitary life. He'd have Greer and through her, Brenyn and her bonded. It was Emerald and Warren all over again, only this would be amplified to the extreme. He'd dipped his toe into the quicksand of caring with the young couple and it had ended with a chest filled with arrows and a mind damaged by drugged wine. This time he'd jumped headfirst and might very well end up far more damaged after.

Greer touched his elbow, startling him out of his thoughts. One look in her eyes and all his worries evaporated. He settled his mind—on her. Them. She mattered and these people mattered. Even the old man did, he admitted.

"What does he mean, 'lines' that are being tested?" he asked.

"Fiacre uses magical wards. The lines are light blue to your sight, if you can see magic," she added with a questioning lift of one delicate eyebrow.

He frowned. "I can't see magic."

"You have other skills, though," Greer said, as if he needed to hear something positive. "Can you sense magic when it's used?"

"Yes, if it's near…like now. What's he doing? I can only tell he's doing something, not what."

Fiacre sighed. "I'm reinforcing my spells so they can't see her. They are growing stronger."

Greer sighed and rolled her shoulders. "We're running out of time, aren't we, Fiacre?"

Fiacre held a hand over Brenyn's pale face and didn't answer. There were age spots and his knuckles were swollen, but his hand was steady.

"We can't be running out of time." Jacob shoved his hair off his brow. "Even if Brenyn recalls her life, does that mean they can sense her? Are her memories linked with them?"

"No. Her memories are held back by a potion." Fiacre whispered words that made Jacob's skin crawl, then added in recognizable speech, "I believe we still have time, but there is more here than I can see."

Jacob clenched his fingers around his sword hilt. He needed to fight something, yet he knew better. With magic like this, there was no enemy to face.

"What of the spell on this garden? Did the magic here cause this? Her remembering before you were ready?" Jacob asked.

Fiacre shook his head and took a few deep breaths. "It's difficult to say. This garden has an evilness all its own. This part of the palace predates all the other sections. It was built long ago, during a time when such excesses were...unheard of," he whispered, then shook his head slightly. "It matters not. Or if it does, I can't spare the time to delve deeper." He met their gazes. The frown lines around his mouth deepened. "Her memories are rousing Brenyn before we thought they would." He seemed to come to some conclusion, because he added, "Still, that might be just as well. The longer she has to learn who she is — what she is — the better her chances of surviving the battle."

"You can't mean for her to" — Greer glanced at Jacob, then back to Fiacre — "fight."

Fiacre stared down at the woman in his arms. "We will all fight. Now, no more questions." Fiacre eyes blazed bright blue. "This night isn't over yet. They test us. Perhaps we can trick them into trying for more than they can achieve."

Jacob shifted his feet. "That doesn't sound safe, old man."

"There's no time to argue." Fiacre rested his hand on Brenyn's forehead and whispered to her in a language that made Jacob shiver.

Brenyn stirred, then blinked her eyes until she met Fiacre's.

"Calm, child." Fiacre was gentler than Jacob would have given him credit for.

Brenyn tried to sit and succeeded in pulling away enough from Fiacre to sit on her own.

"I saw it. The end. They're aware. They know. They see us. He'll come soon. He'll arrive and — "

Fiacre rested his hand on her forehead. "No one will force you to that end again."

She closed her eyes and tears slipped past her lids. "It's true. It's all true. Greer will suffer. He will suffer. And I will kill — "

"No." Fiacre took her hand in his and she opened her eyes. "Not this time. This time we will break their hold. Already Greer is free. Soon Oisin will be here."

Brenyn's eyes flashed with something that looked like fire. She didn't appear convinced. She drew her legs to her chest and rubbed her face on her dirty gown. After only a moment though, she lifted her head. There was a smudge on her forehead. It made her appear more fragile to Jacob than ever before. She looked like a lost girl, hopeless and alone.

"He has already broken from them. They seek us, realizing they've lost him. And there's nothing I can do to save him, to save you." She included them in her frightened gaze.

"Calm yourself. When he arrives, he will aid us, Bren. Together, we can end this." Greer squatted near Brenyn and, taking her hand, she helped her to her feet.

Brenyn inhaled and exhaled shakily, gaining control of herself bit by bit. She wiped at her mouth with her sleeve, wincing at a slight cut in her bottom lip.

Greer squeezed Brenyn's hand. "We will win this time."

Brenyn shook her head slightly, a frown saying she couldn't believe Greer. "No, we won't win. We can't defeat them."

Jacob had his doubts about winning this battle, too, but the way Brenyn said 'we' made him worry. Did she think she could do something alone that they couldn't? He'd have to discuss his concern with Fiacre.

"We will, Bren. We will." Greer released her only when Fiacre moved to take Brenyn off to the side. With a sad expression pulling at her smooth brow, Greer returned to stand beside him. He replaced his sword in its scabbard and put an arm around her shoulder, feeling a sense of rightness with the way she fit perfectly against his body.

Fiacre tipped Brenyn's chin and examined her closely. Perhaps he'd heard the emphasis she'd used as well. After only a minute of silently scrutinizing Brenyn, Fiacre smiled, seemingly satisfied with whatever he saw. "Brenyn, you are well."

"Yes. I... I have been seeing...more."

"Of your past?"

Though there was a shimmering to her eyes, she didn't let the tears overflow. "More than my past. I saw a woman in the wood."

"A woman?" Fiacre asked sharply.

"She was there when Jacob arrived. She…warned that Oisin was free."

Fiacre's eyes glowed with light. His ancient wrinkles deepened and, under his fierce gaze, Brenyn met his eyes steadily. After far too long like that, the old man slowly faded and seemed to shrink. Brenyn let a tear fall.

"I see. A warning. I was not there for you, Brenyn. I apologize, my dear." Fiacre brushed the tear off her cheek with a knuckle crooked and swollen with age, yet he smiled painfully as he did it. "If you've ever trusted me, trust me in this. You will survive this time. You will win your freedom this time."

"I've always trusted you," she murmured.

"Good. Then keep it so. They will strike at me, thinking I have weakened. When they do, I will try to take advantage if I can and see what they are up to, and if I can't?" Fiacre smiled. "I will show them not to think me weakened."

An enormous flock of ravens suddenly swooped down, cawing shrilly as they winged above them. The wind swirled the leaves again. A sound like a locomotive roared through the corridor and garden. A limb from a tangled mass of an apple tree cracked and fell to the ground. It toppled a small statue of a child with a basket of apples. The child fell to the paving stones of the path and crumbled to pieces. The ravens cawed in laughter at the destruction.

"They are bold." Fiacre cast them a fierce smile, as if he were enjoying himself. "Shall we show them not to stick their noses where they don't belong?"

It was rhetorical, but Jacob winced. "Old man, don't be too bold. If they had a part in Brenyn recalling her lives before this one, even a small part, then you're playing with fire."

"Do you worry that I'll be burned?" Fiacre asked.

"I worry you'll burn the palace down," Jacob replied.

Brenyn covered her mouth with her hand, her eyes wide and watching them.

Greer frowned fiercely. "Fiacre... Jacob... Let us not poke a sleeping bear. Instead, let's reassure it that winter is still the sleeping season."

"Good idea." Jacob folded his arms over his chest.

Fiacre breathed in through his long nose and exhaled in a grumbled snort. "If you two are done giving me advice, step aside. Out of the garden." He lifted his shaggy eyebrows at them.

Jacob found himself being drawn away from the fountain by Greer. Brenyn followed, still hesitant and holding her hand to her mouth.

"You know what to do if this goes wrong." Fiacre waited until Greer turned to face the garden. "I'll ensure the bears don't wake too early." Not waiting for a rejoinder, Fiacre thrust his staff at the sky and spoke in a language only mages understood.

The swarm of ravens screamed as they flapped their midnight wings overhead — then their cries were muffled. They were still there, only now they were not so painfully shrill.

The corridor, Fiacre, the garden and everything in it appeared as if he were staring through a dirty window separating him from the world. And the world beyond that dirty window suddenly looked like hell. Leaves swirled up and around Fiacre. There were so many that he was lost in the storm of them. The cyclone circled and pulled the debris from the garden, effectively revealing what had once been its beauty. Only it slept, cold, gray and brown, the beauty sapped from it. And in the center now, where once had stood a fountain, a storm of evil swirled, growing larger and larger.

Jacob fisted his hands and considered his options — one being getting two women out of hell before it spilled over to drag them all down into it. The rest were lost to him as the storm erupted. As he watched in horror, Fiacre held the witches at bay. None of the wind, the flinging leaves or diving ravens touched them.

He hoped none of it would reach the frail old mage.

Chapter Seventeen

The tantalizing scent of woman clung to the ground under a massive oak. Alrick traced his palm over the flattened turf. He imagined he could feel her warmth, but it was wishful thinking. She was gone.

How is it that I can't track one woman? How does she appear and disappear so easily?

He stood and surveyed the clearing. An army had camped there—a Faye army led by King Edric. They were a few days ahead of him, but he would close the distance this day. Would she still be with them? After months of tracking her, Alrick had begun to doubt her existence. The spot where she'd lain last night solidified his faith.

Now the only question he couldn't answer troubled him. If she proved to be a mage, what then?

A breeze stirred the air, bringing with it the scent of spring. He rubbed his face with both hands, reminded of how filthy he'd become. His hands were rough with callouses. A beard grew unchecked. Even his hair now reached his shoulders. His gear showed signs of his travels. There was a hole in his breeches where he'd been caught up in a tangle of undergrowth. That damn bramble patch had left him scratched, torn and ripped in places he still felt stinging.

What a way to meet the woman who I will share this life with.

If she proved to be a mage, he'd accept her. At this point, if she were a Vampire, he'd not blink an eye.

Why did she travel with the Faye? If they stayed on this path, they'd reach Fiacre. They might be heading to join in the fight against The Three. Just as easily, they could be heading into battle with the cursed witches. The scent of evil lingered on the meadow. It was a light scent, true, but there all the same. Pockets of it were not fully present but not completely gone either. The Faye were still caught in whatever spell held their king.

What if she serves those evil women? What then?

He stared at the spot where he could still make out her slight form from the way the grass had been flattened. He bent and drew in a deep breath. No scent of evil lingered there, but he wasn't certain he'd be able to pull something like that from such a small spot unless the person had given their soul to the service of the darkest of oaths. There was something there, though — something he couldn't pinpoint. Something…wrong. Not precisely good or bad, just…odd.

Another scent intruded on the field. His attention snapped to full alertness and he drew his sword in one swift move. Across the meadow, six wolves walked out of the forest. They were still three football fields away at least, but Alrick could scent the Vampires on them. No Vampires were with them. It was the bond forcing on them that he scented.

The lead wolf shifted to a man. He wore the browns and greens of the forest and had a sword at his hip but didn't draw it as he walked forward. His lean frame could have used a few more meals, but what he lacked in padding he made up for in muscle. There wasn't a wasted ounce of him. Alrick considered his own trail-worn body and shook his head. They were the same, the two of them, hardened down to the animals they were.

"That's close enough," Alrick warned. "What do you want?"

"To speak with you." There was a trace of humor in the man's tone. "I'm called Silverback."

Alrick considered the man. Strength and courage shone in his eyes, along with fairness and honesty. The years of his bondage to the Vampires had hardened him but not broken the essential goodness of his spirit. He kept his thoughts to himself and tested the other man by asking, "You are bonded to the Vampires. What could you possibly want of me?"

"Freedom."

The other five stayed back, still in their wolf forms, watching as their chosen leader stood before him. Even across the distance, Alrick could sense their loyalty. It was as tight as Alrick's own people to him — or those who hadn't betrayed him and all he'd fought to give them. Silverback would be a king to them.

"I can't give you freedom. You have to win your own." Alrick sheathed his sword and walked forward to stand closer to the man. "The Vampires are weakening. Soon, you'll have your time. Perhaps in time, you'll even form alliances with them. But I can't help you. Not here."

"You are Alrick, a king among Lykae."

"I am. In my own realm, not here. Can you hear me? Can you feel my mind?" Alrick folded his arms and cocked his head to the side as Silverback stared at him with growing acceptance.

"How do you know their control is weakening?" Silverback asked.

"You're here, aren't you?"

Silverback grinned. The seriousness of his expression vanished and Alrick felt the kinship with him grow. Only Lykae could find humor under such conditions. They were, in essence, slaves to the Vampires of this realm—but not for long, not if Silverback chose to help them break free.

"If you are strong enough, you can lead your people. Take your freedom. Find a way. Fiacre will aid you. The mage has a Vampire with him from my realm. Jacob. He will aid you as well."

"A mage? You trust such?"

"I do. Fiacre is not like other magic users. He has always fought for good. And Jacob? While he is a Vampire and their true king, he has not always been one."

Silverback canted his head. His amber gaze sharpened. "He was bitten."

"Yes. Ages ago. Since then he's been in my realm. He's fought for good. He has found someone here who he'd thought lost. Now he will fight here...for good." That broke it down to the simplest terms, but it seemed to register with the other man.

His gaze scanned the field, then the giant oak where Alrick had found signs of his bonded. Silverback drew in a breath, holding it as was their fashion when they tested the air. He released it and focused back on Alrick. "You seek the Dream Walker."

Alrick felt his grip on the world tilt. Even the ground under his boots turned unsteady and traitorous. Silverback laughed and smacked him on the shoulder, Lykae fashion. "I guess you have never scented a Dream Walker before, Alrick, King of the Lykae."

"Dream Walkers are myth." This was a fact he knew. They were nothing more than a dream.

"Well, so are Vampires and Lykae in some realms." Silverback squinted at him but didn't hide his humor. "I would say you might have a long hunt ahead of you. It is said that Dream Walkers are tethered to far distant realms."

It was also said that Dream Walkers were on their deathbeds and walked their dreams because, in their reality, they couldn't leave their sickbeds.

Does this mean I will find her, only to lose her to death? The blue of the sky seemed suddenly too enormous, too bright, too harsh. *If I can even find her – truly find where she resides outside her dreams.*

* * * *

"What is he doing?" Jacob asked. With his power, he called Greer's boots, socks and leather jerkin. If there was going to be a fight, she wasn't going into it in nothing except a shirt and a pair of trousers. He handed her the clothing and got a hint of her scent – and the sex they'd been enjoying. His mind went off track, but he re-railed it. If they were being attacked, he had to be ready.

She stared at the clothing. "How did – ?"

"I'm a Vampire. Explain what he's doing while you put those on."

"He is preparing for them." Brenyn's voice wavered. She held Greer's jerkin while Greer sat and quickly pulled her socks on, then her boots. Greer stood and Brenyn helped her buckle the jerkin. They moved easily with each other, clearly having done such chores before. *Battle upon battle upon battle. Have they done this hundreds of times? Thousands?*

Greer took Brenyn's hand when she would have moved away. "Are you well, Brenyn?"

There was color back in Brenyn's face. "I'm well. I remember pieces."

"You saw him? Oisin. He's free?"

"There was a woman, the night Jacob arrived. I heard her in my head. Everyone was so busy. Jacob had arrived and you were hurt. I didn't say anything... I should have."

"What do you mean, you heard her in your head?" Jacob asked.

Brenyn tapped her temple and gave him a look that Emerald would have envied. It said louder than words that he wasn't keeping up. "She was here. The woman told me he'd freed himself and they knew, that they always knew."

Greer picked up her sword from where she'd laid it down. She did so gracefully, a warrior in every sense of the word. Brenyn was graceful, but he sensed that her power lay in other areas...frightening areas. She could become a *Dragon*. A legendary Dragon. He had a hard time imagining the kind, quiet woman who brought him his meals and tried not to wrinkle her nose at his goblet of blood becoming one of the fiercest creatures in any of the seven realms.

"We have to wait. If Fiacre is successful, it will buy us the time we need," Greer said.

Her attention was on the garden and the man standing with his back to them. A wind seemed to be blowing harder and harder in there. The mage's robes were pinned to his body, outlining how thin the old man was, his gaze pinned on the rooftops as if he saw something more than the hundreds of ravens. Suddenly, his power glowed like muted blue fire from his eyes. The leaves in the courtyard turned into to flying missiles, capable of slicing unprotected skin. None reached them. Everything inside the spell Fiacre had placed to protect them was still. Brenyn and Greer's breathing was over-loud in the silence.

A wild shriek echoed through to them, loud enough to make him wonder how the mage didn't cover his ears. The doors on the opposite side of the garden crashed outward, falling halfway off their iron hinges. The wind whistled leaves through the opening. Even where they stood watching, it was icy cold. Ancient debris and musty-smelling leaves hit the barrier like bullets and exploded into shards, as if they had been frozen.

Three women swept into the garden. They were dressed in black, with black smeared in a thick path across their eyes, as if they'd painted on masks.

"Holy shit, is that…? Are they—?"

"The Three." Brenyn had a grip on her hands that made her knuckles white. "The Black Queen and her lieutenants."

"They won't beat him," he assured her.

"They aren't powerful enough here," Greer said. "We are safe."

Brenyn didn't appear to hear them. And as the witches settled behind Fiacre's wards, Jacob had his doubts that the mage could hold them off.

The witch in the center had wild, tangled hair that she'd bound with what appeared to be millions of twisted bits of black feathers. The pile of it rose above her head in a crown. Her armor was heavy with golden swirls and gemstones. It had to be magically altered, otherwise she could never have borne the weight. Her thick cloak was lined with white-dappled fur that reminded Jacob of a snow leopard. There were small knots along the cloak's seam running up to her neck and down to the hem of her gown. He realized with horror that the knots were bones the size and shape of a human child's finger bone.

Every inch of her screamed evil. Yet when he met her gaze, he realized how deep that darkness went. Her eyeballs were solid ebony. The lack of white in them made her appear gruesome. But to make it worse, she'd outlined the shape with red. It made her look as if she had bloody holes in her face where her eyes should be. There were smaller red lines scrawled along her cheeks, as if she'd cried bloody tears.

When he glanced down at her arms, he saw that the backs of her hands and the tips of her fingers were also decorated with black and red.

The other two were just as horrifying. Both had the same designs on their skin. The right one wore a small crown of antlers, while the left wore a crown of what he thought might be more finger bones. Neither were as horrifying as the first, though. That one, he knew, held some sort of pact with such evil that he didn't want to get near her.

He could easily imagine them harming Greer and Brenyn. The witches would have thrived on causing them pain—any and all kinds.

He fisted his hands, unable to decide what to do. The mage was on his own. Was he truly strong enough?

The witches didn't walk into the garden as much as they floated inches above the ground, as if on an invisible moving sidewalk. It made his fangs ready to drop. The threat they poised felt impossible to ignore.

"Won't they see you? Recognize you?"

"No. They can't see through Fiacre's spell. We can see them," Greer explained. "They can't perceive us. If they do..."

"It will be bad," Brenyn finished.

Jacob didn't like the odds. Just as he opened his mouth to suggest they leave, the mage struck before the witches had time to float closer. A lift of his staff and a shout that roared through Jacob's mind and rattled the shingles brought to life a whip of bright blue. It hit the three witches, knocked two of them up against the wall and pinned them there. The third was forced down so that her feet rested on the ground. As soon as they did, she shrieked, her head thrown back so that her neck muscles were pulled taunt. The raven on her shoulder rushed upward with a loud cry and struggling wings.

Fiacre struck again. The bird hit the ground and didn't move.

The witch rotated her head to the side and shoved her arm up and out, as if throwing a shot put. What erupted from her palm was a three-headed viper, bigger around than Jacob's waist. It rushed at Fiacre, slithering in the air as if it were whipping through sand dunes.

Brenyn cried out and buried her face against his shoulder. Greer took a step toward the barrier.

Jacob caught her arm and held her in place. "It won't reach him." He hoped.

Another volley of blue air from the mage turned the snake to ice. With a loud crack, it burst into chunks of frozen serpent.

The witch howled. She threw her head back again and really let rip a shriek that would have made Alfred Hitchcock happy. Clearly, she wasn't keen on losing her pets.

Greer didn't try to reach out to Fiacre again. He didn't dare pull her closer. If he did, he might not let her go.

Suddenly, the two pinned witches broke free. They screamed at Fiacre—words, Jacob thought, but he was glad he couldn't hear properly. Even muffled by the barrier, the sound was horrible. If he hadn't been holding Greer's arm, he would have covered his ears.

He'd seen magic before. At his age, he'd seen every kind of magic—white, black and in-between. This was worse than anything he'd ever witnessed. Maybe because the woman he loved stood inches from it and if they realized she did, he'd lose her.

The storm, the ravens, the witches, Fiacre... It all felt too real, more so than anything had since he'd been bitten. *If they break Fiacre, nothing will stop them.*

Jacob held steady, ready to shift the women away should the mage fall.

Fiacre brought his staff down in a wide sweep. Out of the tip, a light so bright it made Jacob's eyes water erupted. The three witches were hit with it. He could feel the impact. It vibrated like a gong. Instead of flattening them to the wall, it seemed to push them away, make them smaller and smaller, until, with a loud cracking sound, they were gone. The silence was deafening.

Jacob's legs nearly gave out as relief took the place of battle-readiness. Greer was silent. She relaxed under his grip. Brenyn, even though she'd lifted her head, still had a death grip on her hands.

The mage turned and, breathless, set the end of his staff on the cobblestones. His eyes shimmered like bright Dragon fire — blue like the hottest of stars. "They know."

Brenyn covered her mouth with her hands. Tears shimmered in her eyes.

The panic returned a hundredfold. *I can't protect them. Not against this.*

"They will come for us." There was no tremble in Brenyn's voice…or fear. Merely acceptance.

"What do we do?" Jacob asked. "Leave?"

"There is nowhere we can go that they would not find us." Brenyn wasn't making sense. There had to be ways to hide, places they could go where the witches would never know to look.

"We can't just accept defeat before we even fight. There's always a way." Jacob looked to Fiacre for support.

The old man had his head bowed.

"Fiacre?" Jacob prompted.

Fiacre raised his head. His eyes still shimmered blue with magic. The light faded slowly until his eyes were back to normal, only they weren't normal. Jacob sensed something had happened, something more devastating than the evil witches knowing the women were here, away from their control.

"We may have time yet." Without another word, Fiacre turned and walked away, his staff clicking against the paving stones, his robes swirling around his legs.

"What?" Jacob shouted. "You know something. Something more happened, Fiacre!"

"Jacob," Brenyn whispered in a voice that sounded as if he'd shocked her. "You mustn't be angry with Fiacre."

"We must trust that he knows what he does, Jacob. Patience." Greer didn't seem upset at all.

Brenyn didn't either.

Both should be.

"The battle is beginning," Greer explained calmly. "This is but the first strike, and from it, we've not been harmed, but they have. When a witch weaves her spells and they do nothing, the cost is transferred to them. We have a bit of time. It will have to be enough."

"While they recover?" Jacob stared from one woman to the other.

Brenyn said, "They do not suffer defeat well. Trust in Fiacre."

"Like you did?" He wanted to take the words back as soon as he'd said them.

"Fiacre has my trust, if for no other reason than I will always have this." The color had drained from Brenyn's face, but she gestured to the keep. "The memory of my time here. If this is all I have, then it will have to be enough. Always before I was born into poverty, starving and near dead when the witches found me and made *that* my only fond memory." Her cheeks flushed now, the pink making her eyes appear as if they were flickering with flames. "This time I will have more." She took Greer's hand then his. "I have you both, and soon, Oisin will be here. We have a chance. I can feel it." She squeezed their hands then let them go.

"I agree. For now, we will keep our faith." Greer touched his arm, drawing his attention to her. She trusted him as well.

Deep inside, his unease grew.

Chapter Eighteen

Karina surfaced back in Meredith's throne room. The enormous hearth lit all four corners of the room, and yet she still saw shadows after the brilliance of Fiacre's spell. Her eyes hurt, as if he'd burned her with his magic. Blinking helped ease the reeling of her head, but the pain remained. Next to her, Delilah moaned, while Meredith stood silently nearby. One glance at her and Karina knew her queen balanced on the edge of madness. Was it time for Karina to give a push, one that might send her over that fragile edge?

"He shall pay," Meredith raged. Her anger was so great the words came out through her clenched jaw. She threw her head back and screamed, then sought something in the room to take her rage out on. Thankfully her gaze slid past Karina. When she found no release in the deserted hall, she pulled her own hair and shouted, "I will wear his guts around my neck to remind me of all the pain I will force upon him!"

She spun and threw a spell at the entrance where an unsuspecting servant had thought to bring them a tray of drinks. The young boy's eyes burst from his sockets and the blood splattered the wall. He fell forward. The goblets crashed and rolled. The wine mixed with the pool of blood haloing the boy's head as his body shook in the grip of dying.

Karina stayed silent and still. When enraged, Meredith struck out without thinking. The boy had been her favorite of the dozen or so houseboys.

After trembling and shuddering for long minutes, the boy finally ceased to move. The scent of death — blood, piss and shit — floated to them. There would have to be candles lit and the floor would need to be scrubbed to get the stench out of the hall.

Immediately after, Meredith shrieked again.

The boy burst into white flames, then in an instant disappeared. At least the smell went with him.

Silence filled the hall. Delilah stood with her shoulders hunched and her head bowed. Karina barely dared breathe while she watched Meredith pacing back and forth, panting.

Karina prayed to all the evil she'd sold her soul to that Meredith gained her balance. If she attempted to strike now, her chances of success were slim. Meredith's power always rose in strength after a battle. Slowly, the pacing eased. The servant's death seemed to have calmed her — for now. When she realized which boy she'd killed, Karina hoped to be far away.

Delilah let out a long, anguished moan. "We need to strike now," she cried. There was blood on her cheeks from where she'd scratched at her eyes.

Karina touched her own cheeks but felt no wetness. There were slices here and there from the turbulent windstorm, but she felt nothing more.

"Let us return now," Delilah cried, "and bring down on him the full force of our will. He will not survive this insult!"

"Together, my queen, we can make him pay," Karina added, not willing to let Delilah give guidance alone.

"Silence!" Meredith flung her hand outward.

The spell hit Karina fully. She was flung across the throne room to land against the farthest of the pillars. A pain like none she'd felt since before she'd sold her soul to darkness blossomed along her spine and spread. Before the pain had settled or she'd had time to scream, a warmth settled over her and the pain disappeared.

Meredith's eyes were bright with insanity, but she said, "Forgive me, sister. I... My mind is elsewhere." She walked closer. The sound of her gown dragging behind her caused panic in Karina. She began to rise but decided to remain still.

Meredith wore her gowns so that the long trains were either folded over her arm or carried by servant boys, two side-by-side. If it touched the ground, the servants would die horribly. Meredith did not allow her clothing to touch the earth.

Now she walked toward Karina with her eyes unfocused, her face slack, as if she'd sustained a blow that had deadened her magic. The defeat by Fiacre had done something to her. Whatever it had done, it hadn't taken away her power. If anything, Karina sensed Meredith's magic was deeper, stronger than ever before — and worse, chaotic.

Halfway to where Karina still reeled from her impact with the marble pillar, Meredith seemed to forget where she was or what she'd been doing. She paused, hunched over, her beautiful face wrinkled in a frown of confusion. Karina dared not speak for fear of her sister's response.

"Sister," Delilah called, "we must not let this mage worry us. We are strong. You are undefeatable."

At her words, Meredith lifted her head and some of the insanity left her eyes. Karina stayed silent, grateful for Delilah's words but not certain she wouldn't be killed for them. Delilah had cleaned the blood from her face, but wrinkles still etched themselves deeply down from her lips and across her once-smooth forehead. Fiacre had drained them. Karina could feel her guise slipping.

After an extended pause, Meredith walked over to Delilah. Karina wasn't certain, until she spoke, that Delilah hadn't earned her death sentence. "He will pay?"

It was a question.

"Yes, my queen." Delilah looked regal and strong, but Karina had no doubt that she chose her words carefully. "He has our Hawk, sister."

Karina cursed her. Of all the words, those were the ones she should have said. Delilah always managed to win their Meredith over — even if it was pure dumb luck.

Meredith cocked her head to the side and regarded the mirror hanging on the wall above her bone chair. She raised her left hand and formed a claw, lifting first one crooked finger, then another. The words of power trembled through the air, chilling her flesh as much as they caressed it like a lover. Within the depths of the murky silver, a woman's face—a warrior's face—surfaced. Her strong features were feminine but filled with an inner strength even the darkest spells hadn't been able to vanquish. Their Hawk. Meredith's favorite. The dark queen had tricked the girl when she'd been too young to know the lies that witches spun. Since then, she had fed Meredith's considerable power with her pain—and the pain she inflicted on others.

"See, my queen? She has returned."

Karina had never been more grateful to Delilah. She forgave her sister all her weaknesses and sins. If there was one soul Meredith would not release, it was the woman in the mirror, and Karina knew why. The girl's pain fed her magic, but it also fed her ego. The warrior who had been her father had once denied Meredith. *The tale is as old as time, but as potent as ever.* Karina took a breath and vowed that soon, she would be the one wearing the crown, and others' pain would be the fuel that burned her magic bright. Let Delilah grovel and choose her words. *I will choose the time, and when it is given to me, take it. There will be no Black Queen. I will be a god to those that bow to me.*

"Since the beginning, she has been ours. She will be so again." Meredith had completely lost the look of confusion as she turned to focus on Delilah. "Ready the fire. Prepare the sacrifice. It's time to call in our lost hawk."

To Karina she called, "Rise, sister. We will not lose what we fought so hard to build to an old mage with dreams of retribution. Prepare the potion. We need to ensure she stays ours."

Karina rose to her feet and hid her excitement. The potion had always been hers to make, but this time she would do more to it—or less—than she had before. Freeing a hawk might be the small shove needed to break the weak control Meredith had on her mind. Bringing Greer back to them, without her being bound, would create an opening that Karina could use.

"No one breaks free from me," Meredith muttered. "I have armies at my bidding. And she will lead them. This time, I will ensure she kills them all. There will be such blood spilt, my sister, such blood spilt."

"The lands will run with it," Karina agreed. *And among that blood will be yours.* Karina held her power in the palms of her hands. The tingle of it reminded her of all she'd lost to gain the power she now took for granted. Nothing and no one would take it away.

Not even her queen's addled mind.

Chapter Nineteen

Greer studied the map spread out over the table. War drew them near and yet the map revealed how truly far apart they were. War would be upon them within days. She could feel it. *Who will come to our aid?*

The Twins were small triangles on the parchment. There were more jagged peaks trailing along them to indicate other mountain ranges and huge expanses of forests, as well as deserts and frozen tundra. The oceans and lakes encompassed much of the map, making it clear that the Silkies and Merfolk needed to join this war if they hoped to win it.

Fiacre's keep, what was left of her beloved Rose Kingdom, was merely one castle compared to the territories and kingdoms others controlled — or tried to control. Some of the names she didn't recognize. Some she knew too well and had hoped they'd been wiped out, while others she'd hoped had grown were now merely small fortresses scattered among their enemies.

The Greenway still covered the western portion of the map, while the territories of the Vampires were a dark crescent-shaped land along their southeastern borders. Northeast of the Greenway lay the Faye forest, and north of them all lay the icy kingdom of the Dragons. Greenway was surrounded with only the non-threatening Silkies and Merfolk on their western border. The alliances with the Seven Kings of Greenway had dissolved. The once-mighty kingdom was no more. The fortresses where once the seven kings ruled in unison were cut off from one another. That isolation had been a trick of the Black Queen. Her skills at dividing and conquering were legendary for a reason.

Fiacre's keep, once the home of the Rose Kingdom, had been a gateway to the other lands. From the north, a pass through the Twins led to the Faye, and if desired, onward to the Dragon Lands. From there, going west another pass — far more dangerous — through the Broken Back Mountains led to Greenway. During her lifetime, most had used the sea to travel down around the Vampires' lands, and up to the shores of Golden Towers, the Greenway's largest town.

King Edward of the Rose Kingdom, her father for a short period of her many lives, had created many alliances with his neighbors. The Seven Kings had called him 'brother', and the Silver King had often come to court to enjoy the festivities of the seasons. Silkies had dined with them, while proud Merfolk had journeyed to offer their friendship. Her brothers had traveled the seas for years, even under them, learning all they could of the sea folk.

The dinners, discussions, laughter and merriment rang like distant bells throughout the now-silent hall.

Were all the alliances that Robert the Fair had created dead? Were those brave people no longer willing to fight?

Questions filled her, and yet it was she, with Brenyn and Oisin, who had destroyed those peaceful times. She had betrayed them all. If there were memories of the joy from that short lifetime of being a princess, there were more—many more—of the horrors she had done to thousands upon thousands.

"Greer. We need you here, now." Fiacre covered her hand with his, drawing her back from the sorrow that came with such thoughts.

"What? What is it?" Jacob's concern helped her more than Fiacre's reminder. She didn't wish to worry him.

"It's nothing."

"She remembers the kingdoms of our world." Brenyn hugged herself and closed her eyes. She too had to be suffering from memories. "We have done so many terrible things," she whispered. "Who will come to our call? Why would they come?" She gave Fiacre a searching glance, one filled with pain, but Greer recognized the unsaid worries. There was as much horror in her eyes as Greer felt. Why would anyone wish their aid now, after all they'd done to this realm?

Brenyn exhaled a shaky breath. "We massacred thousands, Fiacre. Why trust us now? The queen will call and when she does, we will go. There is no stopping that."

Greer shivered, trying hard not to lose her nerve. It was true. Every word. How could Fiacre save them?

"We don't know that," Fiacre said with so much confidence that Greer took a breath free from the tight grip her fear had started to take on her. "Brenyn. For you, aye, and you, Greer, the path to freedom is open.

We must take this chance. And as to who will come when you call, everyone who wishes the same." Fiacre scowled at the map and tapped the symbol for the keep they stood in. "We are all a small piece of something larger. To win, we must continue to fight. They tested my defenses and found them strong. Aye, they gained knowledge, but within a day or two, we would have had to reveal ourselves." Fiacre sighed heavily and leaned on his staff. "I have reinforced the spells on the keep, but it is not here that we will stay, hidden behind the walls. We must prepare for battle and forget the past for a while longer, eh?"

Jacob snorted and shook his head. "We'd better hope we have allies. She will bring an army, and as good as we all are in battle, three against thousands isn't odds I want to bet on. Who is with us?"

Fiacre studied the map, drawing his finger from the Twins to the distant north, then down again to the sea. "The water kingdoms are with us."

She was not surprised that the merfolk's watery world stood with them. They had always resisted the Black Queen. She studied the shoreline. The Sirens were no more. Their lands lay in the distant mountain ranges that ran raggedly along the sea. They had been destroyed by the Black Queen through her control of the Faye. *Does Edric know that he hunted down and killed the very people who nearly destroyed all three of the witches?* She doubted it.

Fiacre moved his finger to the bottom of the map and to the west of the Greenway—the Silkies' rocky islands and their turquoise seas. They were fierce fighters and had always fought the darkness. Among them were lore masters who knew the ways of all the realms. Their continued existence infuriated the Black

Queen. Like the Merfolk, the Silkies were among the very few she'd sought but could not have. "The Silkies will join us. Their forests are overrun by Faye still caught and held by the queen's spells. We need them free." Fiacre tapped the Silver Wood. "Edric is our key. When he breaks free, he will bring more than his own folk."

Jacob crossed his arms, seemingly satisfied—for now, at least. She suddenly wasn't as sure.

"If Edric has broken her spell, will he be our ally when he's lost so much? Won't he turn to a darker, deeper despair?" she asked Fiacre.

"He will come. There is much strength in him." His gaze was strong and his words filled with a conviction she couldn't share. "There will be several kings present in the final battle, you included, Jacob. Whether you want it or not, you are the true king of the Vampires in this realm." He held up a hand. "They will sense that33333 when they draw closer. There is no denying it now. Later, aye, you may, and perhaps will, appoint someone else in your stead. But for now, we must have faith that our allies will come to our aid. If this does not happen—"

"I will be here." Greer said. She felt an insistence, as if she knew that if she weren't here, none of this would be worth the risk. But it wasn't merely that she had to be here. It was more...something she couldn't put her finger on. All eyes were on her as she tried to explain. "Until they draw me to them, I will be here."

"I will, as well," Brenyn offered in a voice filled with emotion.

Greer's heart filled with warmth at her friend's declaration. She hadn't been a good friend to Brenyn since she'd arrived. Now she regretted the way she'd kept her emotions distant.

Fiacre patted Brenyn's hand before Greer could speak. "You will have to leave soon, Brenyn. If I am not mistaken…" He turned his head to stare at the far end of the hall. A smile appeared on his face. "I believe someone has arrived to guide you."

Brenyn rose to her feet. "Shall I prepare rooms?"

"You are no longer a servant, not that you ever were." He took her hand in his and smiled. "My dear, you are done pretending, aren't you?"

"We still need rooms readied if there are to be guests," she argued.

"Let them ready their own rooms, then. You won't be doing it," a man called.

Greer startled at that voice. Brenyn let out a small cry and spun to face the man standing at the far entrance to the hall. His hair was windswept and wild, his gear muddy and drenched from the rain. He looked like he'd just left the bow of a ship after months on a stormy sea. None of that stopped Brenyn from running into his arms. He dropped a bag at his feet and caught her. He held her tight, his head tucked to hers with his arms wrapped around her.

Greer's heart did a funny flip and took off at a gallop. The surge of adrenaline was pure happiness. Tears clouded her eyes but she forced them away.

"Who's that? I didn't sense him sneaking in until he was standing there."

Greer smiled over at Jacob's suspicious frown. "Oisin, Brenyn's sword."

"I guess Brenyn remembers *him*, eh?" Jacob had a laugh in his tone and a grin on his face. It made Greer's heart ache to see it. Memories of other times — safer, happier times — rushed her on a fast stream of images and sensations. Not all their time serving the queen had been horrifying. There had been slices of free moments when the three of them had celebrated what little they had. *Friendship. We had friendship and that was no little thing. It grew as the time went by. She never understood the power of that. She may not even now.*

"She does," Fiacre said. "Perhaps we will win this war after all."

"That *is* the plan," Jacob reminded him. "Should we leave them alone?"

Brenyn broke their embrace and cupped her hands on both sides of Oisin's face. Whatever they said to each other, they were too far for Greer to hear. Oisin kissed Brenyn once more, then turned them and walked over with her hand in his. He dwarfed her, but they fit each other as only those who truly share a deep love can.

Oisin caught her eyes, and his smile grew warmer. She couldn't help but return it. Oisin had eyes like no one she'd ever met and a smile that had always been contagious. But his were truly a mirror to his soul. Now they radiated happiness so complete that Greer's stomach flipped, because she could easily remember when they had been filled with such sorrow that she feared seeing it again. *Can we win this war?*

She hoped with all her heart that she never witnessed Oisin's eyes turning black with despair again, but was that hope enough? He and Brenyn deserved happiness, a life together — one without pain.

"Greer." Oisin spoke her name the way only he had, with inflections on the vowels so the 'r' at the end was almost lost. More memories tried to overtake the happiness of the moment. She refused them and clung to the here and now. "It gladdens me to see you well."

Her throat was too tight to speak, so she closed the distance and suddenly found herself in his embrace. Brenyn was included, so the three of them were hugging each other close and laughing. Some of the fear diminished. Oisin was free. There were no bonds tying him to the queen. If he could win his freedom, so could they.

She knows where I am. If she knows, she will come.

"We will stay free. We will beat them," Oisin said in a voice choked with emotion.

She shoved her doubts aside, for them. They all had to win their freedom. Doubt lead to darkness. With a smile she felt deep inside, she clasped Oisin's arm, warrior-to-warrior. "We will, won't we?"

Oisin's grin grew. "We will." He turned to regard Fiacre. "Fiacre." He bowed with his hand over his heart. The ancient form of respect was saved for kings. Oisin gave it to Fiacre, and with his head still bowed, said, "I owe you more than I will ever be able to repay. You've kept her safe and freed me from the Black Queen's spell."

"It was not I who freed you from them. I merely opened a door for another. If I had done such a thing, they would have known. I could not jeopardize all your freedom in such a way." Fiacre took Oisin's hand from his heart and forced the other man to straighten. "You will keep her safe now. We will win this war, Dragon Guard. You need to show her how to trust herself. Soon, there will be need of her fire. She will have to be ready."

Oisin gripped Fiacre's shoulder. "It's Brenyn who possesses the strength to save us all."

"All of you have that strength." Fiacre included Jacob in his gaze. "All of you."

Brenyn cleared the tears from her cheeks with an impatient swipe of her hands and exhaled shakily. "I remember how to control it. I also remember how many times I lost control. We must go to the north...to our homeland." Her expressive eyes filled with tears again, but she fought them. "I don't want to go. It's happening so fast. Greer? Don't you feel it? The rush? The fear?"

"Yes, I feel it. But we have a chance."

"We must take it," Brenyn said before she could.

Greer took her friend's hand. It was icy cold. "We must take it."

Brenyn squeezed her hand, trying for a smile, but it was a sad attempt.

"The Dragon Lands will give you all you need," Fiacre agreed. "You must be ready. Jacob will do his part, and so will Greer and me, but we will need you both to be strong."

Oisin eyed Jacob, and after a moment offered his hand.

Jacob took it without hesitation, grasping forearms with Oisin as if they'd known each other for years, not merely minutes. "I need to thank you for all you've done for Greer. She's shared some of her life." He shook his head slightly and added, "I guess I mean lives. In all of them, the two of you have given her friendship."

Oisin grimaced. "Always. Greer has been there from the beginning. She has saved my life as many times as I have saved hers. This time we will end this cycle." Oisin took Jacob by the shoulder as he had Fiacre and smiled. His grin was fierce and contagious. "We won't fail them, eh?"

"No, we won't fail them." Jacob finally seemed satisfied. He'd found a warrior, she supposed.

"Do you leave now?" Greer asked when the two men broke apart. Brenyn wrapped her arm around Oisin's waist while Oisin put his arm over her shoulders and pulled her in closer. He had turned to thoughts of strategy. She could tell by the way his forehead creased and his eyes grew chilly.

"We must. The Faye are on the march. There is one with them I'm not familiar with. She is waking the king with questions he can't answer. I followed their path for two days. He rides next to her and says very little. It may take days to wake him, though. His people are leery, some of them openly confused over his behavior."

"We heard word of her as well. The scouts thought she posed as a Greenway spy." Greer glanced at Jacob for confirmation. "They seemed to think she was Alrick's mate."

"Or that Alrick thought she was his," Jacob corrected.

"Is it a witch, do you think? One of theirs?" Brenyn asked, sounding fearful. "What if she is and she is Alrick's mate? Such a thing would be…terrible. They would use him."

"No, she was not a witch." Oisin's assurance seemed to calm Brenyn. She drew in a slow breath and let it out just as slowly. Greer glanced at Fiacre, but his gaze was distant, as if he heard them but was elsewhere. If Brenyn grew too upset…

"She struck me as very powerful, all the same," Oisin added. "The Faye seemed not to realize that next to him rode a woman with power enough to light the sky during the darkest of nights. Edric is blind to the world. Perhaps she will help him see again."

"Who do you think it was, then?" Brenyn asked Fiacre.

"A Dream Walker," Fiacre said.

Greer exchanged a glance with Oisin then Brenyn. Neither knew what he spoke of.

Jacob grunted and raised an eyebrow. "There haven't been Dream Walkers in ages," he said. "They were legends."

Fiacre smiled. "Much like Vampires."

"No, we always knew Vampires were real." Jacob shoved his hair off his brow. "A Dream Walker travels their dreams and enters other realms."

Oisin frowned deeper. "I have heard of such, but I thought as Jacob. They are stories" — he grinned — "to scare children with and keep them in their beds."

"Aye, much as were told of the Dragons," Jacob countered.

"Or Vampires," Oisin said with enough of a laugh in his tone to get a grin from Jacob.

"Dream Walkers are rare, but as real as you and me," Fiacre explained, sounding testy. "This one is as powerful as the sun at the solstice. She will wake him today." His far-off gaze snapped back to them, as if they'd asked something of him. "Then, I believe, she will open the door to awaken King Aden."

Greer stared at Fiacre, struck silent with disbelief.

Brenyn was the first to recover. "How? It takes Dragon fire to wake him. Is she...a Dragon, too?"

"She is a Dream Walker. She woke Oisin with a potion and the Silver King with words, and she will bring someone who can awaken the Dragon when the time is right."

Oisin shook his head but was first to ask, "A Dream Walker broke the Black Queen's spell?"

"Dream Walkers can rework the flow of magic. They can also see the flow of power from realm to realm — the connections between our worlds, so to speak. Some can even walk through a land that links all the realms. It was foretold that they would return when the balance needed to be regained." Fiacre scratched his short beard. "I sense it is the Dream Walker who will aid us in the rebalancing."

"Then we won't have to fight?" Jacob asked doubtfully.

Fiacre gave him a grumpy frown. "Of course, we will have to fight. They do not directly change our lives. They use methods that are more…indirect."

Jacob grunted. "They broke Oisin from the Black Queen's control."

Shaking his head, Fiacre seemed to re-evaluate his words. "*They* did not. *One* did, though." He touched his finger to the side of his nose and winked. "One did." With that he turned away, muttering to himself, his staff tapping out his fast progress.

"There he goes again." Jacob smiled, though, and bowed his head a little toward Brenyn's frown. "With all due respect, Bree, he does wander off in mid-conversation."

"He is thinking," Brenyn said in his defense.

Greer wondered. There were so many threads that Fiacre was attempting to weave. Had he forgotten that the witches now knew she lived again? Had they also seen Jacob? What of Brenyn?

"Is he strong enough?" Oisin asked quietly when they could no longer hear his footfalls or his staff clicking against the stone floor.

She shared a look with the three of them, seeing doubt and fear reflected at her. "He will be strong enough. He convinced me to return, didn't he? He found and raised you, Brenyn. He did his part in opening the gate for the Dream Walker to wake you, Oisin. No one may enter the Dragon Lands uninvited. He left a door open for her, no doubt about it. And he rescued you, Jacob."

"If he left a door open, is it still open?" Jacob had crossed his arms again over his chest. He studied her with that look of intelligence she knew so well. "And you rescued me, didn't you?"

"I couldn't have broken you free without him."

"And the door? Is it still open, do you think?" Jacob insisted.

She understood his cynicism. Unlike him, she had chosen to return and try to find her freedom. She had to trust in Fiacre. "If it is, Oisin and Brenyn will close it."

"First we must wait for Fiacre to return. Surely he doesn't want us to leave now. While he is still...thinking." Brenyn bit her lip. "Oisin?"

Oisin smiled and bent his head to brush a kiss to her forehead. "We will have to wait for Fiacre. He has learned something new right now. We will let him think on it."

"True." Brenyn still didn't look convinced. "I want to wait. I also want to go. It's...confusing." Brenyn worried her hair, twisting and twisting the ends. "I can remember more now. I can also remember my first day here. If we manage this —"

"*When* we manage this," Oisin corrected, pulling her closer. "We *will* manage this."

"*When* we do," she said, tugging at the short beard on his chin, "I want us to all live in the Dragon City."

Jacob barely held in a groan. "Are you serious? Never put the cart before the horse, Bree. *Never*. We haven't even hit the battlefield and you're planning the celebration!"

Oisin laughed, and after a moment, Greer and Brenyn joined in. It felt good. The echo of it filled the hall, reminding her of a time when many voices had been lifted in such a way.

There would be a when. She would ensure it. No matter the cost, she would not let her friends down.

Chapter Twenty

The steady beat of his mount's feet on the ground, along with the sharp sounds of metal on rocks as his army marched, served as a backdrop to the journey Edric made through the mountain's high passes. *How many times have I made this march to war?*

He'd lost count. The weariness of that realization had him reining in his horse. "Here is far enough."

"Of course." Drustan immediately turned his horse back down the lines.

The spy gave him a shake of her head in disapproval. "Everyone does your bidding, don't they?"

He had considered her comments from every angle. Over the past few days, he'd thought of little else other than what this woman questioned so airily. Her comments circled in his mind like ravens over a battlefield.

There had always been an order to his people. They found joy in harmony and happiness in the beauty of understanding the way the world — their world — worked.

Or do they?

For the first time since he couldn't remember when, he'd noticed those around him. Many of his soldiers were unknown to him. He hardly saw a face he knew as they marched through the Silver Wood. Such a thing was rare. In a realm of immortals, he felt he should know everyone. And yet, there were only a handful of soldiers each day whom he recognized. Worse, some of them looked away from his gaze when he would have spoken to them. Only Drustan followed him, spoke to him and lingered near him as night covered the land and they stopped for their mounts to rest.

"Drustan is an old companion."

"Is he? I assumed he was a servant." She turned her gaze to him and the keenness of it again spoke to him of much more than he could decipher in her azure eyes. "Is there no one that you call 'friend'?"

He scoffed at the question then realized that she spoke from a true curiosity, which called to question why he didn't possess such friends — not that she'd asked. It was implied. Worse, he realized she might know he had no friends and not wonder about it at all.

Have I cut everything from my life so completely? And for what? A trick pulled on me by a Siren and a witch?

In the suddenly awkward silence, he said, "Kings often find little time for companionship."

"Well, you must have family."

"Must I?" he murmured, just to see her reaction.

She rolled her eyes and opened her pretty mouth to ask more questions.

"Do you have family?" he asked before she could speak.

"Tons."

One-word responses abounded from her. While she drilled him for answers, hers barely revealed anything about her. "Highly improbable." He studied her features, still unable to find a flaw. Her smooth skin appeared without blemish. Even though they'd ridden in the full brightness of the winter sun, no redness colored her nose or cheeks. There were no dirty smudges from their ride and camping and not a single wrinkle near her eyes or along the skin between her expressive eyebrows from all the frowning at him she did. "How old are you?"

"Is that a polite question, your majesty? What do they teach you in royal school? Not manners," she said then laughed.

Her laughter caused a stir among his people. They openly stared until they glanced at him, then they turned away. In fear? Or out of politeness for her odd ways?

"I did not attend school. Such a thing is unnecessary. Faye are naturally curious and highly intelligent. We are the experts in anything we choose to learn."

"And so modest, too." She smiled, but this time there were daggers in it.

He wasn't offended. She often tried to upset him. After days in her company, he could see that now. "We are modest...and cultured. Our music is the melody of all living creatures. All folk honor our songs with their rapt attention. You have only to attend one of our festivals to know the joy found in all living things when they are near us."

"Ah, so you honor living things in your banquets?"

He studied her smooth, high cheeks and evenly spaced, white teeth. A dimple appeared when she truly meant her smile. Her eyes glowed luminescent and could have been from an ancient merfolk relation. "We honor all living things. It is not the Faye way to kill without need. Even this march to battle can be ended with a truce if we can find a way to come to terms over my people's unnecessary and brutal murder."

All around them, the troops began to set up camp. He guided her to the shelter of a mountain growth of aspens, still with their bright yellow leaves. "Here we will rest our mounts for the night." After watching her ride, he wasn't surprised when she dismounted before a groom could aid her. She stayed quiet, perhaps for once contemplating the truth he'd tried to explain to her — that his people were the victims of enemies who wanted them gone from this realm.

"If such a thing were true, then how do you explain the capture and torture of warriors by your people? And the warriors forced to fight in arenas for sport? How do you explain that?"

Drustan appeared as she plunked her fists on her hips and faced him. "Can you? Explain that?" she demanded of him, then included his captain in her fierce gaze.

He examined her closely to see if she'd meant what she'd said or had been jesting. Her humor had struck him as odd before. This seemed far from funny to him. Clear-eyed, if not simmering with anger, the girl believed what she said.

He turned his attention to Drustan, whose gaze had stayed fixed above the tree line, far off into the distance. Only when Edric took a step closer did Drustan dip his eyes to his. His gaze widened in alarm and he took a step backward.

"Majesty, your tent will be —"

"Explain to her that we have never tortured warriors, nor have we used them for sport."

Drustan glanced from him to the girl then back and stepped closer to speak in a low, confidential tone. "Perhaps we should speak on this in private, your majesty."

Edric tilted his head, unsure he'd heard correctly. The implications spiraled, circling...circling just like the other words the girl had said, coming together to form a picture he couldn't bear to bring into focus too sharply.

"Your majesty, you have not been yourself," he heard Drustan say, as if suddenly far off. "Others have made decisions."

Edric was certain Drustan had said more, but it was lost under a rushing sound like water filling his ears. He scanned the faces of his people and saw truth on their downward gazes, in their slumped shoulders and hesitant behavior. Only a few met his eyes, and in their gaze, the truth, the brutal, horrific reality of what he'd let happen revealed itself.

His people had suffered. They had changed. The evil that lay so tempting and dark had taken hold here, among his beloved Faye. They sought battle, not to avenge the fallen. They were eager for blood. That animalistic need buried deeply within the gentlest of Faye had taken root and grown from his lack of attention.

He backed away from them, stumbled into his horse and caught the reins to secure himself from falling flat on his back. Before he recognized that he'd mounted, he was back in his saddle, galloping back the way they had come, urging his horse through the lines, weaving in and out of his people as he sought to escape the reality rushing at him from all sides.

It wasn't until he'd reached the far side of the river that he stopped. By then, his mount trembled as it blew great billows of a misty breath into the twilight.

Edric feared the poor creature would not survive and swung down to rest his hand on the beast's forehead as he walked it. The gelding hung its head near his and walked beside him. Edric hung his head as well and walked. He didn't stop until the light left the world. Clouds hung high overhead, blocking the moon and stars.

It didn't matter to him. He could see in light and the darkest of darks. The velvet blackness of the night sky didn't hide the world from him. There were other senses. Sight was only one.

Slowly, he drew in a deep breath and released it. The night creatures were wide awake around him. The rushing sound in his ears receded. There was nothing between him and the truth — and that truth was terrible. It was as dark and horrible as any nightmare — if he had such things.

For the first time in ages, he walked alone. He couldn't remember the last time he'd walked among the trees or the last time he'd sat with his people, celebrating the seasons. There had been a mist in front of his eyes. Now there was nothing blurring the reality. His heart sorrowed, but just as powerfully, it filled with rage.

After an unknown amount of time, he heard horses approaching. He wasn't surprised to see Drustan. Loralei and his nephew, Thane, surprised him, though.

"Well, you didn't kill the horse, at least." Loralei jumped down from hers and dropped the reins with a sweep of her hand that ended in a low, mocking bow. "Are you awake now, your majesty?"

"What have you done?" he shouted, then realized he had and backed away from her. How could one woman draw such emotions from him?

"I think you've slept long enough. I tried humor. I tried jabs at your pride. I think the truth is the only thing you will accept."

"Stop! I don't wish to hear another word. Leave me in peace." He sounded weak. Enraged. Desperate.

"Peace? Do you truly believe you have been at peace?" She laughed and it was a mocking, unpleasant sound. "You slept. And while you did, your people turned evil—or most of them did." She glanced at Drustan and gave him a half salute as if to say he'd passed a test. "Some did not. But those who turned evil tortured good people and killed a ton more. So, the question is, now that you know, what will you do? Go back to pouting over being fooled into thinking someone was yours then realized she wasn't, or are you going to take up the mantle of your kingship and rule your people?"

Drustan stormed past Thane to reach Loralei. "Woman, I warned you that speaking to him like that won't aid him!"

Thane appeared wild-eyed, unsure of what to do while Drustan shouted at Loralei.

"At least I did something! What did you do? When you knew it was wrong, did you do anything?" she shouted.

"I have been by his side, more than you can say!" Drustan shouted back at her.

"Enough!" Edric pushed them apart. Loralei tried to take a swing at Drustan. Shocked, Edric caught her tiny fist and held it firmly but carefully in his hand. "Explain this to me, Drustan." He shook her hand in his to get her attention. "Not you. You've said more than enough."

Her eyes blazed pure rage at him. With a scoffing exhale, she pulled free. Instead of arguing, she crossed her arms and smiled. "Very well. Begin."

Drustan shot her an angry glance then focused on Edric. Slowly, something like hope filled his expression. "You've been…we believe poisoned by Lilith. We tried to stop her. We could never get close enough. She sensed it, and whenever someone tried to…remove her, she accused them of treason and had them executed." He grimaced and continued, "That is one reason you know so…few of our people. For the march, we had to bring in everyone."

Edric tilted his head, unsure he'd heard correctly. "Explain that. What do you mean 'everyone'?" His people stretched to the sea and far over the mountains to the east. They protected the trees, the meadows, the rivers and oceans of this realm. "And executed? Never."

Executions never happened. They might, at times, isolate individuals to let them find solace in their solitude, but execute them? Never.

Drustan sent his nephew a glance.

Thane stepped closer. His armor had once belonged to Edric's brother. They'd both been given matching sets by their mother. "Uncle, what she's said is true. You've been…gone. In your absence, the witch Lilith—"

"Lilith is from the oldest family! How can you think her a witch?" Edric demanded.

"She lied and tricked you," Thane said with vehemence. "She is no Faye. She is a witch."

Edric scanned his nephew's face and saw that Thane believed what he said was the truth, but how could it be?

Loralei uncrossed her arms and stepped closer to lightly grip his arm. "The Black Queen has many faces. Her sisters have even more. It was her who poisoned you. It was the Black Queen in her rage at your rebuff of her offer that sent your kingdom to become the darkest Faye Kingdom to ever exist. She killed Lilith and took on her form. She used you. She killed your people when they tried to save you. She killed others with your peoples' aid. Good people died and some people turned bad. The Black Queen tricked you, but now you are no longer under her spell. So, the question remains, what will you do?"

The question was simple, the impact on him vast.

He turned away from them and opened his mind to his kingdom. He snapped into full awareness, and in that moment, he saw everything. From the very center of his kingdom the land unfolded, and the lives of his Faye spread before him. He stared, struck to the heart at the destruction and death. He waved his hand and the deepest, most gruesome dungeons ever created broke open. The cells were unlocked and the Faye ruling over the poor starving prisoners choked and died. From one end of his kingdom to the other, he washed away the evil tainting it until he stared into his own soul and saw the blackness there.

"No. Not so fast, your majesty." A hand touched his, bringing him back to the mountain meadow and the woman who had joined his company a short few days before. "Your life is not blackened—perhaps bruised, but nothing time won't heal."

He stared at her shimmering eyes. The clouds had vanished and, under the moonlight, she appeared more elfin in feature than any of his own folk. "Who are you?"

"Me? I told you—"

"*What* are you?"

"Ah." Her eyes grew brighter, clearer and more powerful. She seemed to weigh him and, for whatever reason, she found him worthy of the truth. "I am a Dream Walker, your majesty." She tilted her head and smiled softly as she released his hand. "My path now lies elsewhere, to waken another king who is lost in a chilly sleep. Can I trust you to find your way to the light? I believe you left all your people back on that mountain top. They need someone to lead them."

"Wait." He caught her hand and stopped her from walking away. "Who sent you?"

"I saw what was needed and came. It was my own will, the will of one woman. Perhaps you should consider that not all women are bad—perhaps just as not all witches, Sirens or your Faye are bad."

He nodded, too stunned to do more. His nephew and captain walked over, both filled with concern and no little amazement. The girl bowed her head to him in respect, then sent him a saucy grin and turned, disappearing in a burst of snowy scenery that winked out as soon as she took a few steps. All that was left were a few snowflakes and the crisp scent of winter on the air.

They stood in silence, then Thane cleared his throat. "Was that truly a Dream Walker?" he asked in a subdued tone.

Drustan suddenly started to chuckle. "It would seem so."

"Then it's true," Thane said in a wondering tone. "They can change a path."

Edric didn't know for certain what the Dream Walker had done beyond waking him. He was certain of one thing, though. "We need to get to Fiacre. There is more than our kingdom at stake here." If he wasn't mistaken, she'd just entered the Dragon Lands. And there was only one person who could help them free the lands from the Black Queen.

The Dragon King. *May the light guide us.*

Chapter Twenty-One

Fiacre settled his gaze on the four people sitting around the hearth. He had known kings, warriors, witches and ordinary folk in his long life, but few touched his heart as deeply as these four. The path he'd chosen would break them free — or break them.

It was the news of the Dream Walker that worried him more than the attack by the Black Queen. He sensed the dark magic in the queen had weakened in her madness. Her lack of control posed a dangerous crossroads on their path. Cornered animals were always more dangerous and so were their offspring. Her sisters...worried him.

After seeking guidance from the weaves of the worlds, he'd felt Evie's light touch, a featherlight caress to warn him that the pieces were falling into place. The time was here to put his players on the gameboard. And yet he stood at the entrance to the hall feeling as if he were poised on a knife edge. There were paths yet not traveled by them. If he stepped one foot on this one, other steps would have to be taken. The Black Queen's madness was not a complete surprise to him. It had been foretold in a prophecy so old that very few now lived who had ever read the scribbles of the mad seer. But he also knew that her evil ran deep. Such a path cost.

His heart missed a beat then thudded painfully in his chest. He'd grown old. Beyond old, he knew, waiting for a chance to fix what he'd helped break. *Will I have to sacrifice one of these lives that have grown so close to my heart?* Such a thought strengthened him. He would not sacrifice one life in this journey.

"Oisin, Brenyn." He walked into the room, feeling the weight of his decision. The couple had ties so tight that they glowed between them. "It is time for you to journey north. I had hoped you would have time to rest," he said, "but with the news you bring and the attack, we cannot wait."

"We will leave now." Oisin rose to his feet and drew Brenyn to hers.

Brenyn's beloved face was filled with worry and no little fear. She was a Dragon, without the training she needed or the time to accept what lay ahead of them. He hoped she could find the strength in Oisin to burn her own. She possessed more strength than she realized. He hoped she would learn that. Suddenly all he hadn't said filled him with regrets and worries. To win, they had to remain strong — he knew that — and yet this step would require another, then another and on until they won.

He had to believe that fate did not decide their course. He must help by sending this couple down this path. "I will open a gate. You will be able to rest when you arrive. There will be visitors. They will arrive soon. Be prepared for them by the full moon. No longer."

Brenyn nodded bravely then broke away from Oisin and surprised him with a tight hug and a tearful kiss on his cheek. "I will do my part, Fiacre. Trust me."

He brushed her tears aside, but more joined them. Brenyn was the strongest in many ways, but also the most fragile. "Don't cry, my dear. I trust you. You are strong. You will have your life with Oisin and the two of you will have many children to keep you company."

Oisin laughed and joined them. "I doubt you've seen that clearly, Fiacre, but it is something to fight for, eh?"

"And if we do have a dozen little ones, one will be called Fiacre." Brenyn kissed his cheek once more and went to stand beside Oisin. She took his hand. "We're ready."

"You will find supplies there. Look for the old courtyard within the King's Fountain. Off the courtyard, I have left enough to carry you through several weeks. Look for the Dream Walker before the week is out."

Greer stepped forward and hugged first Brenyn then Oisin. "We will do our part here. Until we meet again..." She kept her emotions in check, but Fiacre could sense how much fear she held at bay.

"Until we meet again," Jacob said and clasped hands with Oisin. To Brenyn he said, "Take care of yourselves."

Brenyn hugged him, clearly surprising the Vampire as much as Fiacre had been surprised. "Take care of yourself," she said. "And trust in Fiacre, Jacob. Greer does."

Fiacre lifted an eyebrow at Jacob's guilty glance in his direction.

"Come," Oisin said and held out his hand to Brenyn.

With that, they were ready. There should have been fanfare and song, a banquet and music, but for the two of them, all they had was each other. It was such a small force to turn the tide. Fiacre steadied himself and drew from his link with all things living. Carefully he called a gate to the Dragon City. The snowy landscape appeared in a large circle in front of the hearth. Snowflakes erupted from it, but the couple stepped through and turned, waving back to them. Brenyn wore her simple blue gown while Oisin wore his battle gear. Neither needed more. They were from the lands of the Dragon and, as such, would never suffer from the cold.

Fiacre closed the gate and bowed his head. *Light guide us.*

"Will we leave, too?" Greer asked, sounding subdued but prepared.

"No. Not yet." The way wasn't clear. There were forks in the road he had not foreseen, but the closer they grew to what they wanted, the more would arise. "For now, I believe we wait. The Faye are on their way, and now I know they come in peace, to aid us. Our only worry is whether we must go to them or they will come to us."

"They will be attacked?" Jacob asked.

"It is possible. She will know she has not only lost them but that he's aware of what she's done." He said no more but turned and left them, uneasy this night with the changes in the wind.

* * * *

Edric heard the cries before he broke through the woods and entered the clearing. His folk were surrounded. Everywhere he looked, the silver-and-black fought with ragged bands of warriors wearing rough, dirty leathers and long, unkept hair and beards.

If that wasn't enough to identify them as the wild mountain men, their fiercely tattooed bodies proclaimed to all who saw them that they bowed to the will of the Black Queen. Only her minions inked themselves with the black lines of interwoven ravens.

Drustan and Thane caught his eye. They were ready. Edric felt the surge of battle adrenaline soar through him, capturing his senses and alerting his mind to all and everything. "Let them know we have come." It was only fair. Even the wild men would be given a chance at leaving the field alive—if they chose to drop their weapons now. Either way, they would leave the field—walking or passing on to the next plain.

His nephew lifted his horn and sounded their charge. The sound brought gladness to Edric's heart as he watched his people spin toward the sound and begin to regroup. The wild men paused in their assault and stared. With a savage cry, they rushed forward.

"They will not lay down their arms. Perhaps that is for the best. The fewer who fight for the Black Queen, the better." Edric drew his sword. The hilt fit his palm. Weighing it, he felt the last wisp of cobwebs leave his mind. "I want one alive."

"The rest?" Thane asked.

"They have chosen their paths."

Drustan waited with his sword drawn, but at Edric's words, the worry creasing his brow eased.

How long have you waited, worry your only companion, for me to awaken?

"Fiacre will need our aid," Drustan murmured.

"Yes. Let us help him now, then." But instead of charging down the steep incline, he took a moment. Drustan and Thane watched him. Both were warriors he would gladly die to protect. He could not stop them from this fight, though. He could not stop any of them. The battle had found them. "To battle."

"To battle," Thane said, Drustan a second behind him.

They spurred their mounts down the hill, swords drawn and ready. His people were already there, waiting for him. He rode through the lane they opened and charged, first into battle. Each swing of his blade took heads and ended lives. The wild men attacked him from the sides, front and back, but his horse was battle-trained and took as many lives as he did. All around him the clash of metal was met with screams from the wild men. They died, dozens at a time as his people worked with silent efficiency through them. Even when his ranks passed on to the next path, they did so silently. Sorrow beat at him with as much force as battle adrenaline as he plowed through the opposition. Each life lost was a song forever silenced from their home. Each song would only linger in their memories when they returned to what was left of their sacred wood.

He took down an enormous wild man with bones in his beard and tangled raven claws in his long braids. The warrior nicked Edric on the thigh, but without the force necessary to mortally wound him. Instead, Edric used the pain to fuel his strength and swung his long double-edged sword in an arc that sliced the warrior's head from his broad shoulders. His head flew into the field and bounced as it rolled to the feet of a silver-haired warrior standing on the sidelines of the fight.

The man bent, picked up the head by its long braids and shouted out a grief-filled curse, then dropped the head and drew his sword as he ran forward.

Edric waited. Here, he knew, was their leader.

His nephew battled near him. As Edric watched, he dispatched his opponent with a sword to his throat, then a kick to get the man off his blade. Immediately his gaze found Edric's, then the man running toward them. Sweat and dirt smeared Thane's forehead, but in that moment, he resembled his father to the point that Edric felt a pang of loss for his brother that he hadn't experienced in centuries.

"What is it, Uncle?" Thane had grown concerned.

Will I always worry them? Edric pushed his regrets aside and focused on the leader. "He is the one I want."

The wild man had reached them, cursing him in his barbaric tongue. Thane jumped from his mount and killed the four men with their leader before any of them could counter his attack. Edric waited, sword in hand but not needed, as Thane caught the old man by the throat with a blade resting along his jugular.

Around them, his people still fought their way through the wild men, but there were very few of their enemy still standing. The remaining band tried to halt their passage. Desperation hung over them, and with it, the understanding that they were no match for the full assault of a Faye army.

He turned his attention to the leader. There were massive tattoos covering his face in the twisted script of his people. Ravens flying in tight circles decorated his hands, up his arms, and on his neck. Perhaps there would be even more under his filthy rags. "How did you learn we would march?"

The man spat. Thane jerked him backward. A line of crimson fell from where the blade had sliced his throat.

"He will not speak. He knows nothing. It was sheer luck they found us. Luck for us." Thane tightened the man's arms behind his back until he had to bend slightly backward. "Less of your scum to help the witch."

"You might be correct, nephew. I thought this one might have some wisdom, but he is as lost to her as I was, even more so, since he freely gives himself to her."

"She is a god. She will destroy you all and give us the lands we deserve! Lands you stole, elf!"

Edric thought that if the man didn't slow down, he might die from whatever had him breathless. His already large nose and puffy cheeks darkened to an unhealthy color as he trembled. Spittle sprinkled his beard as he shouted, "You stole what was ours — you and all your filthy Faye."

"I dare say we are cleaner than you and your men, but what is this? We have not taken your lands. The wood has always been our sacred home. Before your kind traveled here, we planted the seeds that grew to a forest. Where were you when the saplings sang during the festivals of our kind? Not here. She has poisoned you, but tell me how you knew we would travel this way and I will let you go to your mistress."

"Liar! Your forked tongue speaks only lies."

"I assure you my tongue is not forked." Edric turned his attention to his folk. They had taken the field and now waited. A few had minor injuries. A handful, though, had left this field and would walk this realm no more. "Kill him. He has nothing to add —"

"Wait! Wait." The man seemed to have calmed. At the least, his face had lost the horrible purple-and-red flush. His hollow eyes and the dark circles under them seemed all the darker without the horrid coloring. Now he appeared defeated, gray and without the rage he'd possessed moments before. *A trick? Or did the sight of his dead finally bring reason to his mind?*

"I'm listening." Edric waited, not taking his eyes off the man.

"We had word that we should stop you here."

"From?"

"Her. She sent word through our...seer." The man seemed to search Edric's face for something.

"And? Why stop us here? Why not in the pass? Is it not easier there?"

"We were not near the pass."

"You live in the mountains. How could you not be near the—?" Edric paused. If they were not in the mountains, then this field was nearer to another pass that led to the Rose Kingdom—or what was left of it. Was he saying that their forces were entering the ancient forest guarding his southern border, between his lands and the Greenway? Those forests were filled with shadows and steeped in magic. Even his people lingered there only with the most respect for those ancient trees. "You will go through the ancient Gold Wood?"

The old man shuddered and shook his head violently—or as much as he could with Thane still holding him under his blade. "We go around, through the Greenway," he admitted, sounding reluctant.

It would be best to kill him, no matter his promise. But he had given his word. He motioned to Thane. No matter what the old man said, the witches would force them through that wood, and if they entered, they might not ever leave it. But one thing was clear. Edric needed to get his people there—or as near as they could. The battlefield had been decided, it would seem.

"Release him. Go. Do not tarry. If we see you again, your life will end."

Thane dropped his hold and backed away, keeping himself alert for any tricks. But the old man spat again and made a sign in the air. "She will win. We will rule over all the lands, with her as our queen."

"Light protect us from that fate," Thane muttered.

The old man turned and walked a few steps then began a hunched-over, shambling run. He disappeared into the forest within seconds.

"Do we send a scout after him?" Drustan asked.

"Yes...two. Let them stay far back, but don't lose him. Send word when he reaches his people — or wherever he ends up." Edric turned his gelding in a slow arc and faced his people, surveying the damage. Many had lost their song on this field. They would never again walk under the silver light of the stars and welcome the seasons. Those remaining were blood-soaked, some of them barely standing, but to a one, they faced him silently with an expectation he could sense. Drustan and Thane were among them, and their presence brought hope to his heart.

"I have slept too long. Today I will cleanse our line. All those who wish to remain and journey with us to aid Fiacre have my oath that I will lead you as one of you. To any who wish to return to our wood, I will send escort so that you might arrive safely. No longer will I languish in sorrow, blind to the pain of my people, blind to the evil that some of our kind have brought unjustly to others. We will aid the light or we will perish."

Silence settled over the field. Then, with a rush, his people lifted their voices in a joyous shout.

Thane rode up to his left and Drustan on his right.

"I want scouts. Two flanks to either side of our main force." Edric settled his gaze on the still dying wild men. Most had journeyed on. Some still suffered in the mud and blood. Their leader hadn't spared them a glance. Edric gestured to them. "See to them, but be quick. We have much ground to cover before we reach the Rose Kingdom. If what the old man said is to be trusted, they will try to gain access to Fiacre through the Gold Wood."

Drustan slipped from his saddle.

Edric gripped Thane's wrist when he would have moved away. "See to our wounded. If they cannot travel, prepare an escort for them back to our home."

A cry from above drew his eyes. A raven, its black wings spread wide, circled once before winging off to the south. The witches were already aware and watching. Would they speed up their attack? If so, they had very little time to reach the battle.

"And get me a messenger. We need to send word to Fiacre."

Chapter Twenty-Two

As Fiacre's footsteps retreated from the great hall, Greer met Jacob's eyes. Heat sizzled in hers — not for battle, but for him. She took his hand and his temperature spiked. "I wish to share what is left of our time here with you."

He brought her hand to his lips, and holding her gaze, kissed her palm. "You have me. Now. Forever. I found a place" — he kept her hand in his as he added — "for us. For this."

"Then take us there."

So simple, yet so life changing. He closed the distance between them and shifted them through the keep's walls and on until they were flying above the crumbling remains of their childhood.

Greer didn't speak and she didn't tighten her grip on him in fear. She breathed against his neck and caressed her hand through his hair as he lifted them skyward. He wanted to have her to himself, without fear of interruption, this first time he loved her. There was a network of caves with warm pools of water that he had found centuries before. He had sought them out and discovered them not far from the keep.

He traveled there with her now. It was like a dream, yet more real than anything else in his long life. Even the wind against his face felt realer than it ever had before. She weighed so little in his arms. He tightened his grip to keep her as close as possible. She was so small, so fragile and yet so strong. He loved her until there was no room for anything other than her.

"I love you more than any man has a right. I have always loved you," he said.

She lifted her head and kissed him. The taste of her nearly drove the location of the caves from his mind. He had to pull away. At the same time, he couldn't. He couldn't stop himself from sucking on her full bottom lip as he shifted them to the spot he wanted.

He settled her down on her feet, ensuring she was safe while he kept her in his arms. She took over and kissed him again, sucking on his lip once in retaliation. His body pulsed with demands. The skin on his erection had never been so tight, had never ached this badly.

"Greer." He pulled up from her luscious mouth. There was love in her eyes — love and desire. His throat closed and he couldn't speak for the pain of it. He kissed her as tenderly as he could. She softened like she had before, settling against him so he could support her. No one had taken her burden from her, not even this much, not even for a small slice of time. She had endured such pain, so many deaths, so many painful deaths, and still she survived. He would make her life better. He would do all he could to ensure she never hurt again, least of all by his lovemaking. "Don't be afraid."

"I'm not." She framed his face with her hands and stared into his eyes, and there, again, he saw what he should have from the first—a woman who loved him.

"I love you. *You*." He tightened his hands on her wrists and made sure she saw the truth in his eyes. "It doesn't matter how deeply you hide. I've always seen you."

Tears shimmered in her eyes. None fell, thankfully. Without a word, she gently broke his hold so she could slip her arms around his neck. With a sigh, she laid her head on his chest. He knew she could hear his heartbeat. It beat again—for her. "I have always loved you, too, Jacob."

He couldn't stop his arms from tightening on her. She was strong. A warrior. To him, she was so much more. She was more precious than anything else in this world or any other. With a rush of adrenaline, he bent his knees and picked her up.

She laughed and stared down at him like he was crazy. Slowly, he lowered her until she was at eye level. Staring into her eyes, he saw the truth there. As carefully as he could, he brought her in closer, letting her feel the effect of her kisses. Her eyes flared with pleasure and she pressed her hips against him. He lowered her to the sandy shore of the underground hot springs.

He groaned at the pleasure of pressing his hips between her welcoming thighs. It was too good. He had to take hold of her waist and draw her away from his cock so he could think. He had to take his time. This was about her. She managed to glide back over his erection with her inner thigh. It felt so good, and he tightened his hold on her lush hips. He decided this was about them. It had to be about them both sharing as much of each other as they could.

"I want to bond with you," he murmured against the warm skin of her throat. "Do you know what that means?"

She stiffened and her hands, which were driving him insane with their soft touch, turned tight on him.

He forced himself to lift his head, afraid that no matter how much she said she didn't care about him being a Vampire, she did. Her expression was intense with the love still shimmering in her eyes. He saw fear there also — and the stubbornness that he knew so well.

"No. We can't. Not yet," she added with a light touch of her palm to his face. "Once I'm free of them," she whispered fiercely, "nothing will ever come between us. But not yet. Not now."

She was right. They had no idea what would happen if he bonded to her. It might draw their attention. It might alert them.

He was too overwhelmed with love to speak. He let her pull his head down to kiss him. She pressed her body to him, fiercely demanding her wants.

She was so responsive, so sweet and eager that he had a hard time keeping the pace slow. The first touch of her skin under his palm was enough to drive him crazy. The first touch of her hand on his skin set him on fire. He couldn't get enough of her, taste enough of her, touch enough of her. She broke the kiss, breathlessly pulling at his tunic. He lifted enough to tear the shirt off over his head, then kissed her lips again. The sweet taste of her, the delicate shape of her mouth and heat of her passion branded him.

She stroked her hands up and down his back, using her nails with a small sound of passion that made him shudder. When she tugged at his trousers, he pulled away and kissed her neck then licked down her throat and brushed her shirt aside to sample her collarbone.

"Jacob..." Her tone was rich with passion and he knew he'd never be able to live without it.

There were no words. He gently pulled her shirt over her head. She wore a tissue-thin chemise that accentuated her pink nipples and drove him wild. His erection flooded with blood, stiffening so hard that he reached down to soothe it with a few quick strokes.

"So beautiful." He sounded hoarse, as if he'd swallowed sawdust.

She arched her back and her full breasts pressed up against the fabric, driving him crazy.

He captured one stiff peak in his mouth and shoved his cock against her soft thigh for relief. She moaned loudly and gripped his hair in both hands. Whether it was to hold him there or pull him off, he didn't know. He had to have her, needed to feel her slick flesh along his aching erection.

He broke away and watched as she pulled her chemise off in a rush that made her plump breasts bounce. He had to taste every inch of her.

First, he had to get control of himself. Slowly, so as not to rush things, he bent his head and kissed her lips then her cheek and on to her neck. There he got lost in the feel of her body pressed to his, her scent filling his senses as he knew he'd soon be filling her. He traced the lines of her ribs with his hands while he used his mouth to kiss her collarbones then rose above her to meet her gaze. No woman had ever been so beautifully created.

Her eyes were the deepest of blues now. He smoothed his hands over her hair, marveling at the smoothness and the weight of her braids. He lifted the twisted length and breathed them in. They smelled sweet, like her.

She pulled his head down and kissed him. This time he let her unlace her trousers. He felt a jerk that meant she'd taken her boots off and, with a groan, realized she was stripping down completely as she kissed him.

He let her lips go long enough to remove his boots and his trousers. His erection hung heavy and ready for attention. As soon as he realized how enormous he'd gotten, he hoped it wouldn't startle her. But her hand on it was firm and all his worries evaporated. The pleasure of her touch blew his mind.

"So ready. Yes?" She squeezed him with both hands and bit him on the chest.

He growled playfully and picked her up. They landed with him on his back. She laughed then began running kisses over his jaw and down to his ear. The sensation sent a shot of lust so hard though him that he feared losing control.

"I'm not going to last if you don't stop."

"We have all night. I'm certain you can last several times."

True. At this rate, he'd never grow soft.

She licked the spot again and he had to close his eyes and concentrate, otherwise he'd throw her down and simply lose himself in her. Even as he thought it, he knew he would never do so. She was his—Gwen or Greer—forever.

He gained some control at the thought and rose to sit with her in his arms. She smiled breathlessly at him. "What?"

"I think you'll enjoy the water. What do you think?"

She looked around, as if first seeing where he'd taken her. "The hot springs." Her smile burned into his consciousness. "You remembered."

He couldn't speak—again his throat was trapped with emotions—but he smiled and brushed a bead of sweat from her brow.

She got to her feet and pulled his hand until he stood as well. Together they walked into the pool. The luxurious heat eased him, and he walked them carefully out until he could dip them both into the water to their shoulders.

"Oh!" She gripped his forearms for balance. Her face had flushed pink and her eyes shimmered with blue. He picked her up. She wrapped her arms around his neck and her legs around his waist. "It's perfect."

"You're perfect." He couldn't help himself from kissing her again. She clung to him as desperately as he held her. She made that little sound in her throat once more and rubbed her body against him. The slip of her warm, wet skin along his had his knees weakening. He tightened his muscles, not about to drop her, not even for a moment. As carefully as he could, he let her feel his erection against her. She bit her lip and arched her back then made his body tremble when she rubbed her pussy against him. The heat her of her slick lips slid along his sensitive cock. It was unbearably good.

They both groaned when he tightened his grip on her ass and shoved forward along her heat. He eased their kiss and met her eyes. She was ready. It was there in her gaze. If he didn't do something, she would.

"Easy. Let me."

"If you don't—"

"You will. I know."

She smiled then bit her lip and stroked his shoulders as if to calm him.

"I want this to be for you." He watched her passion blossom higher as he guided his cock to the entrance of her body. She stunned his senses as she pressed down to take more of him. Worried he'd not last, he sucked on her shoulder, panting with the needs urging him to penetrate her as fast as possible.

"Jacob." Her voice dripped with passion—and need. "Not so slow. I want you."

"Right. Right. I want this to be good."

"It is good. Faster, though…faster."

He nodded, afraid to say anything for fear of sounding like a wild animal. He wrapped his arm around her waist and held her bottom with his other hand to guide her downward this time. She took him. Her body was so hot, so slick and ready that he had to close his eyes to concentrate on what he wanted—her pleasure.

"Oh, yes. *Yes*."

"Yeah, Greer, it's so good."

She met his eyes and hers were bright with passion. "Yes, yes, it's so good. Don't stop, Jacob."

"I won't." The heat of her was nearly too much. The sheer pleasure of sinking his body into hers had him unable to do more than hold her to keep her still so he could gain control. It was *so* good…almost too good. Her body was a hot, tight caress around his. He already felt like he was on a hair trigger. Her ultra-delicate, ultra-soft heat clutched at his erection, giving him telltale signs he couldn't at first believe. Then, with a small gasp, he felt it.

She climaxed.

The spasms drove him to clench every inch of his muscles to stop from joining her.

"Jacob, oh, Jacob, it's so good." Her body went a little limp and the contractions on his cock slowed. She moaned in pleasure then bit his shoulder, making him groan.

"I have to move."

"Yes. Yes, move," she whispered, already sucking a line up his neck to that spot again.

He began moving her up and down more firmly. Her orgasm had slicked her body for him, and with the pre-cum he'd been loosing, she was ready. His first full penetration made his body shiver. His sac drew up. The tingle along his spine began to warn that no matter what he wanted, his body was going to dive into orgasm soon. *Not yet. Not yet. Gain control.*

He held her in place and captured her lips for a kiss that they didn't end until each thrust bounced them too hard to keep on kissing. They broke apart. Greer was breathless, pink with a flush that filled her beautiful face with passion and excitement. He thrust harder, making them both want more, until with a cry, she started bucking into him.

The pleasure grew to impossible heights. He felt lightheaded with it. The urge to bite her started to build. He fought it and concentrated on her golden skin and blue eyes. She was his. Finally, they had each other again.

Suddenly Greer dug her nails into his shoulders and her gaze went inward. She gasped. Then with a shiver that made her rounded breasts shake, she fell backward in his arms, trusting him to catch her. At the same time, she caught his shoulders and tightened on his cock. Her slender waist and flat, sexy stomach flexed. He watched her sob out a breath. Her delicate ribs were detailed under her skin, then her body tensed and trembled.

In awe, he held her and couldn't hold in his groans as he watched her. He was caught between heaven and hell as she climaxed for him for the second time. The delicious stimulation of her squeezing around his erection tortured him. Within seconds, he felt tremors at the base of his cock and the tingle along his balls. Then, with a shout, he climaxed with her. Searing jets of seed burst from him. The orgasm seemed to shoot up from his toes and course through his body with dizzying urgency.

When he could see, he was still deeply possessing her.

He lifted his head and met her eyes. She smiled, and any worry that he'd been too much vanished.

She wiggled down on his still-very-hard cock. "I want to stay just like this."

"For as long as we can," he assured her. He felt no difference. The urge for sex had grown, if anything. His erection was tight, so hard, he worried over her. But she smiled, happy and clearly excited. "That might be a long time."

She sighed happily at his warning then kissed his shoulder. Her heart still beat wildly. The feel of her naked body against his filled him with a sense of satisfaction. *I belong here...in her arms.* The truth was that he'd never felt like he'd belonged anywhere, except with her. Now, with her, he finally knew why. *I needed her. No matter where we go from here, I belong.*

He kissed her neck against her pulse, savoring the beat of her life against his lips. He wished suddenly that they had more time, more of this, before they entered a world filled with dangers. The risks were enormous and so was the battle they were going to have to face. He brushed another kiss to her throat and hoped that whatever Fiacre had seen him doing was possible. If not, he'd have to find another way to bring the Vampires to their side. He wasn't letting anyone destroy this for them.

Chapter Twenty-Three

The wind blew hard and cold from the north. Billows of snow blurred the landscape, no matter which way Aubrey looked. If there was a blue sky, it was hidden behind the snow.

Greyson stood like a solid pillar of warmth to her left. The presence of Evie and her two guards peeked in and out of sight ahead of them. The snow swirled in sheets, hiding them one minute, revealing them the next. One lone figure stood out against the white — the Dream Walker. For her the snow bent, avoiding her as if she were an arrow slicing through air.

Since they'd made their decision to come here, she'd left them for a few days then returned and demanded that now was the time. So here they were — here in the Dragon Lands.

Aubrey missed those few days of peace, even though they hadn't truly been peaceful. They'd been filled with tense demands from Greyson to know more, and his insistence that they include the rest of the Immortal Council in her decision to go when the Dream

Walker returned. Evie, surprisingly, had helped Greyson see that the fewer who knew of the Dream Walker and their plans, the better.

Evie's two guards had helped Greyson stock up on warm clothes and other winter gear. Aubrey could have told them that they wouldn't need any of it, but it kept the three men busy and out of her hair. Evie seemed to agree.

The seer had slept for a full day and night. Greyson had not commented, but he'd lifted an eyebrow at Aubrey a few times when she'd returned from checking on the seer. If he'd wanted an explanation, she had none to give. Her opinion was that the seer had needed the rest. Her two men hadn't seemed worried, so she'd kept silent on her own concerns for Evie.

The Dream Walker had returned with news that the Faye king, Edric, had broken free from the Black Queen's spells. He led his people now. Whether or not he'd endanger them in a final battle was another matter.

Aubrey wasn't as sure that he would. She knew how evil some of his people had become. They had willingly served the Black Queen. They had enjoyed torturing her, fed on the helplessness and pain she'd endured. That kind of evil wasn't easy to stop. Edric, as the Faye ruler in the Heartland, could stem it. He could cut the rot out. If he did, he would have very few of his people left. Above all, he knew that those remaining were his responsibility. Would he endanger them after making them suffer another's rule — for surely the Black Queen had ruled his lands for so long while he slumbered in his sorrow? She worried the problem from as many angles as she could and, in the end, left it to the decision of the Faye king. He would do as his path willed.

She had opened herself to see the magic of the Heartland and sensed that the queen's magic had begun to deteriorate. Her spells were a tangled mass of black, but they felt rotten, as if they'd been too long in the dark and were now little more than moldy silk—no longer strong and supple enough to hold its shape. That didn't mean the dark queen couldn't gather enough of an army to destroy Edric and his Faye, Fiacre and anyone else who tried to stop her, however.

There was the threat of her sisters, too.

The two were as dangerous as the queen. Delilah had been a curse on the lips of many witches. But compared to Meredith, Delilah was gentle. Then there was Karina. Of the three, Aubrey feared her the most. She was hidden, often the serpent in the bed, striking before one knew it was there. What if she knew of her sister's decline? How could she not? Was she even now planning something that would move her into position to take over as queen? And Delilah... What of her? She'd lost a coven, but she had others at her beck and call. The Faye had done her bidding. What if she had severed their ties to Edric? What if she held them to her and used them to gain a win for Meredith? Or herself?

There were too many threads. She had a seer with her, and yet Evie was as good as blind. She could tell Aubrey nothing of the Black Queen and her followers. If she did, Aubrey feared Evie would also have to use her gift for the Black Queen. Such a fate would not have ended well for Evie.

Aubrey shivered. The tremble was more for what they were about to do than the cold of the Antarctic-like weather. She still couldn't believe this was the path they should take. There were reasons the Dragons slept and reasons that Aden had chosen sleep over life. What if she woke him, only to have him still suffer from the insanity that had driven him to his sleep?

"Are you certain this is the correct path?" Aubrey shouted to be heard above the blast of wintery wind.

"It is here that we need to be." Evie didn't turn to face them. She simply kept walking. Her two warriors flanked her, but they glanced back. Both looked intent but not worried.

If this was where they should be, what would follow? The spells to wake the Dragons could very well kill her. *Am I such a coward? Do I fear death when the knowledge of how to wake the king is part of my oath?*

"Do you trust her?" Greyson asked, when she didn't move to follow.

She met his strong gaze and thought of all the things she wished he would say — or that perhaps she should say. Women of the new era spoke of their feelings before their men. But such was not her way. She turned away from his gaze. *I am more cowardly than I ever would have believed.*

"Aubrey? Do you trust her?"

"I have no choice." Aubrey pulled her scarf up higher over her face. The cold made her wounds ache fiercely.

"Then follow her. The sooner we do, the sooner we are out of the cold."

Always practical. If only he was as passionate. She followed, not about to admit that she'd been standing there freezing. The wind blew hard enough to make her eyes water, but when she blinked them clear, she stopped again. Awe filled her. The walls of the Dragon Citadel rose up and up and up out of the swirling snow. From where they stood, she could see no end to their height, nor an end to them when she looked either direction. She knew from legends that the walls curved around the city like the wings of the Dragon, but in the blustery wind, she couldn't believe the enormity of them.

"This is the Dragon Citadel?" Greyson sounded impressed.

"Yes. I had no idea we were already so close." The walls were slick with ice but built out of white marble. They would withstand any attack — and had. The Black Queen had broken legions on them and not gained entrance. *But she defeated the Dragons all the same.*

Greyson stepped to her side, blocking some of the fierce wind with his bigger frame. "Where's the entrance?"

"I have no idea."

The immediate frown was classic Greyson. *Will he miss me when I'm no longer here to pester him with unwanted answers?*

"What? How's that possible? Evie said you were a Dragon."

She refused to discuss this with him. There was no time, and if she did answer him, it would only bring up more questions — and more questions after that, none of which she wished to talk about. But suddenly there was something she wanted to ask, something that spun in her mind like a cyclone. Why had he never kissed her? Why he'd never opened her bedroom door and slipped into her bed or come up behind her when she'd been at the hearth and kissed her neck. Why had he never spoken to her of any of the emotions she saw simmering in his gaze? *Too late. It's for the best. Whatever his reasons, it's too late.*

"We have to keep up." She started walking again, but Greyson stopped her with a hand on her arm. He rarely touched her. She stopped and turned her head. His handsome face was filled with concern.

"What is it?"

"What do you mean?"

"What aren't you telling me?"

She laughed. There was so much. *Where to start?* "I can't even begin to answer that as fully as you deserve." She turned back and started walking, spotting Evie and her darker guards through a swirl of snow. She hurried after them, aware of Greyson muttering next to her. He would keep on until she finally broke down and answered him—at least, answered some of what he wanted.

"I have never been to the Dragon Lands. The way is cursed. The Dream Walker gained entrance somehow," she explained, unsure why his grumblings upset her so much. She thought it might be because his natural silence had to be broken when he grumbled. *Or, you hate not doing what he wishes.*

"And now we go here to do what?"

She dreaded answering *that* question. There was a pause, filled with Greyson's frustration and her stubbornness. If she admitted that she might never leave this land again—or least for ages—what would he do? Demand she not do what she was bound to do by an oath?

A loud whoosh of wind hit them—different from the rest and far more powerful. She was knocked into Greyson's chest. He held her close, apparently not impacted by the hurricane winds.

The wind died down. Out of the swirling snow a woman and a man appeared, walking calmly toward them. Neither were dressed for the cold, but neither appeared bothered by it. The man was tall, far taller than the slim woman who held his hand. She wore a gown better suited to warmer climates. The man wore a sword and armor, but his tunic and trousers weren't made for the weather.

"Dream Walker," he called in a voice laced with respect. He bowed from the waist, fist over his heart, and said, "I owe you a great debt. We both do." He indicated his companion with a sweep of his hand. She had long, brilliant hair, the color of sable—thick, rich and flowing with the wind currents. Her eyes were dazzling amber that Aubrey realized weren't amber at all but flames.

Aubrey went to one knee in the snow and bowed her head, fist over her heart. "Dragon Lords."

"No, no, do not kneel," the woman said in a rush. "I know you. You are Aubrey. Your family has long served the honor of the Dragons." Hands gripped her on the arms, and she was brought to her feet to meet the gaze of the youngest daughter of the Dragon King. "Your lineage is there for us to sense, much as mages sense all things magical."

Aubrey stared. She had no words. The eyes of the daughter of the Dragon held her and found her worthy. She could not speak for fear of what she would say.

"I'm Brenyn. You are most welcome to our lands. Fiacre said to expect you...all of you." She stepped back, smiling brilliantly. Her happiness flowed from her and encompassed the warrior who smiled at them with a sparkle in his eyes. They both possessed the happiness that only those who are truly at peace could own. And yet Aubrey knew who these two were, and more, what they had been forced into and might—if this battle did not go as they wished—become again.

"We are at the end, aren't we?" he asked, as if reading her thoughts. "We will face it bravely and hope that our suffering will be enough of a price to earn all our freedom." He dipped his head. "I'm known as

Oisin." He cocked an eyebrow at Evie. "You've been busy since I last saw you, seer."

"You gave me time," Evie responded, no little awe in her tone. "I thought it best to use it wisely."

Oisin laughed. The sound was so out of place, yet at the same time, so right, that Aubrey glanced at Greyson to see him shaking his head. "He's been pushed too far."

"You've clearly never seen me being pushed too far, my friend." Oisin slapped Greyson on the shoulder. "I'm enjoying the days I have." He dropped his hand and took Brenyn's hand in his. "We're using our time wisely, as well. Come. Fiacre said you would be able to help us."

"He did?" Aubrey asked.

"With what?" Greyson asked.

"Waking the Dragon King, my dear Aubrey," the Dream Walker said. "This one I can't wake alone. I'll need a Dragon Mage."

Several things became crystal clear in the next moment, as if she had senses like a Vampire. Greyson stiffened next to her. The wind died. Brenyn's smile grew and softened to reveal the swirls of deep sorrow coloring her happiness. Oisin's eyes glittered brilliant blue with the power of his considerable strength. And the Dream Walker watched her as the hawk regarded her prey.

But the Dream Walker wasn't the true hawk. That was reserved for another who might also break free from the Black Queen if what they wanted Aubrey to do succeeded in bringing to the world a sane, powerful Dragon.

And if she woke the grief-ridden, insane Dragon? Then what? It was said that Dragon fire killed instantly.

Only Evie, out of all her companions, looked as pale and as frightened as Aubrey felt.

Chapter Twenty-Four

The scent of sex clung to the air. Greer lightly stroked her fingers down her skin, marveling at the texture. Had her skin ever been so responsive? So ready for a warm press of flesh on flesh? She ran her fingertips down her stomach, lingering over the velvet smoothness. Jacob needed to hurry. After so many lifetimes, she now knew the heat and pressure of wanting. She ached with emptiness. Jacob could fill it.

He'd surprised her. She'd anticipated him being cold. Vampires were supposed to be chillingly cold. A Vampire, in her mind, would be like marble stored in dark, deep caverns. Jacob burned with heat. His mouth made her feel faint with needs she'd never considered or experienced before. She craved him in ways she hadn't anticipated.

There was more of his scent on the bedding. She breathed him in and curled around the pillows, wishing he would hurry. There was no need for food...only him. They'd had these past few nights to themselves, all the while waiting for Fiacre's call for them to join the fight. *Three nights I've had him to myself. Is it a gift before it's all taken away?*

No. She'd do what she could. Fight, just like Brenyn would for her man.

Her stomach growled, but she smiled and rolled over onto her back. The moonlight cast the room in shadows and darker crevices where the corners refused to be exposed. She didn't mind. She didn't even mind that the fire had long since died and the breeze coming in off the ocean chilled her skin. Jacob would warm it soon enough. Another rumble from her stomach made her smile again and stretch. Hunger really didn't matter. She wanted him first and whatever food he'd made second.

The first real painful tug in her abdomen caught her by surprise. She froze in mid-stretch, cataloguing the depth of pain and comparing it to hunger for far too long. Another tug, this one unmistakable. Cold suffused her skin, chilling it to the point that gooseflesh broke out all over her naked flesh.

I should have known. I should have been ready. Have they called Brenyn? Have they taken her happiness away?

No. They are safe. They have to be safe.

She sat and stared at the high corners of the room. The absolute darkness there in the corners had grown to devour it. Soon it would cover the entire wall.

A stab of pain, lasting longer this time, sliced up her stomach then downward through her legs before it faded.

Fiacre could not stop this. Jacob would die trying. She hoped Brenyn and Oisin had learned to control Brenyn's fire. She hoped they were safely away, too hidden under the spells of the Dragons and Fiacre to be found.

The next agonizing tug brought her to her knees, clutching her bare stomach and breathing through her nose to stop a scream. When she'd recovered, the shadows along the western wall had grown into a monstrous blackness. There was no time, not with Jacob a few floors below, not with Fiacre still here. She could be summoned and go to them — or worse, controlled from afar and forced to kill them.

There was no need for clothing. She straightened and walked to the shadows, knowing when she did that her death was inescapable. Nothing that happened from now until then mattered — except keeping Jacob and her friends alive.

Darkness covered her like a cold sheet left out on the line during a thundershower. Goosebumps raced down her skin, skin that had so recently been loved and caressed by a man she'd given her soul to, a man that she would love no matter how many times she had to live and die.

The blazing fire ahead of her came as a surprise. So did the warmth. The three women didn't. She knew them well. Tonight, they were dressed in war gear. The black stains of their magic shimmered along their eyes and darkened their hair at the temples. The blood they used to mix the pigment had come from boy-children. They would drain the child and carve his body into pieces that they buried in the peat pits. Slaves would dig up the bones and line the walls of their amphitheater. There were millions of skulls, one on top of the other, all the way up and down the three chambers and three domes. It was horrific on purpose. Anyone who stood before them should know that their lives were a fragile thread, easily snipped.

How could I ever believe that they lived in the Siren's homes? They needed this to instill the horror they loved.

"My Hawk. You've returned to us."

Greer knelt. The agony in her stomach had grown impossible to ignore. She sought a balance by taking deep breaths. The attempt to control the ever-growing torture had failed, as she'd known it would. The Black Queen sought to hurt her and hoped to see Greer show it. Such was always the case. They fed on pain. It was their nourishment and their enjoyment. They had contrived with the vilest of evil to live longer than was their due, but the cost was a need for more — more horror, more suffering, more death, more and more and more. They didn't understand that their needs would far outpace what she or anyone else could supply. What then? Greer imagined they would die — either at their own hands, or by some evil far greater than they ever imagined. *Fiacre believes they can be killed on a battlefield. Will the Dragons be powerful enough?*

"Bring her gear. She is bare." A laugh from the queen, followed by scurrying sounds of servants.

Greer kept her eyes on the floor. The light of the massive central hearth warmed the room and provided light. There was only the circular hole in the roof far above the hearth to let in light. They preferred the dark. Greer knew this, and yet the silvery light from the moon cast the floor in a muted glow she'd never noticed before. It was a softer light, she thought, than the red and orange glow of their fire.

"She is more than bare. She has been touched by a man. What punishment shall she receive? Surly she deserves one." Delilah's singsong voice was as horrible as the witch-queen's deeper tenor.

"Sister, shall we break our sword when it misses a throat? Or shall we wield it more wisely?" Meredith sounded sane, wise, kind even. But there was madness there. Greer, who had known her time upon time, age upon age, heard the difference. She glanced at Karina, the cunning one, and saw her gaze skip from her queen to her sister, Delilah. Was there division among them? If there was, she might have a chance.

"Ah, here we are." Meredith motioned to the boys who'd brought her gear. "Stand, so that you can be as you should be. Strong. Fierce. Our Hawk. Our beloved warrior."

"You jest? A few stripes with the whip are needed, surely," Delilah cried.

Greer didn't indicate that she'd heard. She stood, calmly lifting her arms so the servant—a boy with a shaved head and bare except for a loin cloth of transparent white material—could dress her. The whip was a common punishment. It had nine lines, all of them studded with hard, sharp metal hooks that ripped the skin as they hit, digging in so that it tore away flesh with the upstroke.

"If we whip her, she will not be able to lead, sister." Again, the passive, wise tone so unlike the Black Queen. *Could it be that the madness of her magic has finally broken her?*

Greer lifted her arms higher for the servant to strap her armor in place and she dared to scan the dais where the queen sat upon her carved bone throne. The bones were from a sacred white stag, cut down with no regret by Karina. It should have lived a life protected, and yet nothing had saved it from Karina's bow. The Black Queen had simply wanted it and gotten what she desired. Nothing could stop her, not even madness.

The crimson smear of spells lined her eyes and were as familiar to Greer as her own reflection in the mirror. More so, in fact. The intricate symbols did more than declare the dark queen's love of the black arts. They muddled the mind of anyone trying to meet her gaze. Greer could discern no difference from the last time she'd been called to service, but she still suspected it. Her instincts warned her to use caution. *Don't hope.*

"We should at least question her. She has been with our enemy." Delilah sounded pleading now, as if fearful to speak and equally as anxious not to give her advice.

Always before, the queen had ruled, giving orders that everyone obeyed. Not even her sisters had dared to offer advice, unless asked. But this was different.

Could it be that the sisters were battling? Such a thing had never occurred before. The Black Queen's lieutenants had bowed to her every design. If they were at odds, they might fail to realize that she had not been called to this life by them.

"She needs to be purged," Delilah insisted. "She is not ours, not completely. She could lead Fiacre to us."

The hope that she'd been trying to resist but had built anyway died out. There would be no escape from them. There never had been.

Her armor was complete. The servant backed away from her, bowing as he went. She knew why. The Hawk killed without thought—or her own thought. She carried out the will of the women who owned her. The Queen of all that was evil.

She glided over now, and the tiny chance that she could give her soul to Jacob and save a bit of herself disappeared.

There was no madness in her eyes—no more than there always had been, at least. Greer dug down deep and buried her emotions as the Black Queen reached out with one hand. Her fingers were stained black, with red from the end of her sharp nails to her first knuckles on each finger. Some said it was blood. Greer knew it was worse. It wasn't the life force of her kills that stained her hands. It was their souls.

With one finger, she tipped Greer's head so that Greer was forced to meet her gaze. "You have been missing for far too long. Did you love the Vampire? Is that why you betrayed us?"

Greer kept her lips closed. It was difficult. The urge to respond grew with each breath. She didn't break. If she did, Jacob's life would be forfeit. Even now, she knew, it hung in the balance. Surely, she would be ordered to kill him. She knew they would demand it. Fiacre had to know as well, which meant they would find a way to stop her. They had to. She could not bear to waken to Jacob no longer in this world.

"I think you did. I think you forgot that love is a lie," the queen whispered. "A game for fools. You are mine. This." She didn't drop her gaze or the tight grip she had on Greer's chin as she picked up Greer's hand. It felt as though the ravens burned into her palm were trying to claw and peck their way out of her flesh. "This means you are mine, Dragon Guard." She spat the last words as one would a curse and dropped Greer's hand.

A moment passed, then two. Suddenly Greer felt the agony of her curse intensify until she had to drop to one knee and clutch her stomach. She expected blood to pour from her mouth when she coughed. None splattered the gray marble. Instead she coughed again and again, unable to handle the degree of agony.

Then, as suddenly as it hit, the pain vanished and, with it, everything else. Despair threatened to do what the pain could not—break her, until she sought that place, that part of herself they'd never been able to reach, that place where Brenyn and Oisin, and her parents, and her brother and sisters, existed. There she added Jacob, Fiacre and her mare, and the keep where she'd learned to live again.

With one more enormous effort she dug her fingernails into her palm, cutting half-moon slices into the ravens.

Remember. Remember there is more. Remember there is hope. I can cut their bonds as easily as this.

The Black Queen's palace became indistinct, shadowy, then with one more breath, blackness took her away.

Chapter Twenty-Five

Jacob dropped the tray of food he'd made for Greer. His senses flared. *Magic.*

His fangs dropped. He shifted to Greer's room, already sensing panic strangling him. The bed was empty. He knew the moment he sensed the dark magic that it would be. The reality of Greer not waiting there hit hard enough to drop him to his knees. He wasn't aware he was bellowing her name until someone struck him on the face.

Fiacre stood with his eyes blazing blue. When their gazes met, Jacob knew the mage understood everything. Still, he managed to force his lips to form the words.

"They have her."

Fiacre stared into his eyes and Jacob glimpsed a despair to match his own.

"Jacob, you must shift to her. We have no time." His eyes flared brightest blue. Magic tingled through the air. "We can't let them have her. I made her a promise. We shall not abandon her to them."

"How do I find her? We did not bond! There was no time," he added more to himself than Fiacre.

"I can find her. I will open a door, much as I did for Oisin and Brenyn. When I do, we must reach her quickly. They will sense my magic. Once we have her, we must travel to the Dragon Citadel. Above all else, do not let her attack," Fiacre said, squeezing his shoulder hard for an old man. "Put her to sleep as you did before when we freed you from the Faye. Only this time"—Fiacre met his gaze—"do *not* let her waken."

Jacob called his sword and, after a moment, called a shield he'd seen in the armory. He buckled it on and stood lifting the weight to test the balance. It fit him well. "And if we are separated, old man? Then what?"

"Then take her where you can keep her safe."

"Is there such a place?" Jacob prepared himself for what lay ahead. Battle. He could feel it in his bones. He was ready. It was as if his entire existence had prepared him for this one last battle...for saving her. "They will draw her back, won't they? Is there a safe place?"

"Yes. Of course." Fiacre smiled and chuckled. "A dungeon. Bars will keep her until we can kill the Black Queen and her sisters."

"So, fight whatever forces lie between us and Greer. Put her to sleep before she can kill me. Then you want me to take her to a dungeon? I only know one."

"Yes. And there, in the Silver King's lands, she will be safe. It is the last place they would think to look. Remember... It was chance that led them here. They did not sense her waking, rather a spell unfurled in Greer, drawing her to them."

"Every time?"

"Save one."

Jacob didn't ask when that one time had been. He knew. Greer had been Gwen that one time. He steadied his hands. He'd let her down before. He'd left her, lost his way when he should have returned and helped save her and her family, this kingdom. He wouldn't let her down now. "Where is she?"

Fiacre's frown grew into a network of deep wrinkles. His eyes lost focus. For a minute, then another, Jacob waited, thinking while he did of all the horrible things the Black Queen might be doing to Greer to get information out of her. Torture…worse than torture.

"Ah, they have played themselves into a corner." Fiacre sounded glad about that. Jacob wasn't as sure. Cornered animals fought all the harder.

"Where is she?"

"They are near the ancient wood, Gold Wood. Do you know it?"

"The cursed one that lies between here and Greenway? Why would they go there? That wood hates evil." If the rumors were true, the wood hated everything, evil *and* good.

"It's there we will find her — or near enough," Fiacre whispered. "She has the wild men at her side…and the Vampires. The Faye will aid us. Who else will come, I have no word. My hope is the Dragon King. With his army, we can win this battle. It's what we wanted" — Fiacre winced — "just too early by far. They may not arrive. We may be alone, left only with ourselves to win her freedom. Prepare yourself."

Jacob took a moment to let the news settle. He'd been alone most of his life. If aid came, it came. If not, they would get her out of there or he'd die trying.

"I'm ready." He drew in a deep breath, knowing as he did that he would have to find her scent as soon as they arrived. The Vampires would sense Fiacre. *And me.* He would have to blend in and walk among them unseen, if they were there. To do that, he would need to stop breathing, stop pretending to be anything other than what he was—a Vampire.

* * * *

Alrick reached the top of the rise and stared down at the army beneath him. They were a rag-tag bunch of roughly dressed warriors. Most were milling around, disorganized and not what he would call worthy opponents. But they were in somewhat straight lines, and they did appear ready to enter the forest…only they weren't.

"There's Celenia. She's near the front, by the dark one."

Silverback pointed and Alrick followed the line of his arm. A woman wearing crimson stood out, like a red flag. Her gown even had a train that trailed along behind her. "She wears a gown to battle?"

"She doesn't need to carry a sword. She *is* a weapon," Silverback reminded him.

There weren't as many Vampires as he'd imagined. The wolves were there, but they'd not shown sign of sensing them. "Does your pack know you are here?"

"Yes. I've advised them. They will not break from the Vampires until I give the signal."

"Good." The less prepared the Vampires were, the easier it would be. Some were believed to be on Silverback's side, but even those needed to be in the dark. Any leak of the intentions of the pack, and they would be stopped. "We need a way around them. If we stay out of sight and arrive when the battle begins, it will be easier in the confusion to break away from the Vampires. They will be busy with other things, you see?"

"Yes. In battle, they are at their most vulnerable. But not all will oppose us. The queen should die though. If she is gone, many will side with our freedom."

"So you've said." Alrick didn't trust easily, and definitely didn't believe the word of a Vampire often at all. There were exceptions, of course. He scanned the field, then the forest. For some reason, it held them back. Magic of some sort—and not one that the witch could counter. Yet.

"Do you see the woman on the horse, in the middle of the wild men? With the golden hair?"

Alrick saw her and bit off a curse. "She's not one of them."

"No? She is the Hawk. She kills everything that stands in her way. If the Vampires have sided with the darkness and she is here, soon other names out of legend will come and they will be unstoppable."

Alrick snorted. "Legends, eh? She is good. I would even say the best warrior I've seen in a while, but she is a woman. And she has a mate. Jacob."

"Jacob is the Vampire? Your friend?"

The dark one, as Silverback called him, was in a fit. Even from where he stood, he could sense her rage. A young boy brought her something in a cup and was struck down with a scream from the witch. Two more boys dragged him away, not daring to look at the witch.

"If they want to go through the wood, we'll go around. How big is it?"

"It will take us an hour, two. In wolf form, we will move faster. The spells keeping them out... They are not from the wood, are they?"

"I sense more than the forest is behind them. But Fiacre? Something else? I don't know. The woman, Hawk" — he pulled Silverback close so he could see his seriousness — "she is not to be harmed. No one tries to kill her. I don't know what is going on, why she is here with them, but it is not by choice. This I know."

Silverback's amber eyes glowed as his wolf checked in. "No one would willingly serve such evil." He pulled away and his gaze lingered on the field. "Except for the wild scum, that is. They have the stench of evil all their own."

"Then we head off around. Hopefully we'll locate the Faye, or Fiacre, or...some kind of allies." Alrick ran a hand over his neck. He'd lost the girl again. This time she had gone so far north that he barely had a scent of her. This battle would come first, then he would see about finding out if his future was as bleak as he believed. Surely there were Dream Walkers who weren't mortally ill. And if there were, weren't they all human? He shook his head and met Silverback's gaze, then checked in with his men. All were good warriors, men he'd be proud to have as part of the pack. "Let's do this."

He owed Jacob a debt. If not for having to save him, he'd have not come to this land. In a twisted way, Jacob had brought him his mate. Now it was up to Alrick to help bring Jacob closer to his. *Greer. What are you doing?* He shifted to his wolf form and took off, tearing up the turf with his massive paws and, for once, feeling at right with the world.

At least until I can find one very busy Dream Walker.

Chapter Twenty-Six

The drums of war beat a steady rhythm. If Greer looked back, behind her, she would see acre after acre of fighters. Most of them were Vampires, but among them, legions of warriors also marched. They were the wild men. For generation upon generation, they had served the queen. Most were dressed in black cloth with wolf pelts covering their shoulders and fangs woven into their black beards. The army covered the lands behind her as far as she could see, as well as the lands on either side of the road. They destroyed crops, killed cottagers and broke walls. Nothing stood in their way, certainly not trees. And yet they had stopped at the edge of an ancient wood. The canopy rose hundreds of feet above their heads, and within their shadowy shelter, they'd sent scouts who hadn't returned. That had been hours ago — and still they waited.

From the front of the line, the witch-queen paced from left to right. She had dismounted and raged at her sisters then at a Vampire woman, who seemed unable to offer the answers the queen demanded. Once already the queen had struck the Vampire on the face. Two other Vampires had immediately come forward to help the woman up from where she'd fallen. They gestured to the forests, seeming to offer whatever counsel they could to calm Meredith.

Greer wasn't certain anything would end the queen's rage. The forest blocked them from entering. Magic, obviously stronger than the three witches, was at work. Nothing they did seemed to penetrate. There was no obvious resistance, but here they stood, waiting.

Since they'd started out, there had been no resistance, no attacks, only more and more legions of warriors joining them. The barren lands of the Vampires had gone by in a haze of overcast skies and heated desert sands.

Only once had Greer felt something wasn't right. It had been a warrior—one of the Vampires' Lykae. His gaze had settled on her long enough to draw her attention. Their eyes had met and, instead of glancing away, he had met her gaze for a long moment then turned and jogged out of sight.

She'd ignored him. Many warriors wanted to gain her attention. It was the legend they sought. None earned more than a glance. There were only two who'd earned her trust and they were absent. Greer rubbed her nose with her wrist, suddenly unable to recall what she'd been thinking.

Officers stood beside her on their own horses. None were faces she knew. But she knew they were waiting for entrance to the wood. Now she waited. An army at her back, ready for her to lead them into a battle.

Greer's armor bit into her neck. She adjusted the leather strap on her shoulder, trying to keep her eyes on the queen, the forest and the men. The heat was almost unbearable. Almost. She wiped her brow and shifted in the saddle. Her mount sighed heavily. The mare wasn't one she'd ridden before, and because of that, she didn't trust the beast as she should. But even in the heat and dull waiting, the mare held up to her training. Her black mane was tangled where the reins had fallen. Greer settled it. It would not do to grow attached to the horse. She would most likely not survive the battle.

A boy ran through the lines with water, stopping whenever anyone lifted their hand. He and other boys his age would run up and down the lines all day, providing water to anyone who asked.

It was useless, since most warriors had a water skin. The boys would run the ranks or be without food and the meager shelter the queen provided. When they were older, they would fight for her. And when they were too old, she would release them with a death on a battlefield.

Greer shook her head to clear the constant stream of thoughts. A ragged, hollow-eyed boy walked over, but she ignored him and tried to keep her focus alert.

A shriek — an order from Karina, the queen's second — and the drums stopped. Another shout and two dozen men near the front ran toward the forest. Greer could hear the ring and chime of their armor and the heavy, dull beat of their boots pounding the ground. As a line, they shoved through the undergrowth and disappeared beneath the shadowy canopy.

She frowned, squinted at where they had entered and couldn't track them.

Another shriek, this one with understandable words, reached her. "What are you waiting for? Follow them. Now. Everyone!"

The drums stumbled then steadied. Soldiers on either side of her glanced around then began to form lines and move forward. Into the trees they went, each line disappearing. Greer scanned the forest's edge and saw no other option. She followed, shifting her visor down in preparation for trouble as she rode.

The warriors on either side of her had to control their mounts as they neared the tree line. Hers blew out a nervous breath but kept up her pace. Greer secured her shield, guiding the mare with her legs as she drew her broadsword.

Warriors near her did the same.

The anticipation of war grew, vibrating through the ranks of soldiers as they readied for whatever battle lay ahead.

"Prepare yourselves." The warning came from a lone rider ahead of her on a chestnut horse. His eyes were a fierce blue within the shadow of his visor. He raised his sword and shouted then charged in between two massive trees.

She followed, feeling the instant she crossed from meadow to beneath the dark, shadowy canopy. The air felt heavier, as if there were more moisture weighing it down. More, it felt dangerous. Her vision narrowed and focused. She saw no enemy to engage among the heavy, twisted greenery. All around her, warriors trampled through the forest, some calling out suddenly as if in pain, some shouting as if fighting an enemy.

In the chaos her mount veered to the left, dodging around a tree and forcing her to duck to avoid a low-hanging limb. An incline created more mayhem and she ended up in a small valley created by a seasonal river that merely trickled along a sandy riverbed. Above her, shouts and fighting echoed oddly to her, then another scream from the queen split the air, this one full of dark magic. Greer's skin shivered and her mare reared. She leaned forward and calmed her mount with a whisper and gentle hand on her neck.

Suddenly, everything went up in flames. She turned the mare, trying to find a gap in the fires raging at the top of the ravine. Only one path existed, downstream. She kneed her mount into a run on the sandy shore. Agonized screams filled the air and trees made horrible cracking sounds as they split then landed heavily

A tree crashed down in front of her, taking two smaller saplings down with it. Their tangled web of branches roared with flames. She pulled the mare up short and turned in a circle, scanning for a passage but seeing no way to bypass the blaze. Her horse neighed in a frightened scream. Its sides trembled and she had to fight to keep it from running off blindly. A look behind showed only one avenue and it was up. She turned her mount and kicked her into a lunging run so she could lean over her neck and prepare for the upward sprint. There was but a slim opening in between the blazing tree trucks, but every second it grew smaller and smaller as more of the dense foliage caught fire. With two heavy lunges, the mare made it through.

Warriors were sprawled on the ground, dead from either the smoke or some magic. Their blackened faces and bulging eyes said their deaths hadn't been easy. Vampires formed a contingent on her left, and within them, the black guise of the queen's painted mask shimmered.

Greer approached, careful of the fallen men still gasping for life.

The queen spotted her. "Hawk! Go ahead of us. Lead our armies to the other side! We will show these Faye death and destruction."

Wild shouts and yells from the Vampires accompanied her words. Next to her, Delilah rode, but Karina was nowhere to be seen. It didn't matter. The three witches were one when it came to what they wanted. Death…always death.

Greer rode forward, hearing fighting as she left the heavily wooded area. Up ahead, the true battle raged. Warriors suddenly flanked her, riding beside her to form a line of attack.

Their enemies were not merely Faye. She spotted the blue swirls of the ancient men of the north alongside the black capes of the Silkies and, in their midst, the shimmering green and blue of the Merfolk.

Greer didn't speak. There was no need. She dropped her reins and raised her shield as she lifted her sword and charged their ragged ranks. The first wave she cut down with her sword and horse. Beside her, the other warriors did the same. They broke through the lines and engaged. Within minutes of hard battle, she'd won to the far side of the field. She turned her mount and cut down a warrior's battle cry with a slice of her sword. A kick, then a swift stab of her sword to his chest and he fell to the ground. His cry died on his lips along with him.

"Onward. Don't stop until the field is bathed in their blood!" The witch's shout carried on the breeze, and with it came the rest of her army.

Greer charged forward, shouting as arrows suddenly filled the sky and pinged off her helm, shield and armor. None penetrated her skin. Nothing could touch her. She brought death wherever she was told.

"Not always. Once you were a woman with a heart and soul...with freedom."

The woman's voice broke through Greer's concentration the way a flood breaks a child's stone dam. Her shout died on her lips. The world dimmed. A rush of images paraded through her mind—men, women, families, farms, cities, warriors, bakers, weavers, coinsmiths, children and elders—all of them turned to stare at her with sorrow in their expressions.

As quickly as they had appeared, the parade of dead vanished. A man dressed in the battle gear of the Dragon walked toward her. His silver helm and heavy plate-mail armor were blackened and charred from battle. He held no weapon ready, and even though she knew the battle must still be raging, he walked slowly to her through a slight mist that hung to the cold ground. He reached up and removed his helm, revealing a bearded warrior with fierce blue eyes and long brown hair tied back from his face.

An archer must have hit her directly in the chest. She felt it—a pain so great that it brought tears to her eyes. She blinked to clear her sight, instantly fearing he'd disappear again. He stopped a mere foot from her, allowing her to soak up every forgotten detail of his beloved features.

"Greer. My brave daughter, you must stop fighting. You must stop and put down your arms."

Chills raced over her skin. "Is it truly you?" She reached out and startled when her fingers touched warm flesh. She no longer sat on her horse, no longer heard battle. The madness and death were happening to someone else, somewhere else.

Her father took her hand in his and brought her closer with it. His head bent to hers, he smiled, but his familiar face was filled with pain. "It is truly me, little one. You must stop. When you return, you must put down your sword and not pick it up again until you are called by your true king."

"How? How are you here? They killed you. No matter what I did, they were always going to kill you." She sobbed out a breath. "I should have listened. I should have known."

"Nay, how could you? You were a child." He touched her face and she could feel the warmth of his hand against her cheek, just like when she'd been a child. "I failed you. I didn't protect you like a father should have. King Aden was right. Until the Black Queen and her sisters have been destroyed, none of us has earned peace. But you can win it." His gaze grew intense, the power of it chilling. "You can win your freedom, daughter. You are strong. Show them how strong."

She knew what he asked. The fog the witches put on her had lifted. Her mind had returned. The compulsion to do what the witch had bid was gone. In her mind's eye, she saw Jacob, his handsome face so close that she could only see him — the way he shoved his hair out of his eyes — and she felt the fear that she hadn't been enough. Then she'd understood the way he'd been worried over not being enough for her, the feel of his body on hers, *in* hers, the heat of him — Jacob in all the multitude of ways she knew him, inside and out. She knew without a witch's sight that he fought to reach her. She saw Brenyn and Oisin...and beside them Fiacre. Near them were other warriors, men and women from the different races of this realm, ready to die to end the Black Queen's rule.

And just as clearly, she saw them perish.

"They will live if I do this."

Her father brought her hand up to his lips. "They will live. This realm will know a time of peace."

"I must die?"

"One more time, my brave daughter. One more time."

"You did not fail me," she managed past the emotions trying to close her throat. "You were the best father. I loved you. I love you."

"And I, you. My time is done here. Know that I have been nothing but proud of you, daughter."

She sniffed back the tears but more flowed, blurring him. As quickly as he had come, he was gone and she was on her horse in the middle of the battle. Sights and sounds assaulted her.

"Attack. Kill them all! The Faye will perish for their trickery. Kill them all, every one of them, my bright hawk. Fulfill your destiny," the queen shouted.

Greer felt no compulsion to do as ordered. She tested it by dropping her sword. No pain blossomed. Nothing happened except that her sword fell to the forest floor. She kneed her mount and headed to the clearing, disarming as she rode. Her shield hit the turf, followed by her helm. A breeze blew against her heated face, drying the sweat from her cheeks and forehead. The sun broke from the clouds. Smoke still shifted through the fighting, but the sun revealed the battle in all its horrible detail.

"Hawk! You will obey me or die!" The queen rode up, her face startlingly white and black in the brightness of the sunshine. The lines of paint she'd smeared on her battle visage made her look hideous. Wrinkles were revealed under the warpaint.

A weakness perhaps?

It was a glorious day to die. The sun brought warmth and the wind carried the scent of climbing pink roses.

She dismounted and unbuckled her armor. *I will not die in her colors.* A hard tug and the heavy armor came free. She threw it down and took a deep breath of clean, fresh air, unburdened by the weight of war. Her sword belt followed. Finally, she stood in a loose blouse and her breeches.

"You dare to defy me?" The Black Queen threw her head back and screamed. The sound brought a halt to the battle near them.

Greer didn't flinch. She felt no compulsion, no heat or pain of spells.

"How dare you do this? I made you. I made you strong and you show your respect by defying me?" Her formidable gaze bore down on Greer. There was madness and death in her eyes.

"I will no longer kill for you."

The lines of age that marred her face deepened. "I will make you wish you had never been born."

Greer refused to explain that the witch had done that long before. The multitude of lives Greer had been forced to live crowded her, as if she had her own army of selves at her back. All of them stood strong, uncompromisingly sure of her path. Greer felt their support like a warm fire at her back.

Delilah rode up. She dismounted and smacked Greer on the face before Greer had an idea that the blow was coming. "How dare you disarm! We are in the midst of a battle, you whore!"

"She has refused to fight."

At the queen's quiet words, Delilah jerked Greer by her hair and bent her backward by it. Greer allowed it. The grip wasn't painful, but the helplessness of not fighting back made her stomach feel hollow.

"What are your orders? Shall we kill her?"

"We will teach her a lesson."

Wildness flickered in Delilah's eyes, but she released her grip. Greer stumbled backward but stayed on her feet.

Warriors stood in a circle around them. More stood behind those, and so on in row upon row to keep the fight away from their queen. Greer didn't look to them for aid. They were as evil as the witches, if not more so in their own way.

Shouts and curses reached them, but within the circle, there was little sound. Meredith regarded her, panting as if she'd run a race. She was unused to losing so soon. Or was it the madness coming to the surface? Her black gown was splattered with blood. More crimson glittered on her hands. She carried no weapon. She needed none. Her fingers were poison, her words death to only the most stalwart. But there was an unsteadiness to her, and the obvious signs of age on her once-glowing youthful features.

Greer did not linger on the hope that the witch would die before she did. Her father had been clear. She needed to give her life, and when she did, many others would survive this day, and even better, live on free from this evil hag.

"Drag her to a tree and flog her. When she can no longer stand, she will be drawn and quartered."

The words felt as if they weighed the air down with their viciousness. Greer tried not to let herself hear, to find that buffer that always surrounded her when she fought a battle. It was gone. The savagery of her upcoming death seemed to have stolen it away. Every detail was crystal clear in her mind. She even felt the air differently upon her skin.

Delilah shrieked with laughter.

Meredith limited herself to a chuckle and motioned to a warrior. "Take her."

He immediately dismounted.

"The next time you enter this realm, you will remember this death and your betrayal."

The warriors in the circle cheered.

The man who'd dismounted beckoned to another and together they approached, looking worried. She stood with her arms down, her head up. There would be no resistance, even though her body screamed out for her to fight. Jacob was out there. At this very moment, he might enter the field, then he would die as well.

When the men realized she would offer no resistance, they took hold of her arms in a tight grip and dragged her to the trees. She didn't resist. The nearest one proved to be too wide for their rope. Cursing at her as if she were to blame, they slammed her into the next tree. The painful blow was nothing compared to what lay in store. She exhaled a shaky breath and shook her head. The one that had shoved her grabbed her by the hair and jeered at her. His teeth were a mishmash of yellow kernels that stank of rot.

"Not going to fly away this time, are you, Hawk?"

"Cut her hair off," the queen called. "I want her shaven. She will remember what defiance earns her."

The man's disgusting breath was unbearable, but Greer kept her expression blank as he yanked her by the hair, and with his knife, sawed through her braids. The loss of the weight of her hair hit hard. The pain steadied her. With a meaty, filthy hand, he squeezed her neck and used his blade to shave her head. The additional stings and slices of his blade firmed her resolve. This much hate in the world had to be stopped.

More stings and warm blood followed. She ignored him and his disgusting breath and kept her focus on her goal — death. *Once more and I will truly be free.*

The queen's laughter grew. "How ugly our shorn hawk looks, sister." With one more jerk of the blade, the man released her neck. "Tie her."

He shoved her forward into the tree again and quickly bound her wrists, so she was forced to hug the tree but with her arms stretched over her head. They used the rope to tighten her waist to the trunk too, then with a vicious, sharp pull, cut off all circulation to her hands.

"Use the barbed cat-o-nine," Meredith instructed. "I want each strike to rip her flesh from her bones. Put your back into it."

The men howled with laughter, shouting coarse curses at her.

"Wait!" The one word silenced the men. Greer held her breath, fear that the queen would change her verdict racing through her mind.

The man behind her dared ask, "Your majesty?"

"Rip her shirt open. I want to see the flesh ripped to shreds."

Relief settled over Greer. She had no modesty. Battle after battle, she'd stripped and cleaned without a care of who saw her. None would have touched her or been seen looking at her. The laughter from the men, more from the queen's sister, didn't affect her except to solidify her decision. This evil had to be stopped.

Her shirt was torn from collar to hip. The breeze felt cool and wonderful. She drew a steady breath, knowing that soon she would be unable to do so. Soon the screams would be torn from her. The pain would force them from her. But for now, she drew in deep, steadying breaths and hoped that her death would be quick enough to save Jacob from joining her.

"Now, your majesty?"

"On my count, my dear, eager man." Meredith rode her horse closer.

The breeze carried with it a bit of moisture, as if dusk were approaching and there might be mist over the meadow. She loved it when the fog blanketed the landscape and hid the signs of battle.

"I hope you remember this, my dear. No one crosses me. No one. I will rip the guts from your lover's body. I will string Poison from his intestines. And your Dragon? I'll give her to the men to use until nothing is left of her. And the best part? Poison will watch it all before he earns his own death."

Greer refused to close her eyes at the painful images. Her friends were safe. They were safe. *Jacob is safe. Brenyn and Oisin are in the north. They will be free. We will be free.*

"And when you are reborn, I will do the same thing to you until you learn that you are mine. You swore an oath. I own you." She sneered and turned to the warrior with the whip. "I want you to make each stroke count."

"Yes, your majesty."

There was an eagerness in his tone that disgusted Greer. She didn't close her eyes though. She stared out into the forest and hoped for strength.

"You may begin. I think fifty should do it, but if she's still able to stand, give her fifty more. I want her begging before you stop."

"Yes, your majesty."

"Now. Begin."

Greer didn't tense. There was nothing she could do to stop the pain that would follow. There was nothing but enduring it and hoping that this time she would die and never be reborn. *Jacob, I love you. Always.*

Chapter Twenty-Seven

Jacob scanned the forest. It was charred and in places still burning. There was smoke on the air, masking the scents of death, but not completely. He had no sense of smell—of anything. They'd walked for hours, lost in the Gold Wood. It looked little like a golden wood to him. It was broken, and the magic in it was...wrong.

"Are we too late?" He fisted his hand on his sword hilt. It shouldn't be, but fate was a fickle bitch. "I still can't find her scent. Are we too late? Is she gone?" He could barely say the words. Hurt like he'd never felt before hit him. A bottomless pit of it. Her scent wasn't on the air. It wasn't here. If she were gone... If they'd simply killed her...

"No. This fire is the queen's doing and it's fresh. Greer still lives. I sense..." Fiacre paused, and his vision did that off-and-about that Jacob had never liked. Now he hoped that meant he could find Greer. "She's awakened." A frown deepened the wrinkles.

"What do you mean? She's awakened?"

"She's not bound to them. The link is…gone."

"What? How?" Hope built up where despair had held him down.

"There's no time. They will be… We must hurry. She's near. We must hurry." Fiacre gripped his arm. "You must find her. *Now!*"

Jacob drew in another breath, but he couldn't pick up her scent. "I can't. There's no hint of her." He couldn't ask, couldn't bear to think that she'd broken her bond to them with her death.

"Then we find her. Follow me. There's no time to waste." Fiacre didn't wait. He walked ahead, a gray-robed old man with a staff, heading toward the sound of battle. If the sun stayed behind the clouds, Jacob could stay within the shadows of the trees. It was his nightmare come to life. But the wind was blowing and the clouds were thinning above him.

"She is here. I sense it," Fiacre said. "Don't give up hope, Jacob. Hope is essential."

Jacob held in his immediate need to shout at the old man. It wasn't Fiacre's fault. It was his. *I should have bonded her. If we'd bonded, I could sense her. Talk to her. See what she sees.*

Fiacre stepped over a fallen warrior and bent to examine the next. "Faye. The battle has come. Greer is…"

"What? Greer is what?"

"Essential, Jacob." Fiacre's eyes were always disturbingly intense, but the strength in them now spoke of something painful. "Jacob. Listen to me. There is no time. We must find her. I fear—" His gaze slid above Jacob's head, but Jacob grabbed his shoulder and brought him back. There was no time to go off in his head, not now, not when Greer was in even more danger than before.

"You fear what? Tell me."

"I fear she will sacrifice herself."

The world was suddenly ablaze with sunlight as the wind shifted the clouds away from the sun. Still under the shadows of the trees, Jacob felt as if he'd already been burned to his soul. "I will not lose her."

Fiacre's eyes blazed brightest blue. "No. We will not. Follow me."

* * * *

Brenyn took Oisin's hand in hers. The warmth and strength of his bigger hand comforted her. Ahead of them, the mage Aubrey and her warrior walked with space between them, but Brenyn saw the unsettled and unspoken love there. It created a tension that couldn't be hidden by not speaking of it.

"I had forgotten you were a romantic."

She smiled up at Oisin and bumped his side with her shoulder. "You never forget anything."

"Not about you. No. Is she strong enough?"

Brenyn watched Aubrey lift her head to stare up at the ceiling then down the walls of the corridor. Her beauty was pale, but there was fire in her eyes — strength and courage. "Fiacre believes she is. The Dream Walker is here. She must also believe. Do you doubt?"

"She is a wee bit smaller and younger than I thought she'd be."

"Size does not matter. Look at me."

"You? I could scoop you up and carry you for weeks." Oisin laughed, a sound she wanted to hear daily — and would if Aubrey could wake her brothers and sisters, and her father.

"I think she is powerful enough. I can…feel it." She touched her chest.

Oisin's gaze lingered on her face then turned to scan the entrance to the Dragon's Heart. She did the same. It had been a long time since she'd walked these halls. She'd been a mere child, too young to truly be allowed down here where the Dragons ruled their realm.

"Fiacre broke an evil spell that had been placed on this door," Aubrey said. "His spells are still strong. The floor will be spelled. Don't look at it too long." She lifted her hand and circled it. Blue lines appeared in the air and more rose on her hand, as if she'd burned tattoos of blue there.

Brenyn felt the magic grow. Oisin did as well and drew her closer to his side, likely for protection.

Aubrey murmured something in a language that made Brenyn's skin tingle. A crack sounded and the door disappeared from the middle to the sides of the arch.

"It's broken!" The arch lay in ruins on the stone floor, but the keystone still held strong in the very center of the arch, ensuring that the entire thing didn't topple. Carved words were half-missing but Brenyn couldn't stop herself from smiling as she read what remained. "You enter the Heart of the Dragon. Beware, enemies, for within lies your death," she read aloud. "It is still secure."

"Aye. Fiacre re-positioned the spells to hide the damage, but they are still intact," Aubrey whispered. There was awe in her tone as she went on, "We have reached the Dragons." She entered the hall and turned in a circle, gazing around with wonder clear on her face.

Brenyn tightened her grip on Oisin and stepped through the entrance. At once she heard the heartbeat of her family. Tears stung her eyes. "I hear them."

"Easy, they live. We knew they lived," Oisin murmured, cradling her closer to his chest.

She breathed in the scent of him and soaked in the steady thud of his heart blending with that of her family. "I doubted so long. All this time they were here. Sleeping."

"We could not have come to them. You know that. It will take the mage to wake them. Even Fiacre cannot bring them out of their sleep."

She sniffed back her tears and turned her head to stare over at Aubrey. Her warrior, Greyson, stood near her, the seer off to the side, huddled in on herself with her two guards on either side of her. Evie clearly suffered from the cold. Soon the hall would be lit with fires and she would no longer feel the chill. The Dream Walker had left them with the advice to hurry. Brenyn worried over that advice but knew that the only way to help Greer was to free her family. Aubrey did not seem affected by the cold, further proof that she was the Dragon Mage.

"Are you strong enough?" Oisin asked her.

Greyson cast him a steady frown that made Brenyn smile. "He meant no disrespect, Greyson. Time is short. Greer needs us…all of us."

Aubrey blew out a cloud of breath. She looked anxiously from Brenyn to Oisin. "I will be strong enough. My family swore an oath. Many have suffered to ensure that I stood here, at this time, for this purpose."

Brenyn settled herself. It was enough.

"Stand to the sides," Aubrey murmured. "I will wake your brothers and sister first. The king... He is deeper in his sleep. Do you sense them?"

"Aye. I sense them." She could feel something from her brothers, as if her presence had disturbed their slumber. Eden and Conleth had been much older than her, she remembered. They'd had many duties and responsibilities, but both had always shown her love. So had Keegan, her elder sister. They had all been a part of her life until their world had been turned inside out. "Wake them, mage. Hurry."

Aubrey glanced at Greyson and motioned him back. "I will need to stand alone. The magic I call will be...unpredictable." She undid her cloak and coat and held them out to Greyson. The warrior took them slowly and the two shared a look that pierced Brenyn's heart.

"He fears she will give her life to this."

"Aye, perhaps he has reason to fear. The magic will be powerful." Oisin pulled them to the wall.

Greyson stepped away from Aubrey and stood to the side where she'd gestured. Aubrey smoothed her sweater and took a deep breath. She looked nervously at them, then focused on the domed ceiling far above their heads.

"You were born to do this, Aubrey Mac Cinaed," Evie called. "Everything you've done has been to help you have the power to waken the Dragons."

"Agreed," Brenyn said. "You are the Dragon Mage. Our blood runs in your veins, mage."

"We will aid you, if you have need," Oisin added.

Aubrey straightened, nodding as she drew in another deep breath. "The magic will be powerful.

Make sure you stay far back. When they waken, they may waken in their Dragon forms."

Oisin laughed. "Aye, I believe they might."

Brenyn smiled. She had practiced her Dragon form until she could shift to it on the run. Her siblings were much more able. "I will be here. They will know me."

"Aye." Aubrey blew out a mist of breath and closed her eyes. She lifted her right hand again and circled the air, creating a path of blue. Murmured words flowed from her, growing louder and louder. Her boots lifted from the tiles and her hair blew from a breeze she had to be making. Oisin drew them back to the side of the hall. Evie and her men did the same. Only Greyson stood, watching her to the exclusion of all else.

When she was five feet in the air, the words she spoke rumbled and echoed through the cavern. A sudden stirring near her made Brenyn's heart race. The wall opposite her cracked and drew aside to reveal a dark-haired man with his head bowed and his hands clasped on a sword hilt. The tip of the blade rested on the floor, but as she watched, it lifted, and as it did, the man slowly raised his head. *Eden.* Her heart raced and heat shimmered over her skin.

His eyes remained closed. Brenyn held her breath. With a suddenness that had her jumping closer to Oisin, Eden opened his eyes and leaped from his chamber. He didn't shift to dragon but shouted a battle cry that echoed through the cavern.

Along the chamber two more doors opened. Conleth emerged from one, his auburn hair pulled back from his strong features and his sword in his hand. Keegan vaulted from her chamber with a bow in her hand, her arrow already notched. She jerked her head to dislodge a strand of dark hair from her eye, then very slowly lowered her bow.

Another crack sounded above Aubrey's chanting.

Her brothers and sister slowly eased their positions as recognition entered their eyes.

Brenyn's vision blurred and tears she couldn't stop flowed. Her eldest brother saw her and his face changed from aggression to wonderment then joy. "Brenyn!"

Keegan and Conleth moved as one but froze as Aubrey's magic suddenly flooded the chamber with brilliant blue light. Every inch of the massive room was detailed in it. It grew brighter than the sun.

"Don't move!" Evie shouted. "She wakens your father now."

Her heart felt near to bursting with joy. "It's them. Oisin, it's truly them."

"Aye, little one. Your family."

"And yours." She hugged him tight around his waist and brushed back her tears. She couldn't decide where to look, for she wanted to see all of them at once.

Aubrey suddenly screamed. It sounded painful but filled with purpose. Her blue tattoos grew so bright that it was impossible to look at her straight on. The power in the chamber grew until giant icicles dropped from the ceiling and crashed onto the floor. Oisin tightened his grip on her and pressed them back against the wall. A tingle trickled down her skin. She stepped away from Oisin—or tried to. "Oisin, let me go. I…sense something. She needs us."

"Careful, Brenyn."

"I am in control." She felt the Dragon coming. Her eldest brother stood straight across from her. He too felt it.

"She is correct," he shouted. "We need to aid her." He sheathed his sword and, with a hunch of his shoulders, he burst to Dragon.

Brenyn drew in a breath as her siblings all shifted to their Dragons. She sent her love to Oisin and let go of her control.

Aubrey's eyes opened and blue flames were present to Brenyn's Dragon sight. The fire blazed brighter and brighter until, with another determined scream, Aubrey spread her arms wide. Magical flames lit her from her fingers and flowed from her body until Brenyn had to squint.

The floor beneath Aubrey suddenly disappeared, and from the depths of his lair, her father's eyes shone with brilliant flames.

In that instant, Aubrey fell, and through her link with the world, Brenyn sensed Greer. She was not with Fiacre, not safe, not secure with Jacob. She was once again at death's door.

Brenyn roared in pain and locked eyes with her father. "Father, we cannot let her die!"

"She will not give her life again," he roared.

Her father's promise burned in her breast. She only hoped they were not too late.

Chapter Twenty-Eight

Jacob's shoulders ached from wielding his sword. He'd been attacked from the moment he'd stepped out of the burned remains of the ancient wood. At least two thousand warriors fought for no apparent reason other than the sheer need to destroy each other. He'd cut through dozens. Most wore bones threaded through their beards and had dark charcoal around their eyes with a white paste smeared over their foreheads and in angles on their cheeks. It was a ghastly sight. They stank of rank, sweet flesh left out to rot. Their ragtag bands seemed to be circled around the exact area he wanted to reach. He wanted to shift but wasn't clear where to go. The smoke and stench of death confused Greer's scent.

His frustration mounted the longer he had to deal with the black-bearded fools. From his flank, he scented Vampires. Scanning the field, he saw them. Dressed in black battle gear and helmetless, they stood out simply because they fought side by side with cold efficiency.

Near them, he thought he thought he spotted Alrick with a band of Lykae, but they were engaged in fighting off the disgusting black-beards. But Alrick might have a better gauge on where Greer was in this chaos. He shoved his sword in the gut of a burly black-beard, jerked it free and took off in Alrick's direction.

"Alrick!"

The king of the Lykae tossed a tall, rangy warrior over his shoulder and spun to impale the man in the throat. He ripped his sword free, effectively cutting the man's head off. "Jacob."

"Do you scent her? Greer?"

Alrick scowled and shook his head. He was sweaty and breathless, but when Jacob took a step closer, he narrowed his eyes and held up a hand. "Let me catch my breath."

"The golden warrior is in trouble."

Jacob looked behind him and faced a Vampire with silvering black hair. He bowed slightly and gestured to the band of wild men Jacob had been trying to get past. "She is there, behind the Black Queen's warriors."

"This is Brock. He's helped the Lykae free themselves from the Vampires." Alrick waved between them. "This is Jacob."

"Our true king," Brock said politely.

"Look... All that's great. And later, I'll congratulate you, but right now —"

"She's important," Brock said. "I can aid you. *We* can aid you. They will break if enough force is applied. They outnumber us. That is their only advantage."

A sudden change in the air and Jacob spun, catching a black-bearded man in the shoulder. Alrick fought next to him, and nearby the others were suddenly under assault. Jacob traded blow after blow with the giant before finally driving his sword into his stomach when the man overstepped and floundered to find his footing on the increasingly muddy ground. Over the man's dying groans, a pain-filled scream reached him. His entire body felt dipped in ice. He knew that voice. Knew *her* voice. Through the chaos, he spotted Fiacre racing toward him.

"Greer!" Whatever caused her to make such a sound terrified him to the bottom of his soul.

Fiacre reached him and steadied him with a hand on his shoulder. "It's Greer. We need to reach her."

"I can't find her! The smoke is in the way!"

Fiacre held up his hand and whispered words that made Jacob's skin crawl. Brock and Alrick both looked serious while the other men stood and acted as a buffer from the fighting. A wind picked up and suddenly her scent reached him. "There." Where Brock had indicated, but clearer, along the tree line. His relief was short-lived. The scent of her blood saturated the air. "She's hurt. We must hurry!"

"I agree," Fiacre said, not releasing him. "Stay with me. Let me see if I can't force this wind to bring us some cloud cover."

"Who cares about the clouds?" he shouted as he took off in a run toward the sound of Greer's second scream.

"The sun is returning. You'll be killed!"

"Jacob, wait a goddamn second!" Alrick yelled.

He didn't wait. His skin sizzled from the sun, but he was strong. He could last. Nothing mattered more than reaching her. His greatest fears had come to life. She was suffering and his limitations would *not* stop him. He vaulted over a warrior instead of engaging him. He landed poorly and felt his knee buckle. Without slowing, he let himself roll and rose to his feet still running. He could hear Alrick swearing as he kept up, and he knew that the Vampires had joined them. They were keeping the black-beards back from him and that was all that mattered.

The third scream tore through the forest and ripped his soul to shreds. He burst through a weaker link of the black-beards and frantically scanned the battlefield before him. Faye fought everywhere he looked. Beside them were the colors of the Silkies and Merfolk. The warriors from before, the ones with blue on their skin, Aubrey's kin, were there as well.

His skin began to blister. A sudden blast of wind and clouds billowed over the meadow, making it look like twilight.

"Damn it, Jacob. Look at your hands and neck, man!"

Jacob ignored Alrick's grumbling and tried to see her.

Through the battle sounds, the sickening crack of a whip hitting flesh and the grunt of the person wielding it reached him.

He exchanged a startled glance with Alrick and Fiacre. They'd heard it too.

A scream, this one filled with sobbing breath and pain, reached him. There was no time. Not now. Without knowing exactly where she was, he shifted to the other side of the clearing. He'd guessed right. A quick strike, and he shoved his sword through the back of a man wielding a barbed whip. Two other warriors attacked him, but he broke one's neck with a hit of his hand and toppled the other with a spin and slash of his sword. From behind him, he sensed Alrick and his team, along with Fiacre. He let them deal with the rest and turned toward Greer.

He nearly fell to his knees at the sight of her.

Her back wasn't simply slashed with lines from a whip. It was torn and ripped open. Blood bathed her from her neck down to her breeches. More blood pooled at her feet. Her golden hair no longer hung in marvelous braids down her back. Her head had been shaved roughly, leaving chunks of skin missing and golden stubble in uneven patches. But that wasn't the worst. Her back. Her beautiful back…

"Jacob, easy, man. She's alive. She'll recover. She's strong," Alrick said.

Jacob lost the words in a roar that seemed to fill his mind.

"Jacob. Wait. Wait!" Fiacre passed him and reached her first. He touched her forehead. Her head slumped to her shoulder and her body eased in the ropes they'd used to keep her upright. Her breathing slowed, and when it did, Jacob realized Fiacre had sent her to sleep.

He felt like his head had filled with sludge. His thoughts were disjointed, the voices around him muffled. All he could see was Greer and the torture they'd put her through. He stood, helpless and unable to process the impact of her pain.

Horses, galloping closer, had him turning, sword ready. He lowered it at the sight of two riders. A Faye warrior bowed his head respectfully, but it was the other familiar face that made him straighten and lower his weapon. "Aubrey."

"Jacob!" Aubrey slipped from her horse, only to reveal Greyson, the human warrior he knew from the Immortal Council, behind her. Aubrey scanned his face. "Jacob, you are free."

"I am." He shook his head and felt a painful tightness in his throat. "Can you heal her, Aubrey?"

Her gaze fell upon Greer and she raised a hand, holding it to her lips. Tears filled her eyes. "The sacrifice."

Jacob shook his head. "No. She lives. She lives." He could hear her heart. It was faint, but there. He wasn't losing her. Not now. She'd broken free. She'd ended the curse.

"Aubrey knows that, Jacob. She can—" Fiacre paused, and Jacob glanced at him, then at where the old man stared off into the heavy clouds above them.

"They come," the Faye warrior murmured, dismounting.

"They? Who?" If it was the witches, he would kill them.

Alrick still had his sword out, ready to aid him. His warriors were also alert, but they had their heads cocked to the side, as if they scented something but couldn't trust it. Jacob drew in a breath and held it. The scent was wild, filled with power and something else.

"The Dragons." Aubrey walked to Greer's side as she spoke, her focus clearly on Greer. "I freed them. They come to destroy the Black Queen."

Jacob shook his head. He didn't care about the Black Queen or Dragons. "Can you help her, Aubrey?"

"Fiacre has taken her away from the pain." Aubrey covered Greer's forehead with her hand. She bowed her head and the tattoos on her arms shimmered blue.

"She's done enough magic for one day, Jacob," Greyson murmured. "She shouldn't do more."

Jacob didn't bother to answer the man. It was clear he was worried about Aubrey, but Aubrey's back wasn't a painful mass of bleeding flesh.

"I cannot heal her, but there is one who will," Aubrey said, standing as she spoke. "I'm strong, but not strong enough to heal her as quickly as you'd no doubt like, Jacob."

"Who can?"

"The Dragon King." Aubrey pointed to the clouds. "He can heal her."

"They come," Alrick whispered, sounding unlike himself.

A wind billowed through the meadow, flattening Jacob's cloak to his legs and making him hold up an arm to keep the dirt out of his eyes.

He squinted out from the protection in time to watch a golden Dragon drop down from the clouds. It landed gracefully, but the men on the ground scattered. The remaining black-beards ran, as if the devil was at their feet. The other warriors went to one knee in respect.

In the sky above the field, other Dragons winged into sight. An enormous golden one arrowed downward, grabbed a black-clothed woman and crushed her in its talons. Another dragon and another swept downward, each grabbing running warriors and tossing them aside. A screamed curse cut through the sound of mighty wings. The light went out of the day.

Jacob stepped backward toward Greer. Whatever this new magic was, he would kill anyone who dared approach her.

Fiacre shouted and a bright blue flame shot from his staff. It went high overhead, and where it traveled, the battlefield was revealed again. Alrick had moved to stand beside him, protecting Greer with him, and next to him stood Brock, his face impassive, sword out.

Aubrey joined Fiacre, and with her swirling tattoos blazing bright under her skin, she cried out a spell that formed an arch to meet Fiacre's.

Greyson stood impassive on the side, watching Aubrey to the exclusion of all else. To Jacob, she appeared strong and hale. The human didn't understand the power of her — or any of them — if he questioned her ability.

The enemy warriors, those that remained, dropped their swords and ran, covering their faces while they tried to flee, as if the blue light hurt them. Faye warriors on horses pursued them.

Silence settled on the field of battle. The depth of it was like nothing Jacob had ever experienced before. It felt sacred.

A Dragon flew through the arched flames unharmed and rose in the air with another witch in its claws. Wherever she'd been hiding hadn't been far enough. She appeared to fight back, but another Dragon soared in and took hold of her, and together they ripped her body in two.

The warriors on the field cheered.

None of that mattered. Jacob turned back to Greer and felt his legs grow weak all over again. He forced himself to walk to her before they gave out, then fell to his knees beside her. Head bowed, he could barely bear to look at her mutilated back. The blood scent was strong. Her blood. Her heart beat fragile, as if she barely held on. *I will die this day if she leaves me.*

Footsteps behind him alerted him to someone approaching, then the familiar scent of Brenyn was there. Her face was flushed from battle and Oisin was a step behind her. Both wore expressions of concern. He couldn't bear it.

"I couldn't protect her."

"She put down her weapons. She refused to fight." Brenyn touched his shoulder, drawing his head up. "She defied them."

He shook his head. "I don't know what you mean. I don't care. I want her healed. She was in such pain."

"She defied the queen, Jacob," Aubrey said softy, too gently.

Brenyn knelt beside him. "She sacrificed herself, and when she did, she freed us. Without her sacrifice, the queen would have been more powerful. Too powerful. She did this to help us win."

"You don't...understand. None of that matters." He fisted his hands. "I can't lose her."

"You won't lose her." Oisin squeezed his shoulder. "We always died in battle. We never refused to fight."

"You did." Brenyn rose to her feet and touched Oisin's cheek.

"Only when I killed myself, and by doing so, ensured I was theirs again. But Greer? She always died in battle."

"And? Why tell me this now!" He couldn't bear to see the mass of broken flesh on her back, the horrible split skin, but he couldn't bear not to look. "Just heal her, Brenyn. Get the Dragon King!"

Oisin took him by the arm and almost lost his. "This means she may have broken the curse. If the cursed witches are dead..."

"The Dragons killed two of them," Greyson said to the field.

"Karina has escaped," offered the Faye.

Jacob had no idea who he was, but he spoke with assurance. All Jacob wanted was for Greer to be free of this pain.

A dark-haired man with a beard threaded with silver came into sight. He wore the crimson and silver of the Dragon Guard. He was a legend walking, but Jacob had no time for any of them.

"Unless he can heal Greer" — he had to clear his throat to continue — "I don't have time for him."

"Jacob." Oisin squeezed his shoulder, harder this time. "He can and will. He is the king. Our king, the Dragon King."

Oisin and Brenyn each gave the man a respectful bow of their heads, but the king smiled and shook his head. "Neither of you two will bow to anyone, least of all me, daughter," he said. He reached Brenyn, cupped her neck with his hand and lowered his head so his forehead rested against hers. "Daughter, you have saved our people."

"It was not just I, Father. Oisin, Greer, Fiacre, Aubrey and her warrior Greyson...and this man, Jacob."

"Man?" The king's stare was strong, but Jacob had grown up with kings. "Are you not a Vampire?"

"I am. Once, I was merely a man who loved a woman. This woman. Can you heal her?" Jacob forced himself face her broken body again. His throat tightened.

"Greer, the daughter of my most trusted warrior. To her I would offer my kingdom. Healing her will be the least I will do, Jacob."

He knows my name, which means he knows who I am and who Greer is to me. The panic eased. "Then stop talking and do it."

Brenyn sucked in a shocked breath.

The king stepped closer and drew Jacob's eye. There was no anger in his expression, only understanding.

Jacob didn't want any of it. Through gritted teeth he said, "She's hurting."

"Not any longer. She is asleep," the king observed, lending him a hand to rise to his feet. "I will take her home. Fiacre will show you the way, I am certain."

"I can take him," Brenyn offered.

Oisin grinned and smacked him on the shoulder. "I hope you're not afraid of heights."

Jacob didn't answer. He watched as the Dragon King knelt on one knee next to Greer and whispered to her. He placed a hand on her head then turned to Jacob. "Untie her and I will take her home."

The words, with the action, did it. Fear, panic, guilt and love so deep that it felt bottomless all attacked him, and he bowed his head, trying to manage the chaos of his emotions. It took only a moment, but he felt as if the world had stopped while he battled. "I will repay this debt with all I am. I give you my word."

"There is no debt, Jacob. You have brought her back to us. For this, you have my thanks. Untie her. Let us leave this place of death."

The bonds were so tight that Greer's hands were white from lack of blood. When Jacob carefully cut the rope, her arms dropped like heavy weights and she fell backward. If Jacob hadn't been there to catch her, she would have fallen. He gathered her carefully closer so as not to disturb her back. Oisin knelt next to him and helped shift her so that Jacob could carry her over his shoulder.

"I will hold her. Make the gate, Fiacre. I will carry her to the Dragon Lands. I'm not about to ride a Dragon with her in my arms."

Brenyn laughed. "I think he's afraid of heights."

"Mayhap," Oisin offered.

Fiacre simply opened a gate to a land of snow and ice. Jacob stood, lifting Greer's weight easily. Alrick nodded to him. Brock did the same. All around him, the people he knew and had just met formed a protective circle. Not that many of the enemy remained. There was Karina, but she would not dare.

He reached out and clasped Fiacre's shoulder.

"Thank you."

Fiacre smiled and in it, Jacob saw a brief glimpse of the younger, happier man he'd once been. Then Fiacre released him, and Jacob stepped through the gate with Greer.

Epilogue

Something warm cocooned Greer. She moved her fingers to test the sensation. It was warm and wet. Water. There was more to the water — something special, *someone* special. She couldn't open her eyes. Her lids were too heavy, the darkness too comforting. It was not as comforting as the warm arms that held her, but the pull of sleep was strong.

"Don't go. I can't bear it if I lose you again."

That voice. The cadence of it, the pitch, the warmth in the tone tugged at her. Memories of a boy with jet-black hair and soft brown eyes filled her mind's eye. It floated along the stream of consciousness that tried to claim her. Another glimpse of him, this one of his face firmed with age, a shadow of bristle on his jaw as he said goodbye. *Leaving me.*

"I only meant to be gone for a short while. I never meant to leave you."

"You did leave me. I stood and drowned in sorrow and you did nothing to stop it. You caused it."

She shared the painful memory, once again caught in the loneliness of being deserted by the one she loved most in all the world, and the days after, when she had hoped against all odds that he would return, followed by the months when she had realized he would not and, finally, the cold acceptance that she had never mattered.

"Not true. You were all that mattered. Come back to me. I will prove it for the rest of eternity."

Will I live that long?" Eternity. Hadn't she already endured eternity through lives she had never wanted to live?

"You won't need to if you don't want to."

The silliness of the sentence did something to her. She smiled and opened her eyes. A face took shape. His face. *Jacob.* His expression was lined with pain and worry. His eyes were darker, the bruises under his eyes unfamiliar, but the depth of his love was there.

"Jacob."

He curled his arms and she was closer to his warm chest, his wet, warm chest. She felt as weak as a babe. With effort, she raised her hand and touched his jaw. He let her go enough to look up at him again. He grinned, a quick flash of happiness that stabbed her painfully. "I thought I would lose you."

At his words, the crack of the whip shocked her into sitting upright. Pain flashed down her back then disappeared as if it were only a memory.

"It's over. You're here. We're both here. The Black Queen is dead, Greer. She's dead."

Disbelief rushed her, then a surge of something so joyous, so right that she felt as if she could fly. She hugged him close and pressed her face against his warm neck. "It's true? You aren't lying?"

"It's true." His voice sounded choked. She loosened her hold on him but still hugged him to her. It felt so good, so right. His heart beat in time with hers. They were one—or would be. "You're free of her."

"You both are."

That voice. She stiffened and released Jacob to scan her surroundings, immediately spotting a man dressed in the scarlet and gold of the Dragons. His eyes... His eyes glowed with flames, but it was his serious expression that stilled her.

"Greer, you have done your family proud." He pressed his right hand over his heart and bowed his crowned head.

"You..." She tried to gain her feet and couldn't. She was sitting in a fountain. The warm waters lapped around her. "You..."

"The Dragon King. He healed you." Jacob tightened his hand on hers. "You were... I failed you, Greer. You were—"

"No." She stopped him with a hand to his mouth. "You did not fail me, Jacob." She lowered her hand and took his. "My father came to me. He told me the path I had to take. And...it worked? I am truly free?" She scanned Jacob's dear face and saw that he believed that to be truth. She turned to her king.

"You are free of their spells. You are both free."

She tilted her head. "Jacob was spelled by them?"

"Not by them, but he has gone with you into my healing waters. He is now free of his Vampire curse."

Next to her, Jacob stiffened to the point that she worried he'd harm himself. She took his face in her hands and stared into his beautiful eyes. He was warm. His heart was racing. She could feel his pulse under her palms. "You are unhappy with this?"

"What?" He covered her hands with his, brought them to his mouth and kissed them. She'd thought she'd never feel that caress again, never have him, and here he was. They had each other.

Grinning, he pulled her to her feet then lifted her in his arms. "I'm stronger now. Nothing can take you from me ever again."

"Only death. You won't live an eternity now," she reminded him.

"But we will live, and we are going to live a long, long life, Greer." He spun her and his grin was contagious. When he set her down, he grimaced. "We're wet."

"But not cold," Greer noted.

"As well you shouldn't be. Have you never wondered who you are, Jacob?" The Dragon King wore a smile that reminded her of her father. He was up to something.

At the king's question, Jacob paused in the act of helping her from the pool. He gazed at Aden with suspicion. "No."

Aden smiled. "I find myself doubting your truthfulness. But let me assure you that both of you will have long lives. The blood of the Dragon runs through you. It will be for me to decide how long you live. And if you choose a normal length of time, I shall ensure this, but I would not lose either of you quickly."

"What? I'm... How can I be a Dragon?" Jacob demanded. "I was found in the Rose Kingdom. That's a hell of a distance from here."

"Aye, 'tis." The king straightened and sighed. "I have much to do, and the two of you should change. Your friends would dearly like to see you both happy and whole. I dare say my daughter will not wait much longer to assure herself of your wellbeing, Greer."

At the mention of Brenyn, Greer couldn't contain her happiness. "And Oisin? He is here as well?"

"Everyone is here, even the Faye King. There is a battle on the horizon. But for now, we have earned a slice of peace. Use it wisely." With that, Aden turned and strode from the courtyard.

Greer met Jacob's eyes and in them saw what she felt reflected back at her. "If I can choose, I will love you for eternity."

"Eternity it is, my love."

He lifted her again and swung her in a circle with such joy on his handsome face that she thought she'd burst. A winter wind blew in through the courtyard, bringing the cold, clean scent of snow with it. But on that wind, she detected no roses. Instead, the winds brought change—the kind that she had never dared dream of.

She drew in a deep breath and, holding Jacob's face between her hands, she let her happiness fill the space between them. "Even eternity will never be enough."

Want to see more from this author? Here's a taster for you to enjoy!

Love's Command: Running Scared
Billi Jean

Excerpt

There has to be some kind of mistake.

The MapQuest directions sat on the truck seat next to Lacey, outlining that this was the right exit. She hadn't accidentally decided to take a wrong turn. Besides, there weren't any decisions in her life right now, only directions. She smiled at the thought. Yeah, her attempts at making colossal, life-changing decisions had landed her here, in the middle of nowhere, with no one and nothing around her.

Well, not exactly nothing. There were mountains everywhere. Huge, monstrous mountains, like the kind you could see on the travel channel seconds before some giant paw-waving, open-mouthed, roaring grizzly ate the cameraman.

Oh, yeah, this had to be some kind of mistake. Lacey needed the beach. And people. At this point, she'd settle for a pizza from her favourite beach shack. To hell with anyone else. She needed out of this truck, she realised, surprising herself with a broken mini-sob.

There wasn't a car in sight when she pulled her truck off the turn lane and stopped a few hundred yards onto the cracked asphalt of the old highway.

Two fumbles at jerking the door handle open, and she jumped down, the map in her hand. Blue sky, a cold November breeze, clean air and mountains filled her senses immediately. One deep breath, two, and half the tension simmering along her skin disappeared. Not the unease, though. The breeze felt different from home. Smelt different. Was different.

This has to be a mistake.

She rubbed her hand through her hair at the thought. Yeah, sure, this had to be a mistake, right? Wrong. Throughout this mess, she'd kept thinking that any time now she'd wake up, that this couldn't be happening, that there had to be some kind of freaking mistake. Life couldn't turn from normal to horrible in the blink of an eye. A decision to go outside a club trying to avoid a creepy guy couldn't destroy everything she'd worked so hard to build.

But, yeah, one look at the rugged, wilderness reminded her that, yeah, one thoughtless decision had ripped her life to shreds.

If she could reverse time, she'd—what? If she'd known that by leaving the bar she'd witness a mob hit, would she have taken her chances with the creepy guy? Probably not.

So here she was, standing on the side of a road on what looked like some crazy Wild West movie set.

Reality sucked. Delusions worked so much better—at least for about ten seconds. Lacey hadn't witnessed a murder. She hadn't been beaten to within an inch of losing her life. She hadn't spent months in a hospital trying to breathe on her own. She hadn't been forced to testify against some of the nastiest criminals in the world. She hadn't been left out to dry like this, forced to move, alone, to a place so remote and far from normal she might as well have been on another planet.

She was used to people, sunshine that smelled like the ocean...heck, music and noise, for God's sake. She was used to delis filled with adorable little old Italian men, smiling at her and asking about her day. She was used to Jewish bakeries with bagels that she'd get up at seven for on a Sunday morning. She was used to coffee shops brewing wicked espresso by the cup. She was used to nice people. Beaches. Safety.

The landscape facing her she was not used to. Big open grasslands, lined with the brilliant colours of fall foliage. Yellow and burnt cinnamon, deep green pines next to the white bark of some other kind of tree — beech or aspen, she didn't know — all created a wildly beautiful picture.

The view gave her the creeps. Maybe she was afraid of wide-open spaces. Agoraphobia was a possibility.

Humour bubbled up and she rubbed her face with both hands. The map crumpled a little, reminding her of the brutal reality of her new life. She was running scared. Nothing was going to change that. Not standing here, not staring off at the mountains, nothing.

So many regrets washed over her. Tears stung her eyes — she felt like they were clogging her throat. Lacey fought them and ignored the deep hollow pit in her stomach.

She needed a plan. Action washed all the turmoil aside — always had. She'd always filled her life with action. Being forced to sit in a truck for days on end had driven her slightly insane, no doubt.

The real estate office in Troy couldn't be too far. She'd find that, then her home, and see her new address for the next... Ah, God, who knew how long she'd be here?

Forever?

And didn't that thought put a huge dollop of pity into her pity-party sundae? Two blinks and the tears held off, so she focused on the mountains. The peaks looked white, possibly ten feet deep in snow by now. She could hike up to that snow; feel the cold on her face, maybe trail run along the ridges and ravines? They would be a challenge. Something to do. Later, maybe, after she'd settled in.

A truck slowed behind her, bringing the heartbeat she'd settled down to normal skyrocketing. What felt like ice water flooded her veins, while goosebumps beaded along her arms and a huge whoosh of adrenaline raced through her veins. The FBI agents had been clear: do not act anything but normal. What that meant, really, after all she'd endured, was a bit unclear. She didn't feel normal in her own skin, let alone here in this wilderness. Besides, she doubted she would look normal to a small western town filled with redneck cowboys. She was a beach babe, had always been one, and didn't think the changes of hair and scenery were going to make a difference.

Truck doors closed and she turned to face two guys—two cowboys, she corrected herself, taking in their jeans, rough looking tan jackets, scuffed boots and dusty black cowboy hats. Both walked over, and she panicked. What was she supposed to say?

They don't look Russian. The thought ran a frantic circle in her mind, followed by, what does a Russian hitman actually look like? God, did he have to be Russian? Or even a he? A humorous hysteria built up, but she took a deep breath and clenched her hand around the map. She steeled herself not to take a step backward as both men walked right up, almost breaking her bubble of personal space.

"Miss, can we help ya out?"

Home of Erotic Romance

Sign up for our newsletter and find out about all our romance book releases, eBook sales and promotions, sneak peeks and FREE romance books!

About the Author

Billi Jean was born in California but didn't stay put for long. She's lived in New York, Indiana, Missouri, Arizona, Colorado, Florida, Massachusetts and Vermont. She's lived in and worked from ranches to beach-side coffee shops to the woods in western Massachusetts. Now living and working in China, she continues to write for Totally Bound Publishing.

Billi Jean has been writing since high school when she couldn't wait for Robert Jordon to write his Wheel of Time series faster. As an adult, she still finds herself drawn to fantasy-adventure stories, but with an erotic romance flair. Her books are extremely hot, with a focus on strong characters that are shoved into fast-paced adventures. Her unique style of incredible journeys infused with hot passion leave her fans hoping for more.

Billi loves to hear from readers. You can find her contact information, website details and author profile page at https://www.totallybound.com